HINDU
Mythology

The author's purpose has been to collect materials so that they may be arranged in such a way that the reader can conveniently gain a good general idea of the names, character and relationship of the principal deities of Hinduism. These deities have been described, discussed and classified so far as possible according to the words of the sacred books of the Hindu scriptures so that subjective prejudice or bias have been eliminated in favour of an objective approach to the subject. The many illustrations have been copied from the designs of Hindu artists and therefore reflect the attitudes and interpretations of those to whom the religion is a living thing. The method of classification is intended to afford the reader a clear general view of Hindu mythology.

Durgā

Ganesa   Lakshmi   Sarasvati   Kartikeya

The Demon Durgā

HINDU
Mythology

W.J. Wilkins

RUPA

Published by
Rupa Publications India Pvt. Ltd 1975, 2013
7/16, Ansari Road, Daryaganj
New Delhi 110002

Sales centres:
Allahabad Bengaluru Chennai
Hyderabad Jaipur Kathmandu
Kolkata Mumbai

Edition Copyright © Rupa Publications India Pvt. Ltd 1975, 2013

ISBN: 978-81-291-2981-9

First impression

10 9 8 7 6 5 4 3 2 1

Printed at Shree Maitrey Printech Pvt. Ltd., Noida

Contents

Part II
THE PURĀNIC DEITIES

Part III
THE INFERIOR DEITIES

Preface

On reaching India, one of my first inquiries was for a full and trustworthy account of the mythology of the Hindus; but though I read various works in which some information of the kind was to be found, I sought in vain for a complete and systematic work on this subject Since then two classical dictionaries of India have been published, one in Madras and one in London; but though useful books of reference, they do not meet the want that this book is intended to supply. For some years I have been collecting materials with the intention of arranging them in such a way that any one without much labour might gain a good general idea of the names, character, and relationship of the principal deities of Hinduism. This work does not profess to supply new translations of the Hindu Scriptures, nor to give very much information that is not already scattered through many other books. In a few cases original extracts have been made; but, generally speaking, my work has been to collect and arrange translations ready to hand. It has been my endeavour to give a fair and impartial account of these deities, as far as possible in the words of the sacred books; such an account as I should expect an honest-minded Hindu to give of God from a careful study of the Bible. I have honestly striven to keep free from prejudice and theological bias; and, wishing to let the sacred books speak for themselves, have refrained from commenting on the passages quoted, excepting where some explanation seemed necessary. I have not selected those texts which describe the darker side only of the Hindu gods, nor have such been altogether suppressed. There was much that could not be reproduced. Of what was fit for publication I have taken a proportionate amount, that this, together with what is worthy of commendation, may give a faithful picture. To magnify either the good or the evil is the work of the advocate—a work I, in this book, distinctly disclaim. An honest effort has been made to give a reliable account of the things commonly believed by millions of our Hindu fellow-subjects.

In order to render the work more interesting and instructive, a number of illustrations of the principal deities have been introduced. Most of them have been copied from pictures drawn by the Hindus themselves, and which may be seen in the houses of the people. No attempt has been made to idealize them; they are, what they profess to be, *faithful representations of the designs of Hindu artists.* For their kindness in making these drawings from the original highly-coloured pictures, I am very greatly indebted to my friends the Rev. A. J. Bamford, B.A., and Messrs. H. T. Ottewill and C. A. Andrews, B.A.

By the introduction of a full index it is hoped that this work will serve as a classical dictionary of India; whilst the classification of the gods will enable the student to obtain a general view of Hindu mythology, and of the relation in which one deity stands to others. And as many legends are given at some length, the book can hardly fail to be interesting to the general reader, who may not have time or opportunity to refer to the sacred writings from which they are taken.

A word of explanation respecting the classification of the deities is called for. It will be noticed that some of those described as belonging to the Vedic Age appear under the same or other names in the Purānas; whilst others spoken of as belonging to the Purānic Age have their origin, traceable indeed with difficulty in some cases, in the Vedas. It was a common practice with the writers of the later books to claim a remote antiquity, and the authority of the Vedas, for the more recent additions to the Pantheon. In some instances an epithet, descriptive of one of the old deities, is attached as the name of a later one. And by this means the old and the new are linked together. The Vedic gods are those whose description is *chiefly* to be found in the Vedas, and whose worship was more general in the Vedic Age; the Purānic are those who are more fully described in the Purānas, and whose worship was more general in the Purānic Age. Any very rigid classification it is impossible to make.

W. J. W.
CALCUTTA, *February* 22, 1882.

Preface to the Second Edition

As a large edition of this work has been sold out, and a new one called for, an opportunity is presented of adding a few words to what was said eighteen years ago. The reception given to it both in India and in England was most gratifying, practically the only serious condemnation of it being that I had not pronounced judgment on much that I had quoted from the Hindu sacred books. This was a task that I distinctly disavowed in my preface. I set out with the intention of rigidly abstaining from comment, commendatory or condemnatory. I feel that a mere statement of much that was written in books professedly inspired by God, carried its own condemnation. And at the same time it was a pleasure to indicate how, amid much evil, there was also much good. The sages of India were not in complete darkness. As we examine the earlier writings, the light was bright indeed contrasted with what came later. It is most instructive to notice the marked deterioration in the quality of the teaching, deities as described by the earlier sages being vastly better than their successors declare them to be. "Non-Christian Bibles are all developments in the wrong direction. They begin with some flashes of true light, and end in darkness." As Max-Müller says, "The more we go back, the more we examine the earliest germs of any religion, the purer I believe we shall find the conceptions of the Deity."

In this edition there is some added matter. Errors have been corrected, and an attempt made to render certain passages more clear that were somewhat obscure. Substantially the book remains the same. An account of the ordinary worship and the festivals of these gods will be found in another work— "Modern Hinduism."

W. J. W.
1900.

PART I

THE VEDIC DEITIES

Chapter I

The Vedas

Before speaking of the Vedic Deities, it is necessary that something be said concerning the Vedas themselves, the source of our information concerning them. The root of the word is *vid*, "to know;" hence the term *Veda* signifies *knowledge;* and as these books were not *written* for centuries after they were originally composed, it signifies knowledge that was heard, or orally communicated. The Vedas are not the work of a single person, but, according to popular belief, were communicated to a number of Rishis or saints, who in their turn transmitted them to their disciples. The Seer Vyāsa is styled the arranger, or, as we should now say, the editor, of these works.

The instruction contained in these writings is said to have been breathed forth by God Himself. Other writers teach that it issued from Him like smoke from fire. Sometimes the Vedas are said to have sprung from the elements. The accounts of their origin, though differing in form, agree in teaching that they were the direct gift of God to man; and hence they are regarded with the greatest veneration. They are the special property of the Brāhmans. As early as Manu, the nominal author or compiler of a law book probably not more than two or three centuries later than the Vedas, though some suppose it to have been no earlier than A.D. 500, it was regarded as a grave offence for a single word of these divinely given books to be heard by a man of a lower caste.

The Vedas are four in number; of these the Rig-Veda is the oldest, next in order was the Yajur-Veda, then the Sama-Veda, and last of all the Atharva-Veda. Each of these Vedas consists of two main parts: a Sanhita, or collection of mantras or hymns; and a Brahmana, containing ritualistic precept and illustration, which stands in somewhat the same relation to the Sanhita as the Talmud to the Law. In these are found instructions to the priests who conduct the worship of the gods addressed in the hymns. Attached to each Brāhmana is an Upanishad, containing secret or mystical doctrine. These are regarded as of lesser authority than the Mantras and Brāhmanas. For whilst they are spoken of as *Sruti,* i.e. heard, the Upanishads are *Smriti,* learned. Though based on the older compositions, if there is any discrepancy between them, the teaching of the later ones is rejected. The Sanhita and Brāhmana are for the Brāhmans generally; the Upanishads for philosophical inquirers. Yet, strange to say, whereas the older portions had, until recent years, been almost entirely neglected, with some parts of the Upanishads there was considerable acquaintance amongst the learned pundits of Benares and other places. In many parts of India not a man could be found able to read and interpret them. Of the Sanhitas, the "Rig-Veda Sanhita—containing one thousand and seventeen hymns —is by far the most important; whilst the Atharva-Veda-Sanhita, though generally held to be the most recent, is perhaps the most interesting. Moreover, these are the only two Vedic hymn-books worthy of being called separate original collections;"* the others being almost entirely made up of extracts from the Rig-Veda. Between the time of the composition of the Rig-Veda and that of the Atharva, considerable changes in the. religious faith of the people had come about. The childlike trust of the earlier hymns has disappeared, and the deities now seem more cruel, and there is greater need of propitiatory offerings. Probably the old religion of the people whom they had conquered had begun to tell on that of the Aryans.

The Sanhitas of three of the Vedas are said to have some peculiarity. "If a mantra is metrical, and intended for loud recitation, it is called *Rich* (from *rich,* praise) whence the name Rig Veda; *i.e.* the Veda containing such praises. If it is prose (and then it must be muttered inaudibly), it is called *Yajus* (*yaj,* sacrifice, hence, literally, the means by which sacrifice is effected); therefore Yajur-Veda signifies the Veda containing such *yajus.* And if it is metrical, and intended for chanting, it is called *Sāman* [equal]; hence Sāman Veda means the Veda containing such *Samans.* The author of the Mantra, or as the Hindus would say, the inspired 'Seer,' who received it from the Deity, is termed its *Rishi;* and the object with which it is concerned is its *devata* —a word which generally means a 'deity,' but the meaning of which, in its reference to *mantras,* must not always be taken literally, as there are hymns in which not gods nor deified beings, but, for instance, a sacrificial post, weapons, etc., invoked, are considered as the *devata.*"* It should, however, be noticed that the deifying of a "sacrificial post" or a "weapon" is in perfect harmony with the general pantheistic notions which prevailed amongst the people then as now: so that there is nothing unnatural according to their religious ideas in speaking even of inanimate objects as deities. There is little doubt that the Brahmanas are more recent than the Sanhitas.

The Vedas have not come down to the present time without considerable dispute as to the text. As might have been expected, seeing that this teaching was given orally, discrepancies arose. One account mentions no less than twenty-one versions (Sākhās) of the Rig-Veda; another gives five of the Rig-Veda, forty-two of the Yajur-Veda, mentions twelve out of a thousand of the Sāman-Veda, and twelve of the Atharva-Veda. And as each school believed that it possessed the true

Veda, it anathematized those who taught and followed any other. The Rig-Veda Sanhita that has survived to the present age is that of one school only, the Sākala; the Yajur-Veda is that of three schools; the Sāma-Veda is that of perhaps two, and the Atharva-Veda of one only.

"The history of the Yajur-Veda differs in so far from that of the other Vedas, as it is marked by a dissension between its own schools far more important than the differences which separated the school of each [of the] other Vedas. It is known by the distinction between a Yajur-Veda called the Black—and another called the White—Yajur-Veda. Tradition, especially that of the Purānas, records a legend to account for it. Vaisampāyana, it says, a disciple of Vyāsa, who had received from him the Yajur-Veda, having committed an offence, desired his disciples to assist him in the performance of some expiatory act. One of these, however, Yājnavalkya, proposed that he should alone perform the whole rite; upon which Vaisampayana, enraged at what he considered to be the arrogance of his disciple, uttered a curse on him, the effect of which was that Yājnavalkya disgorged all the Yajus texts he had learned from Vaisampayana. The other disciples, having been meanwhile transformed into partridges *(tittiri)*, picked up these tainted texts and retained them. Hence these texts are called Taittiriyas. But Yājnavalkya, desirous of obtaining Yajus texts, devoutly prayed to the Sun, and had granted to him his wish—'to possess such texts as were not known to his teacher.'"* And thus there are two Yajur-Vedas to this day; the Black being considered the older of the two.

As to the date of the Vedas, there is nothing certainly known. There is no doubt that they are amongst the oldest literary productions of the world. But when they were composed is largely a matter of conjecture. Colebrooke seems to show from a Vaidick Calendar that they must have been written before

---

*Art. "Vedas," Chambers's Cyclopædia.

the 14th century B.C. Some assign to them a more recent, some a more ancient, date. Dr. Haug considers the Vedic age to have extended from B.C. 2000 to B.C. 1200, though he thinks some of the oldest hymns may have been composed in B.C. 2400. Max-Müller gives us the probable date of the Mantra, or hymn portion of the Vedas, from B.C. 1200 to B.C. 800, and the Brāhmanas from B.C. 800 to B.C. 600, and the rest from B.C. 600 to B.C. 200.

There is nothing whatever in the books themselves to indicate when they were *written*. All references in them are to their being given orally, learned, and then again taught audibly to others. Probably for centuries after the art of writing was known in India it was not employed for preserving the sacred books, as in the Mahābhārata those who *write* the Vedas are threatened with the punishment of hell.

Chapter II
The Vedic Gods Generally

Yaska (probably the oldest commentator on the Vedas) gives the following classification of the Vedic gods. "There are three deities, according to the expounders of the Vedas: Agni, whose place is on the earth; Vāyu or Indra, whose place is in the air; and Surya, whose place is in the sky. These deities receive severally many appellations in consequence of their greatness, or of the diversity of their functions."* In the Rig-Veda itself this number is increased to thirty-three, of whom eleven are said to be in heaven, eleven on earth, and eleven in mid-air. 'Agni, the wise god, lends an ear to his worshippers. God with the ruddy steeds, who lovest praise, bring hither those three-and-thirty." This is the number usually mentioned, though it is by no means easy to decide which are the thirty-three intended, as the lists found in various places vary considerably; whilst in another verse it is said that "three hundred, three thousand, thirty-and-nine gods have worshipped Agni."

These deities, though spoken of as immortal, are not said to be self-existent beings; in fact their parentage in most cases

---

*Muir, 0. S. T., v. 8.

is given; but the various accounts of their origin do not agree with each other. Agni and Savitri are said to have conferred immortality upon the other gods; whilst it is also taught that Indra obtained this boon by sacrifice. An interesting account is given in the Satapatha Brāhmana* of the means by which the gods obtained immortality, and superiority over the asuras or demons. All of them, gods and demons alike, were mortal, all were equal in power, all were sons of Prajāpati the Creator. Wishing to be immortal, the gods offered sacrifices liberally, and practised the severest penance; but not until Prajāpati had taught them to offer a particular sacrifice could they become immortal. They followed his advice, and succeeded. Wishing to become greater than the asuras, they became truthful. Previously they and the asuras spoke truthfully or falsely, as they thought fit; but gradually, whilst they ceased from lying, the asuras became increasingly false; the result was that the gods after protracted struggles gained the victory. Originally the gods were all equal in power, all alike good. But three of them desired to be superior to the rest, viz. Agni, Indra, and Surya. They continued to offer sacrifices for this purpose until it was accomplished. Originally there was not in Agni the same flame as there is now. He desired, "May this flame be in me," and, offering a sacrifice for the attainment of this blessing, obtained it. In a similar manner Indra increased his energy, and Surya his brightness. These three deities form what is commonly described as the Vedic Triad. In later times other three took their place, though an attempt is made to show them to be the same.

It will be noticed that each of the gods is in turn regarded by the worshipper as superior to all the others. In the Vedas this superlative language is constantly employed, and identical epithets are indiscriminately given to various deities. Professor Max-Müller says, "When these individual gods are

---

*Muir O. S. T., iv. 54-62.

invoked, they are not conceived as limited by the power of others, as superior or inferior in rank. Each god, to the mind of the supplicants, is as good as all the gods. He is felt at the time as a real divinity, as supreme and absolute, in spite of the limitations which, to our mind, a plurality of gods must entail on every single god. All the rest disappear for a moment from the vision of the poet, and he only who is to fulfil their desires, stands in full light before the eyes of the worshippers. …It would be easy to find, in the numerous hymns of the Rig-Veda, passages in which almost every single god is represented as supreme and absolute."

The will of these gods is sovereign; no mortal can thwart their designs. They exercise authority over all creatures. In their hands is the life of mortals. They know the thoughts and intentions of men, and whilst they reward the worshipper, they punish those who neglect them.

When the Puranic deities are described it will be noticed that the representations of the deities of that age are far more clearly defined than those of earlier times. Though the Vedic gods are spoken of as possessing human forms and acting as human beings, there is considerable vagueness in the outline. But as time goes on this is lost. The objects of worship are no longer indistinct and shadowy, but are so minutely described that their portraits could be easily painted. And as their physical features are no longer left to the imagination, so their mental and moral characters are fully delineated. They are of like passions with those who depict them, only possessing vastly greater powers.

Professor Williams says* "that the deified forces addressed in the Vedic hymns were probably not represented by images or idols in the Vedic period, though doubtless the early worshippers clothed their gods with human forms in their own

---

*"Indian Wisdom," p. 15.

imaginations." Professor Müller* speaks more positively: "The religion of the Veda knows of no idols. The worship of idols in India is a secondary formation, a later degradation of the more primitive worship of ideal gods." The guarded language of Professor Williams seems to be better suited to the facts, as far as they are known, for Dr. Bollensen† speaks quite as strongly on the other side. He writes, "From the common appellation of the gods as *divo naras*, 'men of the sky,' or simply *naras*, 'men,' and from the epithet *nripesas*, 'having the form of men,' we may conclude that the Indians did not merely in imagination assign human forms to their gods, but also represented them in a sensible manner. Thus a painted image of Rudra (Rig-Veda, ii. 33, 9) is described 'with strong limbs, many-formed, awful, brown, he is painted with shining colours.'" "Still clearer appears the reference to representations in the form of an image. 'I now pray to the gods of these (Maruts).' Here it seems that the Maruts are distinguished from their gods, *i.e.* their images.'" "There is in the oldest language a word, '*Sandris*,' which properly denotes 'an image of the gods.'"

We shall now proceed to the consideration in detail of the deities as described in the Vedas.

---

*"Chips from a German Workshop," i. 38.
†Muir, O. S. T., v. 453

Chapter III
Dyaus and Prithivi

The general opinion respecting Dyaus (Heaven) and Prithivi (Earth) is that they are amongst the most ancient of the Aryan deities, hence they are spoken of in the hymns of the Rig-Veda as the parents of the other gods.* They are described as "great, wise and energetic;" those who "promote righteousness, and lavish gifts upon their worshippers;" And in another place they are said to have "made all creatures," and through their favour "immortality is conferred upon their offspring." Not only are they the creators, but also the preservers of all creatures; and are beneficent and kind to all. In other passages Heaven and Earth are said to have been formed by Indra, who is declared to transcend them in greatness, whom they follow "as a chariot follows the horse." They are described as bowing down before him; as trembling with fear on account of him; and as being subject to his control. Again, they are said to have been formed by Soma; and in other verses other deities are said to have made them. This confusion of thought respecting the origin of the gods led very naturally to the question being asked in other hymns, "How have they

---

*Muir, O. S. T., v. 23.

been produced? Who of the sages knows?"

There seems to be considerable ground for the opinion that Indra gradually superseded Dyaus in the worship of the Hindus soon after their settlement in India. As the praises of the newer god were sung, the older one was forgotten; and in the present day, whilst Dyaus is almost unknown, Indra is still worshipped, though in the Vedas both are called the god of heaven. The following statement of Professor Benfey* gives a natural explanation of this. "It may be distinctly shown that Indra took the place of the god of heaven, who, in the Vedas, is invoked in the vocative as Dyauspitar (Heaven-father). This is proved by the fact that this phrase is exactly reflected in the Latin Jupiter, and the Greek Zeū-pater as a religious formula, fixed, like many others, before the separation of the languages. When the Sanskrit people left the common country, where for them, as well as for other kindred tribes, the brilliant radiance of heaven appeared to them, in consequence of the climate there prevailing, as the holiest thing, and settled in sultry India, where the glow of the heavens is destructive, and only its rain operates beneficially, this aspect of the Deity must have appeared the most adorable, so that the epithet Pluvius, in a certain sense, absorbed all the other characteristics of Dyauspitar. This found its expression in the name In-dra, in which we unhesitatingly recognize a word (which arose in some local dialect, and was then diffused with the spread of the worship) standing for Sind-ra, which again was derived from Syand, 'to drop.' The conceptions which had been attached to Dyaus were then transferred to Indra." The opinion that Indra has taken the place of Dyaus is now pretty generally believed, and the above explanation appears natural.

Of Prithivi we hear again. The "Vishnu Purāna" † gives the following account of her birth. There was a king named Venā,

---

*Muir, O. S. T., v. 18.
†Page 103.

notorious for his wickedness and general neglect of religious duties. When the Rishis of that age could bear with his impiety no longer, they slew him. But now a worse evil happened; anarchy prevailed, and they felt that a bad king was better than none at all. Upon this they rubbed the thigh of Venā, when there came forth a black dwarf, resembling a negro in appearance. Immediately after his birth the dwarf asked, "What am I to do?" He is told, "Nisida" (sit down), and from this his descendants are called "Nisidis" unto this day. The corpse was now pure, as all sin had left it in the body of this black dwarf. The right arm was then rubbed, and from it there came a beautiful shining prince, who was named Prithu, and reigned in the place of his father. Now during his reign there was a terrible famine. As the Earth would not yield her fruits, great distress prevailed. Prithu said, "I will slay the Earth, and make her yield her fruits." Terrified at this threat, the Earth assumed the form of a cow, and was pursued by Prithu, even to the heaven of Brahmā. At length, weary with the chase, she turned to him and said, "Know you not the sin of killing a female, that you thus try to slay me?" The king replied that "when the happiness of many is secured by the destruction of one malignant being, the slaughter of that being is an act of virtue." "But," said the Earth, "if, in order to promote the welfare of your subjects, you put an end to me, whence, best of monarchs, will thy people derive their support?" Overcome at length, the Earth declared that all vegetable products were old, and destroyed by her, but that at the king's command she would restore them "as developed from her milk." "Do you therefore, for the benefit of mankind, give me that calf by which I may be able to secrete milk. Make also all places level, so that I may cause my milk, the seed of all vegetation, to flow everywhere around."

Prithu acted upon this advice. "Before his time there was no cultivation, no pasture, no agriculture, no high-ways for merchants; all these things (or all civilization) originated in the reign of Prithu. Where the ground was made level, the king induced his subjects to take up their abode. ... He therefore having made Swayambhuva Manu the calf, milked the Earth, and received the milk into his own hand, for the benefit of mankind. Thence proceeded all kinds of corn and vegetables upon which people now subsist. By granting life to the Earth, Prithu was as her father, and she thence derived the patronymic appellation Prithivi."

In a note Professor Wilson adds,* the commentator observes that "by the 'calf,' or Manu in that character, is typified the promoter of the multiplication of progeny:" Manu, as will be seen in the account of the Creation, being regarded by some of the Purānas as the first parent of mankind. This legend, with considerable variation, is found in most of the Purānas; Soma, Indra, Yama, and others taking the place of Manu as the calf, whilst Prithu's place as the milker is taken by the Rishis, Mitra, etc. In the same note Professor Wilson says, "These are all probably subsequent modifications of the original simple allegory, which typified the earth as a cow, who yielded to every class of beings the milk that they desired, or the object of their wishes."

It should be noticed that, later in the "Vishnu Purāna," Prithivi is said to have sprung from the foot of Vishnu.

---

*"Vishnu Purāna," p. 104.

Chapter IV

Aditi, and The Ādityas

Aditi has the honour of being almost the only goddess mentioned by name in the Rig-Veda, as the mother of any of the gods; but it is by no means an easy task to delineate her character, as the most contradictory statements are made concerning her. She was invoked as the bestower of blessings on children and cattle: and she is declared to be the mother of Varuna, and other deities, sometimes eight, sometimes twelve in number. She is supposed to be the impersonation of "infinity, especially the boundlessness of heaven, in opposition to the finiteness of earth." Another supposition is that Aditi is the personification of "universal, all-embracing Nature or Being." This latter idea seems to be the more correct from the following verses,* where a man about to be immolated says, "Of which god, now, of which of the immortals, shall we invoke the amiable name, who shall give us back to the great Aditi, that I may behold my father and my mother?" Whatever may have been intended by the poets to be expressed by this name, or whatever may have been the precise power personified by Aditi, she is connected with the forgiveness of sin. Thus,

---

*Muir, O. S. T., v. 45.

"May Aditi make us sinless." "Aditi be gracious, if we have committed any sin against you." "Whatever offence we have, oh Agni, through our folly committed against you, oh most youthful god, make us free from sins against Aditi." "Whatever sin we have committed, may Aditi sever us from it."* Probably the term Aditi "the boundless," was originally employed as an epithet of Dyauspitar, the Heaven-father. When the heavens came to be divided into a number of parts, over each of which a ruler was nominated, a mother was wanted for them, and the name Aditi was given to her.

In the account of the Creation given in the Rig-Veda, Aditi is said to have sprung from Daksha, and in the same verse Daksha is called her son. There is also a reference to her other sons. In the "Vishnu Purāna" we have no less than three somewhat differing accounts of the origin of Daksha the father of Aditi. In the first account, his name appears amongst the mind-born sons of Brahmā; and in this connection he is said to have had twenty-four daughters; but Aditi is not mentioned as one of them. In the second account of Daksha, Aditi is said to have been one of his sixty daughters, and was given in marriage to Kasypa, by whom she had twelve sons—the Adityas. Elsewhere we read that Vishnu, when incarnate as the Dwarf, was a result of this marriage. In the third account of Daksha, Aditi is again mentioned as his daughter, and the mother of Vivasat (the Sun). The sons of Aditi are termed

THE ADITYAS

This name signifies simply the descendants of Aditi. In one passage in the Rig-Veda† the names of six are given: Mitra, Aryaman, Bhaga, Varuna, Daksha and Amsa. In another passage they are said to be seven in number, though their

---

*Muir, O. S. T., v. 46, 47.
†Ibid. v. 54.

names are not given. In a third, eight is the number mentioned; but "of the eight sons of Aditi, who were born from her body, she approached the gods with seven, and cast out Mārttānda (the eighth)."* As the names of these sons given in different parts of the Vedas do not agree with each other, it is difficult to know who were originally regarded as Ādityas. Judging from the number of hymns addressed to them, some of these deities occupied a conspicuous position in the Vedic Pantheon; whilst others are named once or twice only, and then in connection with their more illustrious brethren. In the "Satapatha Brāhmana," and the Purānas, the number of the Ādityas is increased to twelve. In addition to the six whose names are given above, the following are also described in some hymns of the Rig-Veda as the offspring of Aditi: Surya, "as an Āditya identified with Agni, is said to have been placed by the gods in the sky;"† Savitri, and Indra too, are in one passage addressed as an Āditya along with Varuna and the Moon. In the Taittiriya Texts, the following are described as Ādityas:—Mitra, Varuna, Aryaman, Amsu, Bhaga, Indra, and Vivasvat (Surya).

Professor Roth says‡ of these deities, "In the highest heaven dwell and reign those gods who bear in common the name of Ādityas. We must, however, if we would discover their earliest character, abandon the conceptions which in a later age, and even in that of the heroic poems, were entertained regarding these deities. According to this conception they were twelve Sun-gods, there being evident reference to the twelve months. But for the most ancient period we must hold fast to the primary significance of their names. They are inviolable, imperishable, eternal things. Aditi, Eternity, or The Eternal, is the element which sustains them, or is sustained by them. The eternal and inviolable element in which the Ādityas dwell, and which

---

*Muir, O. S. T., v. 49.
†Ibid. v. 54.
‡Ibid. v. 56.

forms their essence, is the celestial light. The Ādityas, the gods of this light, do not therefore by any means coincide with any of the forms in which light is manifested in the universe. They are neither the sun, nor moon, nor stars, nor dawn, but the eternal sustainers of this luminous life, which exists, as it were, behind these phenomena."

As noticed above, the text of the Rig-Veda says,* "Of the eight sons who were born from the body of Aditi, she approached the gods with seven, but cast away the eighth." In the commentary, the following explanation of this circumstance is given. "The eighth son was deformed. His brothers, seeing his deformity, improved his appearance. He was afterwards known as Vivasvat (the Sun). From the superfluous flesh cut off his body an elephant was formed, hence the proverb, 'Let no man catch an elephant, for the elephant partakes of the nature of man.'"

According to a passage quoted in Chapter II.† from the "Satapatha Brāhmana," Agni, Indra, and Surya, obtained superiority over the other gods by means of sacrifice. By whatever means this position was obtained, it is certain that they were the most popular deities of the Vedic Age. Agni stands in a class by himself; but with Indra and Surya there are other deities closely associated, and possessing very similar attributes. Nearly the whole of the more conspicuous Vedic deities may be classified as follows:—(1) Agni, the god of Fire; (2) Sun Gods, or gods of Light; and (3) Storm Gods, or those associated with Indra.

---

*Muir, O. S. T., v. 49.
†Page 10.

Chapter V
Agni

Agni, the god of Fire, is one of the most prominent of the deities of the Vedas. With the single exception of Indra, more hymns are addressed to him than to any other deity. Professor Williams gives the following spirited description of Agni:—

'Bright, seven-rayed god, how manifold thy shapes
Revealed to us thy votaries: now we see thee
With body all of gold; and radiant hair
Flaming from three terrific heads, and mouths,
Whose burning jaws and teeth devour all things,
Now with a thousand glowing horns, and now
Flashing thy lustre from a thousand eyes,
Thou'rt borne towards us in a golden chariot, Impelled
by winds, and drawn by ruddy steeds,
Marking thy car's destructive course with blackness."

Various accounts are given of the origin of Agni. He is said to be a son of Dyaus and Prithivi; he is called the son of Brahmā, and is then named Abhimāni; and he is reckoned amongst the children of Kasyapa and Aditi, and hence one

of the Ādityas. In the laterwritings he is described as a son
of Angiras, king of the Pitris (fathers of mankind), and the
authorship of several hymns is ascribed to him. In pictures he
is represented as a red man, having three legs and seven arms,
dark eyes, eyebrows and hair. He rides on a ram, wears a poita
(Brāhmanical thread), and a garland of fruit. Flames of fire
issue from his mouth, and seven streams of glory radiate from
his body. The following passage, for every sentence of which
Dr. Muir* quotes a text from the Vedas, gives a good idea of
the character and functions of this deity in the Vedic Age.

Agni

Agni is an immortal who has taken up his abode with
mortals as their guest. He is the domestic priest who rises
before the dawn, and who concentrates in his own person and
exercises in a higher sense all the various sacrificial offices

*Muir, O. S. T., v. 119 ff.

which the Indian ritual assigns to a number of different human functionaries. He is a sage, the divinest among the sages, immediately acquainted with all the forms of worship; the wise director, the successful accomplisher, and the protector of all ceremonies, who enables men to serve the gods in a correct and acceptable manner in cases where they could not do this with their own unaided skill. He is a swift messenger, moving between heaven and earth, commissioned both by gods and men to maintain their mutual communication, to announce to the immortals the hymns, and to convey to them the oblations of their worshippers; or to bring them (the immortals) down from the sky to the place of sacrifice. He accompanies the gods when they visit the earth, and shares in the reverence and adoration which they receive. He makes the oblations fragrant; without him the gods experience no satisfaction.

Agni is the lord, protector, king of men. He is the lord of the house, dwelling in every abode. He is a guest in every home; he despises no man, he lives in every family. He is therefore considered as a mediator between gods and men, and as a witness of their actions; hence to the present day he is worshipped, and his blessing sought on all solemn occasions, as at marriage, death, etc. In these old hymns Agni is spoken of as dwelling in the two pieces of wood which being rubbed together produce fire; and it is noticed as a remarkable thing that a living being should spring out of dry (dead) wood. Strange to say, says the poet, the child, as soon as born, begins with unnatural voracity to consume his parents. Wonderful is his growth, seeing that he is born of a mother who cannot nourish him; but he is nourished by the oblations of clarified butter which are poured into his mouth, and which he consumes.

The highest divine functions are ascribed to Agni. Although in some places he is spoken of as the son of heaven and earth, in others he is said to have stretched them out; to have formed them, and all that flies or walks, or stands or moves. He formed the sun, and adorned the heavens with stars. Men tremble at his mighty deeds, and his ordinances cannot be resisted. Earth, heaven, and all things obey his commands. All the gods fear, and do homage to him. He knows the secrets of mortals, and hears the invocations that are addressed to him.

The worshippers of Agni prosper, are wealthy, and live long. He watches with a thousand eyes over the man who brings him food, and nourishes him with oblations. No mortal enemy can by any wondrous power gain the mastery over him who sacrifices to this god. He also confers and is the guardian of immortality. In a funeral hymn, Agni is asked to warm with his heat the unborn (immortal) part of the deceased, and in his auspicious form to carry it to the world of the righteous. He carries men across calamities, as a ship over the sea. He commands all the riches in earth and heaven; hence he is invoked for riches, food, deliverance, and in fact all temporal good. He is also prayed to as the forgiver of sins that may have been committed through folly. All gods are said to be comprehended in him; he surrounds them as the circumference of a wheel does the spokes.

The main characteristics of this deity are taught in the following verses by Dr. Muir : — *

"Great Agni, though thine essence be but one,
    Thy forms are three; as fire thou blazest here,
    As lightning flashest in the atmosphere,
In heaven thou flamest as the golden sun.

"It was in heaven thou hadst thy primal birth;
    By art of sages skilled in sacred lore
    Thou wast drawn down to human hearths of yore,
And thou abid'st a denizen of earth.

---

*Muir, O. S. T., v. 221.

"Sprung from the mystic pair,* by priestly hands
  In wedlock joined, forth flashes Agni bright;
  But, oh! ye heavens and earth, I tell you right,
The unnatural child devours the parent brands.

"But Agni is a god; we must not deem
  That he can err, or dare to comprehend
  His acts, which far our reason's grasp transcend;
He best can judge what deeds a god beseem.

"And yet this orphaned god himself survives :
  Although his hapless mother soon expires,
  And cannot nurse the babe as babe requires,
Great Agni, wondrous infant, grows and thrives.

"Smoke-bannered Agni, god with crackling voice
  And flaming hair, when thou dost pierce the gloom
  At early dawn, and all the world illume,
Both heaven and earth and gods and men rejoice.

"In every home thou art a welcome guest,
  The household tutelary lord, a son,
  A father, mother, brother, all in one,
A friend by whom thy faithful friends are blest.

"A swift-winged messenger, thou callest down
  From heaven to crowd our hearths the race divine,
  To taste our food, our hymns to hear, benign,
And all our fondest aspirations crown.

"Thou, Agni, art our priest: divinely wise,
  In holy science versed, thy skill detects
  The faults that mar our rites, mistakes corrects,

---

*The two pieces of wood from which fire is produced.

And all our acts completes and sanctities.

"Thou art the cord that stretches to the skies,
    The bridge that scans the chasm, profound and vast,
    Dividing earth from heaven, o'er which at last
The good shall safely pass to Paradise.

"But when, great god, thine awful anger glows,
    And thou revealest thy destroying force,
    All creatures flee before thy furious course.
As hosts are chased by overpowering foes.

"Thou levellest all thou touchest; forests vast
    Thou shear'st, like beards which barber's razor shaves.
    Thy wind-driven flames roar loud as ocean's waves,
And all thy track is black when thou hast past.

"But thou, great Agni, dost not always wear
    That direful form; thou rather lov'st to shine
    Upon our hearths, with milder flame benign,
And cheer the homes where thou art nursed with care.

"Yes ! thou delightest all those men to bless
    Who toil unwearied to supply the food
    Which thou so lovest—logs of well-dried wood,
And heaps of butter bring, thy favourite mess.

"Though I no cow possess, and have no store
    Of butter, nor an axe fresh wood to cleave,
    Thou, gracious god, wilt my poor gift receive :
These few dry sticks I bring—I have no more,

"Preserve us, lord; thy faithful servants save
    From all the ills by which our bliss is marred;
    Tower like an iron wall our homes to guard,

And all the boons bestow our hearts can crave,.

"And when away our brief existence wanes,
    When we at length our earthly homes must quit,
    And our freed souls to worlds unknown shall flit,
Do thou deal gently with our cold remains.

"And then, thy gracious form assuming, guide
    Our unborn part across the dark abyss
    Aloft to realms serene of light and bliss,
Where righteous men among the gods abide."

"In a celebrated hymn of the Rig-Veda, attributed to Visishtha, Indra and the other gods are called upon to destroy the Kravyāds (the flesh-eaters), or Rākshas, enemies of the gods. Agni himself is a Kravyād, and as such takes an entirely different character. He is then represented under a form as hideous as the beings he, in common with the other gods, is called upon to devour. He sharpens his two iron tusks, puts his enemies into his mouth, and devours them. He heats the edges of his shafts, and sends them into the hearts of the Rākshasas."*

"In the Mahābhārata, Agni is represented as having exhausted his vigour by devouring too many oblations, and desiring to consume the whole Khāndava forest, as a means of recruiting his strength. He was [at first] prevented from doing this by Indra; but having obtained the assistance of Krishna and Arjuna, he baffled Indra, and accomplished his object."†

According to the Rāmāyana, in order to assist Vishnu when incarnate as Rāma, Agni became the father of Nila by a monkey mother; and according to the "Vishnu Purāna," he married Swāhā, by whom he had three sons—Pāvaka, Pavamāna, and

---

*Dowson, "Dictionary of Hindu Mythology."
†ibid. *s.v.*

Suchi.

Agni has many names; those more generally known are the following : —

Vahni, "He who receives the *hom,* or burnt sacrifice."
Vītihotra, "He who sanctifies the worshipper."
Dhananjaya, "He who conquers (destroys) riches."
Jivalana, "He who burns."
Dhūmketu, "He whose sign is smoke."
Chhāgaratha, "He who rides on a ram."
Saptajihva, "He who has seven tongues."

Brihaspati and Brahmanaspati are generally regarded as being identical with Agni. Nearly the same epithets are applied to them, with this additional one—of presiding over prayer. In some few hymns they are addressed as separate deities. In "The Religions of India," M. Barth, regarding these as names of one and the same deity, thus describes him : —

"Like Agni and Soma, he is born on the altar, and thence rises upwards to the gods; like them, he was begotten in space by Heaven and Earth; like Indra, he wages war with enemies on the earth and demons in the air; like all three, he resides in the highest heaven, he generates the gods, and ordains the order of the universe. Under his fiery breath the world was melted and assumed the form it has, like metal in the mould of the founder. At first sight it would seem that all this is a late product of abstract reflection; and it is probable, in fact, from the very form of the name, that in so far as it is a distinct person, the type is comparatively modern; in any case, it is peculiarly Indian; but by its elements it is connected with the most ancient conceptions. As there is a power in the flame and the libation, so there is in the formula; and this formula the priest is not the only person to pronounce, any more than he is the only one to kindle Agni or shed Soma. There is a prayer in the thunder, and the gods, who know all things, are not ignorant of the power in the sacramental expressions. They possess all-potent spells that have remained hidden from men and are as ancient as the first rites, and it was by these the world was formed at first, and by which it is preserved up to the present. It is this omnipresent power of prayer which Brahmanaspati personifies, and it is not without reason that he is sometimes confounded with Agni, and especially with Indra. In reality each separate god and the priest himself become Brahmanaspati at the moment when they pronounce the mantras which gave them power over the things of heaven and of earth."

Chapter VI

Sun Or Light Deities

1. SURYA

Surya and Savitri are two names by which the Sun is commonly addressed in the Vedic hymns. Sometimes one name is used exclusively, sometimes they are used interchangeably, and sometimes they are used as though they represented quite distinct objects. It is supposed that Savitri refers to the sun when invisible; whilst Surya refers to him when he is visible to the worshippers. This at any rate gives *some* reason for the two names being employed, though it may not explain the case satisfactorily in every instance.

Although the hymns in which Surya is addressed are not very numerous, his worship was most common in the olden time, and has continued to the present hour. It is to him that the Gayatri, the most sacred text of the Vedas, is addressed at his rising by every devout Brāhman. Simple in its phraseology, this short verse is supposed to exert magical powers. It is as follows: —

"Let us meditate on that excellent glory of the divine
    Vivifier;
May he enlighten (or stimulate) our understandings."*

As a specimen of the language employed in some of the later writings in reference to this verse, read the following few lines from the "Skanda Purāna":— "Nothing in the Vedas is superior to the Gayatri. No invocation is equal to the Gayatri, as no city is equal to Kasi (Benares). The Gayatri is the mother of the Vedas, and of Brāhmans. By repeating it a man is saved. By the power of the Gayatri the Kshetriya (Warrior caste)

Surya

Vishvamitra became a Brāhmarsi (Brāhman saint), and even

___

*"Indian Wisdom," p. 20.

obtained such power as to be able to create a new world. What is there indeed that cannot be effected by the Gayatri? For the Gayatri is Vishnu, Brahmā, and Siva, and the three Vedas."*

With promise of such blessings, it is not to be wondered at that the worship of Surya should continue.

The following translation† of hymns from the Rig-Veda gives a fair specimen of the language used in addresses to Surya:—

"Behold the rays of Dawn, like heralds, lead on high
The Sun, that men may see the great all-knowing god.
The stars slink off like thieves, in company with Night,
Before the all-seeing eye, whose beams reveal his
    presence,
Gleaming like brilliant flames, to nation after nation.
With speed, beyond the ken of mortals, thou, O Sun !
Dost ever travel on, conspicuous to all.
Thou dost create the light, and with it dost illume
The universe entire; thou risest in the sight
Of all the race of men, and all the host of heaven.
Light-giving Varuna! thy piercing glance dost scan,
In quick succession, all this stirring, active world,
And penetrateth too the broad ethereal space,
Measuring our days and nights, and spying out all
    creatures.
Surya with flaming locks, clear-sighted god of day,
Thy seven ruddy mares bear on thy rushing car.
With these, thy self-yoked steeds, seven daughters of thy
    chariot
Onward thou dost advance. To thy refulgent orb
Beyond this lower gloom, and upward to the light
Would we ascend, O Sun! thou god among the gods."

---

*Kennedy's "Hindu Mythology," p. 345.
†"Indian Wisdom," p. 19.

Surya, as we have already noticed, is regarded as a son of Aditi; at other times he is said to be a son of Dyaus. Ushas (the Dawn) is called his wife, though in another passage he is said to be produced by the Dawn. Some texts state that he is the Vivifier of all things; whilst others state that he was formed and made to shine by Indra, Soma, Agni, and others.

From the character ascribed to Savitri in some hymns, it seems more natural to regard him as the sun shining in his strength, and Surya as the sun when rising and setting. Savitri is golden-eyed,* golden-handed, golden-tongued. He rides in a chariot drawn by radiant, white-footed steeds. He illuminates the earth; his golden arms stretched out to bless, infusing energy into all creatures, reach to the utmost ends of heaven. He is leader and king in heaven; the other gods follow him, and he it is who gives them immortality. He is prayed to for deliverance from sin, and to conduct the souls of the departed to the abode of the righteous.

In the Puranic Age, Surya sustains quite a different character. He is there called the son of Kasyapa and Aditi. He is described as a dark-red man, with three eyes and four arms: in two hands are water-lilies; with one he is bestowing a blessing, with the other he is encouraging his worshippers. He sits upon a red lotus, and rays of glory issue from his body. In addition to the daily worship that is offered to him by Brāhmans in the repetition of the Gayatri, he is worshipped once a year by the Hindus of all castes, generally on the first Sunday in the month of Māgh; and in seasons of sickness it is no uncommon thing for the low-caste Hindus to employ a Brāhman to repeat verses in his honour, in the hope that thus propitiated he will effect their recovery.

In the "Vishnu Purāna"† we find the following account of Surya. He married Sangnā, the daughter of Visvakarma; who,

---

*Mnir, O. S. T., v. 162 ff.
†Book iii. chap. ii.

after bearing him three children, was so oppressed with his brightness and glory that she was compelled to leave him. Before her departure, she arranged with Chhāya (Shadow) to take her place. For years Surya did not notice the change of wife. But one day, in a fit of anger, Chhāya pronounced a curse upon Yama (Death), a child of Sangnā's, which immediately took effect. As Surya knew that no mother's curse could destroy her offspring, he looked into the matter and discovered that his wife had forsaken him, leaving this other woman in her place. Through the power of meditation, Surya found Sangnā in a forest in the form of a mare; and, in order that he might again enjoy her society, he changed himself into a horse. After a few years, growing tired of this arrangement, they returned in proper form to their own dwelling. But in order that his presence might be bearable to his wife, his father-in-law Visvakarma, who was the architect of the gods, ground the Sun upon a stone, and by this means reduced his brightness by one-eighth. The part thus ground from Surya was not wasted. From it were produced the wonder-working discus of Vishnu, the trident of Siva, the lance of Kartikeya (the god of war), and the weapons of Kuvera (the god of riches).

The "Bhavishya Purāna" says, "Because there is none greater than he (*i.e.* Surya), nor has been, nor will be, therefore he is celebrated as the supreme soul in all the Vedas." Again, "That which is the sun, and thus called light or effulgent power, is adorable, and must be worshipped by those who dread successive births and deaths, and who eagerly desire beatitude." In the "Brahmā Purāna"* is a passage in which the sun is alluded to under twelve names, with epithets peculiar to each, as though they were twelve distinct sun-deities: —

"The first form of the sun is Indra, the lord of the gods, and the destroyer of their enemies; the second, Dhata, the creator of all things; the third, Parjanya, residing in the clouds, and

---

*Kennedy's "Hindu Mythology," p. 349.

showering rain on the earth from its beams; the fourth, Twasta, who dwells in all corporeal forms; the fifth, Pushan, who gives nutriment to all beings; the sixth, Aryama, who brings sacrifices to a successful conclusion; the seventh derives his name from almsgiving, and delights mendicants with gifts; the eighth is called Vivas'van, who ensures digestion; the ninth, Vishnu, who constantly manifests himself for the destruction of the enemies of the gods; the tenth, Ansuman, who preserves the vital organs in a sound state; the eleventh, Varuna, who, residing in the waters, vivifies the universe; and the twelfth, Mitra, who dwells in the orb of the moon, for the benefit of the three worlds. These are the twelve splendours of the sun, the supreme spirit, who through them pervades the universe, and irradiates the inmost souls of men."

Surya is said to have Aruna (Rosy), the Dawn, the son of Kasyapa and Kadru, as his charioteer.

According to the Rāmayana, Sugriva, the king of the monkey host which assisted Rāma in his great expedition to regain possession of Vitā his wife, was a son of Surya by a monkey. According to the Mahābhārata, the hero Karna also was the son of this deity; and when he was in the form of a horse, he became father of the Asvins, and communicated the white Yajur-Veda.

When speaking of the planets, Surya will be noticed again under the name of Ravi.

Among the many names and epithets by which this deity is known, the following are the most common : —

Dinakara, "The Maker of the day."

Bhāskara, "The Creator of light."

Vivaswat, "The Radiant one."

Mihira, "He who waters the earth;" *i.e.* he draws up the moisture from the seas so that the clouds are formed.

Grahapati, "The Lord of the stars."

Karmasākshi, "The Witness of (men's) works."

Mārtanda, "A descendant of Mritanda."

2. PUSHAN

Pushan is the name of a sun-god to whom some hymns are exclusively addressed, and whose praise at other times is sung in connection with that of Indra and other gods. In these hymns his character is not very clearly defined. He is said* to behold the entire universe; is addressed as the guide of travellers, and the protector of cattle. He is called upon to protect his servants in battle, and to defend them as of old. He is invoked in the marriage ceremonial, and asked to take the bride's hand, to lead her away, and to bless her in her conjugal relations. He is said also to conduct the spirits of the departed from this world to the next. In one text he is called "the nourisher," as Vishnu in later times was called "the preserver." By far the greater number of prayers addressed to him seem to regard him as the guide and protector of travellers, both along the ordinary journeys of life and in the longer journey to the other world; and as he is supposed to be constantly travelling about, he is said to know the road by which they have to go.

The following is a specimen of the hymns addressed to Pushan in the Rig-Veda:—" Conduct us, Pushan, over our road; remove distress, son of the deliverer; go on before us. Smite away from before us the destructive and injurious wolf which seeks after us. Drive away from our path the waylayer, the thief and the robber Tread with thy foot upon the burning weapons of that deceitful wretch, whoever he be. O wonder-working and wise Pushan, we desire that help of thine wherewith thou didst favour our fathers! O god, who bringest all blessings, and art distinguished by the golden spear, make wealth easy of acquisition! Convey us past our opponents; make our paths easy to travel; gain strength for us here. Lead us over a country of rich pastures; let no new trouble (beset our) path. Bestow, satiate, grant, stimulate us; fill our belly. We do not reproach

---

*Muir, O. S. T., v. 171 ff.

Pushan, we praise him with hymns; and we seek riches from the wonder-working god."* "May we, O Pushan! meet with a wise man who will straightway direct us and say, 'It is this.' May Pushan follow our kine; may he protect our horses; may he give us food. ... Come hither, glowing god, the deliverer, may we meet."† In the Purānas Pushan occupies a far less exalted position. It seems almost like a burlesque to see him, who in the Vedas is reverently approached as the giver of good to his worshippers, described as being obliged to feed upon gruel, because his teeth have been knocked out of his mouth. The earliest form of the legend describing this event is found in the Taittiriya Sanhita. Rudra, the name by which Siva was then known, not being invited to a great sacrifice that Daksha, his father-in-law, was celebrating, in his anger shot an arrow which pierced the sacrificial victim. Pushan ate his share, and in doing so broke his teeth. In describing Daksha,‡ an account of this sacrifice will be given. In the "Vishnu Purāna" Pushan appears as one of the Ādityas.

3. MITRA AND VARUNA

These deities are most frequently named together in the hymns; Varuna is often addressed alone, but Mitr very seldom. The idea of the older commentators was that Mitra represented and ruled over the day, whilst Varuna was ruler of the night. "Varuna is sometimes visible to the gaze of his worshippers; he dwells in a house having a thousand doors, so that he is ever accessible to men. He is said to have good eyesight, for he knows what goes on in the hearts of men. He is king of gods and men; is mighty and terrible; none can resist his authority. He is sovereign ruler of the universe." "It is he who makes the

---

*Muir, O. S. T., v. 175.
†Ibid. v. 177.
‡Part iii. chap. i.

sun to shine in heaven; the winds that blow are but his breath; he has hollowed out the channels of the rivers which flow at his command, and he has made the depths of the sea. His ordinances are fixed and unassailable; through their operation the moon walks in brightness, and the stars, which appear in the nightly sky, vanish in daylight. The birds flying in the air, the rivers in their sleepless flow, cannot attain a knowledge of his power and wrath. But he knows the flight of the birds in the sky, the course of the far travelling wind, the paths of ships on the ocean, and beholds all the secret things that have been or shall be done. He witnesses men's truth and falsehood."*

Varuna

---

*Muir, O. S. T., v. 58 ff.

The following is a metrical version of one of the hymns of the Rig-Veda as given by Dr. Muir : — *

"The mighty lord on high our deeds as if at hand espies;
The gods know all men do, though men would fain their
      deeds disguise:
Whoe'er stands, whoe'er moves, or steals from place to
      place,
Or hides him in his secret cell, the gods his movements
      trace.
Wherever two together plot, and deem they are alone,
King Varuna is there, a third, and all their schemes are
      known.
This earth is his, to him belong those vast and boundless
      skies,
Both seas within him rest, and yet in that small pool he
      lies.
Whoever far beyond the sky should think his way to
      win,
He could not there elude the grasp of Varuna the king.
His spies descending from the skies glide all this world
      around;
Their thousand eyes, all scanning, sweep to earth's
      remotest bound.
Whate'er exists in heaven and earth, whate'er beyond
      the skies,
Before the eye of Varuna the king unfolded lies.
The secret winkings all he counts of every mortars eyes;
He wields this universal frame as gamester throws his
      dice.
Those knotted nooses which thou flingst, O god ! the bad
      to snare,
All liars let them overtake, but all the truthful spare."

---

*Ibid. v. 64.

Professor Roth says of this hymn, "There is no hymn in the whole Vedic literature which expresses the divine omniscience in such forcible terms;" and it would not be easy to find in any literature many passages to surpass it in this respect.

In other hymns we learn that the affairs of men are under his control; he is asked to prolong life, to punish transgressors; and a hope is held out that the righteous shall see him reigning in the spirit world in conjunction with Yama, the ruler of that region. Varuna in fact has attributes and functions ascribed to him in the Vedas, of a higher moral character than any other of the gods, and therefore men call upon him for pardon and purity. "Release us," they say, "from the sins of our fathers, and from those which we have committed in our own persons." And again, "Be gracious, O mighty god, be gracious. I have sinned through want of power; be gracious."

In the hymns addressed to Mitra and Varuna together, almost the same terms are employed as when Varuna is addressed alone. Both are spoken of as righteous, and as the promoters of religion. They are said to avenge sin and falsehood.

In the Vedic literature, though Varuna is not regarded chiefly as the god of the ocean, as he is in the later writings, but rather, as the above hymns show, as one of the gods of light, yet there are passages which describe him as being connected with the waters of the atmosphere and on the earth, which afford some foundation for the later conceptions of his kingdom. Thus, for instance, we read, "May the waters which are celestial, and those which flow; those for which channels are dug, and those which are self-produced; those which are proceeding to the ocean, and are bright and purifying, preserve me! May those (waters) in the midst of which King Varuna goes...preserve me!"* In other places he is said to dwell in the waters as Soma does in the woods. Professor Roth gives a

---

*Muir, O. S. T., v. 73.

probable explanation as to the manner in which Varuna, who was originally the god of the heavens, came to be regarded as the god of the ocean. He says:* "When, on the one hand, the conception of Varuna as the all-embracing heaven had been established, and, on the other hand, the observation of the rivers flowing towards the ends of the earth and to the sea had led to the conjecture that there existed an ocean enclosing the earth in its bosom, then the way was thoroughly prepared for connecting Varuna with the ocean."

In the Brāhmana of the Rig-Veda† is an interesting legend showing that probably human sacrifices were at one time offered to Varuna. A certain king named Harischandra had no son. Being greatly distressed on this account, as a son was necessary to the due performance of his funeral ceremonies, the king, acting upon the advice of Nārada the sage, went to Varuna, saying—

> "Let but a son be born, O king! to me,
> And I will sacrifice that son to thee."

Varuna heard the prayer, and granted a son. When the boy grew up, his father told him of the vow he had made; but unfortunately the son was not willing to be sacrificed, and left his home. Varuna, not being at all pleased at the non-fulfilment of the king's vow, afflicted him with dropsy. For six years the boy wandered in the forest; at length, happening to meet with a poor Brāhman with his three sons, the prince proposed to purchase one of them to offer to the god as a substitute for himself. The father could not give up his firstborn, the mother would not yield her youngest; the middle one was therefore taken. The prince then returned home, taking with him the Brāhman's son. At first the king was delighted at the prospect

---

*Muir, O. S. T., v. 75.
†"India" Wisdom," p. 29.

of being able to keep his promise to the deity; but a difficulty now arose as to who would slay the boy. After some time, on the consideration of a large present being made to him, the boy's father consented to do this The boy was bound, the father ready to strike, when the boy asked permission to recite some texts in praise of the gods. Of course this was granted; and as a result the deities thus lauded were so pleased with the boy's piety, that they interceded with Varuna to spare him. Varuna granted their request, suffered the boy to live, and Harischandra recovered from his sickness.

In the Purānas, as mentioned before, Varuna is described as the god of the ocean. After a great conflict between the powers of heaven and earth, when order was again restored, the "Vishnu Purana" records the position assigned to the various deities. In that account Varuna is said to rule over the waters. In the same Purāna we read that an old Brāhman named Richika was most anxious to obtain in marriage a daughter of King Gādhi, who was really an incarnation of Indra. Gādhi refused to give his daughter to Richika except on one condition: that he would present him with a thousand fleet horses, each having one white ear. Horses of this colour were special favourites of Indra; hence those sacrificed to him usually had this peculiarity. The Brāhman is said to have propitiated Varuna, the god of the ocean, who gave him the thousand steeds, by means of which he was able to obtain the princess in marriage.

Varuna is represented in pictures as a white man sitting upon a fabulous marine monster called a *makara*. This animal has the head and front legs of an antelope, and the body and tail of a fish. In his right hand he carries a noose. He is occasionally worshipped in seasons of drought, and by fishermen as they cast their nets, but nowadays no images of him are made.

The following legend is found in the "Padma Purāna."* On one occasion Rāvana, the demon king of the island, was

---

*"Ward on the Hindoos," i. 57.

travelling home to Ceylon, carrying with him a stone *linga,* the emblem of Siva. He was desirous of setting up the worship of the great god there, and was taking the image from the Himalayas for this purpose. But the gods, fearing he would grow too powerful through his devotion to Siva, wished to frustrate his purpose. Siva, in giving the stone, made Rāvana promise that wherever it first touched the ground, after leaving Siva's abode, it should remain. Aware of this fact, the gods tried to induce him to let it rest on the earth before he reached Ceylon. At last it was agreed that Varuna should enter Rāvana's body, so that, in attempting to free himself, he might be compelled to loose his hold of the *linga.* Accordingly Varuna entered Rāvana, and caused him such intense pain that he could scarcely bear it. When thus suffering, Indra, in the form of an old Brāhman, passed by, and offered to take hold of the stone. No sooner did Rāvana entrust it to him, than he let it fall to the ground. It is said that it sank into the earth, the top of it being visible at Vaidyanāth in Birbhum to this day. The river Khursu is said to have taken its rise from Varuna when he left Rāvana at this place; and, as a result, the Hindus will not drink of its waters.

Although Varuna is described in the Vedas as a holy being, according to the teaching of the Purāna his heaven is a place of sensual delights. He sits with his queen Varunī on a throne of diamonds; Samudrā (the sea), Ganga (the Ganges), and the gods and goddesses of different rivers, lakes, springs, etc., form his court. And stories are told of conduct the very opposite to what would be expected in one who once was addressed in such language as is found in the Vedic hymns. He is said, conjointly with Surya, to have been enamoured of Urvasi, a nymph of Indra's heaven, by whom they had a son named Agastya, one of the most eminent of Hindu ascetics.

Varuna is also known as Prachetas, the wise; Jalapati, the lord of water; Yādapati, the lord of aquatic animals; Amburaja, the king of waters; Pasī, the noose-carrier.

4. THE ASVINS

From the hymns addressed to these deities it is not at all easy
to know who or what they are. Yaska, the commentator of the
Vedas, deriving the name from a root meaning "to fill," says
they are called Asvins because they pervade everything, the
one with light, the other with moisture. Another commentator
says they are called Asvins because they ride upon horses.
Some say that by them heaven and earth are indicated; others
that they are day and night; others, again, that they are the sun
and moon. Professor Roth says, "They hold a perfectly distinct
position in the entire body of the Vedic deities of light. They are
the earliest bringers of light in the morning sky, who hasten on
in the clouds before the Dawn and prepare the way for her."*
In some hymns they are said to be sons of the sun (*vide* Surya);
in others are called children of the sky; in others, again, as the
offspring of the ocean. They seem to represent the transition
from night to morning— night when it is passing into day.

The Asvins are said to have had Suryā, the daughter of
Savitri, as their common wife. She chose them, as her life was
lonely. Her father had intended her to marry Soma; but, as the
gods were anxious to obtain so beautiful a bride, it was agreed
that they should run a race, Suryā being the prize of the winner.
The Asvins were successful, and she ascended their chariot.†
In another passage Soma is said to have been her husband; the
Asvins being friends of the bridegroom.

The Asvins are regarded as the physicians of the gods,
and are declared to be able to restore to health the blind, the
sick, the lame, and the emaciated amongst mortals. They are
the special guardians of the slow and backward; the devoted
friends of elderly women who are unmarried. They are said
to preside over love and marriage, and are implored to bring

---

*Muir, O. S. T., v. 235.
†Muir, O. S. T., v. 236.

together hearts that love.*

A number of legends are found illustrating the power of the Asvins in healing the sick and assisting those in trouble, from which we learn that they could restore youth and vigour to the aged and decrepit; they rescued a man from drowning, and carried him in safety to his home. The leg of Vispalā, that was cut off in battle, they replaced by an iron one. At the request of a wolf, they restored sight to a man who had been blinded by his father as a punishment for slaughtering a hundred and one sheep, which he gave to the wolf to eat. They restored sight and power to walk to one who was blind and lame. As a result of these and other similar legends, the Asvins are invoked for "offspring, wealth, victory, destruction of enemies, the preservation of the worshippers themselves, of their houses and cattle."

The following legend of the cure they effected on Chyavana, from the "Satapatha Brāhmana,"† will illustrate the peculiar features of the work of the Asvins :— Chyavana, having assumed a shrivelled form, was abandoned by his family. Saryāta, a Rishi, with his tribe settled in the neighbourhood; when his sons seeing the body of Chyavana, not knowing it was a human being, pelted it with stones. Chyavana naturally resented this, and sowed dissension amongst the family of Saryāta. Anxious to learn the cause of this, Saryāta inquired of the shepherds near if they could account for it: they told him that his sons had insulted Chyavana. Saryāta thereupon took his daughter Sukanyā in his chariot, and, apologizing for what had been done, gave his daughter to the decrepit man as a peace-offering.

Now the Asvins were in the habit of wandering about the world performing cures, and, seeing Sukanya, they were delighted with her beauty and wished to seduce her. They

---

*Ibid. v. 234.
†Muir, O. S. T., v. 250.

said, "What is that shrivelled body by which you are lying? Leave him and follow us." She replied that whilst he lived she would not leave the man to whom her father had given her. When they came to her a second time, acting on her husband's suggestion she said, "You speak contemptuously of my husband, whilst you are incomplete and imperfect yourselves." And on condition that they would make her husband young again, she consented to tell them in what respect they were imperfect and incomplete. Upon this they told her to take her husband to a certain pond. After bathing there, he came forth with his youth renewed. Sukanyā told the Asvins that they were imperfect because they had not been invited to join the other gods in a great sacrifice that was to be celebrated at Kurukshetra. The Asvins proceeded to the place of sacrifice, and, asking to be allowed to join in it, were told that they could not do so, because they had wandered familiarly among men, performing cures. In reply to this, the Asvins declared that the gods were making a headless sacrifice. The gods inquiring how this could be, the Asvins replied, "Invite us to join you, and we will tell you." To this the gods consented.

In another account of this legend, it is said that, as the Asvins were physicians, they were consequently unclean; hence no Brāhman must be a physician, or he is thereby unfitted for the work of a priest; but as the work of the Asvins was necessary, they were purified, and then allowed to join the gods. They then restored the head of the sacrifice.

Professor Goldstucker* says, "The myth of the Asvins is one of that class of myths in which two distinct elements, the cosmical and the human or historical, have gradually become blended into one. ...The historical or human element in it, I believe, is represented by those legends which refer to the wonderful cures effected by the Asvins, and to their performances of a kindred sort; the cosmical element is that

---

*Chambers's "Cyclopaedia."

relating to their luminous nature. The link which connects both seems to be the mysteriousness of the nature and effects of light and of the healing art at a remote antiquity. It would appear that these Asvins, like the Ribhus, were originally renowned mortals, who, in the course of time, were translated into the companionship of the gods."

5. USHAS

This goddess, representative of the Dawn, is a favourite object of celebration with the Vedic poets, and "the hymns addressed to her are among the most beautiful — if not the most beautiful — in the entire collection."* She is described as the daughter of the Sky, has Night for her sister, and is related to Varuna. She is at times spoken of as the wife of the Sun; at other times Agni is given as her lover; the Asvins are her friends. Indra is at one time regarded as her creator; at another time he assumes a hostile position, and even crushed her chariot with his thunderbolt.

Ushas is said† to travel in a shining chariot drawn by ruddy horses or cows. Like a beautiful maiden dressed by her mother, a dancing girl covered with jewels, a gaily-attired wife appearing before her husband, or a beautiful girl coming from her bath, she, smiling and confiding in the irresistible power of her attractions, unfolds her bosom to the gaze of the beholders. She dispels the darkness, disclosing the treasures it concealed. She illuminates the world, revealing its most distant extremities. She is the life and health of all things, causing the birds to fly from their nests, and, like a young housewife, awaking all her creatures, sends them forth to the pursuit of their varied occupations. She does good service to the gods, by causing the worshippers to awake, and the sacrificial fires to

---

*Muir, O. S. T., v. 181.
†Ibid. v. 194.

be lighted. She is asked to arouse only the devout and liberal, while she allows the niggardly to sleep on. She is young, being born every day; and yet she is old, being immortal, wearing out the lives of successive generations, which disappear one after another, whilst she continues undying. The souls of the departed are said to go to her and to the sun.

In the following lines* will be found the main teaching of the Vedas respecting this goddess:—

> "Hail, ruddy Ushas, golden goddess, borne
> Upon thy sinning car, thou comest like
> A lovely maiden by her mother decked,
> Disclosing coyly all thy hidden grace
> To our admiring eyes; or like a wife
> Unveiling to her lord, with conscious pride,
> Beauties which, as he gazes lovingly,
> Seem fresher, fairer, each succeeding morn.
> Through years and years thou hast lived on, and yet
> Thou'rt ever young. Thou art the breath and life
> Of all that breathes and lives, awaking day by day
> Myriads of prostrate sleepers, as from death,
> Causing the birds to flutter in their nests,
> And rousing men to ply with busy feet
> Their daily duties and appointed tasks,
> Toiling for wealth, or pleasure, or renown."

In the following verses by Dr. Muir† we have a still more vivid picture of this goddess as represented in the Vedic hymns:—

> "Hail, Ushas, daughter of the sky,
> Who, borne upon thy shining car

---

*"Indian Wisdom," p. 20.
†Muir, O. S. T., v. 196.

By ruddy steeds from realms afar,
And ever lightening drawest nigh—

"Thou sweetly smilest, goddess fair,
    Disclosing all thy youthful grace,
    Thy bosom bright, thy radiant face,
And lustre of thy golden hair—

"She shines a fond and winning bride,
    Who robes her form in brilliant guise,
    And to her lord's admiring eyes
Displays her charms with conscious pride—

"Or virgin by her mother decked,
    Who, glorying in her beauty, shows
    In every glance her power she knows
All eyes to fix, all hearts subject—

"Or actress, who by skill in song
    And dance, and graceful gestures light,
    And many-coloured vestures bright,
Enchants the eager, gazing throng—

"Or maid, who, wont her limbs to lave
    In some cold stream among the woods,
    Where never vulgar eye intrudes,
Emerges fairer from the wave—

"But closely by the amorous Sun
    Pursued and vanquished in the race,
    Thou soon art locked in his embrace,
And with him blendest into one.

"Fair Ushas, though through years untold
    Thou hast lived on, yet thou art born

A new on each succeeding morn,
And so thou art both young and old.

"As in thy fated ceaseless course
  Thou risest on us day by day,
  Thou wearest all our lives away
With silent, ever-wasting force.

"Their round our generations run:
  The old depart, and in their place
  Springs ever up a younger race,
Whilst thou, immortal, lookest on.

"All those who watched for thee of old
  Are gone, and now 'tis we who gaze
  On thy approach; in future days
Shall other men thy beams behold.

"But 'tis not thoughts so grave and sad
  Alone that thou dost with thee bring,
  A shadow o'er our hearts to fling—
Thy beams returning make us glad

"Thy sister, sad and sombre Night,
  With stars that in the blue expanse,
  Like sleepless eyes, mysterious glance,
At thy approach is quenched in light;

"And earthly forms, till now concealed
  Behind her veil of dusky hue,
  Once more come sharply out to view,
By thine illuming glow revealed.

"Thou art the life of all that lives,
  The breath of all that breathes; the sight

Of thee makes every countenance bright,
New strength to every spirit gives.

"When thou dost pierce the murky gloom,
    Birds flutter forth from every brake,
    All sleepers as from death awake,
And men their myriad tasks resume.

"Some, prosperous, wake in listless mood,
    And others every nerve to strain
    The goal of power or wealth to gain,
Or what they deem the highest good.

"But some to holier thoughts aspire,
    In hymns the race celestial praise,
    And light, on human hearths to blaze,
The heaven-born sacrificial fire.

"And not alone do bard and priest
    Awake —the gods thy power confess
    By starting into consciousness
When thy first rays suffuse the east;

"And hasting downward from the sky,
    They visit men devout and good,
    Consume their consecrated food,
And all their longings satisfy.

"Bright goddess, let thy genial rays
    To us bring store of envied wealth
    In kine and steeds, and sons, with health,
And joy of heart, and length of days."

In the later writings we find merely the name of Ushas. The
people lost much of their poetic fire; hence the more human

and practical deities caused the more poetical ones to pass into oblivion. Some of the figures in the preceding extracts are most beautifully drawn. The changing colours of the dawn are compared to the many-coloured robes of the dancing girl; the golden tipped clouds that appear ere the sun shines in his strength, are like the jewels of a bride decked for her husband; whilst the quiet modesty of the dawn herself is like a shy maiden, conscious indeed of her beauty, entering society under the protection of her mother. And from the last four lines of the metrical sketch it will be noticed that she was believed to be able to bestow upon her worshippers cattle, horses, sons, health, joy, and length of days.

Chapter VII

The Storm Deities

1. INDRA

As was noticed previously, Indra, together with Agni and Surya, by means of sacrifice obtained supremacy over

Indra.

the other gods; and if we may judge from the number of hymns addressed to him in the Vedas, he was the most popular deity.

He is the god of the firmament, in whose hands are the thunder and the lightning; at whose command the refreshing showers fall to render the earth fruitful. When it is borne in mind that in India for months together the earth, exposed to the scorching rays of the sun, becomes so hard that it is impossible for the fields to be ploughed or the seed to be sown, it will not be regarded as wonderful that the god who is supposed to bestow rain should frequently be appealed to, and that the most laudatory songs should be addressed to him. To the poetic minds of the Vedic age, the clouds that the winds brought from the ocean were enemies who held their treasures in their fast embrace until, conquered by Indra, they were forced to pour them upon the parched soil. And very naturally when, in answer to the cry of his worshippers, the genial rains descended, and the earth was thereby changed from a desert to a garden, songs of thanksgiving and praise, couched in the strongest terms, were addressed to him. The attributes ascribed to him refer principally to his physical superiority; and the blessings sought from him are chiefly of a physical rather than a spiritual character.

Indra is not regarded as an uncreated deity. In some hymns he is spoken of as the twin-brother of Agni, and therefore the son of Heaven and Earth; whilst, in other hymns, heaven and earth are said to have been formed by him. Although his parents are often referred to, it is but seldom that they are named; and when they are named, they are not always the same. He is the king of the gods; and in post-Vedic ages his reign is said to extend for a hundred divine years only; at the end of which time he may be superseded as king by some other of the gods, or even by man, if any be able to perform the severe penance necessary to obtain this exalted position.

In pictures, Indra is often represented as a man with four

arms and hands; with two he holds a lance, in the third is a thunderbolt, whilst the fourth is empty. He is also sometimes painted with two arms only, and, having eyes all over his body, is then called Sahasrāksha (the thousand-eye). He is generally depicted as riding upon the wonderful elephant Airavata, who was produced at the churning of the ocean,* carrying a thunderbolt in his right hand and a bow in his left. In the Vedic Age his worship was far more popular than it is at present.

The position and attributes of Indra as taught by the Vedas will be seen from the following description, abbreviated from that given by Dr. Muir:— †

> "Come, Indra, come, thou much invoked,
> Our potent hymn thy steeds has yoked.
> Friend Indra, from the sky descend,
> Thy course propitious hither bend.
> But, Indra, though of us thou thinkest,
> And our libations gladly drinkest,
> We, mortal men, can only share
> A humble portion of thy care.
> We know how many potent ties
> Enchain thee in thy paradise.
> Thou hast at home a lovely wife,
> The charm and solace of thy life.
> Thou hast a ceaseless round of joys
> Which all thy circling hours employs;
> Joys such as gods immortal know,
> Unguessed by mortals here below."

Being invoked by mortals, Indra is born. The Sky and the Earth trembled at his appearance, and the Sky exclaimed—

---

*See part ii. chap. iv.
†Muir, O. S. T., v. 126.

"Thy father was a stalwart wight;
Of most consummate skill was he,
The god whose genius fashioned thee."

Immediately after his birth the god gave unmistakable evidence of his divinity. Grasping his weapons, he cried—

"Where, mother, dwell those warriors fierce,
Whose haughty hearts these bolts must pierce?"

Borne in his chariot, hastened by the prayers of his people, the god appears.

"Yet not one form alone he bears,
But various shapes of glory wears,
His aspect changing at his will,
Transmuted, yet resplendent still.
In warlike semblance see him stand,
Red lightnings wielding in his hand."

Ready prepared for him is a feast, the principal attraction of which is the Soma juice.* Indra was particularly fond of this intoxicating drink. It is a most strange circumstance that, whilst the Hindus of the present day are prohibited from the use of intoxicants, Indra is described as being addicted to the Soma; whilst the drink itself is deified and worshipped as a god. Indra on his arrival is invited to quaff the invigorating cup:—

"Thou, Indra, oft of old hast quaffed
With keen delight our Soma draught.
All gods the luscious Soma love,
But thou all other gods above.

---

*See chap. viii.

Thy mother knew how well this juice
Was fitted for her infant's use.
Into a cup she crushed the sap,
Which thou didst sip upon her lap.
Yes, Indra, on thy natal morn,
The very hour that thou wast born,
Thou didst those jovial tastes display,
Which still survive in strength to-day."

Indra, after singing the praises of the Soma juice, drinks
the proffered cup, and as a result is most graciously disposed
towards the worshippers, ready to give whatever they ask.
When thus strengthened by the draught, he goes forth to meet
the great enemy he came to conquer. This enemy is Vritra
(Drought). And in the conflict and victory are seen the peculiar
blessings to the earth and man that Indra is able to grant. Vritra
is thus described : —

"He whose magic powers
From earth withhold the genial showers;
Of mortal men the foe malign,
And rival of the race divine;
Whose demon hosts from age to age
With Indra war unceasing wage;
Who, times unnumbered crushed and slain,
Is ever newly born again,
And evermore renews the strife
In which again he forfeits life."

The battle is described at length; in which we have a graphic
description of the commencement of the rainy season, with the
severe thunderstorms which usually accompany this change
of the seasons. At last the conflict is over:

"And soon the knell of Vritra's doom

Was sounded by the clang and boom
  Of Indra's iron shower.
Pierced, cloven, crushed, with horrid yell,
The dying demon headlong fell
  Down from his cloud-built tower."

As a result of the victory of the god, the rains descend and the earth is made fruitful:

"Now bound by Sushna's spell no more,
The clouds discharge their liquid store;
And long by torrid sunbeams baked
The plains by copious showers are slaked;
The rivers swell, and seawards sweep
Their turbid torrents broad and deep.
The peasant views with deep delight,
And thankful heart, the auspicious sight.
His leafless fields, so sere and sad,
Will soon with waving crops be glad;
And mother Earth, now brown and bare,
A robe of brilliant green will wear."

After this blessing has been received, the sun shines, and earth again is bright; the gods come with their congratulations to their king, and men present their thanksgivings.

Such was Indra in ancient times; and though worshipped still, he occupies a very inferior position in the present age. As mentioned previously, according to the teaching of the later books, his rule over the gods continues for a hundred divine* years; at the expiration of which time he may be superseded by another god, or even by a man. The Purānas teach that, in each age of the world, a different being has enjoyed this position. In

---

*See part ii. chap. x.

the "Vishnu Purāna"* is the following story of a man raising himself to the throne of Indra.

There was a war between the gods and demons; both parties inquired of Brahmā which would be victorious. Brahmā replied, "The side for which Rāji (an earthly king) shall take up arms." The demons called first upon Rāji to invoke his aid. He promised to assist them provided they would make him their Indra or king. They could not promise this, as Prahlāda their Indra's term of office was not yet expired. The same condition being proposed to the gods, they consented, and Rāji became their Indra. He fought for them, and conquered. Upon this, Indra bowed down before him, and, placing Rāji's foot upon his head, said, "Thou hast preserved me from a great danger. I acknowledge thee as my father: thou art king over all; I am thy son." Rāji, however, was contented to remain as king on earth, and appointed Indra to continue as his representative on the throne of heaven. On the death of Rāji, his sons wished to assume the position their father had declined. This Indra opposed, but was at length compelled to yield. After a time, being sad because deprived of his share in the sacrifices of mortals, Indra met with his spiritual preceptor Vrihaspati, and asked him for a morsel of the sacrificial butter. The teacher replied that, had Indra applied to him earlier, he would not have been reduced to such straits; but "as it is," he said, "I will regain your sovereignty in a few days." Upon this he commenced a sacrifice, with the special purpose of obtaining power for Indra. The result was, that Rāji's sons were led into sin, they became enemies of the Brāhmans, despised the Vedas, and neglected their religious duties. When thus weakened, Indra fell upon and slew them.

The most effectual way by which a mortal could obtain the position of Indra was by the sacrifice of a hundred horses;

---

*Book iv. chap. ix.

and, as will be seen in the account of Gangā,* the Indra of that time did not object to play the part of a thief, so as to prevent the completion of the rites by which he was to be deprived of his sovereignty. The most common and generally successful method by which these ambitious mortals were frustrated in their design was by his sending down some celestial nymphs, called Apsaras, who, by their beauty, distracted the thoughts of the devotees, and rendered them unfit to offer this great sacrifice.

In the "Vishnu Parāna,"† there is a legend of a conflict between Indra and Krishna, in which Indra is overcome. Krishna, accompanied by his wife Satyabhālmā, visits Indra in his heaven. On her arrival, this lady was most anxious to obtain possession of the wonderful Pārijātā tree, which was produced at the churning of the ocean, and planted in Indra's heavenly garden. This tree was beautiful in form, was adorned with lovely and sweet-scented flowers, and bore most luscious fruit. The flowers had this virtue, that, worn in the hair by a wife, they enabled her to retain the love of her husband; whilst those who ate the fruit of this tree could remember what had occurred in their previous states of existence. At the request of his wife, Krishna took the tree, and placed it upon Garuda, his wonderful bird-vehicle. Immediately there was an uproar in heaven; but though Indra and his attendant deities tried to prevent the removal of his property, they could not do so. Krishna caught a thunderbolt of Indra in his hand, and, returning home unhurt, planted the tree in his garden.

The Rāmāyana has a story showing that Indra was believed to have been guilty of the grossest immorality — the seduction of the wife of his spiritual teacher. He is said to have visited the house of Gautama, in the form of a sage, hoping to be mistaken by the preceptor's wife for her husband, who was absent from

*Part iii. chap. viii.
†Book v. chap. xxx.

home. But although Ahalyā knew him to be Indra, she yielded
to his wishes. As Indra was about to leave, Gautama returned,
and, knowing what had happened, cursed the god and his
wife. Indra in consequence lost his manhood; and Ahalyā
was doomed to live for many years invisible in a forest, until
Rāma should come to restore her to her former state.* Another
account of this curse of Gautama was that Indra was compelled
to carry a thousand disgraceful marks upon his body, that all
might know the sin of which he had been guilty. At the god's
earnest request these were changed from their original form
into eyes; which by the ignorant came to be regarded as an
indication of his omniscience.

The heaven of Indra must not be passed over without
notice, as it is there the good on earth hope to go for a time, as
a reward of their holy lives. To go to Swarga, as his heaven is
named, is not the highest happiness a man can obtain, because
he cannot remain there for ever. When his allotted years of
happiness are over, he must return to earth and live other lives,
until he becomes perfect and fit to enjoy the highest felicity —
absorption into the Divine Being. The "Vishnu Purāna"†
says: "Not in hell alone do the souls of the deceased undergo
pain: there is no cessation even in heaven; for its temporary
inhabitant is ever tormented with the prospect of descending
again to earth. Again must he be born upon earth, and again
must he die. Whatever is produced that is most acceptable to
man becomes a seed whence springs the tree of sorrow."

The home of Indra is situated on Mount Meru.‡ It has

---

*One result of this sin of Indra was the fact that a son of Rāvana,
a demon king, who ruled in Ceylon, was able to carry him off as
a captive, when he made war upon the gods; and it was not until
Brahmā promised immortality to this warrior, that he consented to
release his prisoner. Brahmā gave this prince the name of Indrajita
(conqueror of Indra).
†Book vi. chap. v.
‡Meru is a fabulous mountain, supposed to be the centre of the earth.

beautiful houses for its inhabitants; and the splendour of its capital is unequalled in the universe. Its gardens are stocked with trees that afford a grateful shade, yield the most luscious fruits, and are adorned with beautiful and fragrant flowers. Most beautiful nymphs (Apsaras) charm the happy inhabitants, whilst choristers and musicians, unrivalled in the universe, discourse sweet music. The city was built by Visvakarma. It is eight hundred miles in circumference, and forty miles high. Its pillars are diamonds; its palaces, thrones, and furniture, pure gold.*

In Bengal this deity is worshipped one day in each year. His image is made of mud, prettily painted; on the day after it has been worshipped it is cast into the river. At the commencement of a sacrifice, too, he is invoked, in the hope that he will convey the prayers and offerings to the deity specially worshipped at that time, or that he will conduct the deity into the presence of the worshippers. In seasons of drought special offerings are made to him in some parts of the country, that through his power the clouds may pour their streams upon the parched country.

The more common of Indra's other names are the following:—Sakra, the able one; Divapati, the lord of the gods; Bajrī, he who wields the thunderbolt; Vritrahā, the destroyer of Vritra; Meghavāhana, he who rides on the clouds; Mahendra, the great Indra; Swargapati, the lord of heaven.

2. INDRĀNI.

It is believed to be somewhere to the north of the Himalayas. The heavens of the other gods are situated in its vicinity. From the fact that they regarded heaven to be near their former home, it would seem that the Indo-Aryans retained pleasant recollections of the place whence they migrated; or perhaps the inaccessibility of these mountains was a reason for heaven being placed on their summits.

*"Malābhārata," quoted by Ward, ii. *36.*

Of Indrāni, the wife of Indra (called also Sachi), very little is said. In the Rig-Veda* we read, "Among all females Indrāni is the most fortunate; for her husband shall not at any future time die of old age." This may be explained by the fact that Indrāni is wife to all who successively attain to the throne of Indra. There is always some one ruling in heaven; the office is perpetual, and as she is the wife of the reigning king, whoever he may be, her husband can never die of old age. Though kings may come and go, she continues queen. She is said to have a son, Chitragupta by name, who was born of a cow; for, owing to a curse pronounced by Umā, none of the goddesses could become a mother. She practised austerities, in order that, she might not be childless; and by means of this expedient her desire was gratified. At the birth of this child, the reputed mother suffered all the pains attendant on childbirth, and was able to nurse him.

3. PARJANYA

There are a few hymns addressed to this deity in the Rig-Veda; but from the character and functions ascribed to him it is difficult to see wherein he differs from Indra. Professor Roth† says, "Taking a review of the whole, we find that Parjanya is a god who presides over the lightning, the thunder, the rain, and the procreation of plants and living creatures. But it is by no means clear whether he is originally a god of the rain, or a god of the thunder." In another essay he says Parjanya is "the god of the thunderstorms and rain, the generator and nourisher of plants and living creatures. Seeing that the hymns addressed to this deity are so very similar to those sung to Indra, may not Parjanya (whose name signifies one acting for another) be merely another name for Indra?" In these hymns are the

---

*Muir, O. S. T., v. 82.
†Ibid. v. 142.

following passages,* all of which are in perfect harmony with those in honour of Indra:— "Laud Parjanya, worship him with reverence—the procreative and stimulating fructifier. ... He splits the trees; he destroys the Rakshasas (cloud demons who withhold the rains). The whole creation is afraid of his mighty stroke; even the innocent man flees before the vigorous god, when Parjanya thundering smites the evildoers. Like a charioteer urging forward his horses with a whip, the god brings into view his showery scouts. From afar, the lions' roarings arise when Parjanya charges the clouds with rain. The winds blow, the lightnings fall, the plants shoot up, the heaven fructifies; food is produced for all created things when Parjanya thundering replenishes the earth with moisture. Raise aloft thy vast water-vessel, and pour down showers; let the discharged rivulets roll on forward, moisten the heaven and earth with fatness; let there be well-filled drinking-places for the cows."

In all this there is not a single idea that was not expressed in the hymns to Indra noticed previously. In the Purānas Indra is generally styled the king of the gods; whilst Parjanya is spoken of as the ruler over, and as dwelling in, the clouds.

4. VĀYU

Another of the storm-gods is Vāyu, the god of the winds. He is often associated with Indra, and is regarded, equally with him, as representing or ruling over the atmosphere. He won the race for the first draught of the Soma juice; and, at Indra's request, allowed him to have a quarter of it. He does not occupy a very prominent position in the Vedic hymns. In one passage† we read, "The two worlds (heaven and earth) generated him for wealth." This may be intended to teach his parentage; and Dr. Muir says that he is not aware of any other passage where his

---

*Muir, O. S. T., v. 140.
†Muir, O. S. T., v. 140

Vāyu

parentage is declared. He is said to be the son-in-law of Tvastri (Visvakarma); but here a difficulty occurs: only one daughter of Tvastri is mentioned, and, as was noticed in the account of Surya, he was said to be husband of this girl.

Vāyu is described* as being most handsome in form; one who moves noisily in a shining car, drawn by a pair of red or purple horses. At times the number of horses is increased to ninety-nine, a hundred, or even a thousand. This latter number would probably be employed during a cyclone. He is seldom mentioned in connection with the Maruts (storm-deities), though in one place he is said to have begotten them by the rivers of heaven.

Another name for Vāyu in the Vedas is Vāta. The praise of Vāta is sung in the following hymn:— † "(I celebrate) the glory of Vāta's chariot; his noise comes rending and resounding. Touching the sky, he moves onward, making all things ruddy; and he comes propelling the dust of the earth. The gusts of air rush after him, and congregate upon him as women in an

---

*Ibid. v. 143.
†Mnir, O. S. T., v. 146.

assembly. Sitting along with them on the same car, the god [Indra] who is king of this universe is borne along. Hasting forward…he never rests. Friend of the waters, first-born, holy, in what place was he born? His sounds have been heard, but his form is not (seen)."

In a later age, when it was thought necessary to connect the heroes, whose exploits are then sung, with the gods, Vāyu, or Pavan as he is then called, is said to have had a son, Hanuman, by a monkey mother. Hanuman played a most conspicuous part in Rāma's expedition in search of Sita. In the Mahābhārata, Bhima (the Strong), one of the bravest of the warriors whose history is given there, is also said to be a son of Vāyu. Kunti, the mother of Bhima, had a boon granted as a reward of her devotion, that she could obtain a child by any of the gods she might wish. As her husband, owing to a curse, could not become a father, she employed this charm, and so Vāyu became the father of Bhima.

Vāyu or Pavan (the Purifier) is represented in pictures as a white man riding on a deer, and carries a white flag in his hand. In the Purānas he is said to be son of Aditi.

Other names by which this deity is known are the following :— Anila, breath; Mārut, air that is necessary to life; Sparsana, he who touches; Gandhavaha, he who carries odours.

5. THE MARUTS

In one passage in the Rig-Veda these gods are said to be one hundred and eighty in number; in another text, twenty-seven is the number given; whilst in the Purānas they are said to be forty-nine. In the Vedas they are called the sons of Rudra. They are the companions of Indra; at times they worship him, and thus acknowledge his superiority; at others they seem to assert their inherent power, and remind Indra of the aid they have given him. They are addressed in the following strain : — * "Spears rest upon your shoulders, ye Maruts; ye have anklets on your feet, golden ornaments on your breasts, lustre in your ears, fiery lightnings in your hands, and golden helmets placed on your heads." They are armed with golden weapons and lightnings; they dart thunderbolts, gleam like flames of fire, and are borne along with the fury of boisterous winds. They split Vritra (Drought) to pieces, are clothed with rain, create darkness during the day, water the earth, and avert heat. They cause the earth and the mountains to quake. They were accustomed to the use of the soma; and were appealed to, to bring healing remedies, which are described as abiding in the (river) Sindhu, the seas, and the hills.

In the "Vishnu Purāna" † we find quite a different account of the Maruts. They are there said to be the sons of Kasyapa and Diti. Diti having lost her children, propitiated her husband, who promised her a boon. She asked that she might have a son of irresistible prowess and valour, who should destroy Indra. The Muni promised to grant this request on one condition. "You shall bear a son," he said, "who shall slay Indra, if with thoughts wholly pious, and person entirely pure, you carefully carry the babe in your womb for a hundred years." Diti accepted the boon with this condition. Indra hearing of this, tried his best to distract her mind, and so prevent the birth of this wonderful child. When ninety-nine years had passed, an opportunity offered itself. Diti retired to rest one night without having washed her feet, and thus violated a rule of ceremonial purity. Indra, ever-watchful, availing himself of this neglect, was able to accomplish his purpose. With his thunderbolt he cut the embryo into seven parts. The children cried bitterly, and Indra was unable to console them. Incensed at their obstinacy in crying, he cut each of these seven parts into seven, and thus formed the forty-nine Maruts. The name Maruts was

---

*Muir, O. S. T., v. 147 ff.
†Book i. chap. xxi.

given to them from the words "Ma rodih" (Weep not), used by Indra when trying to quiet them; and they became subordinate deities—the associates of the wielder of the thunderbolt.

It is not difficult to see how the dwellers in India should have imagined that one god, even though he was the king of the gods, should sometimes need assistance in the management of the winds.' The farther the Aryan immigrants travelled south and eastward, the fiercer were the storms they experienced. Hence arose the hymns addressed to the lesser deities who were invoked to assist Indra in his mighty task of controlling them.

Chapter VIII
....
Soma

Soma, according to the Vedic hymns, is the god who "represents and animates the juice of the Soma* plant." He was the Indian Bacchus. Not only are all the hymns of the ninth book of the Rig-Veda, one hundred and fourteen in number, besides a few in other places, dedicated to his honour, but constant references occur to him in a large proportion of other hymns.† In some of these hymns he is extolled as the Creator, or Father of the gods. Evidently at that time he was a most popular deity. Indra, as was stated before, was an enthusiastic

---

*The Soma-plant of the Rig-Veda is the *Asclepias acida* of Roxburgh. It is a creeping plant, almost destitute of leaves. It has small white fragrant flowers collected round the extremities of the branches. Roxburgh says that it yields purer milky juice than any other plant he knows; and that this juice is mild, and of an acid nature. The tender shoots are often plucked by native travellers. It grows on hills of the Punjab, in the Bolan Pass, in the neighbourhood of Poona, etc. In the Brāhmana of the Rig-Veda (Hang's Translation), is a most interesting account of the Soma sacrifice. This is occasionally made in the present day, but very few priests are acquainted with the ritual of this once celebrated sacrifice.
†Muir, O. S. T., v. 258.

worshipper of Soma.

The following lines will show the warmth of feeling that was cherished towards him:—

"This Soma is a god; he cures
The sharpest ills that man endures.
He heals the sick, the sad he cheers,
He nerves the weak, dispels their fears;

The Soma-Plant

The faint with martial ardour fires,
With lofty thoughts the bard inspires;

The soul from earth to heaven he lifts;
So great and wondrous are his gifts,
Men feel the god within their veins,
And cry in loud exulting strains :

'We've quaffed the Soma bright
   And are immortal grown:
We've entered into light,
   And all the gods have known.
What mortal now can harm,
   Or foeman vex us more?
Through thee, beyond alarm,
   Immortal god, we soar.'"*

From the Vedas the following account of Soma is derived.† In some passages the plant is said to have been brought from a mountain and given to Indra; in others, King Soma is said to have dwelt amongst the Gandharvas, a race of demi-gods that form the choir in Indra's heaven. The gods, knowing the virtues of this king or plant—for the two terms seem to be indiscriminately applied—wished to obtain it. Not knowing how to get it, Vach (the goddess of speech) said, "The Gandharvas are fond of women; let me go, and I will obtain it for you." The gods said, "How can we spare you?" She replied, "Obtain the god; and I will then return to you, whenever you may want me."

Another account of this affair is, that whilst the gods were living on earth, Soma was in the sky. Wishing to possess it, they sent Gāyatri (a name of Brahmā's wife or daughter) to fetch it. She went in the form of a bird, and was returning with it, when the Gandharvas seized it, and only gave it up when the goddess Vach went amongst them as narrated above.

---

*Muir, O. S. T., v. 130.
†Ibid. v. 263 ff.

When Soma was brought to the gods, a dispute arose as to who should have the first draught. At length, this was decided by a race. Vāyu first reached the goal, Indra being second. Indra tried hard to win, and when near the winning post proposed that they should reach it together, Vāyu taking two-thirds of the drink. Vāyu said, "Not so! I will be the winner alone." Then Indra said, "Let us come in together, and give me one-fourth of the draught divine!" Vāyu consented to this, and so the juice was shared between them.*

Soma is said to have had thirty-three wives, the daughters of Prajāpati; of these Rohini was the favourite. Being dissatisfied with the partiality shown to their sister, the other wives returned to their father. Soma asked that they might come back to him; the father consented to restore them, provided Soma would treat them all alike. Soma promised to do this; but, failing to keep his promise, he was smitten with consumption for breaking his word.

In the verses descriptive and songs in praise of Soma, the actual juice, and the god supposed to dwell in and manifested by it, are not at all distinct. All the gods drink of it; and Soma, the god in the juice, is said to clothe the naked and heal the sick. Many divine attributes are ascribed to him. He is "addressed as a god in the highest strains of adulation and veneration. All powers belong to him; all blessings are besought of him, as his to bestow." He is said to be divine, immortal, and also to confer immortality on gods and men. "In a passage where the joys of paradise are more distinctly anticipated and more fervently implored than in most other parts of the Rig-Veda, Soma is addressed as the god from whom the gift of future felicity is expected. Thus it is there said, "Place me, O purified god, in that everlasting and imperishable world, where there is eternal light and glory. O Indu (Soma), flow for Indra! Make me immortal in the world where Vaivasvata lives, where is the

---

*Muir, O. S. T., v. 144.

universal sphere of the sky, where those great waters flow."*

From the hymns addressed to this deity it is evident that at one time it was considered right for the Hindus to use intoxicants. Now as a rule they are forbidden. Amongst the members of one branch of the worshippers of Kāli they are commonly indulged in, but with almost this single exception, the people do not touch them, and Soma, in his Vedic character has ceased to be worshipped.

In later years the name Soma was, and still is, given to the moon. How and why this change took place is not known; but in the later of the Vedic hymns there is some evidence of the transition. In the following passage Soma seems to be used in both senses—as god of the intoxicating juice, and as the moon ruling through the night. "By Soma the Ādityas are strong; by Soma the earth is great; and Soma is placed in the midst of the stars. When they crush the plant, he who drinks regards it as Soma. Of him whom the priests regard as Soma (the moon) no one drinks."† In another passage this prayer is found: "May the god Soma, he whom they call the Moon, free me." Again, "Soma is the moon, the food of the gods." "The sun has the nature of Agni, the moon of Soma."

In the "Vishnu Purāna"‡ we read, "Soma was appointed monarch of the stars and plants, of Brāhmans and plants, of sacrifices and penance." In this Purāna we have quite a different account of the origin of Soma; but it must be borne in mind that in this account the term refers only to the moon. At the time the "Vishnu Purāna" was written, intoxicants were strictly forbidden; hence Soma, as the god of the intoxicating juice, was no longer known and praised. According to that Purāna,§ Soma was the son of Atri, the son of Brahmā. He

---

*Ibid., v. 266.

†Muir, O. S. T., v. 271.

‡Book i. chap. xxii.

§Book iv. chap. vi.

performed the Rājasuya sacrifice, and from the glory thence acquired, and the immense dominion with which he had been invested, became so arrogant and licentious, that he carried off Tārā, the wife of Vrihaspati, the preceptor of the gods. In vain Vrihaspati sought to recover his bride; in vain Brahmā commanded, and the holy sages remonstrated. In consequence of this there was a great war; the gods fighting with Indra on the one side trying to recover Tārā; Soma with the demons on the other. At length she appealed to Brahmā for protection, who thereupon commanded Soma to restore her. On her return, Vrihaspati finding she was pregnant, refused to receive her until after the birth of her child. In obedience to his orders, the child was immediately born; who being wonderful in beauty and power, both Vrihaspati and Soma claimed him as their son. Tārā being referred to, was too much ashamed to speak. The child was so indignant at this, that he was about to curse her, saying, "Unless you declare who is my father, I will sentence you to such a fate as shall deter every female from hesitating to speak the truth." On this Brahmā again interfered, pacifying the child, and saying to Tārā, "Tell me, my child, is this the child of Vrihaspati or Soma?" "Of Soma," she said, blushing. As soon as she had spoken, the lord of the constellations, his countenance being bright, embraced his son and said, "Well done, my boy; verily thou art wise;" and hence his name was Budha.*

---

*This Budha, son of Soma, and regent of the planet Mercury, must not be confounded with Buddha, the teacher whose tenets are held by the Buddhists of the present day. The two beings have nothing in common; and the names are identical only when one or other of them is misspelt.

Chapter IX
Tvastri or Visvakarma

Tvastri, or, as he is called in the later works, Visvakarma, is the architect and workman of the gods — the Hindu Vulcan. The heavenly places were formed by him, and the warlike gods are indebted to him for their wonderworking weapons. He sharpens the iron axe of Brāhmanaspati (Agni), and forges the thunderbolts of Indra. He is intimately associated with men; he forms husband and wife for each other from the womb, and blesses the married couple with offspring. This accounts for the fact that the wives of the gods are his most constant companions. He made the world and all that is in it; and he is the protector of the creatures he has made. He shares with the other gods in the sacrifices offered by mortals.*

Tvastri is in several passages connected with the Ribhus. These were sons of a man named Sudhanvan; who, owing to their great skill in working, obtained immortality and divine honours. The Ribhus made Indra's chariot and horses; also by their great austerities restored their parents to youth. They are spoken of as the pupils of Tvastri. It was through their skill in manufacturing four sacrificial cups out of one their master

---

*Muir, O. S. T., v. 224.

had fashioned that they became divine. This exhibition was made at the command of the gods, and exaltation to deity the promised reward. Tvastri was very angry at their success; and, ashamed of being seen, hid himself amongst the women. It is said that he even tried to slay his pupils. According to other accounts, he admired their skill and was pleased at the result. Tvastri was the father-in-law of Vivasvat (the Sun).

Indra is occasionally described as being in a state of hostility towards Tvastri and his son Visvarūpa, and ultimately caused the death of both. This Visvarūpa had three heads, called respectively, the Soma-drinker the Wine-drinker, and the Food-eater. On one occasion he declared in public that the sacrifices should be shared by the gods only; but in private he said the asuras (demons) should share them too. And as it is customary to keep promises that are privately made, Indra was afraid that the asuras, obtaining a share of the sacrifices, would be so strengthened as to be able to overthrow his kingdom; he therefore cut off the heads of Visvarūpa with his thunderbolt. The three heads were turned into birds: the Soma-drinker became a Kapinjala (a Francoline partridge), for Soma was of a brown colour; the Wine-drinker became a Kalavinka (sparrow), because when men are intoxicated they make a noise like a sparrow; the Food-eater became a Tittiri (partridge), which consequently has a great variety of colour, for its body appears to be sprinkled with *ghi* and honey. Tvastri, enraged because Indra had slain his son, made a libation to the gods, but did not invite Indra to it. Indra, noticing this slight, by force took the vessel containing the Soma juice, and drank it. But he drank more than was good for him. Tvastri, being angry, at once broke off the sacrifice, and used the few drops of Soma left to give effect to a curse. He employed the right formula for accomplishing the death of Indra, but unfortunately laid stress upon the wrong word. So, instead of slaying Indra, he was himself slain by him.*

In the Purānas, Tvastri appears under the name of Visvakarma. In the "Vishnu Purāna" he is styled "the author of a thousand arts, the mechanist of the gods, the fabricator of ornaments, the chief of artists, the constructor of the self-moving chariots of the deities, by whose skill men obtain subsistence." Though not named as an Āditya in the Vedas, he is generally reckoned as one in the Purānas. In other places he is called a son of Brahmā. In pictures he is represented as a white man with three eyes. In his right hand he carries a club. He wears a crown, and is adorned with a necklace and bracelets of gold. He is worshipped once, twice, thrice, or four times each year, according to the devotion of his worshippers. Nowadays, no images of him are set up; each man worships the implements of his trade, as representatives. The carpenter bows down to his hammer, saw, etc.; the bricklayer to his trowel; the peasant to his plough; the student to his books; the clerk to his pen. When the worship is over, the day is spent in feasting and enjoyment.

Though, as we have seen in the Vedas, he is regarded in some hymns as the Creator and the Preserver, in the later books he occupies a much lower position. Brahmā is styled the Creator, and Vishnu the Preserver—whilst Visvakarma becomes a valued servant who fulfils the behests of his superiors. It is for skill and power to work in their ordinary avocations that his aid is now sought.

---

*Muir, O. S. T., v. 232.

Chapter X

Yama

Yama, the judge of men and king of the unseen world, was the son of Vivasvat (the sun) and Saranya, the daughter of Tvastri. He was born before his mother had become afraid of

Yama

her glorious husband. He was twin-brother of Yami, and, in the opinion of Professor Roth, they were regarded as the primeval pair from whom the human family has sprung. In another verse of the Rig-Veda they are described as the offspring of the heavenly choristers, the Gandharvas. As there were no others to perpetuate the race, Yami entreated Yama to become her husband. She urged the fact that Tvastri had formed them as man and wife in the womb; and therefore it was useless for him to refuse her request, as none can act contrary to the ordinances of Tvastri. But Yama was firm, and resisted her overtures on the ground that it was monstrous for those who are preachers of righteousness to act unrighteously.* It is not at all easy to determine what was intended to be represented by these deities. Max-Müller understands Vivasvat to be the sky, Saranya the dawn, Yama the day, and Yami the night. Others suggest that Yama may be the hot air current caused by the rising sun, and Yami the cooler air of the night, and their antagonism would be represented by Yama repelling the advances of Yami.

Yama was the first of mortals who died, and, having discovered the way to the other world, is the guide of those who depart this life, and is said to conduct them to a home which is made secure for them for ever. He is a king, and dwells in celestial light in the innermost sanctuary of heaven. He grants bright homes to the pious who dwell with him.†

"In the Rig-Veda, Yama is nowhere represented (as he is in the later mythology) as having anything to do with the punishment of the wicked. Nevertheless he is still to some an object of terror. He is said to have two insatiable dogs, with four eyes and wide nostrils, which guard the road to his abode, and which the departed are advised to hurry past with all possible speed. These dogs are said to wander about among

---

*Muir, O. S. T., v. 289.
†Ibid., v. 284.

men as messengers, no doubt for the purpose of summoning them to the presence of their master, who in another place is identified with death, and is described as sending a bird as the herald of doom."*

"When the remains of the deceased have been placed upon the funeral pile, and the process of cremation has commenced, Agni, the god of Fire, is prayed not to scorch or consume the departed, not to tear asunder his skin or his limbs, but, after the flames have done their work, to convey to the fathers the mortal who has been presented to him as an offering. Leaving behind on earth all that is evil and imperfect, and proceeding by the paths which the fathers trod, invested with a lustre like that of the gods, it soars to the realms of eternal light in a car, or on wings, and recovers there its ancient body in a complete and glorified form: meets with the forefathers who are living in festivity with Yama; obtains from him, when recognized by him as one of his own, a delectable abode, and enters upon more perfect life, which is crowned with the fulfilment of all desires, is passed in the presence of the gods, and employed in the fulfilment of their pleasure." †

In this kingdom, over which Yama reigns, friends meet with their departed friends—husband with wife, children with parents—and together live in a state of blessedness, free from the evils and infirmities that belong to the present life. As the gods are described as enjoying the pleasures common to men on earth, the kingdom of Yama, the abode of the departed, is not at all less sensual than the present world; and when mortals have been privileged to enter this, happy land, they become objects of veneration to their descendants still living, and joyfully partake of the oblations they offer to them.

In the following lines Dr. Muir‡ has given an epitome of

---

*Muir, O. S. T., v. 302.
†Ibid., v. 302 ff.
‡Muir, O. S. T., v. 327.

the teaching of the Vedas respecting Yama :—

"To great King Yama homage pay,
    Who was the first of men that died,
    That crossed the mighty gulf and spied
For mortals out the heavenward way.

    *   *   *   *

"By it our fathers all have passed;
    And that same path we too shall trace.
    And every new succeeding race,
Of mortal men, while time shall last.

"The god assembles round his throne
    A growing throng, the good and wise—
    All those whom, scanned with searching eyes,
He recognizes as his own.

"Departed mortal, speed from earth
    By those old ways thy sires have trod;
    Ascend, behold the expectant god
Who calls thee to a higher birth.

    *   *   *   *

"And calmly pass without alarm
    The four-eyed hounds that guard the road
    Which leads to Yama's bright abode;
Their master's friends they dare not harm.

"All imperfections leave behind :
    Assume thine ancient frame once more—
    Each limb and sense thou hadst before,
From every earthly taint refined.

"And now with heavenly glory bright,
    With life intenser, nobler, blest,
    With large capacity to taste

A fuller measure of delight,

"Thou there once more each well-known face
    Shalt see of those thou lovedst here;
    Thy parents, wife, and children dear,
With rapture shalt thou soon embrace.

"The father, too, shalt thou behold,
    The heroes who in battle died,
    The saints and sages glorified,
The pious, bounteous kings of old.

"The gods whom here in humble wise
    Thou worshippedst with doubt and awe,
    Shall there the impervious veil withdraw
Which hid their glory from thine eyes.

"The good which thou *on* earth hast wrought,
    Each sacrifice, each pious deed,
    Shall there receive its ample meed;
No worthy act shall be forgot.

"'In those fair realms of cloudless day,
    Where Yama every joy supplies,
    And every longing satisfies,
Thy bliss shall never know decay."

In the Purānas, Yama is called the judge of men, and is said to rule over the many hells in which the wicked are made to suffer. Thus the "Padma Purāna" says: "Yama fulfils the office of judge of the dead, as well as sovereign of the damned; all that die appearing before him, and being confronted with Chitragupta the recorder, by whom their actions have been registered. The virtuous are then conveyed to Swarga (Indra's heaven), whilst the wicked are driven to the different regions of Naraka (hell)."* In the "Vishnu Purāna" the names of the different hells are given, and it is there stated that "there are many other fearful hells which are the awful provinces of Yama, terrible with instruments of torture and fire." In the same Purāna† it is said that "all men at the end of their existence (life) become slaves to the power of Yama, by whom they are sentenced to painful punishments." Inquiry is then made as to how men can be free from his authority. The answer is that "Yama is the lord of all men, excepting the worshippers of Madhusūdan (Vishnu). Worship him in one of his many forms, and Yama can exert no authority over you."

According to the popular ideas now prevailing, Yama is represented as a green man, clothed in red garments. He has a crown on his head, and a flower in his hair; is armed with a club, and rides upon a buffalo. He is regularly worshipped once a year; and daily a little water is poured out to him. For a whole month each year unmarried girls present offerings to him in the hope that he will provide them with a husband; and that, having granted this boon, he will not recall his gift, and leave them widows. In his presence the good and evil deeds of the departed are weighed: according to the turn of the scale, the soul goes to heaven or hell. The soul is believed to reach Yama's abode in four hours and forty minutes; consequently a dead body cannot be burned until that time has passed after death.

In the "Bhavishya Purāna "the following legend of Yama's marriage is found. He was exceedingly pleased with a girl named Vijaya, a Brāhman's daughter. When first she saw him she was greatly alarmed, alike at his appearance and on learning who he was. At length he allayed her fears; and, although her brother tried to dissuade her, she consented to become his wife. On her arrival at Yama's abode, he particularly cautioned her

---

*"Vishnu Purāna," p. 207, note.
†Ibid., p. 286.

against going into the southern quarter of his kingdom. After a time, thinking he must have another wife there, her curiosity overpowered her, and going into the forbidden region, she was greatly distressed, as she saw the wicked in torment: Amongst other sufferers was her own mother. Meeting Yama there, she tried to obtain her release. Yama declared that this could not be granted unless some one then living on earth would perform a certain sacrifice, and transfer the merit of the act to the poor woman then suffering. After some difficulty, one was found willing to perform this act of kindness, and Yama's mother-in-law obtained release.

Stories are told in the Purānas to show how the power of Vishnu is exercised on behalf of his worshippers in rescuing them from Yama's bonds. If a man repeat his name in teaching it to his parrot, or utter it in death without any intention of asking his help, his messengers will be sent to snatch him from the punishments of hell and conduct him to his blest abode.

It is very strange to notice how the character of Yama's rule and kingdom has entirely changed in the conceptions of the Hindus. According to the Vedas, the pure and good went with gladness to Yama's realm of light; now, as taught in the Purānas, it is the wicked who are sent to him for punishment.

In the Mahābhārata* is a most interesting story, showing that sometimes Yama is propitious to prayer, and will allow those who have entered his abode to return to earth.

A princess named Savitri loved Satyavān, the son of an old hermit, but was warned by a seer to overcome her attachment, as Satyavān was a doomed man, having only one year to live. Savitri replies:

> "Whether his years be few or many, be he gifted with all
>   grace
> Or graceless, him my heart hath chosen, and it chooseth

---

*"Indian Wisdom," p. 305.

not again."

They were married, and the bride strove to forget the prophecy; but, as the last day of the year approached, her anxiety became irrepressible. She exhausted herself in prayers and penances, hoping to stay the hand of the destroyer, yet all the while dared not reveal the fatal secret to her husband. At last the dreaded day arrived, and Satyavān set out to cut wood in the forest. His wife asked leave to accompany him, and walked behind him, smiling, but with a heavy heart. Satyavān soon made the wood resound with his hatchet, when suddenly a thrill of agony shot through his temples, and, feeling himself falling, called his wife to support him.

> "Then she received her fainting husband in her arms,
> and sat herself
> On the cold ground, and gently laid his drooping head
> upon her lap:
> Sorrowing, she called to mind the sage's prophecy, and
> reckoned up
> The days and hours. All in an instant she beheld an
> awful shape
> Standing before her, dressed in blood-red garments,
> with a glittering crown
> Upon his head; his form, though glowing like the
> Sun, was yet obscure,
> And eyes he had like flames, a noose depended from his
> hand; and he
> Was terrible to look upon, as by her husband's side he
> stood
> And gazed upon him with a fiery glance. Shuddering
> she started up,
> And laid her dying Satyavān upon the ground, and,
> with her hands
> Joined reverently, she thus with beating heart addressed

the shape:
'Surely thou art a god; such form as thine must more
   than mortal be!
Tell me, thou god-like being, who thou art, and wherefore
   art thou here?'"

The figure replied that he was Yama, king of the dead; that
her husband's time was come, and that he must bind and take
his spirit.

"Then from her husband's body forced he out, and
   firmly with his cord
Bound and detained the spirit, clothed in form no larger
   than a thumb.
Forthwith the body, reft of vital being and deprived of
   breath,
Lost all its grace and beauty, and became ghastly and
   motionless."

After binding the spirit, Yama proceeds with it towards the
quarter of which he is guardian—the south. The faithful wife
follows him closely. Yama bids her go home and perform the
funeral rites; but she persists in following, till Yama, pleased
with her devotion, grants her any boon she pleases, except the
life of her husband. She chooses that her husband's father, who
is now blind, may recover his sight. Yama consents, and bids
her now return home. Still she persists in following. Two other
boons are granted in the same way, and still Savitri follows
closely on the heels of the king of death. At last, overcome by
her constancy, Yama grants a boon without exception. The
delighted Savitri exclaims:

"'Nought, mighty king, this time hast thou excepted: let
   my husband live;
Without him I desire not happiness, nor even heaven

itself;

Without him I must die.' 'So be it, faithful wife,' replied
the king of death:

'Thus I release him;' and with that he loosed the cord
that bound his soul."

Amongst the many names by which Yama is known, the
following are the most common:—

Dharmarāja, "King of righteousness."

Pitripati, "Lord of the fathers."

Samavurti, "He who judges impartially."

Kritānta, "The finisher."

Samana, "The leveller."

Kāla, "Time."

Dandadhara, "He who carries the rod."

Srāddhadeva, "The god of funeral ceremonies."

Vaivasvata, "The son of Vivasvata."

Antaka, "He who puts an end to life."

PART II

THE PURĀNIC DEITIES

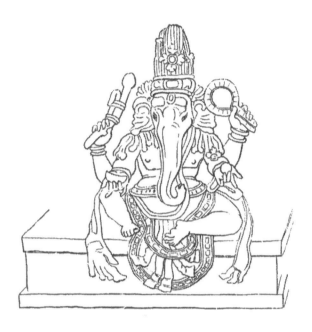

Ganesa

Chapter I

The Purānas

THE chief sources of information respecting the modern mythology of the Hindus are the two great Epics—the Rāmāyana and the Mahābhārata—the Purānas, or "old traditional stories," eighteen in number, and the five principal Tantras.

There is nothing definitely known as to the date of the Epics, beyond the fact that they are later than the Vedas, and earlier than the Purānas. Some place the Rāmāyana as early as B.C. 500, whilst others affirm that it could not have been composed before B.C. 100, and that a considerable portion was added much later. The Mahābhārata is supposed to be fully a century nearer our own time. Unlike the Vedas, they, as well as the Purānas and Tantras, may be read by other than Brāhmans. Each of these books is of immense bulk, and the same stories frequently reappear in them. Yet to this day they retain a firm hold of the faith and veneration of the mass of the people of India. Nor is this to be wondered at when we read such words as these, often repeated in these works: "He who reads and repeats this holy life-giving Rāmāyana [or the Mahābhārata], is liberated from all sins, and exalted with all his posterity to the highest heaven."

It is almost equally difficult to determine the date of the Purānas. It is, however, believed that none of them are older than the 8th century A.D., though some of the legends incorporated in them may have come from much earlier times. That they are considerably later than the two great Epics is evident from the fact that many, who are described there as men and heroes only, in the Purānas, are said to be divine beings. These books differ from the Vedas in this respect, that whilst the older scriptures treat of the religion common to the Hindus of that period, all of whom worshipped the same deities, each Purāna is chiefly concerned with some one god whose excellences are extolled, whilst others are spoken of in a depreciatory manner. There is a general respect shown to the rest of the gods of the Pantheon; yet the particular deity to whose praise the Purāna is devoted, is declared to be supreme; and of him the others are said to be incarnations. Now Brahmā, now Siva, now Vishnu in some of his many forms, is the great god, whose will is that all men should worship him. It may be that originally the Purānas were written in praise of the three great gods, but as the Hindu conquest extended over the continent, there being no central religious authority, a spirit of sectarianism arose and the writers extolled their own special deity at the expense of the others.

The Purānas may be classified as follows:—

I.   Those which are devoted to the praise of Brahmā; viz. the Brahmā, the Brāhmanda, the Brahmāvaivarta, the Mārkandeya, the Bhavishya, and the Vaman.

II. Those which relate to Vishnu; viz. the Vishnu, the Bhāgavata, the Naradiya, the Garuda, the Padma, and the Vārāha.

III. Those which are chiefly connected with Siva; viz. the Siva, the Linga, the Skanda, the Agni, the Matsya, the Kūrma. For the Agni Purāna another called the Vāyu is sometimes substituted.

These Purānas are the authority for nearly the whole of the popular Hinduism of the present day. They are largely read by the people. Parts of some and the whole of others have been translated into the vernaculars from the Sanskrit; and where the people cannot read, it is a common practice for their Guru or teacher to read a portion to them at his periodic visits. By this means the contents of these books are widely known.

The fact that each Purāna is devoted to the praise of some special deity, who, according to its teaching, is supreme, whilst other deities, described in other Purānas in equally extravagant language, are slighted, and in some cases their worship forbidden, seems to prove that these books must have been written at different times and in different places, and probably by those who were ignorant of what others had written. And yet the popular belief is that they were all the work of the great sage Vyāsa, the arranger of the Vedas and the Mahābhārata.

The ideal Purāna—and the Vishnu Purāna approaches more nearly to this ideal than any other—should treat of* five chief topics:—"I. The creation of the universe; II. Its destruction and re-creation; III. The genealogy of gods and patriarchs; IV. The reigns and periods of the Manus (rulers over long periods of time); and V. The history of the two great races of kings, the Solar and the Lunar." The Purānas, as at present known, omit some of these great questions and introduce others. Great discrepancies, too, are found in the different genealogies.†

The last class of religious books to be mentioned here are the Tantras. The word signifies "a means of faith," and they teach that faith in the revelations they record will save from the greatest sin. They are in the form of a dialogue between Siva and his wife. In answer to her questions, the god gives manifold instructions concerning worship. The date of these

---

*Wilson's Preface to the "Vishnu Purāna."
†For an outline of the contents of the different Purānas, see Introduction to Wilson's "Vishnu Purāna."

works is involved in great obscurity; but as far as can be known they probably are not earlier than the 6th century of our era. They form the authority for the faith and ceremonies of the Saktas, as the worshippers of the wife of Siva are called, and are by them regarded as a fifth Veda. The doctrines, or at least a part of the doctrines, of these sects is kept secret and communicated to those only who receive solemn initiation into the mysteries.

In describing the Purānic deities, I shall follow the common order. The Hindus speak of three great gods— Brahmā, Vishnu, Siva, who form what is often spoken of as the Hindu Triad. After giving an account of each of these and their consorts, I shall describe those who are regarded as their incarnations, or descendants; and then proceed to speak of others who have no formal connection with any of them. It will be seen that most of the principal deities are connected with one or other of these three.

Chapter II

Brahma*

Brahma is regarded as the Supreme Being, the God of gods; of whom Brahmā, Vishnu, and Siva are manifestations. It is true that, in some verses of the Vedas, attributes ascribed to him are also ascribed to other deities, and in some of the Purānas various gods are said to be identical with the supreme Brahma; nevertheless Brahma is regarded by the Hindus (for which opinion there is abundant authority in their scriptures) as the Supreme God—the origin of all the others, and of whom they are manifestations. Thus we read in the "Atharva-Veda":—†
"All the gods are in (Brahma) as cows in a cow-house. In the beginning Brahma was this [universe]. He created gods. Having created gods, he placed them in these worlds, viz. Agni in this world, Vayu in the atmosphere, and Surya in the sky. And in the worlds which are yet higher, he placed the gods which are still higher. Then Brahma proceeded to the higher sphere [which is explained by the commentator to mean the Satyaloka, the most excellent and limit of all the worlds]. The gods were originally mortal; but when they were pervaded by

---

*It will be noticed that the final vowel in the name of this deity is *short*, whilst in that of the first incarnation it is *long*.
†Muir, O. S. T., v. 387 ff.

Brahma, they became immortal." In the "Taittiriya Brahmana" it is said: "Brahma generated the gods, Brahma (generated) this entire world. Within him are all these worlds. Within him is this entire universe. It is Brahma who is the greatest of beings. Who can vie with him? In Brahma, the thirty-three gods; in Brahma, Indra and Prajāpati; in Brahma all things are contained as in a ship."

Prof. Monier Williams* says :—"Only a few hymns of the Vedas appear to contain the simple conception of one divine self-existent, omnipresent being; and even in these, the idea of one god present in all nature is somewhat nebulous and undefined." Further on he says: "In the Purusha Sūkta of the Rig-Veda, the one spirit is called Purusha. The more common name in the later system is Brahman, neuter (nom. Brahma), derived from the root *brih,* 'to expand,' and denoting the universally expanding essence, or universally diffused substance of the universe...Brahman, in the neuter, being 'simple infinite being'—the only real eternal essence—which, when it passes into actual manifested existence, is called Brahmā; when it develops itself in the world, is called Vishnu; and when it again dissolves itself into simple being, is called Siva; all the other innumerable gods and demi-gods being also mere manifestations of the neuter Brahman, who is eternal."

In the "Vishnu Purāna" † Brahma is translated as "abstract supreme spirit." Later on‡ the question is asked, "How can creative agency be attributed to Brahma, who [as abstract spirit] is without qualities, illimitable, and free from imperfection?" The answer is, that "the essential properties of existent things are objects of observation, of which no foreknowledge is attainable; and creation and hundreds of properties belong to Brahma as inseparable parts of his essence, as heat is inherent

---

*"Indian Wisdom," p. 12.
†Page 2.
‡Book i. chap. iii.

in fire." The Purāna goes on to say that creation is effected through the agency of Brahmā, the first manifestation of Brahma; and then declares that Vishnu is one with Brahmā.

Again, the same Purāna* says: "There are two states of this Brahma—one with, and one without shape; one perishable, one imperishable; which are inherent in all beings. The imperishable is the supreme being; the perishable is all the world. The blaze of fire burning in one spot diffuses light and heat around; so the world is nothing more than the manifested energy of the supreme Brahma; and inasmuch as the light and heat are stronger or feebler as we are near to the fire or far off from it, so the energy of the supreme is more or less intense in the beings that are less or more remote from him. Brahmā, Vishnu, and Siva are the most powerful energies of God; next to them are the inferior deities; then the attendant spirits; then men; then animals, birds, insects, vegetables; each becoming more and more feeble as they are farther from their primitive source."

The "Vishnu Purāna" † gives the following derivation of the word Brahma:—It "is derived from the root *vrika* (to increase), because it is infinite (spirit), and because it is the cause by which the Vedas (and all things) are developed." Then follows this hymn to Brahma :—" Glory to Brahma, who is addressed by that mystic word *(Om)*, ‡ associated eternally with the triple universe (earth, sky, and heaven), and who is one with the four Vedas. Glory to Brahma, who alike in the destruction and renovation of the world is called the great and mysterious cause of the intellectual principle; who is without limit in time

---

*Page 157.

†Page 273.

‡This word occurs at the commencement of prayers and religions ceremonies. It is so sacred that none must hear it pronounced. Originally the three letters *(a u* m) of which it is formed typified the three Vedas; afterwards it became a mystical symbol of the three deities—Brahmā, Vishnu, Siva.

or space, and exempt from diminution and decay...He is the invisible, imperishable Brahma; varying in form, invariable in substance; the chief principle, self-engendered; who is said to illuminate the caverns of the heart; who is indivisible, radiant, undecaying, multiform. To that supreme Brahma be for ever adoration."

In perfect harmony with this teaching of the "Vishnu Purāna" is the common belief of the Hindus. No phrase is more commonly used by them when speaking of the divine being than this: "God (Brahma) is one without a second." The word used by them for God as distinguished from his manifestations, is Brahma; and when charged with Polytheism, and of violating the primary law respecting the unity of God, they reply that Brahmā, Vishnu, Siva, etc., are only manifestations of the supreme Brahma.*

In the earliest writings Brahma signified a hymn or mantra, whilst Brahmā was the term used to denote a priest or worshipper. It is in the later parts of the Vedas that Brahma is identified with the supreme, and Brahmā becomes his great manifestation. Prajāpati, the lord of creatures, was the Creator according to the earlier teaching of the Vedas, and occupied the position in the earlier Pantheon that Brahmā did in the later. In several texts of the Vedas the two are identified, and thus authority is found for the idea that Brahmā is to be worshipped as the Maker of all things.

This Brahmā, though satisfactory to the priests, was not so to the common people. In process of time local gods absorbed their worship, and the non-Aryan deities of the people whom they had conquered exercised their influence on the Aryans themselves. Rather than lose their hold of the people, the priests adopted these new deities, and found a parentage for

---

*The Theistic sect that arose in Bengal during the present century, for a long time gloried in the name Brahmo Samaj; *i.e.* the Society that worshipped the supreme Brahma or God.

them from amongst the old Vedic gods. By the time the Epics were composed, Vishnu and Siva had been thus assimilated. The different names by which these deities are now known may possibly have been the local names of local or tribal gods; by retaining these the priests also retained their hold upon the people. In the "Satapatha Brāhmana" attempts are made to identify Siva with Agni, as though the writer wished to show that the later triad—Brahmā, Vishnu, and Siva—was identical with the older one composed of Agni, Indra, Vayu, and Surya.

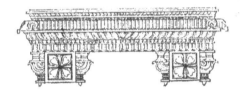

Chapter III
Brahmā and Sarasvati

BRAHMĀ

B rahmā, the first of the three great Hindu gods, is called the Creator; he is the father of gods and men, the Vedic Prajāpati,

Brahmā

the lord of creatures. As nearly all the writers of the Puranas seem to regard it a duty to describe the work of creation as performed by this god, and as each account differs in detail from the others, it is a perfectly hopeless task to attempt to give a harmonized statement of this great event. I shall therefore give Manu's* account of it, which is largely founded upon the teaching of the Vedas, though considerably mixed up with more modern views.

"This universe was enveloped in darkness — unperceived, undistinguishable, undiscoverable, unknowable, as it were, entirely sunk in sleep. The irresistible self-existent lord, undiscerned, creating this universe with the five elements, and all other things, was manifested dispelling the gloom. He who is beyond the cognizance of the senses, subtile, undiscernible, eternal, who is the essence of all things, and inconceivable, himself shone forth. He, desiring, seeking to produce various creatures from his own body, first created the waters, and deposited in them a seed. This (seed) became a golden egg, resplendent as the sun, in which he himself was born as Brahmā, the progenitor of all worlds. The waters are called *nārāh,* because they are the offspring of Nara; and since they were formerly the place of his movement *(ayana),* he is therefore called Nārāyana.† Being formed by that First Cause, undiscernible, eternal, which is both existent and non-existent, that male is known in the world as Brahmā. That lord having

---

*"Dharma Shastra," chaps, i.-v.

†According to the "Brahmā Parāna," another name, Apava (who sports on the waters), is given Brahmā, which has a similar, though not identical, application with Nārāyana. Āpava, according to that Purāna, divided himself into two parts, male and female, from whom proceeded Vishnu, who in his turn created Virāj, who brought the first man into the world. Wilson says "According to the commentator on this passage, the first stage was the creation of Āpava, or Vishistha, or Virāj by Vishnu, through the agency of Brahmā: and the nest was the creation of Manu by Virāj." —Dowson, *s.v.* "Apave."

continued a year in the egg, divided it into two parts by his mere thought."* In the Mahābhārata, and some of the Purānas, Brahmā is said to have issued from a lotus that sprang from the navel of Vishnu.

The egg referred to above is thus described in the "Vishnu Purāna"†:—"Its womb, vast as the mountain Meru, was composed of the mountains, and the mighty oceans were the waters which filled its cavity. In that egg were the continents, seas, and mountains; the planets and divisions of the universe; the gods, the demons and mankind. Brahmā is said to be born; a familiar phrase to signify his manifestation." This wonderful egg, after the Creator had inhabited it for a thousand years, burst open, and Brahmā issuing forth by meditation commenced the work of creation. Seeing that the earth was sunk beneath the waters, he assumed the form of a boar,‡ and, diving, raised it upon his tusks. After this, he continued the work of creation.

In pictures Brahmā is represented as a red man with four heads, though in the Purānas he is said to have had originally five. He is dressed in white raiment, and rides upon a goose. In one hand he carries a staff, in the other a dish for receiving alms. A legend in the "Matsya Purāna"§ gives the following account of the formation of his numerous heads:—"Brahmā formed from his own immaculate substance a female who is celebrated under the names of Satarupā, Savitri, Sarasvati, Gāyatri, and Brāhmani. Beholding his daughter, born from his body, Brahmā became wounded with the arrows of love, and exclaimed, 'How surpassingly lovely she is!' Satarupā turned to the right side from his gaze; but as Brahmā wished to look after her, a second head issued from his body. As she passed

---

*Muir, O. S. T., iv. 31.

†Page 18.

‡In later writings Vishnu, in a special incarnation, is said to have assumed this form.

§Kennedy's "Hindu Mythology," p. 317.

to the left, and behind him, to avoid his amorous glances, two other heads successively appeared. At length she sprang into the sky; and as Brahmā was anxious to gaze after her there, a fifth head was immediately formed. Brahmā then said to his daughter, 'Let us produce all kinds of animated beings, men, suras (gods), and asuras (demons). Hearing this, she descended, and Brahmā having espoused her, they withdrew to a secluded spot where they dwelt together for one hundred divine years;* at the expiration of which time was born Manu, who is also called Swayambhuva and Virāj."†

The following legend‡ occurs, with some variations, in several Purānas, showing why Brahmā was deprived of his fifth head :—

"Once when they were assembled on the top of Meru, the holy sages, having saluted Brahmā, requested him to declare the true nature of the godhead; but the Creator, influenced by the delusion of Mahesha (a demon), and his mind obscured by spiritual darkness, asserted his own pre-eminence, and said: 'I am the womb of the universe, without beginning or end, and the sole and self-existent lord; and he who does not worship me shall never obtain beatitude.' On hearing this, Kratu, a form of Nārāyana (Vishnu), smiled and said: 'Hadst thou not been misled by ignorance, thou wouldst not have made an assertion so contrary to truth; for I am the framer of the universe, the source of life, the unborn, eternal and supreme Nārāyana; and, had I not willed it, creation would not have taken place.'

---

*See Part ii. chap. x.

†The "Bhāgavata Purāna" says there was another son from this marriage, named Priyavrata. Being dissatisfied with the work of the Sun because he illuminated only one-half of the world at a time, he followed him seven times in a flaming chariot of equal velocity, like another sun, and thus turned night into day. Brahmā stopped him. The ruts made by his chariot wheels became the seven oceans; and thus the seven continents were made.—Dowson.

‡Kennedy's "Hindu Mythology," p. 273.

"Thus Vishnu and Brahmā disputed, and at length they agreed to allow the matter to be decided by the Vedas. The Vedas declared that Siva was creator, preserver, destroyer. Having heard these words, Vishnu and Brahmā, still bewildered by the darkness of delusion, said, 'How can the lord of goblins, the delighter in graveyards, the naked devotee covered with ashes, haggard in appearance, wearing twisted locks ornamented with snakes, be the supreme being?' The incorporeal Prāna (Life), then assuming a form, said, 'This is not the real form of Siva; but when united to his energy, he sometimes, under the figure of Rudra, delights himself in various illusive sports.' But even these words dispelled not the spiritual darkness of Vishnu and Brahmā; when suddenly appeared between them a wondrous effulgence filling the heavens, earth, and mid-air. In the midst of this they beheld a human form, vast, uncreated, of a dark hue holding in his hand a trident and a rosary, and wearing a serpent for a Brāhmanical thread. On seeing whom, the fifth head of Brahmā glowed with anger and said, 'I know thee well, O Chandra Shekera, for from my forehead didst thou spring, and because thou didst weep I called thee Rudra. Hasten then to seek the refuge of my feet, and I will protect thee, O my son!' At these proud words of Brahmā, Siva was incensed; and from his anger sprang into existence a terrific form (Bhairava), whom he thus addressed: 'Chastise this lotus-born!' No sooner did Bhairava receive this order, than instantly he cut off the head of Brahmā with the thumb of his left hand. That member which had committed the fault received punishment; and therefore Brahmā was deprived of his fifth head." Upon this Vishnu and Brahmā praised Siva.

In another part of the same Purāna* is another legend, giving a somewhat different account of this circumstance: —

"Formerly all things movable and immovable having been destroyed, nought remained but one boundless ocean;

---

*Kennedy's "Hindu Mythology," p. 276.

nor fire, nor air, nor sun, nor atmosphere, nor stars, nor planets, nor light, nor earth, nor heaven, nor gods nor demons existed then; and all was involved in impenetrable darkness. One being alone, Mahā Kāla (Siva), pervaded all space; who being desirous of creation, churned his left arm with his right forefinger; whence issued a bubble, which increasing in size became an egg resembling gold. This egg Mahā Kāla divided with his hand; of the upper part he formed the heavens, and of the lower half the earth, and in the centre of it appeared Brahmā with five hands and four arms, to whom Mahā Kāla thus said, 'Through my favour effect creation.' Having thus spoken, he disappeared.

"Brahmā having then considered in what manner he could accomplish this object, propitiated his lord Bhava with a severe *tapas* (meditation), and in consequence received from him the four Vedas, and was thus enabled to become the Creator. But as Siva had not revealed himself, Brahmā continued his meditation in order that he might behold that god. Siva was propitiated; but, still invisible, thus said, 'O Brahmā, choose whatever boon thou choosest!' Brahmā craved that Siva would become his son. Siva replied: 'Propitiated by thy piety, I will become thy son under the form of Rudra; but as thou hast craved a boon which ought not to have been asked, I shall on this account hereafter cut off one of thy heads. Nevertheless, though thou shalt afterwards possess but four heads, yet as thou hast been formed by me, from my own substance which is that Brahma, thou shalt in remembrance of this circumstance be denominated Brahmā. Also from my becoming thy son, shalt thou be called Pitāmāha (the great father).'

"Brahmā having obtained both a boon and a curse, proceeded, in order to effect creation, to sacrifice to that fire which had sprung from his own effulgence; and from the heat, perspiration collected on his forehead. In wiping this off with a small piece of wood, a drop of blood fell into the fire, from which by the will of Siva sprang Rudra, of a dark hue, with five heads, ten hands, and fifteen eyes; having a serpent for his Brāhmanical thread, wearing twisted locks, and the moon on his head, and clothed in the skin of a lion. Having seen such a son, Brahmā was delighted, and bestowed on him various appellations. Brahmā having created various classes of beings, they all adored him, except Rudra; to whom Brahmā said, 'Why dost thou not also adore me?' Rudra replied, 'I worship none other than that effulgence from which I sprang!' Having thus spoken, he departed to Siva's abode. But Brahmā from the impurity of his nature became immersed in spiritual darkness, and thought that it was by his own power alone that he had effected creation, and there was no other god equal to him. His fifth head also having read the Vedas, which the other four heads had delivered, acquired a splendour which neither suras (gods) nor asuras (demons) could endure."

The "Padma Purāna"* thus concludes this story: "Unable therefore to approach or behold it, they determined to apply to Siva for relief. Being propitiated by them, Siva granted their request, and proceeded with them to where Brahmā remained inflated with pride. On seeing Siva, Brahmā did not pay him the customary honours. Siva, seeing Brahmā's fifth head inflicting distress on the universe by its effulgent beams, brighter than a thousand suns, approached him and said, 'Oh! this head shines with too much splendour,' and immediately cut it off with the nail of his left thumb, with as much ease as a man cuts off the stem of a plantain tree."

The Mahābhārata says that Siva did not actually cut off Brahmā's head on this occasion, but was only prevented from doing so through the intercession of the gods. It was because of his attempting to seduce his own daughter that Siva decapitated him. This crime was attempted when in a fit of intoxication; hence Brahmā pronounced a curse upon the gods who should hereafter drink spirits.

---

*Kennedy's "Hindu Mythology," p. 276.

In the passages just quoted, Brahmā is represented as worshipping Siva for his own personal benefit; in the "Vishnu Purāna,"* he is described as joining with gods and men in the worship of this same deity, and as officiating as priest on that occasion. And in another part of the Purāna† is the following hymn addressed to Vishnu by Brahmā: — "Thou art the common centre of all, the protector of the world, and all things exist in thee. All that has been, or will be, thou art. There is nothing else but thee, O lord; nothing else has been, or will be. Thou art independent, and without beginning." The object of this laudation was to induce Vishnu to save the earth from its load of sorrow; in answer to it, Vishnu appeared here as Krishna.

At the present time Brahmā is not largely worshipped by the Hindus. "The Brāhmans in their morning and evening worship repeat an incantation containing a description of the image of Brahmā; at noon they present to him a single flower; at the time of burnt-offering, *ghī* is presented to him. In the month of Māgh, at the full moon, an earthen image of him is worshipped, with that of Siva on his right hand, and Vishnu on his left."‡ Brahmā as Creator is supposed to have finished his work; hence, excepting in one place, viz. at Pushkara in Ājmīr, there is no temple to him now existing. It is evident that for centuries the worship of Brahmā, has not been common, for in the "Skanda Purāna "§ is an indelicate legend, in which the charge of falsehood is proved against him, and this fact is given to account for the fact that his worship had ceased. It concludes as follows : — "Since thou hast childishly and with weak understanding asserted a falsehood, let no one henceforth perform worship to thee."

The Mahābhārata says that Brahmā's heaven is eight

---

*Page 102.
†Page 496.
‡Ward, ii. 30.
§Kennedy's "Hindu Mythology," p. 271.

hundred miles long, four hundred wide, and forty high. Nārada declared himself incompetent to describe it. In two hundred years he could not mention all its excellences. He said that it contained in a superior degree all the excellences of the other heavens; and that what ever existed in the creation of Brahmā on earth, from the smallest insect to the largest animal, was to be found there.

In the later mythology, a deity named Dhātā (the Creator), who in the Rig-Veda has no very clearly- defined powers, but is there said to operate in the production of life and the preservation of health, is identified with Prajāpati, or Brahmā; and in the sense of "maker" the term is also applied to Vishnu and Krishna. Sometimes he is said to be a son of Brahmā.*

In addition to the names of Brahmā already referred to, the following are those most commonly known :—

Ātmabhu, "The self-existent."

Paramesthi, "The chief sacrificer." He as the first Brāhman performed all the great sacrifices of the Hindu religion.

Lokesha, "The god of the world."

Hiranyagarbha, "He who came from the golden egg."

Savitripati, "The husband of Savitri."

Adikavi, "The first poet."

SARASVATI

Brahmā's wife is Sarasvati, the goddess of wisdom and science, the mother of the Vedas, and the inventor of the Devanāgari letters. She is represented as a fair young woman, with four arms. With one of her right hands she is presenting a flower to her husband, by whose side she continually stands; and in the other she holds a book of palm-leaves, indicating that she is fond of learning. In one of her left hands she has a string of pearls, called Sivamāla (Siva's garland), which serves as a

---

*Dowson, *s.v.*

rosary; and in the other is a *damaru,* or small drum. At other times she is represented with two arms only, seated on a lotus, playing a kind of banjo. She dwells on earth amongst men, but her special abode is with her husband in Brahmāloka.

Sarasvati having been produced from Brahmā, was regarded as his daughter; hence her union with him was said to be criminal by the other gods. Sometimes she is called the wife of Vishnu, but this difficulty is explained by a legend.* "Sarasvati, by the standard mythological authorities, is the wife of Brahmā. The Vaishnavas of Bengal have a popular legend that she was the wife of Vishnu, as were also Lakshmi and Gangā. The ladies disagreed, Sarasvati, like the other type

Sarasvati

of learned ladies, Minerva, being something of a termagant; and Vishnu, finding that one wife was as much as even a god could manage, transferred Sarasvati to Brahmā and Gangā to

*Wilson's Works, ii. 187.

Siva, and contented himself with Lakshmi alone.

"Sarasvati is a goddess of some, though not of very great, importance in the Vedas...She is celebrated both as a river and a goddess. She was primarily a river deity, as her name, 'the watery,' clearly denotes; and in this capacity she is celebrated in a few separate passages. Allusion is made in the hymns, as well as in the Brāhmanas, to sacrifices being performed on the banks of this river, and of the adjoining Drishadvati; and the Sarasvati in particular seems to have been associated with the reputation for sanctity which...was ascribed to the whole region called Brahmāvartta, lying between these two small streams, and situated immediately to the westward of the Jumnā. The Sarasvati thus appears to have been to the early Indians what the Ganges (which is only twice named in the Rig-Veda) is to their descendants...When once the river had acquired a divine character, it was quite natural that she should be regarded as the patroness of ceremonies which were celebrated on the margin of her holy waters, and that her direction and blessing should be invoked as essential to their proper performance and success. The connection into which she was thus brought with sacred rites may have led to the further step of imagining her to have an influence on the composition of the hymns which formed so important a part of the proceedings, and of identifying her with Vāch, the goddess of speech. At least I have no other explanation to offer to this double character and identification.*

"Sarasvati is frequently invited to the sacrifices along with several other goddesses, who, however, were never, like her, river nymphs, but personifications of some department of religious worship, or sacred science. She is frequently invoked along with other deities.

"In many passages where she is celebrated, her original character is, as I have intimated, distinctly preserved. Thus in

---

*Muir, O. S. T., v. 339.

two places she is mentioned along with rivers, or fertilizing waters: 'Ye opulent waters, command riches; ye possess excellent power and immortality; ye are mistresses of wealth and progeny; may Sarasvati bestow this vitality on her worshipper.' And she is mentioned with the other well-known streams which are there named, the Sindhu, the Ganges, & c. In another place she is said to 'surpass all other rivers, and to flow pure from the mountains to the sea.' In other verses she is called upon to 'descend from the sky, from the great mountain, to the sacrifice;' and is supplicated to combine with the spouses of the other gods to afford secure protection to the worshippers...It is difficult to say whether in any of the passages in which Sarasvati is invoked, even in those where she appears as the patroness of holy rites, her character as a river goddess is entirely left out of sight...

"In the later mythology, as is well known, Sarasvati was identified with Vāch, and became under various names the spouse of Brahmā, and the goddess of wisdom and eloquence, and is invoked as a Muse. In the Mahābhārata she is called the mother of the Vedas, and the same is said of Vāch in the Taittariya Brāhmana where she is said to be the wife of Indra, to contain within herself all worlds, and to have been sought after by the Rishis who composed the Vedic hymns, as well as by the gods through austerity."*

In the Purānas, Sarasvati is spoken of under other titles. A verse in the "Matsya Purāna" gives authority for the belief that one goddess only is intended, though she is called by several names: "Brahmā next formed from his own immaculate substance a female, who is celebrated under the names of Satarupā, Savitri, Sarasvati, Gāyatri, and Brāhmanī." In the following legend from the "Skanda Purāna,"† though by Savitri Sarasvati is intended, Gāyatri represents some other

---

*Muir, O. S. T., v. 337 ff.
†Kennedy, "Hindu Mythology," p. 320.

person who became a *second* wife of Brahmā. Iswara (Siva) is addressing Devi (Parvati) : —

"Listen, O Devi, and I will tell you how Savitri forsook Brahmā, and he in consequence espoused Gāyatri. The Vedas have declared the great advantages which are derived from sacrifice, by which the gods are delighted, and therefore bestow rain upon the earth...To secure therefore the verdure and vitality of the three worlds, I perform sacrifices; and, in imitation of me, sacrifices are performed by gods and men. For the same purpose Brahmā and his wife Savitri, the immortals, and the holy sages repaired to Pushkara; but when all the preparations had been made, with all due rites and ceremonies, for performing the sacrifices, Savitri, detained by some household affairs, was not in attendance. A priest accordingly went to call her; but she replied, 'I have not yet completed my dress, nor arranged several affairs. Lakshmi, and Bhavāni, and Gangā, and Svāha, and Indrāni, and the wives of the other gods and of the holy sages, have not yet arrived, and how therefore can I enter the assembly alone?'

"The priest returned, and thus addressed Brahmā: 'Savitri is engaged and will not come; but without a wife what advantage can be derived from these rites?' The god, incensed at the conduct of Savitri, thus spoke to Indra: 'Hasten, and, in obedience to my order, bring a wife from wherever you can find one.' Indra proceeded accordingly; and as he passed hastily along, saw a milkmaid, young, beautiful, and of a smiling countenance, carrying a jar of butter. He seized her and brought her to the assembly, when Brahmā thus spoke: 'O gods and holy sages, if it seem good unto you I will espouse this Gāyatri, and she shall become the mother of the Vedas, and the cause of purity to these worlds!' Upon this Brahmā was united to Gāyatri, who was led into the bower of the bride, and there arrayed in silken garments, and adorned with the costliest ornaments.

"At this time Savitri, accompanied by the wives of Vishnu,

Rudra, and the other gods, came to the place of sacrifice. Seeing the milkmaid in the bride's bower, and the priests engaged in the performance of the sacred rites, incensed with anger, she thus addressed Pitāmāha: 'O Brahmā! hast thou conceived so sinful an intention as to reject me, who am thy wedded wife? Hast thou no sense of shame, that thus, influenced by love, thou committest so reprehensible an act? Thou art called the great father of gods and holy sages, and yet thou here publicly actest in a manner which must excite the derision of the three worlds. But how can I now show my face; or, deserted by my husband, call myself a wife?' Brahmā replied: 'The priests informed me that the time for the sacrifice was passing away, and that it could not profitably be performed unless my wife were present, ...and Indra having brought Gāyatri, Vishnu and Rudra gave her in marriage to me. Forgive, therefore, this one act, and I will never again offend thee!'

"On hearing these words, Savitri exclaimed, 'By the powers which I have obtained by the performance of *tapas*, may Brahmā never be worshipped in temple or sacred place, except one day in each year...And, Indra, since thou didst bring that milkmaid to Brahmā, thou shalt be bound in chains by thine enemies, and confined in a strange country; and thy city and station shall be occupied by thine enemies.' Addressing Vishnu, she said, 'Since thou gavest her in marriage to Brahmā, shalt thou, in consequence of Bhrigu's curse, be born amongst men, and shalt endure the agony of having thy wife ravished from thee by thine enemy; and long also shalt thou wander, the humble keeper of cattle!' To Rudra she said: 'By the curse of the holy sages, shalt thou be deprived of thy manhood!' To Agni: 'Mayest thou be a devourer of all things, clean and unclean!' To the priests and Brahmans: 'Henceforth shall ye perform sacrifices solely from the desire of obtaining the usual gifts: and from covetousness alone shall ye attend temples and holy places; satisfied only shall ye be with the food of others, and dissatisfied with that of your own houses; and in quest of riches shall ye unduly perform holy rites and ceremonies!'

"Having pronounced these curses, Savitri left the assembly, and was accompanied for a short distance by Lakshmi and the other goddesses, when they all declared their intention of returning. On hearing this, Savitri was incensed, and thus addressed them: 'Since you now forsake me, O Lakshmi! mayest thou never remain stationary in one place;* and mayest thou always abide with the vile, the inconstant, the contemptible, the sinful, the cruel, the foolish, and the barbarian! And, Indrāni, when Indra incurs the guilt of Brāhmanicide by slaying Tvastri's son, then shall Nahusha acquire his kingdom, and, desirous of obtaining thee, shall exclaim, "Am I not Indra? why then does not the young and lovely Indrāni wait upon me? If I do not obtain her, I will slay all the gods." Thou on learning his wishes shalt remain in thy house immersed in grief, and borne down by the weight of my curse!' Savitri then pronounced this curse on the wives of the gods collectively: 'May you all remain barren; and may you never enjoy the pleasure of having children!' Vishnu then tried in vain to appease her."

After Savitri's angry departure from the assembly, Gāyatri modified the curses that had been pronounced. She promised all kinds of blessing, including final absorption into him, to all the worshippers of Brahmā. Though Indra be bound, his son should release him. Though Vishnu lost his wife, he should regain her. Though Rudra be deprived of his manhood, the Linga as his representative should be universally worshipped. Though men made gifts to the Brāhmans, it would be because they reverenced them as gods. And though the goddesses could not have children of their own, this would not cause them regret.

The "Padma Purāna" gives a happier termination to the

---

*Lakshmi is the goddess of fortune.

story. Vishnu and Lakshmi, at Brahmā's request, followed Savitri when she left the assembly, and induced her to return. On re-entering, Brahmā asked what she wished him to do with Gāyatri. Savitri was too bashful to speak; whereupon Gāyatri threw herself at her feet. Savitri raised her, and embracing her said : "A wife ought to obey the wishes and orders of her husband; for that wife who reproaches her husband, who is complaining and quarrelsome, and instead of being his life, deprives him by her conduct of length of years, shall, when she dies, most assuredly go to hell. Considering this, the virtuous wife will do nothing displeasing to her husband; therefore let us both be attached to Brahmā." "So be it," said Gāyatri; "thy orders will I always obey, and esteem thy friendship precious as my life. Thy daughter am I, O goddess! Deign to protect me!" It would appear that between the time when the "Matsya Purāna" was composed and the date of the Padma, considerable change had come in the character of the ideal woman. Or it may be that the writer of the Padma wished to give a better ideal to the wives of his day.

In a legend in the "Varāha Purāna," Sarasvati is addressed as Gāyatri, Sarasvati, Maheshvari (one of the names of Parvati), and also Savitri. Her most common name is Sarasvati, by which name, as the goddess of learning, she is regularly worshipped once a year.

Chapter IV
Vishnu and Lakshmi

VISHNU

Vishnu is called the second person of the Hindu Trimurti, or Triad: but though called *second,* it must not be supposed that he is regarded as in any way inferior to Brahmā. In some books Brahmā is said to be the first cause of all things, in others it is as strongly asserted that Vishnu has this honour; while in others it is claimed for Siva. As Brahmā's special work is creation, that of Vishnu is preservation. In the following passage from the "Padma Purāna," it is taught that Vishnu is the supreme cause, thus identifying him with Brahma, and also that his special work is *to preserve:* — "In the beginning of creation, the great Vishnu, desirous of creating the whole world, became threefold; Creator, Preserver, Destroyer. In order to create this world, the Supremo Spirit produced from the right side of his body himself as Brahmā; then, in order to preserve the world, he produced from his left side Vishnu; and in order to destroy the world, he produced from the middle of his body the eternal Siva. Some worship Brahmā, others Vishnu, others Siva; but Vishnu, one yet threefold, creates, preserves, and destroys: therefore let the pious make no difference between the three."

The essence of the teaching of the "Vishnu Purāna" is given in a few lines.* "Listen to the complete compendium of the Purāna according to its tenor. The world was produced from Vishnu; it exists in him; he is the cause of its continuance

Vishnu

and cessation; he is the world." Immediately afterwards is a hymn addressed to him which commences as follows:— "Glory to the unchangeable, holy, eternal, supreme Vishnu,

---

*"Vishnu Purāna," p. 607.

of one universal nature, the mighty over all; to him who is Hirānyagarbha (Brahmā), Hari (Vishnu), and Sankara (Siva); the Creator, Preserver, and Destroyer of the world." As will be noticed later on, Siva is commonly called Mahādeva (the great god). By those who make him the supreme object of worship, Vishnu is commonly called Nārāyana, though this was originally a name of Brahmā. These generally, to a large extent, disregard his incarnations, and address their praise to him as the greatest of all. And frequently he is indicated by the word Ishwar (God), as though he were *the* God. But this term is far more frequently employed for Siva.

"The word Vishnu in the Purānas is generally said to be derived from the root *vis* (to enter); entering in or pervading the universe, agreeably to the text of the Vedas: 'Having created that (world), he then afterwards enters into it.' According to the 'Matsya Purāna,' the name alludes to his entering into the mundane egg; according to the 'Padma Purāna,' it refers to his entering into or combining with Prakriti, as Purush or spirit." *

In the "Bhāgavata Purāna" † is the following legend to show the superiority of Vishnu: — "Once when the holy sages were performing a sacrifice on the banks of the Sarasvati, a dispute arose amongst them as to which of the three gods was greatest. They sent Bhrigu, the son of Brahmā, to ascertain this point. He first went to the heaven of Brahmā, and, desirous of discovering the truth, entered his court without paying him the usual honours. Incensed at this disrespect, Brahmā glowed with anger; but recollecting that it was caused by his own son, he assuaged the fire of wrath which had risen in his mind. Bhrigu then proceeded to Kailasa; but when Mahesliwara (Siva) hastened to embrace him as a brother, he turned away from the proffered embrace. Enraged at such misconduct, the

---

*"Vishnu Purāna," p. 3, note.
†Kennedy, "Hindu Mythology," p. 240.

god, seizing his trident, prepared to kill the divine sage; but Parvati fell at his feet, and by her words appeased the anger of her lord. Bhrigu next went to Vishnu's heaven, and kicked the god's breast, as he lay slumbering in the lap of Lakshmi. The lord, rising from his couch, and bowing respectfully to Bhrigu, thus addressed him: 'Welcome to thee, O Brāhman! Be seated for a little, and deign to excuse the fault which through ignorance I have committed [in not performing duties due to a guest], and the hurt which your tender foot must have received!' Having thus spoken, he rubbed the foot of Bhrigu with his own hands, and added, 'To-day am I a highly honoured vessel, since thou, O lord! hast imprinted on my breast the dust of thy sin-dispelling foot.' When Vishnu had finished speaking, Bhrigu was so affected by these benevolent words, that he was unable to reply, and departed in silence, whilst tears of devout emotion rushed from his eyes. On his narrating his adventures to the saints on the banks of the Sarasvati, their doubts were immediately dispelled; they believed Vishnu to be the greatest of the three gods, because he was exempt from impatience and passion."

In the "Padma Purāna"* Siva is represented as admitting Vishnu's superiority to himself. Addressing his wife, he says: "I will acquaint thee with the real essence and form of Vishnu: know then that he is in truth Nārāyana, the Supreme Spirit, and Parabrahma (the great Brahma), without beginning or end, omniscient, and omnipresent; eternal, unchangeable, and supremely happy. He is Siva, Hirānyagarbha, and Surya; he is more excellent than all the gods, even than I myself. But it is impossible for me, or Brahmā, or the gods, to declare the greatness of Vāsudeva, the originator and lord of the universe."

In the "Varāha Purāna"† the special work of Vishnu as

---

*Kennedy, "Hindu Mythology," p. 246.
†Kennedy, "Hindu Mythology," p. 246.

preserver is described:—" The supreme god Nārāyana having conceived the thought of creating this universe, considered also that it was necessary that it should be protected after it was created; 'but as it is impossible for an incorporeal being to exert action, let me produce from my own essence a corporeal being, by means of whom I may protect the world.' Having thus reflected, the pre-existing Nārāyana created from his own substance an ungenerated and divine form, on whom he bestowed these blessings:—'Be thou the framer of all things, O Vishnu! Be thou always the protector of the three worlds, and the adored of all men. Be thou omniscient and almighty; and do thou at all times accomplish the wishes of Brahmā and the gods.' The Supreme Spirit then resumed his essential nature. Vishnu, as he meditated on the purpose for which he had been produced, sank into a mysterious slumber; and as in his sleep he imagined the production of various things, a lotus sprang from his navel. In the centre of this lotus Brahmā appeared; and Vishnu, beholding the production of his body, was delighted." The phraseology of this passage gives countenance to what was said before, that in the worship of some of the Hindus, Nārāyana is regarded as identical with Brahmā the Supreme.

In pictures Vishnu is represented as a black man with four arms: in one hand he holds a club; in another a shell; in a third a chakra, or discus, with which he slew his enemies; and in the fourth a lotus. He rides upon the bird Garuda, and is dressed in yellow robes.

The following description of Vaikuntha, the heaven of Vishnu, is from the Mahābhārata.* It is made entirely of gold, and is 80,000 miles in circumference. All its buildings are made of jewels. The pillars and ornaments of the buildings are of precious stones. The crystal waters of the Ganges fall from the higher heavens on the head of Druva; from thence into the hair of the seven Rishis; and from thence they fall and form a

---

*Ward. ii. 14.

river. Here are also five pools containing blue, red, and white lotuses. On a seat glorious as the meridian sun, sitting on white lotuses, is Vishnu; and on his right hand Lakshmi, who shines like a continued blaze of lightning, and from whose body the fragrance of the lotus extends 800 miles.

This deity is worshipped not only under the name and in the form of Vishnu, but also in one of his many incarnations. Whenever any great calamity occurred in the world, or the wickedness of any of its inhabitants proved an unbearable nuisance to the gods, Vishnu, as Preserver, had to lay aside his invisibility, come to earth in some form, generally human, and, when his work was done, he returned again to the skies. There is no certainty as to the number of times he has become incarnate. Some Purānas describe ten Avatāras, as they are called; some mention twenty-four; and sometimes declare that they are innumerable. Ten is the commonly received number, and these are the most important ones. They will be considered in due order. Of these ten, nine have already been accomplished; one, the Kalki, is still future. "Some of these Avatāras are of an entirely cosmical character; others, however, are probably based on historical events, the leading personage of which was gradually endowed with divine attributes, until he was regarded as the incarnation of the deity himself." In the "Matsya Purāna"* is the following legend, which gives a reason for the manifold and varied appearances of this deity:—

"The asuras (demons, lit. non-suras) having been repeatedly defeated by the suras (gods), and deprived of all share of the sacrifices, were meditating to withdraw from the unavailing contest, when Sukra, their preceptor, determined to propitiate Siva by a severe *tapas* (penance), and procure from him a charm by means of which they could conquer. Having left them for this purpose, the asuras said amongst themselves, 'As our preceptor has laid aside his arms and assumed the

---

*Kennedy, "Hindu Mythology," p. 244.

ascetic dress, how shall we be able to gain a victory over the suras? Let us seek refuge with the mother of Kavya (Sukra), and endure this distress till he shall return; and then let us fight!' Having thus resolved, they hastened to Kavya's mother, who, protecting them, said, 'Fear not! remain near me, and no danger shall approach you!'

"The suras, seeing the asuras thus protected, were about to attack them, when the goddess in anger thus addressed Indra: 'If thou desist not, I will deprive you of the sovereignty of heaven.' Alarmed at her angry words, and dreading her magic power, Indra was yielding to her desire, when Vishnu appeared and said to him, 'Yield not, for I will assist you!' The goddess observing that Indra was protected by Vishnu, angrily said, 'Now let the contending foes behold how the power of my devotions shall subdue both Indra and Vishnu.' Finding themselves likely to be overcome, they asked each other, 'How shall we liberate ourselves from this difficulty?' Indra then said to Vishnu, 'Hasten to conquer before she has finished her invocations, or we shall be defeated !' Then Vishnu, considering the detriment that must be incurred by the gods should the mother of Kavya bring her incantations to a successful issue, deemed that the slaying of a woman under such circumstances was allowable, seized his discus, and smote off her head. Bhrigu, seeing this horrid deed of the slaughter of a woman and the death of his wife, was violently incensed, and thus cursed Vishnu: 'Since thou hast knowingly murdered a woman, thou shalt be born seven times amongst men;' he afterwards somewhat modified its force as he said, 'but each birth shall be for the advantage of the world, and for the restoration of justice.' "

It is interesting to know the character of the *tapas* (penance) by which Sukra hoped to gain power over the gods. He was to imbibe the smoke of a fire of chaff with his head downwards for a thousand years. He accomplished this difficult feat, and by it so pleased Siva, that he gave him many boons, including that of superiority over the gods. But the asuras did not profit long by this penance of their preceptor, as they were deceived by the preceptor of the gods, who, assuming Sukra's form, gave them bad advice, which they followed to their hurt.

In the "Vishnu Purāna"* the benefits to be hoped for from the worship of Vishnu are taught. The question is asked, "By what acts can men free themselves from Yama?" The reply given is that which was once told by a holy Muni who recollected his former births, and by whom "what was, and what will be, was accurately told." "Yama, beholding one of his servants with a noose in his hands, whispered to him and said 'Keep clear of the worshippers of Madhusudana (Vishnu), I am lord of all men, the Vaishnavas (worshippers of Vishnu) excepted. I was appointed by Brahmā to restrain mankind, and regulate the consequences of good and evil in the universe. But he who worships Hari is independent of me. He who through holy knowledge diligently adores the lotus-foot of Hari is released from all the bonds of sin, and you must avoid him as you would fire fed with oil.' And again: 'He who pleases Vishnu obtains all terrestrial enjoyments, heaven, and a place in heaven; and, what is best of all, final liberation: whatever he wishes, and to whatever extent, whether much or little, he receives it when Achyuta (the unde caying one) is content with him.' "

The means by which the favour of this god is to be obtained are then explained:—"The supreme Vishnu is propitiated by a man who observes the institutions of caste, order, and purificatory practices; no other path is the way to please him. He who offers sacrifices, sacrifices to him; he who murmurs prayer, prays to him; he who injures living creatures, injures him: for Hari is all things. Kesava is most pleased with him who does good to others; who never utters abuse, calumny, or untruth; who never covets another's wife or another's wealth,

---

*Pp. 287-290.

and who bears ill-will towards none; who never beats nor slays any animate or inanimate thing; who is ever diligent in the service of the gods, of the Brāhmans, and of his spiritual preceptor; who is ever desirous of the welfare of all creatures, of his children, and of his own soul; in whose pure heart no pleasure is derived from the imperfections of love and hatred. The man who conforms to the duties enjoined by scriptural authority for every caste and condition of life is he who best worships Vishnu; there is no other mode."

Of all the deities now reverenced in India, Vishnu in his many forms has perhaps the largest number of worshippers; and the account of his life and the praises presented to him occupy a very large portion of the later Hindu scriptures. This pre-eminence was certainly not recognized in the Vedic Age, as the following passage will show:—

"In the Rig-Veda are the following verses:—'May the gods preserve us from the place from which Vishnu strode over the seven regions of the earth. Vishnu strode over this [universe]; in three places he planted his step; [the world or his step] was enveloped in his dust. Vishnu, the unconquerable preserver, strode three steps.'* In these verses there is probably the germ of the Dwarf Incarnation, and also of the attribute of Preserver. The interpretations of two commentators of the three strides of Vishnu are as follows :—One regards him 'as a god, who, in what are called his three strides, is manifested in a threefold form as Agni on earth, as Indra or Vayu in the atmosphere, and as the Sun in heaven;'† the other interprets Vishnu's three strides as 'the rising, culmination, and setting of the sun.'"‡

Vishnu, in the Rig-Veda, is said "to have established the heavens and the earth; to contain all the world in his strides; to have, with Indra, made the atmosphere wide, stretched out the

---

*Muir, O. S. T., iv. 63.
†Ibid. iv. 78 ff.
‡Ibid.

worlds, produced the Sun, the Dawn, and Fire; to have received the homage of Varuna; whilst his greatness is described as having no limit within the ken of present or future beings. The attributes ascribed to Vishnu in some of these passages are such that, if the latter stood alone in the Rig-Veda, they might lead us to suppose that he was regarded by the Vedic Rishis as the chief of all the gods. But Indra is associated with Vishnu even in some of those texts in which the latter is most highly magnified: nay, in one place, the power by which Vishnu takes his three strides is described as being derived from Indra; in another text, Vishnu is represented as celebrating Indra's praise; whilst in another verse, Vishnu is said to have been generated by Soma. It is also a fact that the hymns and verses which are dedicated to the praises of Indra, Agni, etc., are extremely numerous, whilst the entire hymns and separate verses in which Vishnu is celebrated are much fewer...Vishnu is introduced as the subject of laudation among a crowd of other divinities, from which he is there in no way distinguished as being in any respect superior. From this fact we may conclude that he was regarded by those writers as on a footing of equality with the other deities. Further, the Rig-Veda contains numerous texts in which the Rishis ascribe to Indra, Varuna, and other gods, the same high and awful attributes and functions which are spoken of in other hymns as belonging to Vishnu...If then we look to the large number of texts in which some of the other gods are celebrated, and to the comparatively small number of those in which Vishnu is exclusively or prominently magnified, we shall come to the conclusion that the latter deity occupied a somewhat subordinate place in the estimation and affections of the ancient Rishis."*

Amongst the thousand names of Vishnu, the following, in addition to those already given, are most commonly known:—

---

*Muir, O. S. T., iv. 98.

Madhusudana, the destroyer of Madhu; and Kaitabhajit, the conqueror of Kaitabha. These were two demons who issued from Vishnu's ear as he lay asleep on the serpent Sesha at the end of a Kalpa,* and were about to destroy Brahmā, as he sat on the lotus which sprang from Vishnu's navel, when this deity slew them, and hence obtained these names:—

Vaikunthanāth, "The Lord of Paradise."

Kesava, "He who has excellent hair."

Madhava, "Made of honey; or a descendant of Madhu."

Swayambhu, "The self-existent one."

Pitamvara, "He who wears yellow garments."

Janārddana, "He who causes the people to worship."

Vishvamvara, "The protector of the world."

Hari, "The saviour;" lit he who takes possession of.

Ananta, "The endless."

Dāmodara, "Bound with a rope."

Mukunda, "The deliverer."

Purusha, "The man," or "The spirit."

Purushottama, "The supreme man or spirit."

Yajneswara, "The lord of sacrifice."

LAKSHMI

Lakshmi, or very commonly Sri, is the wife of Vishnu, and under various names appears in this relation in his various incarnations. "As the lord of the worlds, the god of gods, Janārddana descends amongst mankind in various shapes; so does his coadjutor Sri. Thus, when Hari was born a dwarf, the son of Aditi, Lakshmi appeared from the lotus as Padmā, or Kamalā; when he was born as Rāma (Parasurāma) of the race of Bhrigu, she was Dharāni; when he was Rāghava (Rāmachandra), she was Sita; and when he was Krishna, she was Rukmini. In the other descents of Vishnu she was his

---

*See part ii. chap. x.

associate. If he takes a celestial form, she appears as divine; if a mortal, she becomes a mortal too, transforming her own person agreeably to whatever character it pleases Vishnu to assume."*

There are two somewhat contradictory accounts of her origin; the "Vishnu Purāna" explains this.† "The divinities Dhāta and Vidhātā were born to Bhrigu by Khyāti, as was a daughter Sri, the wife of Nārāyana, the god of gods." The question is asked, "It is commonly said that Sri was born from the sea of milk, when it was churned for ambrosia; how then can you say that she was the daughter of Bhrigu and Khyāti?" In answer to this question, a most elaborate account of her virtues is given: "Sri, the bride of Vishnu, the mother of the world, is eternal, imperishable; as he is all-pervading, so she is omnipresent. Vishnu is meaning, she is speech; Hari is polity, she is prudence; Vishnu is understanding, she is intellect; he is righteousness, she is devotion; Sri is the earth, Hari is its support. In a word, of gods, animals, and men, Hari is all that is called male; Lakshmi is all that is termed female; there is nothing else than they." Later on‡ we read, "Her first birth was as the daughter of Bhrigu and Khyāti; it was at a subsequent period that she was produced from the sea, at the churning of the ocean by the demons and the gods."

The account of the churning of the ocean, to which frequent reference is made in the Hindu scriptures, is found in the Rāmāyana, and several of the Purānas; though there are some discrepancies, they agree in the main. The reason for this great act is as follows:— § A saint named Durvāras, a portion of Siva, was travelling, when he met a celestial nymph with a sweet-smelling

---

*"Vishnu Purāna," p. 80.

†Page 59.

‡ Page 80.

§"Vishnu Purāna," book i. chap. ix.

Lakshmi

garland, which at his request she gave to him. Excited with
the scent, he was dancing, when he met Indra, seated on his
elephant. To please the mighty god, the saint presented him
with the garland, who placed it upon his elephant's head. The
elephant in his turn becoming excited, seized the garland with
his trunk and threw it upon the ground. Durvāras, seeing his
gift slighted, cursed the god in his anger, and told him that his
kingdom should be overwhelmed with ruin. From that time
Indra's power began to wane; for though he sought forgiveness,
the Brāhman's anger was not to be appeased. As the effects
of the curse were experienced by the gods, they, fearing they
should be overcome by the asuras, fled to Brahmā for help. He
told them he could not assist them; that Vishnu alone could do
this, whom he advised them to seek. Brahmā conducted them

to Vishnu; and, having sufficiently lauded him, caused him to lend a willing ear to their request. In the following lines,* put into verse, from the "Vishnu Purāna," we have their prayer, Vishnu's advice and its result:—

> "The gods addressed the mighty Vishnu thus:
> 'Conquered in battle by the evil demons,
> We fly to thee for succour; soul of all,
> Pity and by thy might deliver us!'
> Hari, the lord, creator of the world,
> Thus by the gods implored, all graciously
> Replied, 'Your strength shall be restored, ye gods—
> Only accomplish what I now command:
> Unite yourselves in peaceful combination
> With these your foes; collect all plants and herbs
> Of diverse kinds from every quarter; cast them
> Into the sea of milk; take Mandara,
> The mountain, for a churning stick, and Vāsuki,
> The serpent, for a rope; together churn
> The ocean to produce the beverage —
> Source of all strength and immortality—
> Then reckon on mine aid: I will take care
> Your foes shall share your toil, but not partake
> In its reward, or drink th' immortal draught.'
> Thus by the god of gods advised, the host
> United in alliance with the demons.
> Straightway they gathered various herbs, and cast them
> Into the waters; then they took the mountain
> To serve as churning-staff, and next the snake
> To serve as cord, and in the ocean's midst
> Hari himself, present in tortoise form,
> Became a pivot for the churning-staff.
> Then did they churn the sea of milk; and first

---

*Indian Wisdom," p. 499.

Out of the waters rose the sacred cow—
God-worshipped Surabhi—eternal fountain
Of milk and offerings of butter; next,
While holy Siddhas wondered at the sight,
With eyes all rolling, Vārum uprose—
Goddess of Wine. Then from the whirlpool sprang
Fair Pārijāta, tree of Paradise, delight
Of heavenly maidens, with its fragrant blossoms
Perfuming the whole world. Th' Apsarasas,
Troop of celestial nymphs, matchless in grace,
Perfect in loveliness, were next produced.
Then from the sea uprose the cool-rayed moon,
Which Mahādeva seized; terrific poison
Next issued from the waters—this the snake-gods
Claimed as their own. Then, seated on a lotus,
Beauty's bright goddess, peerless Sri, arose
Out of the waves; and with her, robed in white,
Came forth Dhanvantari, the gods' physician.
High in his hand he bore the cup of nectar—
Life-giving draught—longed for by gods and demons."

On Sri's appearance the sages were enraptured, the heavenly choristers sang her praises, and the celestial nymphs danced before her. Gangā and the other sacred streams followed her, and the heavenly elephants took up their pure waters in golden vessels and poured them upon her. The sea of milk presented her with a wreath of unfading flowers; and the artist of the gods decorated her with lovely ornaments. Thus bathed, attired, and adorned, the goddess, in the presence of the gods, cast herself upon the breast of Hari, and, reclining' there, gazed upon the gods, who were enraptured with her. Siva was most violent and wished to possess himself of her. From the demons she turned away; hence they were miserable. Seeing the cup of nectar, they tried to seize it, when Vishnu, assuming the appearance of a beautiful woman, attracted their attention, whilst the gods quaffed the divine cup. The result was that in the conflict which followed the gods were successful.

The following account of Sri is from the Rāmāyana:—

> "When many a year had fled,
> Up floated, on her lotus bed,
> A maiden fair, and tender-eyed,
> In the young flush of beauty's pride.
> She shone with pearl and golden sheen,
> And seals of glory stamped her queen.
> On each round arm glowed many a gem,
> On her smooth brows a diadem.
> Rolling in waves beneath her crown,
> The glory of her hair rolled down.
> Pearls on her neck of price untold,
> The lady shone like burnished gold.
> Queen of the gods, she leapt to land,
> A lotus in her perfect hand,
> And fondly, of the lotus sprung,
> To lotus-bearing Vishnu clung.
> Her, gods above and men below
> As Beauty's Queen and Fortune know."*

As noticed in this last extract, Lakshmi, or Sri, is regarded as the goddess of Love, Beauty, and Prosperity. When a man is growing rich, it is said that Lakshmi has come to dwell with him; whilst those in adversity are spoken of as "forsaken of Lakshmi." In pictures she is painted as a lady of a bright golden colour, seated on a lotus, with two arms.

"The name of Lakshmi as that of a goddess does not occur in the Rig-Veda, though the word itself is found in its signification as prosperity."†

---

*Griffiths's "Rāmāyana," i. 204.

†Muir, O. S. T., iv. 348.

Lakshmi is known also by the following names : —

Haripriyā, "The beloved of Hari."

Padma," The Lotus," and Padmālaya, "She who dwells on a lotus."

Jaladhijā, "The ocean-born."

Chanehalā, "The fickle one."

Lokamāta, "The mother of the world."

Chapter V

The Incarnations or Avataras of Vishnu

1. THE MATSYA OR FISH AVATĀRA

THE earliest account of what was afterwards regarded as an incarnation of Vishnu is found in the "Satapatha Brāhmana." It will be noticed that though in this passage a wonderful fish is described, it is not said to have been an incarnation of any of the gods. The Mahābhārata says that Brahmā assumed this form; whilst the Purānas teach that the fish here spoken of was Vishnu. This transfer of work from one deity to another is not a matter of much surprise, when we remember how frequently it is declared that all the various gods are but forms of one supreme being. "It should be noticed that the Manu here referred to is regarded as a progenitor of the human race, and is represented as conciliating the Supreme Being by his piety in an age of universal depravity." Here is the passage:*

"There lived in ancient time a holy man

---

*"Indian Wisdom," p. 32.

Called Manu, who, by penances and prayers,
Had won the favour of the lord of heaven.
One day they brought him water for ablution;
Then, as he washed his hands, a little fish
Appeared, and spoke in human accents thus:
'Take care of me, and I will be thy saviour.'
'From what wilt thou preserve me? 'Manu asked.
The fish replied, 'A flood will sweep away

The Matsya Avtāra

All creatures; I will rescue thee from that.'

'But how shall I preserve thee?' Manu said.
The fish rejoined, 'So long as we are small,
We are in constant danger of destruction,
For fish eat fish; so keep me in a jar.
When I outgrow the jar, then dig a trench,
And place me there; when I outgrow the trench,
Then take me to the ocean—I shall then
Be out of reach of danger.' Having thus
Instructed Mann, straightway rapidly
The fish grew larger; then he spake again:
'In such and such a year the flood will come;
Therefore construct a ship, and pay me homage.
When the flood rises, enter thou the ship,
And I will rescue thee.' So Manu did
As he was ordered, and preserved the fish,
Then carried it in safety to the ocean;
And in the very year the fish enjoined
He built a ship, and paid the fish respect,
And there took refuge when the flood arose.
Soon near him swam the fish, and to its horn
Manu made fast the cable of his vessel. Thus
drawn along the waters, Manu passed
Beyond the northern mountain. Then the fish,
Addressing Manu, said, 'I have preserved thee,
Quickly attach the ship to yonder tree:
But, lest the waters sink from under thee,
As fast as they subside, so fast shalt thou
Descend the mountain gently after them.'
Thus he descended from the northern mountain.
The flood had swept away all living creatures;
Manu alone was left."

The account from the Mahābhārata which now follows has

also been put into verse by Professor Monier Williams: — *

> "Along the ocean in that stately ship was borne the lord
>   of men, and through
> Its dancing, tumbling billows, and its roaring waters;
>   and the bark,
> Tossed to and fro by violent winds, reeled on the surface
>   of the deep
> Staggering and trembling like a drunken woman. Land
>   was seen no more,
> Nor far horizon, nor the space between; for everywhere
>   around
> Spread the wild waste of waters, reeking atmosphere,
>   and boundless sky.
> And now when all the world was deluged, nought
>   appeared above the waves
> But Manu and the seven sages, and the fish that drew
>   the bark.
> Unwearied, thus for years on years the fish propelled the
>   ship across
> The heaped-up waters, till at length it bore the vessel to
>   the peak
> Of Himavān; then softly smiling, thus the fish addressed
>   the sage:
> 'Haste, now, to bind thy ship to this high crag. Know
>   me, the lord of all,
> The great Creator Brahmā, mightier than all might,
>   omnipotent.
> By me, in fishlike shape, hast thou been saved in dire
>   emergency.
> From Manu all creation, gods, asuras, men, must be
>   produced;
> By him all the world must be created—that which moves

---

and moveth not.'"

The typical Purānic account of this Avatāra is that of the "Bhāgavata Purāna" which is given by Sir William Jones in the "Asiatic Soc. Res."* With this the accounts in the other Purānas agree in the main: some are more condensed, others, as the "Matsya Purāna," are considerably extended; for it was as the fish was guiding the vessel in which Manu was saved that Vishnu, in this form, is said to have dictated the whole of that Purāna. All the Purānas agree in regarding the fish as an incarnation of Vishnu, and not of Brahmā. Now follows the account from the Bhāgavata:—

"Desiring the preservation of herds, Brāhmans, genii, and virtuous men—of the Vedas, of law, and of precious things—the Lord of the Universe assumes many bodily shapes; but though he pervades, like the air, a variety of beings, yet he is himself unvaried, since he has no qualities subject to change. At the close of the last Kalpa there was a general destruction, occasioned by the sleeping Brahmā, whence his creatures in different worlds were drowned in a vast ocean. Brahmā being inclined to slumber, desiring repose after a lapse of ages, the strong demon Hayagriva came near him, and stole the Vedas, which had flowed from his lips.

"When Hari, the preserver of the universe, discovered this deed of the prince of the Dānavas, he took the shape of a minute fish, called Sāphari. A holy king named Satyavrāta then reigned—a servant of the spirit which moved on the waves; and so devout, that water was his only sustenance. He was the child of the Sun, and in the present Kalpa† is invested by Nārāyana with the office of Manu (*i.e.* the progenitor and lord of men), by the name of Srāddhadevā, or the god of obsequies. One day as he was making a libation in the river Kritamāla,

---

*Vol. i. 230 ff.
†See part ii. chap. x.

and held water in the palm of his hand, he perceived a small fish moving in it. The King of Dravira immediately dropped the fish into the river, together with the water which he had taken from it; when the Saphari thus addressed the benevolent monarch: 'How canst thou, O king, who showest affection to the oppressed, leave me in this river water, where I am too weak to resist the monsters of the stream, who fill me with dread?' He, not knowing who had assumed the form of a fish, applied his mind to the preservation of the Sāphari, both from good-nature and from regard to his own soul; and, having heard his very suppliant address, he kindly placed it under his protection in a small vase full of water; but in a single night its bulk was so increased that it could not be contained in the jar, and thus again addressed the illustrious prince: 'I am not pleased with living miserably in this little vase; make me a large mansion, where I may dwell in comfort.' The king, removing it thence, placed it in the water of a cistern; but it grew three cubits in less than fifty minutes, and said, 'O king! it pleases me not to stay vainly in this narrow cistern; since thou hast granted me an asylum, give me a spacious habitation.' He then removed it and placed it in a pool, where, having ample space around its body, it became a fish of considerable size. 'This abode, O king, is not convenient for me, who must swim at large in the waters; exert thyself for my safety, and remove me to a deep lake!' Thus addressed, the pious monarch threw the suppliant into a lake, and, when it grew of equal bulk with that piece of water, he cast the vast fish into the sea. When the fish was thrown into the waves, he thus again spoke to Satyavrāta: 'Here the horned sharks and other monsters of great strength will devour me; thou shouldest not, O valiant man, leave me in this ocean.'

"Thus repeatedly deluded by the fish, who had addressed him with gentle words, the king said, 'Who art thou that beguilest me in that assumed shape? Never before have I seen or heard of so prodigious an inhabitant of the waters, who, like thee, has filled up in a single day a lake a hundred leagues in circumference. Surely thou art Bhāgavat who appears before me; the great Hari, whose dwelling was on the waves; and who now, in compassion to thy servants, bears the form of the natives of the deep. Salutation and praise to thee, O first male, the lord of creation, of preservation, of destruction! Thou art the highest object, the supreme ruler, of us thy adorers, who piously seek thee. All thy delusive descents in this world give existence to various beings; yet I am anxious to know for what cause that shape has been assumed by thee. Let me not, O lotus–eyed, approach in vain the feet of a deity whose perfect benevolence has been extended to all; when thou hast shown us to our amazement the appearance of other bodies, not in reality existing, but successively exhibited.'

"The lord of the universe, loving the pious man who thus implored him, and intending to preserve him from the sea of destruction caused by the depravity of the age, thus told him how he was to act: 'In seven days from the present time, O thou tamer of enemies! the three worlds will be plunged in an ocean of death; but, in the midst of the destroying waves, a large vessel sent by me for thy use shall stand before thee. Then thou shalt take all medicinal herbs, all the varieties of seeds, and accompanied by seven saints, encircled by pairs of brute animals, thou shalt enter the spacious ark, and continue in it secure from the flood, on one immense ocean without light, except the radiance of thy holy companions. When the ship shall be agitated with an impetuous wind, thou shalt fasten it with a large sea serpent on my horn; for I will be near thee, drawing the vessel, with thee and thy attendants. I will remain on the ocean, O chief of men, until a night of Brahmā* shall be completely ended. Thou shalt then know my true greatness, rightly named the Supreme Godhead; by my favour all thy questions shall be answered, and thy mind abundantly

---

*See part ii. chap. x.

instructed.'

"Hari, having thus directed the monarch, disappeared; and Satyavrāta humbly waited for the time which the ruler of our senses had appointed. The pious king having scattered toward the east the pointed blades of the grass *darbha.* and turning his face towards the north, sat meditating on the feet of the god who had borne the form of a fish. The sea, overwhelming its shores, deluged the whole earth, and it was soon perceived to be augmented by showers from immense clouds. He, still meditating on the command of Bhāgavat, saw the vessel advancing, and entered it with the chiefs of Brāhmans, having carried into it the medicinal plants, and conformed to the directions of Hari. The saints thus addressed him: 'O king, meditate on Kesava; who will surely deliver us from this danger, and grant us prosperity.' The god being invoked by the monarch, appeared again distinctly on the vast ocean in the form of a fish, blazing like gold, extending a million of leagues, with one stupendous horn; on which the king, as he had been before commanded by Hari, tied the ship with a cable made of a vast serpent, and, happy in his preservation, stood praising the destroyer of Madhu. When the monarch had finished his hymn, the primeval male, Bhāgavat, who watched for his safety on the greater expanse of water, spake aloud to his own divine essence, pronouncing a sacred Purāna [the 'Matsya Purāna'], which contained the rules of the Sankhya philosophy; but it was an infinite mystery to be concealed within the breast of Satyavrāta; who, sitting in the vessel with the saints, heard the principle of soul, the Eternal Being, proclaimed by the preserving power. Then Hari, rising together with Brahmā from the destructive deluge, which was now abated, slew the demon Hayagriva, and recovered the sacred books."

2. THE KŪRMA OR TORTOISE AVATĀRA.

This incarnation was necessitated by the fact that the gods were in danger of losing their authority over the demons. In their distress they applied to Vishnu for help, who told them to churn the sea of milk that they might procure the *Amrita,* or water of life, by which they would be made strong, and promised to become the tortoise on which the mountain Mandara as a churning stick should rest. As a full account of this operation has been already given when describing Lakshmi, who was one of its chief products, there is no necessity to repeat it here. A few additional particulars will be found in the following extract from the "Vishnu Purāna:" — *

"Hari having been entreated to help the gods, thus spoke: 'I will restore your strength. Do you act as I enjoin. Let all the gods and asuras cast all sorts of medicinal herbs into the sea of milk, and together churn the ocean for ambrosia, depending on my aid. To secure the assistance of the daityas, you must be at peace with them, and engage to give them an equal share of your associated toil; promising them that by drinking of the amrita…they shall become mighty and immortal. I will take care that the enemies of the gods shall not partake of the precious draught; they shall only share in the labour.'"

The gods entered into an arrangement with the asuras, and together they made the necessary preparations. "The assembled gods were stationed by Krishna at the tail of the serpent Vasuki (the churning rope), and the daityas and dānavas at its head and neck. Scorched by the flames emitted from his inflated hood, the demons were shorn of their glory; whilst the clouds, driven by his breath towards his tail, refreshed the gods by vivifying showers. In the midst of the milky sea, Hari himself, in the form of a tortoise, served as a pivot for the mountain, as it was whirled around. The holder of the mace and discus was present in other forms amongst the gods and demons, and assisted to drag the monarch of the serpent race; and in another vast body sat upon the summit of the mountain. With

---

*Page 73.

one portion of his energy, unseen by gods and demons, he sustained the serpent king; and with another infused vigour unto the gods."

The Kūrma Avatāra

Such is the account of this incarnation of Vishnu as taught by the Purānas; but in the earlier books, where the probable origin of this legend is found, it is Brahmā, and not Vishnu, that is said to have assumed the form of a tortoise. In the "Satapatha Brāhmana" are these words: "Having assumed the form of a tortoise, Prajāpati (Brahmā) created offspring. That which he created, he made;" hence the word Kūrma. Kasyapa means tortoise; hence men say, "All creatures are descendants of Kasyapa. This tortoise is the same as Aditya." As the worship of Brahmā became less popular, whilst that of Vishnu increased in its attraction, the names, attributes, and works of the one deity appear to have been transferred to the other.

3. THE VARAHA OR BOAR AVATĀRA

There is the same conflicting account of this as of the two preceding incarnations; the older books, and some of the more modern ones, describing it as an Avatāra of Brahmā; and some of the modern books and popular belief regarding it as the work of Vishnu. There is, however, this distinction, that "in the former, the transformation of the deity into a boar has apparently a purely cosmical character," the earth being immersed in the ocean. Brahmā, the Creator, in the shape of a boar, raised it on his tusk; "whereas, in the latter, it altogether represents the extrication of the world from a deluge of iniquity by the rites of religion."*

The first mention of this incarnation is in the "Taittiriya Sanhitā," † and is as follows:—"The universe was formerly water, fluid. On it Prajāpati (Brahmā) becoming wind, moved. Becoming a boar, he took it up." In harmony with this is a verse in the "Taittiriya Brāhmana":—"This universe was formerly water, fluid. With that (water) Prajāpati practised arduous devotions (saying), 'How shall this universe be (developed)?' He beheld a lotus leaf standing. He thought, 'There is something on which this rests.' He as a boar—having assumed that form—plunged beneath towards it. He found the earth down below. Breaking off (a portion of) her, he rose to the surface." In the "Satapatha Brāhmana" ‡ there is a similar reference, but there

---

*Goldstücker, Chambers's Cyclopædia, *s.v.* "Vishnu."
†Muir, O. S. T., i. 52.
‡ Muir, O. S. T., iv. 33.

the boar is called "Emusha." Formerly the earth was only of the size of a span. A boar called Emusha raised her up.

Dr. Muir* gives two accounts of this incarnation from two recensions of the Rāmāyana. In one, which he considers the older, it is said that Brahmā assumed the form of a boar; in the other, Vishnu *in the form of Brahmā* is said to have accomplished this work. The alteration of the text is very noticeable. "All was water only, in which the earth was formed. Thence arose Brahmā, the self-existent, with the deities. He then becoming a boar, raised up the earth, and created the whole world with the saints his sons." So far the probably older recension. In the later one we read, "All was water only, through which the earth was formed. Thence arose Brahmā, the self-existent, the imperishable Vishnu. He then, becoming a boar, raised up this earth and created the whole world."

In the following account from the "Vishnu Purāna" † it will be noticed that, as in the last quotation from the Rāmāyana, it was Vishnu in the form of Brahmā who became a boar. As the earlier writers had declared this to have been Brahmā's work, it was necessary to identify Vishnu with him.

"Tell me how at the commencement of the present age, Nārāyana, who is named Brahmā, created all existing things. At the close of the last age, the divine Brahmā endowed with the quality of goodness, awoke from his night of sleep, and beheld the universal void. He, the supreme Nārāyana,... invested with the form of Brahmā,...concluding that within the waters lay the earth, and being desirous to raise it up, created another form for that purpose. And as in the preceding ages he had assumed the shape of a fish, or a tortoise, so in this he took the form of a boar. Having adopted a form composed of the sacrifices of the Vedas for the preservation of the whole earth, the eternal, supreme, and universal soul plunged into

---

*Ibid.
†Page 27 ff.

the ocean." In a note on this passage in the "Vishnu Purāna," by Professor Wilson, it is stated that, according to the "Vāyu Purāna," the form of a boar was chosen because it is an animal delighting in water; but in other Purānas, as in the Vishnu, it is said to be a type of the ritual of the Vedas, for which reason the elevation of the earth on the tusks of a boar is regarded as an allegorical representation of the extrication of the world from a deluge of sin, by the rites of religion.

The earth, bowing with devout adoration, addressed the boar, as he approached, in a hymn of great beauty, in which she reminds him that she sprang from him, and is dependent on him, as in fact are all things. Being thus praised, "the auspicious supporter of the world emitted a low murmuring sound, like the chanting of the Sama-Veda; and the mighty boar, whose eyes were like the lotus, whose body was vast as the Nila mountains, and of the dark colour of the lotus leaves, uplifted upon his ample tusks the earth from its lowest regions. As he reared up his head, the waters that rushed from his brow purified the great sages, Sanandana and others residing in the sphere of the saints. Through the indentations made by his hoofs, the waters rushed into the lower worlds with a thundering noise. Before his breath, the pious denizens of Janaloka (abode of men) were scattered, and the Munis sought for shelter amongst the bristles upon the body of the boar, trembling as he rose up supporting the earth, and dripping with moisture. Then the great sages Sanandana and the rest, residing continually in the sphere of the saints, were inspired with delight, and bowing lowly, they praised the stern-eyed upholder of the earth."

Before noticing the hymn of these saints, in which the boar is identified with the various parts of worship, we can gather a little more information from the other Purānas respecting the dimensions, etc., of this animal. The Vāyu says, "The boar was ten yojanas* in breadth, and a thousand yojanas in height; his colour was like a dark cloud, and his roar like thunder. His bulk was vast as a mountain; his tusks were white, sharp, and fearful; fire flashed from his eyes like lightning, and he was radiant as the sun. His shoulders were round, fat, and large; he strode along like a powerful lion; his haunches were fat, his loins slender, and his body smooth and beautiful," With this the Matsya agrees. The Bhāgavata describes the boar "as issuing from the nostrils of Brahmā; at first of the size of a thumb, and presently increasing to the size of an elephant." This Purana adds a legend of the slaying of Hiranyāksha, who, in a former birth, was a doorkeeper of Vishnu's palace. He having refused admission to a number of Munis, so enraged them, that they cursed him; in consequence of this he was re-born as a son of Diti. When the earth sunk in the waters, Vishnu was seen by this demon in the act of raising it. Hiranyāksha claimed the earth, and defying Vishnu, they fought, and the demon was slain.

Now follow the hymns to the Varaha as sung by the saint: "Triumph, lord of lords, supreme! Kesava, sovereign of the earth...cause of production, destruction and existence. *Thou art, O* god! there is none other supreme condition than thou. Thou, lord, art the person of the sacrifice; thy feet are the Vedas; thy tusks are the stake to which the victim is bound; thy teeth are the offerings; thy mouth is the altar; thy tongue is the fire; and the hairs of thy body are the sacrificial grass. Thy eyes, O omnipotent! are day and night; thy head is the seat of all—the place of Brahmā; thy name is all the hymns of the Vedas; thy nostrils are all oblations. O thou, whose snout is the ladle of oblation; whose deep voice is the chanting of the Sama-Veda; whose body is the hall of sacrifice; whose joints are the different ceremonies; and whose ears have the properties of

---

*A yojan is at least four miles and a half; some reckon it at nine miles.

both voluntary and obligatory rites; do thou, who art eternal, who art in size a mountain, be propitious...raise up this earth for the habitation of created beings!"

"The supreme being thus eulogized, upholding the earth, raised it quickly, and placed it on the summit of the ocean, where it floats like a mighty vessel, and, on account of its expansive surface, does not sink beneath the waters." This seems rather to contradict the common notion of the Hindus, that the earth rests upon the back of a tortoise; and that earthquakes are the result of the tortoise changing the foot on which he stands, when weary.

4. THE NRISINGHA OR MAN-LION AVATARA

In the account of the preceding incarnation, it was stated that Vishnu, ere he raised the earth on his tusk, slew a demon named Hiranyāksha. This daitya had a brother named

The Nrisingha Avatāra

Hiranyakasipu, who, the "Vāyu Purāna" says, had obtained a boon from Brahmā, that he should not be slain by any created being; the "Kūrma Purāna" adds, excepting Vishnu. When therefore his pride, fostered by his supposed immunity from danger, had led him to great excesses, so that his death was desired both by gods and men, Vishnu descended in the form of a living being, half-man and half-lion, and so neither man nor animal, and slew him. By the assumption of this form the *letter* of Brahmā's promise was kept. The story of the demon's hatred of the deity, because in a former incarnation he had slain his brother, is a most interesting one. And as it teaches the wonderful efficacy of Vishnu's worship, it is given at some length. It is taken mostly from the "Vishnu Purāna."*

"Hiranyakasipu, the son of Diti, had formerly brought the three worlds under his authority, confiding in a boon bestowed upon him by Brahmā. He had usurped the sovereignty of Indra, and exercised himself the functions of the sun, of air, of the lord of waters, of fire, and of the moon. He himself was the god of riches; he was the judge of the dead; and he appropriated to himself without reserve all that was offered in sacrifice to the gods. The deities, therefore, flying from their seats in heaven, wandered, through fear of the daitya, upon the earth, disguised in mortal shapes. Having conquered the three worlds, he was inflated with pride, and, eulogized by the Gandharvas, enjoyed whatever he desired."

This demon had a son named Prahlāda, who was a very devout worshipper of Vishnu, whom his father hated most intensely. "On one occasion Prahlāda came, accompanied by his teacher, to the court of his father, and bowed himself before his feet as he was drinking. Hiranyakasipu desired his prostrate son to rise, and said to him, 'Repeat in substance and agreeably what during the period of your studies you have acquired.' Prahlāda said, 'I have learned to admire him who is

---

*Page 126 ff.

without beginning, middle, or end, increase or diminution; the imperishable lord of the world, the universal cause of causes.' On hearing these words, the sovereign of the daityas, his eyes red with wrath and his lips swollen with indignation, turned to the preceptor of his son, and said, 'Vile Brāhman! what is this preposterous commendation of my foe that, in disrespect to me, you have taught this boy to utter?' The preceptor denies the charge, and Prahlāda himself replies, 'Vishnu is the instructor of the whole world; what else should any one learn or teach, save him, the supreme spirit?' 'Blockhead!' exclaimed the king, 'who is this Vishnu, whose name you thus reiterate so impertinently before me, who am the sovereign of the three worlds?' 'The glory of Vishnu,' replied Prahlāda, 'is to be meditated upon by the devout; it cannot be described; he is the supreme lord, who is all things, and from whom all things proceed.' The king threatens death; but the son says, 'Vishnu is the creator and protector not of me alone, but of all human beings, and even, father, of you.' The father can bear this no longer, so orders his son to return to his preceptor's house.

"Prahlāda is taken away, but after a time is sent for again. When requested to recite some poetry, he commenced to sing the praises of Vishnu, which so exasperated the king, that he cried out, 'Kill the wretch! He is not fit to live who is a traitor to his friends, a burning brand to his own race.' Upon this the attendants rushed upon Prahlāda with their weapons, and, though hundreds struck him, none could injure him. His father then entreated him to desist from praising Vishnu; but this the son would not do, as he said he had no fear, 'as long as his immortal guardian against all dangers was present in his mind.'

"Hiranyakasipu, highly exasperated, commanded the serpents to fall upon his disobedient and insane son, and bite him to death. The serpents did their worst, but Prahlāda felt them not. The snakes cried out to the king, 'Our fangs are broken; our jewelled crests are burst; there is fever in our hoods, and fear in our hearts; but the skin of the youth is still unscathed. Have recourse, O king of the daityas! to some other expedient.'

"The young prince" (by his father's orders) "was then assailed by the elephants of the skies, as vast as mountain peaks; cast down upon the earth, and trampled on and gored by their tusks; but he continued to meditate on Govinda, and the tusks of the elephants were blunted against his breast.

"Failing in this, the king said, 'Let fire consume him; and do thou, deity of the winds, blow up the fire, that this wicked wretch may be consumed.' And the dānavas piled a mighty heap of wood around the prince, and kindled a fire to burn him, as their master had commanded. But Prahlāda cried, 'Father, this fire, though blown by the winds, burneth me not; and all around I behold the face of the skies, cool and fragrant with beds of lotus flowers.'

"The Brāhmans now interceded with the king on the prince's behalf, promising either to teach him to recant his errors, or to find some means of accomplishing his death; but instead of profiting by their instructions, he spends his time in speaking to all about him of the glory of Vishnu and the happiness of his worshippers. They informed the king of their failure to bring the prince to a right state of mind; whereupon the cooks are ordered to mix poison with his food. But this expedient was futile, as the others had been. The Brāhmans now reason with him, and try to show him that it is the chief duty of a son to honour his father; but their sophistry is unsuccessful. They remind him that they had promised to use incantations to accomplish his death. This menace he meets with these words: 'What living creature slays or is slain? What living creature preserves or is preserved? Each is his own destroyer or preserver as he follows evil or good.' Enraged by this reply, they now produce a magical female figure, enwreathed in a flame of fire, whose tread parched the earth, and who struck Prahlāda upon the breast. Her blow fell harmless upon him; but turning towards the Brāhmans, she slew them all, and disappeared. In answer to the prince's prayer, they were, however, restored to life, and, having blessed Prahlāda, departed and told the king all that had happened.

"Having sent for his son, Hiranyakasipu inquired again, by what magical art he was able thus to protect himself. Prahlāda said that it was not by magic at all, but simply by the indwelling of Vishnu that he was able to ward off evil; and further that the same power was within the reach of all who would trust him. The king, enraged at this avowal, commanded his attendants to cast his son from the summit of the palace where he was sitting, and which was many yojans in height, upon the tops of the mountains, where his body would be dashed to pieces against the rocks. Accordingly the daityas hurled the boy down, but as he fell cherishing Hari in his heart, Earth, the nurse of all creatures, received him gently in her lap, thus entirely devoted to Kesava, the protector of the world."

Hiranyakasipu, seeing that this fall had not injured his son in any way, asks Samvara, the mightiest of enchanters, to try his hand; but though he puts forth all his skill, the boy remains unhurt. After this, the prince goes again to his preceptor's house, where he is instructed in politics. When his education in this science was completed, he is taken to the king for examination; but on being questioned as to his mode of government, he admits that though he has been instructed in these subjects, he does not approve of what his teachers had said, and again sings the praises of Vishnu. His father, "burning with rage, exclaimed, Bind him with strong bands and cast him into the ocean. Death is the just retribution of the disobedient.' The daityas bound the prince with strong bands, as their lord had commanded, and threw him into the sea. As he floated on the waters, the ocean was convulsed throughout its whole extent, and rose in mighty indulations, threatening to submerge the earth. When Hiranyakasipu observed this, he commanded the daityas to hurl rocks into the sea, and pile them closely on one another, burying beneath their incumbent mass him whom fire could not burn...'Here, since he cannot die, let him live for thousands of years at the bottom of the ocean, overwhelmed by mountains.' This was done. But Prahlāda was uninjured. His mind was filled with thoughts of Hari, and he came to recognize his real identity with Vishnu. As soon as Prahlāda, through the force of contemplation, had become one with Vishnu, the bands with which he was bound burst instantly asunder. Prahlāda, after hymning the praises of Vishnu, again returns to his father, who no sooner saw him, than he kissed him on the forehead, embraced him, and shed tears, and said, 'Dost thou live, my son?'"

For a time there was complete reconciliation between them. And only in a very cursory manner does the "Vishnu Purāna" allude to the death of Hiranyakasipu. After speaking of the reconciliation between the father and son, without any intimation of further dispute, it goes on to say: "After his father had been put to death by Vishnu in the form of the man-lion, Prahlāda became the sovereign of the daityas." In the Bhāgavat we are told that Prahlāda had said that Vishnu was in him, in his father; in fact, was everywhere. "Hiranyakasipu says, 'Why, if Vishnu is everywhere, is he not visible in this pillar?' Being told that Vishnu, though unseen, was really present there, he struck the pillar, saying, 'Then I will kill him.' Immediately Vishnu, in the form of a being half-man and half-lion, came forth from the pillar, laid hold of Hiranyakasipu by the thighs with his teeth, and tore him up the middle. Brahmā's boon to this daitya king, as a reward of his religious observances, was that no common animal should destroy him, that he should die neither in the day nor night, in earth or in heaven, by fire, by water, or by the sword. This promise was kept in the letter, for it was evening when Vishnu slew him; this is neither day nor night. It was done under the droppings of the thatch, and this, according to a Hindu proverb, is out of the earth, and he was not killed by a man or an ordinary animal."*

5. THE VĀMANA OR DWARF AVATĀRA

The four Avataras that have already been described are said to have occurred in the Satya-yuga, or age of Truth, corresponding with the golden age of classic writers; it was in the Treta -yuga, or second age, that this incarnation is supposed to have occurred. It is not easy to see how this belief could be formed; for if the story of Prahlāda be regarded as a true picture of the Satya-yuga, it was not very far superior to the present, the last and worst of all.

This incarnation was undertaken to recover heaven for the gods. Bali, a demon, grandson of Prahlāda whose story has just been given, was king over the three worlds—heaven, earth and sky. In the form of a Brāhman dwarf, Vishnu appears, and asks, as a gift, all he could cross over in three steps. This the king grants. Immediately the pigmy becomes a giant, and with one step strides over heaven, and with the second over the earth, and thus fulfils his purpose. The "Skanda Purāna"† gives the following legend as the reason of this incarnation.

In the battle between the gods and asuras for the possession of the amrita produced at the churning of the ocean, the demons were defeated. Bali prepared a costly sacrifice in order that he might regain his power. As he presented his offerings to the sacred fire, he obtained from it a wondrous car drawn by four white horses, a banner displaying a lion, and celestial armour and weapons. The sacred rites being finished, he raised a large army, and in his newly-acquired chariot went and laid siege to Amravati, the capital of Indra's heaven. The gods in terror turned to their preceptor for advice. He told them that their enemies had been rendered invincible by penance. On

---

*Ward, ii. 7, 8.
†Kennedy's "Hindu Mythology," p. 363.

hearing this, they were greatly alarmed, and Indra besought the preceptor, Vrihaspati, to tell them what to do. He advised them to forsake Amravati, assume other forms, and find a home elsewhere. They obeyed; Indra became a peacock, Kuvera a lizard, and the other gods, variously disguised, went to the hermitage of Kasyapa, to whom they related their misfortunes. On hearing their story, the sage desired his wife Aditi to perform a severe penance, in order to induce

The Vāmana Āvatara

Vishnu to become her son, that through him the gods might be

restored to heaven. As the origin of this incarnation is probably found in the metaphorical language of the Vedas, it will be well to consider the teaching of the Hindu scriptures as far as possible in chronological order.

The legend just quoted from the "Skanda Purāna" was written as an answer to the question why Vishnu had appeared in this strange form. In the Rig-Veda* the germ of the story is found: "Vishnu strode over this [universe]; in three places he planted his step." This passage is interpreted by the commentators in various ways. One taught "that the triple manifestation of the god in the form of fire on earth, of lightning in the atmosphere, and of the solar light in the sky, was intended in this hymn." Another understands the three steps of Vishnu to represent "the different positions of the sun at his rising, his culmination, and his setting." According to this, therefore, Vishnu is simply the sun. Frequently in the Rig-Veda the term "wide-stepping" is applied to him. an evident allusion to his three steps.

In the "Satapatha Brāhmana," † the simple statement of the earlier book respecting Vishnu's strides assumes a larger form. "The gods and the asuras, who both sprung from Prajāpati, strove together. Then the gods were worsted; and the asuras said, 'This world is now certainly ours! Let us divide the earth, and let us subsist thereon.' The gods heard of it and said, 'The asuras are dividing the earth: come, we will go to the spot where they are dividing it!' Placing at their head Vishnu, the sacrifice, they proceeded [thither], and said, 'Put us with yourselves in possession of this earth; let us have a share of it.' The asuras grudgingly said, 'We will give you as much as this Vishnu can lie upon.' Now Vishnu was a dwarf. The gods did not reject this offer. They placed Agni in the East, and thus they went on toiling and worshipping. By this means they acquired the

---

*Muir, O. S. T., iv. 63-156.
†Ibid.

whole earth."

The next form of the legend is that of the Rāmāyana. Visvamitra, a sage, addressing Rāma, tells him the story. "Formerly Bali, the son of Virochana, after conquering the chief of the gods, enjoyed the empire of the three worlds, intoxicated with the increase of his power. When Bali was celebrating a sacrifice, Indra and the other gods addressed Vishnu in this hermitage [saying], 'That mighty Bali is now performing sacrifice; he who grants the desire of all creatures; the prosperous lord of the asuras. Whatever suppliants wait upon him, he bestows on them whatever [they wish]. Do thou take the form of a dwarf, aud bring about our highest welfare.' [Kasyapa now appears, and, after praising Vishnu, asks a boon, that Vishnu will be born as the son of Aditi and himself.] Thus addressed by the gods, Vishnu took the form of a dwarf, and, approaching the son of Virochana, begged three of his own paces. Having obtained three paces, Vishnu assumed a miraculous form, and with three paces took possession of the world. With one step he occupied the whole earth; with a second, the eternal atmosphere; and with a third, the sky. Having assigned to the asura Bali an abode in Pātāla (the infernal region), he gave the empire of the world to Indra."

The notice of this Avatāra in the Mahābhārata is not lengthy. Vishnu is represented as foretelling it to Nārada. "The great asura Bali shall be indestructible by all beings, including gods, asuras, and Rākshasas. He shall oust Indra; and when the three worlds have been taken by Bali, and Indra put to flight, I shall be born in the form of the twelve Ādityas, the son of Kasyapa and Diti. I will then restore his kingdom to Indra, reinstate the gods in their several positions, and place Bali in Pātāla."

The "Vishnu Purāna" barely notices this event, but it is fully described in the Bhāgavata. The question is there asked, "Why did Hari, the lord of creatures, ask, like a poor man, three pieces of land from Bali? And why, when he had obtained his object, did he bind him? And why was an innocent being bound by the lord of sacrifice?" The answer given is as follows:—After Bali had been killed by Indra, he was restored by the Brāhmans of the race of Bhrigu, who consecrated him for supreme dominion, and performed a sacrifice to obtain it for him. He then sets out for Amravati, as before narrated; and Indra is told, when he applies to his preceptor for advice, that Bali had obtained this power "by virtue of the Brāhman's sacrifice;" and that, save by Hari, he is unconquerable. "He now reaps the fruit of Brāhmanical power; through contempt of these same Brāhmans he shall perish with all his descendants."

The gods forsake their capital, which is occupied by Bali. Aditi, the mother of the gods, is distressed as she sees the condition of her children; and acting upon the advice of her husband, propitiates Vishnu, who says: "I shall with a portion of myself become thy son, and deliver thy children. Wait upon thy husband, the sinless Prajāpati, virtuous female, meditating upon me, who in this form abide within him." Aditi followed the advice of the god; and Kasyapa knew by meditation that a portion of Hari had entered into him. In due time the son was born, and became a dwarfish Brāhmanical student.

As the Bhrigus are performing a sacrifice for Bali on the banks of the Narmada river, this dwarf visits Bali at Indra's heaven. "Acquainted with his duty, Bali placed upon his head the auspicious water with which the Brāhman's feet had been washed, and said, 'Welcome to thee, O Brāhman! What can we do for thee? Ask of me, student, whatever thou desirest. Son of a Brāhman, I conclude thou art a suppliant; ask a cow, pure gold, an embellished house, food and drink, a Brāhman's daughter, flourishing villages, horses, elephants, and carriages." The dwarf concludes a speech with the semblance of moderation as follows: "I ask from thee a small portion of ground, three paces measured step by step. I desire no more from thee. A wise man incurs no sin, when he asks [only] as much as he needs." The king, though astonished at the smallness of the request, takes a vessel of water in his hand, and is about to confirm the gift; when his preceptor, seeing through Vishnu's device, tries to dissuade his pupil. In a long speech he seeks to show that rather than be left homeless it would be better for him to break his word. But the king persists in fulfilling his promise; even though cursed by his preceptor for doing so. With two steps Vishnu strode over the universe; there was nowhere for him to take a third.

The gods congratulate Hari; Bali is bound by Garuda and then reproached by Vishnu for not fulfilling his promise. "Asura, three paces of ground were given to me by thee; with two paces the entire world has been traversed; find a place for the third. As thou hast not given what was promised, it is my pleasure that thou shouldst dwell in the infernal regions. That man falls downward who, after promising a Brahman, does not deliver to him what he had solicited. I have been deluded by thee." Bali offers his head as a place for Vishnu's foot, saying, "I fear not the infernal regions so much as a bad name." Bali goes to Patala, and is there visited by his grandfather Prahlāda. First Vishnu's wife and then Brahmā intercede with him on the demon's behalf, who, in reply, promises that Bali shall again become Indra; but that in the meantime he must dwell in Sutala, where "by my will, neither mental nor bodily pains, nor fatigue, nor weariness, nor discomfiture, nor diseases afflict the inhabitants." Bali gladly left Pātāla, and went to Sutala, to wait until the time came when, in accordance with the promise of Vishnu, he should again rule over gods and men.

Another legend teaches that Vishnu gave Bali the choice of going to heaven, taking with him five ignorant people, or of going to hell with five wise. He chose the latter, for there is no pleasure anywhere in the company of the ignorant; whilst a bad place with good company is enjoyable.

6. THE PARASURĀMA AVATĀRA

The incarnation of Parasurāma, or Rāma with axe, was

undertaken by Vishnu for the purpose of exterminating the Kshattriya, or Warrior caste,* which had tried to assert its authority over the Brāhmanical. Twenty-one times Rāma is said to have cleared the earth of these men, but by various means some few were preserved alive who were able to perpetuate the race. The story of this incarnation evidently points to a time when there was a severe and prolonged struggle for supremacy between the members of these two classes. Eventually success lay with the Brāhmans. It should be noticed that the scene of Vishnu's exploits in this Avatāra, and in those which follow it, was the earth; and not, as in those preceding, the abode of the gods.

The following legend of the birth of Parasurama is from the "Vishnu Purāna." † A prince named Gadhi, who was himself an incarnation of Indra, had a daughter named Satyavati. Richika, a descendant of Bhrigu, ‡ demanded her in marriage. The king asked from the decrepit old Brāhman a thousand fleet white horses, each having one black ear, as a wedding present. These horses were obtained, by the help of Varuna, and the Brāhman received the hand of the princess.

In order to effect the birth of a son, Richika prepared a dish of rice, barley, and pulse, with butter and milk, for his wife to eat, and, at her request, consecrated a similar mixture for her mother, by partaking of which she hoped to give birth to a prince

---

*There are four chief castes or jātis of Hindus: the Brāhman, or Priestly; the Kshattriya, or Warrior; the Vaisya, or Merchant; and the Sudra, or Servant. These four classes are commonly said to have sprung respectively from the head, arms, thighs, and feet of the Creator, though there is good reason for the belief that in the olden time no such ideas of the divine origin of caste prevailed. The four original castes have become subdivided into an immense number. This subdivision has been brought about by inter-marriage with members of other classes.

† Page 400.

‡See part iii. chap. i.

of martial prowess, Leaving both dishes with his wife, after carefully describing which was for herself and which for her mother, the sage went away into the forest. When the time for eating the food came, the mother said to Satyavati, "Daughter! all mothers wish their children to be possessed of excellent qualities, and would be mortified to see them surpassed by the merits of their brother. Give me, therefore, the mess your husband has set apart for you, and you eat that which was intended for me. The son which it is intended to procure for me, is destined to be the monarch of the whole world; whilst that which your dish will give you must be a Brāhman, alike devoid of affluence, valour, and power." Satyavati consented to this proposal, and they exchanged messes.

The Parasurāma Avatāra

On Richika's return, perceiving what had happened, he said to his wife, "Sinful woman! what hast thou done? I see thy body of a fearful appearance. Thou hast eaten of the consecrated food that was prepared for thy mother; thou hast done wrong. In that food I had infused the properties of power, and strength, and heroism; in thine, the qualities suited to a Brāhman—gentleness, knowledge, and resignation. In consequence of having reversed my plans, thy son shall follow a warrior's propensities, and use weapons, and fight, and slay. Thy mother's son shall be born with the inclinations of a Brāhman, and be addicted to peace and piety." Satyavati, hearing this, fell at her husband's feet, and asked that she might not have such a son as he had described; "but if such there must be, let it be my grandson and not my son." The Muni relented, and said, "So be it." Accordingly in due time she gave birth to a son named Jamadagni, who married Renukā, and had by her the destroyer of the Kshattriya race, Parasurāma, who was a portion of Nārāyana, the spiritual guide of the universe.

This is all we find about Parasurāma's work in the "Vishnu Purāna." The story of his exploits is told at length twice over in the Mahābhārata, and is found in the Bhāgavata, Padma, and Agni Purānas. The following account is from the Mahābhārata.*

Jamadagni, the son of Richika (whose birth was just described), having married Renukā, "conducted the princess to his hermitage, and she was contented to partake in his ascetic life. They had four sons, and then a fifth, who was Jamadagnya (Parasurāma), the last, but not the least, of the brethren. Once when her sons were absent gathering the fruits on which they fed, Renukā, who was exact in the discharge of all her duties, went forth to bathe. On her way to the stream she beheld Chitraratha, the Prince of Mrittikāvati, with a garland of lotuses on his neck, sporting with his queen in the water, and

---

*"Vishnu Purāna," note p. 401; and Muir, O. S. T., i. 447.

she felt envious of their felicity. Defiled by unworthy thoughts, wetted, but not purified by the stream, she returned disquieted to the hermitage. Beholding her fallen from her perfection, and shorn of the lustre of her sanctity, Jamadagni reproved her, and was exceeding wroth.

"Upon this, her sons came from the wood, and each as he entered was successively commended by his father to put his mother to death; but, amazed and influenced by natural affection, neither of them made any reply; therefore Jamadagni cursed them, and they became idiots. Lastly Rāma returned to the hermitage, when the mighty and holy Jamadagni said to him, 'Kill thy mother, who has sinned; and do it without repining.' Rāma accordingly took up his axe [this was the Parasu, or axe, which Siva had given him] and struck off his mother's head; whereupon the wrath of Jamadagni was assuaged, and, pleased with his son, said: 'Since thou hast obeyed my commands, and done what was hard to be performed, demand from me whatever blessing thou wilt, and thy desires shall be fulfilled.' Rāma begged these boons: the restoration of his mother to life, with forgetfulness of having been slain, and purification from all defilement; the return of his brothers to their natural condition; and for himself, invincibility in single combat, and length of days. All these his father bestowed.

"It happened on one occasion that, during the absence of the Rishi's sons, the mighty monarch Kārttavirya, the sovereign of the Haihaya tribe, endowed by the favour of Dattatreya* with a thousand arms, and a golden chariot that went wheresoever he willed it to go, came to the hermitage of Jamadagni, where the wife of the sage received him with proper respect. This Kārttavirya, by reason of his strength, had greatly oppressed the gods, Rishis, and all creatures. The gods and Rishis applied to Vishnu, who, with Indra, devised the means of destroying

---

*A Brāhman saint in whom a portion of Brahmā, Vishnu, and Siva was incarnate.

him. The king, inflated with the pride of valour, made no return for the hospitality of the Rishi's wife; but carried off with him the calf of the milch cow of the sacred oblation, and cast down the tall trees of the hermitage."

In the Rāmāyana is an account of the wonderful cow whose calf this king stole. When commanded by her owner, on the occasion of the visit of a king to the hermitage, to supply the varied wants of the great multitude which accompanied him—

> "'The cow from whom all plenty flows,
> Obedient to her saintly lord,
> Viands to suit each taste outpoured.
> Honey she gave, and roasted grain,
> Mead sweet with flowers, and sugar-cane.
> Each beverage of flavour rare,
> And food of every sort, were there:
> Hills of hot rice, and sweetened cakes,
> And curdled milk, and soup in lakes.
> Vast beakers flowing to the brim
> With sugared drink prepared for him;
> And dainty sweetmeats, deftly made,
> Before the hermit's guests were laid.'

"When Rāma returned, his father told him what had happened; and seeing the cow in distress, he was filled with wrath. Taking up his splendid bow, he assailed Karttavirya, and overthrew him in battle. With sharp arrows Rāma cut off his thousand arms, and he perished. The sons of Kārttavirya, to avenge their father's death, attacked the hermitage of Jamadagni when Rāma was absent, and slew the pious and unresisting sage, who called repeatedly, but fruitlessly, upon his valiant son. Rāma deeply lamented his father's death, performed the last obsequies, and lighted the funeral pile. He then made a vow that he would extirpate the whole Kshattriya race. In fulfilment of which, with remorseless and fatal rage, he destroyed the sons of Kārttavirya; and, after them, whatever Kshattriyas he encountered. Thrice seven times* did he clear the earth of the Kshattriya caste. After he had cleared the world of Kshattriyas, their widows came to the Brāhmans, praying for offspring. The religious Brāhmans, free from any impulse of lust, cohabited with these women, who, in consequence, brought forth valiant Kshattriya boys and girls."

In another passage in the Mahābhārata it is taught that it was in consequence of the curse of a sage named Apava, that Rāma was able to kill Kārttavirya. The king had permitted Agni to devour the hermitage of this Rishi, who, in revenge, declared that his thousand arms should be cut off by Parasurāma.

In the Rāmāyana is an interesting legend in which Parasurāmā, himself an incarnation of Vishnu, is described as meeting with Rāma Chandra, the next avatāra of the same deity, and in which the superiority of Rāma Chandra is declared.†" As King Dasaratha was returning to his capital with Rama (Chandra), he was alarmed by the ill-omened sounds uttered by certain birds. The alarming event indicated was the arrival of Parasurāma. He was fearful to behold, brilliant as fire, and bore his axe and a bow on his shoulder. Being received with honour, he proceeded to say to Rāma, the son of Dasaratha, that he had heard of his prowess in breaking the bow produced by Janaka, and had brought another which he asked him to bend, and to fit an arrow on the string; and offered, if he succeeded in doing so, to engage with him in single combat. Parasurāma went on to say that the bow Rāma had broken was Siva's; but that the one

---

*The reason why Parasurāma had to perform his work so many times was this:—Some Kshattriya children were hidden from his rage amongst the other castes, and in time grew up to be warriors. It was when his work was effectually accomplished, and there was not a single Kshattriya man left, that their widows resorted to the Brāhmans, as noticed above.

†Muir, O. S. T., iv. 175.

he now brought was Vishnu's. The gods, anxious to discover which was the greater, Siva or Vishnu, and considering this a favourable opportunity for doing so, sought Brahmā's help. He thereupon excited the passions of the two Rāmas. A great fight ensued. Siva's bow of dreadful power was relaxed, and the three-eyed Mahādeva was arrested by a muttering. The gods were satisfied, and judged Vishnu to be superior. Parasurāma, however, did not agree to their judgment, so offered Vishnu's bow for his antagonist to try his strength on. Thus challenged, Rāma snatches the bow, bends it, and fits an arrow to the string; and then tells his challenger that as he is a Brāhman he will not slay him, but will either take away his superhuman capacity of movement, or deprive him of the blessed abodes he had gained by austerity. Parasurāma entreats that his power of movement may not be taken away, but consents that his blissful abodes may be destroyed. 'By bending this bow,' he said, 'I recognize thee to be the imperishable slayer of Madhu, the great lord.' Rāma shoots the. arrow, and destroys Parasurāma's abodes."

The explanation of this strange legend seems to be the one that is commonly received by Oriental scholars, that the passages in the Epic poems which speak of Rāma as an incarnation of Vishnu are interpolations of a later date than the original poem; and this interview of Parasurāma with Rāma Chandra was introduced for the purpose of giving a quasi-divine sanction to the teaching of these interpolations. If Parasurāma, an admitted incarnation of Vishnu, acknowledged that Rāma was superior to himself, what stronger proof could be given that Rāma too was divine?

7. THE RĀMA CHANDRA AVATĀRA

In Northern India this is perhaps the most popular of all the incarnations of Vishnu, and certainly the Rāmāyana, in which his history is found, contains some of the most beautiful legends in the whole of the sacred writings of the Hindus.

The Rāmāyana is very largely occupied with the story of Rāma's life, and the poets have found in its legends subjects for their most attractive poems. A whole volume might easily be written, giving a biography of this most popular hero; we must, however, content ourselves with the merest outline of his doings.

Mr. Griffiths, in the preface to his translation of the Rāmāyana, says, "The great exploit and main subject of the Epic is the war which Rāma waged with the giant Rāvan, the fierce and mighty King of Lanka or Ceylon, and the dread oppressor of gods and nymphs, and saints and men." "The army," to borrow the words of Gorresio, "which Rāma led on this expedition was, as appears from the poem, gathered in great part from the region of the Vindhya hills;* but the races which he assembled are represented in the poem as monkeys, either out of contempt for their barbarism, or because at that time they were little known to the Sanskrit-speaking Hindus. The poet calls the people whom Rāma attacked Rākshasas. Rākshasas, according to the popular Indian belief, are malignant beings, demons of many shapes, terrible and cruel, who disturb the sacrifices and religious rites of the Brāhmans. It appears indubitable that the poet of the Rāmāyana applied the hated name of Rākshasas to an abhorred and hostile people, and that this denomination is here rather an expression of hatred and horror than a real historical name." The account of Rāma which follows is taken from the translation of the Rāmāyana in verse by Mr. Griffiths.

---

*It is a strange though real confirmation of the truth of the underlying history of the hero that to this day the aboriginal tribes inhabiting the Vindhya hills have many legends relating to the life of Rāma and Sita, although they are not Hindus, and know but little of Hinduism. These people are not at all like the Hindus in appearance. They are black, have curly hair and thick lips, not very unlike some African races.

The Rāma Chandra Avatāra

Dasaratha, the King of Ayodha, being childless, determined
to make an *asvamedh*, or horse sacrifice, to obtain a son. It
was necessary, in order to make an acceptable offering, that
the horse destined for sacrifice be allowed to wander at will
for a whole year, as a sign that the authority of its owner was
acknowledged by the neighbouring princes. The people loved
their king, and during his reign were very prosperous; but,
owing to the want of a son, the happiness of king and subjects
was incomplete. The sacrifice therefore was determined on, the
holy place fixed, the horse set free, and the king, encouraged by
the Brāhmans, invited the neighbouring princes to attend the

great preparations made. At length the rite was satisfactorily accomplished and the presiding Brāhman addressing Dasaratha said:—

> "Four sons, O monarch, shall be thine,
> Upholders of the royal line.*
> *　　*　　*　　*
> Another rite will I begin,
> Which shall the sons thou cravest win,
> When all things shall be duly sped
> And first Atharva texts be read."†

The gods having graced the assembly the saint who performed the rite thus addressed them :—

> "For you has Dasaratha slain
> The votive steed, a son to gain;
> Stern penance rites the king has tried.
> And in firm faith on you relied.
> And now with undiminished care
> A second rite would now prepare.
> But, O ye gods, consent to grant
> The longing of your suppliant."‡

The gods, pleased with the Brāhman's prayer, led by Indra, proceeded to Brahmā, and presented to him their united petition, in which they mention the great work they wished Rāma, as one of Dasaratha's sons, to perform:

> O Brahmā, mighty by thy grace,
> Rāvan, who rules the giant race,

---

*Griffiths's "Rāmāyana," i. 81.
†Ibid. i. 82.
‡Griffiths's "Rāmāyana," i. 83.

Torments us in his senseless pride
And penance-loving saints beside.
For thou, well-pleased in days of old,
Gavest the boon that makes him bold,
That gods nor demons e'er should kill
His charmed life, for so thy will.
We, honouring that high behest,
Bear all his rage, though sore distrest.
That lord of giants, fierce and fell.
Scourges the earth, and heaven and hell.
Mad with thy boon, his impious rage
Smites saint and bard, and god and sage.
The sun himself withholds his glow,
The wind, in fear, forbears to blow:
The lire restrains his wonted heat
Where stands the dreaded Rāvan's feet,
And, necklaced with the wandering wave.
The sea before him fears to rave.
Kuvera's self, in sad defeat,
Is driven from his blissful seat.
We see, we feel, the giant's might,
And woe comes o'er us and affright.
To thee, O lord, thy suppliants pray
To find some cure this plague to stay."*

To this request Brahmā makes answer—

"One only way I find
To slay this fiend of evil mind.
He prayed me once his life to guard
From demon, god, and heavenly bard,
And spirits of the earth and air;
And I, consenting, heard his prayer.

---

*Griffiths's "Rāmāyaua," i. 83.

> But the proud giant, in his scorn.
> Recked not of man of woman born.
> None else may take his life away,
> But only man the fiend may slay."*

Upon this Vishnu appears, is gladly welcomed by the assembled gods, and asks what request they have to make :

> "King Dasaratha, thus cried they,
> Fervent in penance many a day,
> The sacrificial steed has slain,
> Longing for sons, but all in vain.
> Now, at the cry of us forlorn,
> Incarnate as his seed be born.
> Three queens has he; each lovely dame
> Like Beauty, Modesty, or Fame.
> Divide thyself in four, and be
> His offspring by these noble three;
> Man's nature take, and slay in fight
> Rāvan, who laughs at heavenly might:
> This common scourge, this rankling thorn,
> Whom the three worlds too long have borne." †

Vishnu asks why it is necessary for him to effect their deliverance. Being told of Brahmā's promise to Rāvan, he at length consents to be born as man, in order to slay the giant and his family.

Not long after this, a messenger comes from Vishnu, laden with a golden vase of nectar, which, as he gives it to the king, instructs him to hand it to his queens, assuring them that

> "They the princely sons shall bear,

---

*Ibid. i. 84.
†Ibid. i. 85.

Long sought by sacrifice and prayer."*

To Queen Kausalya the king gave half the nectar, who through it became the mother of Rāma; the other half he gave to his other wives, who in consequence became mothers too — Kaikeya bore Bharat, and Sumitra gave birth to Lakshman and Satrughna.

Before leaving heaven, Vishnu besought the gods, for whose benefit he was about to undertake the work, to assist him, and they did so in various ways, chiefly by begetting powerful sons to enter his army.

> "Each god, each sage became a sire.
> Each minstrel of the heavenly quire,
> Each faun, of children strong and good."†

The names of some of the leaders who assisted Rāma in answer to this prayer run as follows : —

> "Bali, the woodland hosts who led,
> High as Mahendra's lofty head,
> Was India's child. That noblest lire,
> The Sun, was great Sugriva's sire.
> Tāra, the mighty monkey, he
> Was offspring of Vrihaspati:
> Tāra, the matchless chieftain, boast
> For wisdom of the Vānar host.
> Of Gandhamādan, brave and bold,
> The father was the Lord of gold.
> Nala the mighty, dear to fame,
> Of skilful Visvakarma came.
> From Agni, Nila bright as flame,

---

*Griffiths's "Rāmāyana," i. 89.
†Ibid. i. 93.

Who in his splendour, might, and worth,
Surpassed the sire who gave him birth.
The heavenly Asvins, swift and fair,
Were fathers of a noble pair,
Who, Dwivida and Mainda named,
For beauty like their sires were famed.
Varun was father of Sushen;
Of Sarabh, he who sends the rain [Parjanya].
Hanumān, best of monkey kind,
Was son of him who breathes the wind;
Like thunderbolt in frame was he,
And swift as Garud's self could flee.
These thousands did the gods create,
Endowed with might which none could mate,
In monkey forms that changed at will,
So strong their wish the fiend to kill."*

In due time the four sons of Dasaratha were born; and from infancy the strongest affection existed between Rāma the firstborn and Lakshman, and between Bharat and Satrughna.

When Rāma was about sixteen years of age, a saint named Visvamitra came to Dasaratha's court, asking his assistance against two demons, named Maricha and Suvahu, who were commanded by Rāvana to annoy him, and prevent the completion of his sacrifices. At first the king pleaded the youthfulness of his son as an excuse for refusing to allow him to undertake a work so arduous; but at length his scruples were overcome, and Rāma with the faithful Lakshman set out for the hermitage. When the travellers reached the banks of the Sarju, the saint gave Rāma two spells which he was to employ whilst bathing, and which were so to affect him that he should have no equal in heaven or hell.

---

*Griffiths's "Rāmāyaua," i. 93.

> "None in the world with thee shall vie,
> O sinless one, in apt reply,
> In knowledge, fortune, wit, and tact,
> Wisdom to plan, and skill to act."*

On their journey to the hermitage they visit several places of importance, and Visvamitra beguiles the time with numerous legends; he also bestows on Rāma various arms and powers. On reaching the end of their journey, for six days and nights they have to watch for the demons; just as the sacrifice was about to end, these disturbers of the hermitage appear, are conquered by Rāma, and their attendants by Lakshman. The saint, addressing Rāma, says—

> "My joy, O prince, is now complete :
> Thou hast obeyed my will;
> Perfect before, this calm retreat
> Is now more perfect still."†

Next morning the hermits tell Rāma that King Janaka of Mithila‡ had arranged for a sacrifice to which they are invited. Rāma is asked to accompany them, and is induced to do so by the mention of a wonderful bow in possession of the king, which no one was able to bend. The bow was a gift from Siva, as a reward for sacrifice. On the way to Mithila they pass through a grove, in which, unseen by gods and men, Ahalyā, the wife of Gautama the sage, had been undergoing penance for countless ages, on account of her adultery with Indra Though the god came to her in the form of her husband, she saw through his disguise, yet did not resist his overtures. Her husband condemned her to live unknown in the forest until

---

*Griffiths's "Rāmāyana," i. 125.
†Ibid. i. 156.
‡Tirhoot.

Rāma should liberate her. Her hour of release had now come: Rāma sees her, touches her feet, and, the curse being at an end, her husband receives her back.

In due time they reach Mithila. The princes are introduced to the king, who gives them a hearty welcome, and narrates the history of the world-famed bow they have come to see. He tells them it was the bow with which Siva, when angry at not being invited to Daksha's sacrifice, wrought such havoc amongst the assembled gods. It was held by successive monarchs of his line as a mark of sovereignty, and as a means of defence against their foes.

> "This gem of bows,
> That freed the God of gods from woes,
> Stored by our great forefathers, lay
> A treasure and a pride for aye."*

One day, as Janaka was ploughing, an infant sprang from the ground, whom he named Sitā (a furrow), on account of her secret birth. In the "Uttara Kānda"† is a legend, the object of which is to show that Sitā is another form of Lakshmi, and that it was she who wished to accomplish the death of Rāvana. "Rāvana in the course of his wanderings comes to the Himālayas, where he meets with a young woman of marvellous beauty, named Vedāvati, dressed in ascetic garments, and living the life of a devotee. He speaks of love; but she indignantly rejects his overtures, saying that it was her father's wish she should wed Vishnu, and that she had already wedded him with her heart. Rāvana presses his suit, assuring her that he is superior to Vishnu. She says that none but he would contemn that deity. Rāvana replies by touching her hair. Being very indignant at this, she declares that she

---

*Griffitlis's "Rāmāyana," i. 278.
†Muir, O. S. T., iv. 458.

will enter the fire (die) before his eyes. Before doing so, she says, 'Since I have been insulted in the forest by thee, who art wicked-hearted, I shall be born again for thy destruction. For a man of evil design cannot be slain by a woman; and the merit of my austerity would be lost if I were to launch a curse against you. But if I have performed, or bestowed, or sacrificed aught, may I be born a virtuous daughter— not produced from the womb—of a righteous man.' She then entered the blazing fire. It was she who was born as the daughter of King Janaka. The mountain-like enemy (Rāvana), who was virtually destroyed before by her wrath, has now been destroyed by her after she had associated herself with Vishnu's superhuman energy."

Regarding the child thus mysteriously found to be other than of mortal birth, to all suitors for her hand Janaka gave one reply—

> "I give not this my daughter; she
> Prize of heroic worth shall be."*

She was to be the wife of him who could bend the wonder-working bow. Many of the neighbouring princes had tried, but failed. And now Janaka says—

> "This heavenly bow, exceeding bright,
> Those youths shall see, O anchorite.
> Then if young Rāma's hand can string
> The bow that baffled lord and king,
> To him I give, as I have sworn,
> My Sitā, not of woman born." †

The bow is brought, and Rama invited to try his strength. He takes it up easily in his hand, and as he was drawing the

---

*Griffiths's "Rāmāyana," i. 279.
†Ibid. i. 280.

string, it snapped in two, to the wonder and fright of the beholders. Rāma thus becomes the successful suitor of Sitā, and messengers are despatched to invite his father to the wedding. His two brothers also come; and not only Rāma and Sita are united, but his three brothers are wedded to the three other daughters of Janaka. They then return home and live in happiness and prosperity.

After a time King Dasaratha wishes to abdicate in favour of Rāma his firstborn. When he had fixed upon a suitable time, the old man sends for his son, and enjoins him to prepare himself for the great event, by passing the night in holy exercises. The people hearing of the king's intention are delighted; the city is illuminated, and they spend the night in festivities. In the mean time a servant goes to Kaikeya, the mother of Bharata, and succeeds in exciting her jealousy of Rāma to such an extent, that she secludes herself in the room of discontent in the palace. The king visits her, when she says to him—

> "Now pledge thy word, if thou incline
> To listen to this prayer of mine."*

Ignorant of what her petition is, the king foolishly promises to grant it, before it is expressed. She, calling the gods to witness the promise and oath of her husband, reminds him that on an occasion of great danger she alone had stood by him, and that he then promised her a boon. She now requested the fulfilment of that vow; or,

> "If thou refuse thy promise sworn,
> I die despised before the morn,"†

and concludes her address by asking that her son be installed

---

*Griffiths's "Rāmāyana," i. 373.
†Ibid.

as Prince Regent, and Rāma be sent to live a hermit's life in the forest for fourteen years.

The king, almost mad with grief at this request, being bound by word and oath, is compelled to comply. The city is in tears that but yesterday was bright with joy; and the ceremony that was arranged for Rāma is performed in favour of Bharata, much against his will. Rāma tried to persuade Sitā to allow him to proceed to the forest alone; but to this she will not for a moment consent. The interview between them on this occasion is one of the most beautiful and touching incidents in the whole story. She despises difficulties, dangers and discomforts, if she is with her husband; and avers that death would be preferable to separation. Lakshman's entreaty to accompany them is very touching too:

> "I need not homes of god on high,
> I need not life that cannot die;
> Nor would I wish, with thee away,
> O'er the three worlds to stretch my sway."*

At length Rāma, Sitā, and Lakshman depart, amidst the tears of the whole city. When they reach the forest Dandaka, they seek a quiet spot, and at last settle down at Chitrakuta.

Dasaratha dies of grief a short time after their departure, and the city is again flooded with tears. Bharata visits the exiles, with the intention of bringing his brother home to occupy the throne, but to this Rāma will not consent. Bharata therefore continues to rule in his stead, but always regards him as the rightful king, and keeps a pair of his shoes, which are exposed to view on state occasions, to indicate that Bharata is acting only as Viceroy.

The three meet with many adventures in the forest, where they live the life of ascetics. One day they see an immense

---

*Griffiths's "Rāmāyana," ii. 94.

giant, named Viradha, clothed in a tiger's skin, and

> "Three lions, tigers four, ten deer,
> He carried on his iron spear."*

This giant, taking Sītā, aside, threatens to kill and eat her; but after a time, changing his mind, proposes to keep her; and, thinking that he is acting generously towards Rama, offers to allow him to go off unharmed. At length they fight; but as the giant is proof against their weapons, they do not make much progress. After a time he takes up Rāma and Lakshman on his shoulders, and runs away with them. As they are being carried each succeeds in cutting off one of his arms. The giant falls, weak from loss of blood; and, seeing that their weapons cannot deprive him of life, they bury him alive. After this adventure, they reach the hermitage, and Rāma becomes the protector of hermits throughout the district.

When ten years of his forest life were past, Rāma sets off for the hermitage of Agastya, a man who had gained great merit by his austerities. There they build a cottage, but are not able to live in peace very long. As Rāma and Sītā are sitting together under a tree, a giantess named Suparnakhā, the sister of Rāvana, passes by, and falls madly in love with Rāma.

> "She, grim of eye and foul of face,
> Loved his sweet glance and forehead's grace;
> She of unlovely figure, him
> Of stately form and shapely limb;
> She whose dim locks disordered hung,
> Him whose bright hair on high brows clung."†

The giantess questions Rāma as to the reason of his being

---

*Grifliths's "Rāmāyana." iii. 5.
†Ibid. iii. 80.

in the forest. After giving a full account of himself and Sitā, he inquires who she may be. She says she is Rāvanā's sister, and openly avows her love:

> "This poor misshapen Sitā leave,
> And me, thy worthier bride, receive.
> Look on my beauty, and prefer
> A spouse more meet than one like her;
> I'll eat that ill-formed woman there;
> Thy brother, too, her fate shall share.
> But come, beloved, thou shalt roam
> With me through all our woodland home."*

Rama, smiling, told her that as he was married he could not accept her kind offer, but advised her to try his brother. She acts upon this advice; but Lakshman sends her back to Rāma. Thinking that Sitā was the obstacle to the attainment of her wishes, she was about to slay her; Rāma prevented her from doing this, and Lakshman cut off her nose and ears. She fled to her brother Khara, whose anger she roused by the tale of her mutilation, who sent fourteen giants, giving them strict orders to kill Rāma, Sitā, and Lakshman. These giants are easily slain. Khara is terribly angry when he hears of their death; and, quickly raising an army of 14,000 warriors, goes against his foes. Rāma, single-handed, destroyed them nearly all.

One of the giants, named Akampan, rushed away to inform Rāvana of the catastrophe. Rāvana, intensely angry, asks—

> "Who is the wretch shall vainly try
> In earth, heaven, hell, from me to fly?
> Vaisravan, Indra, Vishnu, He
> Who rules the dead, must reverence me;
> For not the mightiest, lord of these

---

*Grifliths's "Rāmāyana," iii. 82.

> Can brave my will, and live at ease…
> With unresisted influence, I
> Can force e'en Death himself to die."*

He then asks particulars of the fight, and determines to avenge his sister. The messenger informs him that it is useless for him to attempt to conquer Rāma by force, and advises him rather to carry off Sitā; for,

> "Reft of his darling wife, be sure
> Brief clays the mourner will endure."†

Rāvana orders his chariot, starts off alone to Maricha, and asks his assistance, who dissuades him from attempting to fight with Rāma; but soon afterwards, when Suparnakhā, with her mutilated face, appears before Rāvana, she arouses his indignation. As he sat on his throne he is thus described : —

> "A score of arms, ten necks, had he,
> His royal gear was brave to see:
> His stature like a mountain height,
> His arms were strong, his teeth were white.
>   *   *   *   *
> "Ten thousand years the giant spent
> On dire austerities intent;
> And of his heads an offering, laid
> Before the Self-existent, made."‡

The giantess retells her tale, exciting her brother's anger afresh. He immediately sets off again for the hermitage of the fiend Maricha, and asks him to assist in his exploit by assuming

---

*Ibid. iii. 143.

† Griffiths's "Rāmāyana," iii. 143.

‡Ibid. iii. 148.

the form of a golden deer with silver spots, by which Sita's attention would be attracted.

> "Doubt not the lady, when she sees
> The wondrous deer among the trees,
> Will bid her lord and Lakshman take
> The creature for its beauty's sake."

Maricha, remembering the power of Rāma when as a mere boy he went to assist the hermit Visvamitra, and how he himself was wounded by him, again tries to dissuade Rāvana. But this time he cannot prevail, and there is not much choice left him, for Ravana declares—

> "Thy life, if thou the task essay,
>   In jeopardy may stand;
> Oppose me, and this very day
>   Thou diest by this hand."*

Rāvana

---

*Griffiths's "Rāmāyana," iii. 185.

Maricha assumes the form of a deer, and, proceeding to the vicinity of the hermitage, attracts the attention of Sitā, who becomes anxious to possess it. Rāma, leaving Lakshman to guard the home, goes in pursuit, and shoots it. As the fiend was dying, assuming Rāma's voice, he cried out loudly enough to be heard by the wife and brother, "Ho, Sita! Ho, Lakshman!" They imagining that some evil had come to Rāma, Lakshman hurried towards the spot whence the cry proceeded; whilst Rāvana, who was waiting near, seized the opportunity to carry off the defenceless Sitā. The demon did his best to induce her to yield herself an easy prey; but though she struggled hard, and cried for help to all who came near, none were able to deliver her. Held in his magical car, they reached Lanka, where she was placed in one of Rāvana's palaces. He tried both by kind words and fearful threatenings to win her love; but kindness and cruelty were equally ineffective. To comfort her, Brahmā sent Indra, who managed to elude the vigilance of her guards, and assured her of the sympathy of the gods, and of the fact that all would yet be well with her husband and herself.

Whilst this was happening at Lanka, Rāma was almost mad with grief. When Lakshman came to him after the deer was slain, he feared some evil had happened; and on their return to the cottage, as Sitā was not to be found, his anguish was intolerable. He wandered about calling upon the trees, mountains, and rivers to tell him what had happened to his loved one; but they were silent as the grave. A vulture at the point of death, who had fought with Rāvana on Sitā's behalf, informs him of her capture by the great fiend. (See part iii. chap, vii.)

In their wanderings, the brothers meet with a giant named Kabandha, who, owing to a curse, had to wear the hideous form in which he appeared, until his arms should be cut off by Rāma. As he was running away with the brothers on his shoulders, they fulfilled this condition, there being no other way of escape for them. On learning who they were, he was delighted, and asked them, as a favour, to burn his body in order that he might regain his proper form, and ascend to heaven. As the flames encircled him, he assumed a heavenly shape, and when in mid-air, told them where Sitā was taken, and advised them to seek the help of Sugriva, the King of the Vānar* (Monkey) tribes, as only through his aid could they recover her. Acting upon this advice, they proceed to Pampa, Sugriva's home; where the sight of the beauty of the lake causes Rāma's lamentations to burst forth afresh:

> "By sights like these of joy and peace,
> My pangs of hopeless love increase." †

When Sugriva saw the brothers, imagining them to be friends of his brother Bāli, by whom he had been deprived of his throne, he was greatly alarmed, and sent Hanumān, his commander-in-chief, to learn who they were, and why they had come. When Hanuman learns the object of their visit, thinking they might be induced to assist his master to regain his kingdom, he promises Sugriva's help, and, taking them

---

*Siva had foretold that Rāma would obtain the aid of the monkeys for the destruction of Rāvansi, when the demon was travelling in the Himālayas. Siva appeared to him as a dwarf, and tried to prevent him from going along a certain road. Havana disregarded the prohibition, and contemptuously asked who Siva was, to give an order that no one should pass that way; he also ridiculed the monkey-like appearance of the dwarf. Nandeshwara (Siva) replied that monkeys in appearance and power would be produced to destroy Rāvana and his family. In order to show his power, Rāvana raised the mountain in his arms; but Siva pressed it down with his toe, and crushed Rāvana in his arms, until he cried out with pain; and not until he had propitiated Siva for a thousand years did he release him. When he released him, He said that his name should be Rāvana, from the cry (Rāva) which he uttered.

†Griffiths's "Rāmāyana," iv. 6.

upon his shoulders, hurries off with them into the presence of the Vānar king. A league is made immediately, and after Rāma had promised that the usurper Bāli should fall that day, Sugriva says of Sitā —

> "Yea, though in heaven the lady dwell,
> Or prisoned in the depths of hell,
> My friendly care her way shall track,
> And bring thy ransomed darling back."*

Sugriva produces a robe, bracelets, and anklets that fell from Sitā as she was being carried off by Rāvana; the anklets Rāma recognizes at once, and is greatly comforted as Sugriva tells him that though at present unable to inform him where Sitā has been taken, he will be able to obtain this information, and assist him in his attempt to rescue her. Sugriva then narrates the story of his quarrel with his brother, but, ere he believes that Rāma can materially assist him, wished to test the wonderful bow of the hero. He was greatly astonished as he saw an arrow Rāma discharged pierce seven palm-trees in line, pass through a hill behind them, and, after traversing six subterranean worlds, return to the quiver. The Vānar king, seeing he has secured no common ally, goes forth fearlessly against his brother; and in the fight, when Sugriva was getting worsted, Rāma sends an arrow which slays his brother. This was regarded by the dying man as an act of gross injustice, because Rāma slew him without informing him who he was; had he only known he would gladly have assisted him in his quest for Sitā.

Sugriva, on the fall of his brother, re-ascends the throne, but is so fully occupied with the pleasures of his position as to forget the promise of help he had given Rāma, by whose prowess his dominion had been regained. Hanumān, ever

---

*Griffiths's "Rāmāyana," iv. 37.

faithful to Rāma's cause, reminds him —

> "The realm is won, thy name advanced,
> The glory of thy house enhanced;
> And now thy foremost care should be
> To aid the friends who succoured thee."*

But this reminder of his duty is insufficient to arouse the king from his selfish enjoyment; it was not until Rāma sends a strong message by Lakshman that he is alive to his duty. When, however, he does move, it is to collect a mighty army. Of the troops collected for this enterprise it is said —

> "Thousands, yea, millions shall there be
> Obedient to their king's decree.
>
>   *   *   *   *
>
> Fierce bears and monkey troops combined,
> And apes of every varied kind,
> Terrific in their forms, who dwell
> In grove and wood and bosky dell."†

The king gave instructions to each leader of a division, as to the limits of the district he was to search for the lost princess; but as Rāvana was believed to have gone towards the south, Hanumān's district, special instruction was given to him; and Rāma entrusted him with a ring which, if successful in discovering Sitā, he could show her as a proof that he was a messenger from her husband. For a long time the search was fruitless, and would have been given up as hopeless, but for Hanumān's perseverance. When they were about to relinquish the search, they met the vulture Sampati, brother of Jatayus, whom Rāvana had slain as he attempted to prevent him from

---

*Griffiths's "Rāmāyana," iv. 149.
†Ibid. iv. 168.

carrying off Sitā. This bird was the first to put Rāma on the right track for obtaining his wife. Sampati, hearing that Rāvana had slain his brother, was most anxious to avenge his death, and willingly rendered all the assistance he could. He informs the seekers that Sita is at Lanka.

> "A hundred leagues your course must be,
> Beyond this margin of the sea;
> Still to the south your way pursue,
> And there the giant Rāvan view."*

But here a difficulty occurred: there were a hundred leagues of water to be crossed; who could make the leap? Hanumān again comes to the front and declares—

> "Swift as a shaft from Rāma's bow,
> To Rāvan's city I will go." †

According to his promise, Hanumān made the marvellous spring. After meeting with various adventures, at length he reaches the capital of Lanka, and, diminishing in size until he is no bigger than a cat, passes through the city unnoticed, and finally enters the Asoka grove where Sitā was confined. He was just in time to witness an unsuccessful attempt of Rāvana to induce his lovely captive to forget her husband, and become his bride. Rāvana's parting words to Sitā on this occasion were not very love-inspiring; he declared that unless within two months she consented to become his bride,

> "My cooks shall mince thy limbs with steel,
> And serve thee for my morning meal." ‡

---

*Griffiths's "Rāmāyana," iv. 254.
†Ibid. iv. 280.
‡Ibid. iv. 334.

When she is alone, Hanumān addresses her. At first, on hearing a monkey speak, she imagines herself dreaming; but the sight of her husband's ring convinces her that the strange messenger is a friend, and she is delighted to hear all he has to tell:

> "'Thou bringest me,' she cried again,
> 'A mingled draught of bliss and pain:
> Bliss that he wears me in his heart,
> Pain that he wakes and weeps apart.'"*

Though Hanumān had found Sitā, and offered to carry her on his shoulders to her long-lost husband, a difficulty arose; she feared that in rising to the height which so long a leap necessitated, she might be giddy, and find it necessary to lay hold of him; but of her own free will she would on no account so much as touch the limbs of living man except those of her husband. Instead, then, of availing herself of the monkey's offer, she prefers to remain where she is for the present, and simply sends back a kind message to Rāma, with a gem to assure him that she has received his. Hanumān does not care to return without having effected some injury on his foe; he therefore destroys the grove and temple, and slays several of Rāvana's heroes. At length he is made captive. When taken before Rāvana, he confesses that he is a messenger from Rāma to Sitā, and earnestly advises her restoration. This so exasperates the giant that he would have slain him at once had he not been an envoy—and an envoy's life is sacred. Some of Rāvana's people, however, set fire to his tail, and though he does not experience much pain, he manages to set fire to the city in several places.

When Hanumān had completed his work in Lanka, he made a return leap to India, placed Sitā's gem in Rāma's hand,

---

*Griffiths's "Rāmāyana," iv. 365.

and told him all that had transpired in Rāvana's capital. The prince was delighted to hear of his wife's constancy; but as the difficulty of transferring an array from the mainland over a hundred leagues of sea seemed impossible to surmount, he despaired of seeing her again. Sugriva, more practical and fuller of resource, says—

> "Thy task must be
> To cast a bridge across the sea,
> The city of our foe to reach,
> That crowns the mountain by the beach;
> And when our feet that isle shall tread,
> Rejoice and deem thy foeman dead."*

The army, which had remained some distance away, now marches to the seashore, and Rāma is very curious to learn by what means so vast a bridge can be built. He in his anguish calls upon the sea to withdraw and allow his followers to march across as on dry land; but although the Ocean will not grant this prayer, he does assist with his advice, as he tells him to enlist the services of a tribe of Dasyas (servants), who, together with the monkey host, construct a bridge in five days. No sooner is this completed than the troops march across, Rāma being carried by Hanumān, and Lakshman by Angad; and though Rāvana hears of their approach, and his spies, terrified at the appearance of the invading army, counsel him to yield, he obstinately refuses, and at last the attack upon his city is made.

After fierce fighting, with considerable loss on both sides, Rāma and Lakshman are dangerously wounded by Indrajit, a son of Rāvana; but on some wonderful herbs being applied to them by Garuda, the marvellous bird of Vishnu, they are restored. A second time they fall, and are again restored by

---

*Griffiths's "Rāmāyana," v. 3.

herbs which Hanumān fetched in an incredibly short space of time from the Himālayas. At last Rāma and Rāvana meet face to face. Rāma's destructive arrows seem at first to have met with a foe as wonderful as themselves:

> "Straight to its mark the arrow sprang,
> And from the giant's body shred,
> With trenchant steel, the monstrous head.
> There might the triple world behold
> The severed head adorned with gold.
> But when all eyes were bent to view,
> Swift in its stead another grew."*

Acting on the advice of Mātali, Rāma, tired of this fruitless toil, launched an arrow "whose fire was kindled by the Almighty Sire," which pierced the giant's heart and laid him dead at his feet. Hanumān is despatched to assure Sitā of the death of her captor, and in a few hours she is carefully sent in a litter by Vibhishan, the brother and successor of Rāvana. This litter Rāma causes to be opened, that the monkeys may see his wife's face, as he says—

> "A woman's guard is not her bower,
> The lofty wall, the fenced tower:
> Her conduct is her best defence,
> And not a king's magnificence."†

This speech struck terror in the hearts of all around, and Sitā especially is almost heartbroken as, instead of the warm and loving welcome she had anticipated, he coolly tells her—

> "Lady, at length my task is done,

---

*Griffiths's "Rāmāyana," v. 254.
†Ibid. v. 271.

And thou, the prize of war, art won.

*　　*　　*　　*

"If from my home my queen was reft,
This arm hath well avenged the theft;
And in the field has wiped away
The blot that on my honour lay.

*　　*　　*　　*

"But, lady, 'twas not love for thee
That led mine army o'er the sea.

*　　*　　*　　*

"I battled to avenge the cause
Of honour and insulted laws.
My love is fled, for on thy fame
Lies the dark blot of sin and shame;
And thou art hateful as the light
That flashes on the injured sight.
The world is all before thee: flee:
Go where thou wilt, but not with me.

*　　*　　*　　*

"For Rāvan bore thee through the sky,
And fixed on thine his evil eye;
About thy waist his arms he threw,
Close to his breast his captive drew;
And kept thee, vassal of his power,
An inmate of his ladies' bower."*

Hearing these cruel and unexpected words, Sitā, makes a most pathetic appeal, in which she vehemently asserts her innocence; but as there are no signs of relenting in her husband, she wishes to die, or to prove her innocence by the fire-ordeal, and asks Lakshman to prepare a funeral pile:

"I will not live to bear this weight

---

*Griffiths's "Rāmāyana," v. 273.

Of shame, forlorn and desolate.
The kindled fire my woes shall end,
And be my best and surest friend."*

Lakshman performs this sad office; and when all is ready, she walks round it, and, before entering the fire, addresses Agni:

"As this fond heart, by virtue swayed,
From Raghu's son has never strayed,
So universal witness, Fire,
Protect my body on the pyre.
As Raghu's son has idly laid
This charge on Sitā, hear and aid." †

Having made this appeal to Agni to proclaim her innocence, she enters the fire. The gods, descending from heaven in their glory, address Rāma, saying:

"Couldst thou, the Lord of all, couldst thou,
Creator of the worlds, allow
Thy queen, thy spouse to brave the fire,
And give her body to the pyre?
Dost thou not yet, Supremely Wise,
Thy heavenly nature recognize?" ‡

Rāma frankly confesses that he believes himself to be only a mortal; Brahmā tries to enlighten him, as he assures him that he is Vishnu incarnate for the purpose of slaying Rāvana, and that Sitā, whom his cruel conduct had driven into the fire, was no other than Lakshmi, his celestial spouse. In confirmation

---

*Ibid. v. 276.
†Griffiths's "Rāmāyana," v. 277.
‡Ibid. v. 278.

of this, Agni appears in the fire, and, taking Sitā by the hand, conducts her to her husband, and declares her to be pure and spotless. Rāma receives her with the greatest joy, and states that he was certain of her innocence all along, but that as others might have doubted her, he had caused her to pass through this ordeal.

Dasaratha, the father of Rāma, now descends from heaven, and tells him that even in that happy place he had been sad to witness the sorrows of his beloved son. Indra next appears, and, at Rāma's request, brings back to life the many Vānars who had perished in his cause; and then other gods thank Rāma for the relief he has given them by the death of Rāvana. When these congratulations are over, Rāma, Sitā, and Lakshman mount a magic car, lent him by Vibhishan, in which in a single day they travel from Lanka to his own city. On arriving near it, Hanumān is sent to inform Bharat of their return; and the joy this intelligence gives to the faithful Bharat, and to the citizens generally, is indescribable. Rāma quickly assumes his position as king and the people enjoy unexampled prosperity:

> "Ten thousand years Ayodha, blest
> With Rāma's rule, had peace and rest.
> No widow mourned her murdered mate.
> No house was ever desolate.
> The happy land no murrain knew,
> The flocks and herds increased and grew,
> The earth her kindly fruits supplied,
> No harvest failed, no children died.
> Unknown were want, disease, and crime,
> So calm, so happy was the time."*

This state of universal happiness does not continue for ever. People in the city have doubts regarding the purity of their

---

*Griffiths's "Rāmāyana," v. 314.

queen, which at length reach the ears of Rāma, who, taking advantage of a wish of Sitā once again to see a hermitage, leaves her to live an ascetic life. When her twin sons, born in her forest home, come of age, she sends them to their father's court. The king on seeing them, deeply feels the injustice he had done their mother, and determines at any cost to reinstate her as his queen. On her arrival he asks her to assert her innocence before the assembled court; but even Sita could not bear this. She calls to the earth which gave her birth now to give her a home; the earth opened and received her into her bosom. After this Rama grows tired of life, and Time comes to inform him that his work is done. Hearing this, the good king goes to the banks of the sacred stream, and forsaking his body ascends to his home in heaven.

Rāma, to a vast number of Hindus, is not merely the King of Ayodha, whose history is so pathetically told in the Rāmāyana; nor the benefactor of gods, as he slew their enemy, Rāvana; but their saviour and friend. As the dead are carried to the river-side to be burned, the friends repeatedly cry, "Rāma, Rāma, Satya Nāma," *i.e.* "Rāma Rāma, the true name." Probably this is owing to the fact that in life his power of intercession for the dead was great; whilst his kindness to and care for his followers were such as to encourage men's trust. He is said to have taken the whole of the inhabitants of his beloved city Ayodha to Brahmā's heaven without their suffering death. At his intercession Rāvana's spies were saved; and the Vānar hosts that had fallen in battle were restored to life. He entreated his father Dasaratha to remove the curse which he had pronounced upon Kaikeya, the mother of Bharata, through whose unkindness Rāma had been exiled.

8. THE KRISHNA AVATĀRA

Professor Goldsücker says* that this "is the most interesting incarnation of Vishnu, both on account of the opportunity which it affords to trace in Hindu antiquity the gradual transformation of mortal heroes into representatives of a god; and on account of the numerous legends connected with it, as well as the influence which it exercised on the Vaishnava cult. In the Mahābhārata, Krishna—which literally means 'the black or dark one' —is sometimes represented as rendering homage to Siva, and therefore acknowledging his own inferiority to that deity, or as recommending the worship of Uma, the consort of Siva, and as receiving boons from both these deities. In some passages, again, he bears merely the character of a hero

The Krishna Avatāra

---

*Chambers's Cyclopaedia, *s.v.*

endowed with extraordinary powers, and in others his divine nature is even disputed or denied by adversaries, though they are eventually punished for this unbelief. As the intimate ally of Arjuna, he claims the rank of the supreme deity; but there are other passages, again, in the Mahābhārata in which the same claim of Siva is admitted, and an attempt is made at compromising their rival claims, by declaring both deities one and the same. Sometimes, moreover, Krishna is in this Epos declared to represent merely a very small portion—'a portion of a portion,' as it is called—of the divine essence of Vishnu. In the Mahābhārata, therefore, which is silent also regarding many adventures in Krishna's life fully detailed in the Purānas, the worship of Vishnu in this incarnation was by no means so generally admitted or settled as it is in many Purānas of the Vaishnait sect; nor was there at that period that consistency in the conception of a Krishna Avatāra, which is traceable in the later works."

In the "Prem Sāgar," the Hindi version of the "Bhāgavata Purāna," is the following account of the object of this incarnation. A king of Mathura, named Ugrasena, had a beautiful wife, who was barren. One day, when walking in a wood, she lost her companions; and when alone, a demon becoming enamoured of her assumed her husband's form, and as a result a son was born, who was named Kansa. When a mere child Kansa manifested a most cruel disposition—his great delight being to catch and kill children—and he grew up to be a source of sorrow to his father, family, and country. He advised his father to give up the worship of Rāma, the god of his race, and to call in secret only on Mahādeva (Siva). His father replied with sorrow: 'Rāma is my lord, and the dispeller of my grief; if I do not worship him, how shall I as a sinful man cross over the sea of the world?" Kanza hearing this, dethroned his father, and having usurped his place issued a proclamation throughout his dominions forbidding men to worship Rāma, and commanding them to reverence Siva; and his tyranny at length became so unbearable, that the Earth, assuming the form of a cow, went to Indra and, complaining of all this, said: "Evil spirits have begun to commit great crimes in the world; in dread of whom Religion and Justice have departed; and if you will permit me, I, too, will abandon the world, and descend into the lower regions." Indra hearing this went in company with the other gods to Brahmā to see what redress could be afforded. Brahmā conducted them to Siva, who, in his turn, conducted them to Vishnu; and reminding him of the deliverance he had afforded to gods and men in his previous manifestations, they induce him again to become a man for the destruction of Kansa. The gods and goddesses, delighted at this assurance of help, promise also to forsake their heavenly homes that they may be his companions during his earthly sojourn; and Vishnu himself arranges that Lakshman, who in the Rāma incarnation had been his brother and constant and faithful companion, and Bharata also and Sutraghna, should accompany him; and that Sitā, under the name of Rukmini, should be his wife.

The "Vishnu Purāna,"* from which most of the following legends are taken, gives a somewhat different account of Vishnu's reply. Krishna was the incarnation of "a part of a part of the supreme being." When entreated to become incarnate, "the supreme lord plucked off two hairs, one white and one black, and said to the gods, 'These my hairs shall descend upon the earth, and shall relieve her of the burden of her distress!'" The white hair was impersonated as Balarāma, and the black as Krishna. "The asuras shall all be destroyed. This my black hair shall be impersonated in the eighth conception of Devaki, the wife of Vasudeva, who is like a goddess, and shall slay Kansa, who is the demon Kālanemi."†

---

*Book v.

†It should be noticed here that a commentator says on this passage that the statement that two hairs of Vishnu became incarnate must

When Vasudeva and his wife Devaki were being driven by King Kansa in a chariot, "a voice in the sky, sounding loud and deep like thunder, addressing Kansa, said, 'Fool that you are, the eighth child of the damsel you are now driving shall take away your life!'" Kansa hearing this drew his sword, and was about to slay Devaki; but Vasudeva interposed, saying, "Kill not Devaki, great warrior! Spare her life, and I will deliver to you every child she may bring forth." Kansa, appeased with this promise, spared the lady, but, to prevent any mistake, placed a guard by day and night over their apartments; and as child after child was born, it was given up to him and slain.

Kansa was under the impression that he had destroyed Devaki's children, but this was not the case. The children that were handed over to him were children of Hiranyakasipu, whom Visbnu slew as the Man-Lion, who were brought from the nether regions by Yoganindra, "the great illusory energy of Vishnu," and lodged in Devaki's womb in order that the cruel Kansa might be overreached. Vishnu said to this goddess: "Go, Nidra (Sleep), to the nether regions, and by my command conduct successively six of their princes to be conceived by Devaki. When these shall have been put to death by Kansa, the seventh conception shall be formed of a portion of Sesha (the serpent-deity), who is part of me; and this you shall transfer before the time of birth to Rohini, another wife of Vasudeva, who resides at Gokula." This child was Balarāma. "The report shall run that Devaki miscarries. I will myself become incarnate in her eighth conception; and you shall take a similar character as the embryo offspring of Yasoda, the wife of a herdsman named Nanda. In the night of the eighth of the dark half of the month Nabhas I shall be born; and you will be born on the ninth. Impelled and aided by my power, Vasudeva shall bear

---

not be taken literally, but that the work to be done by him on this occasion was so small that it could easily have been effected by two hairs. In Krishna, Vishnu himself was manifested.

me to the bed of Yasodā, and you to the bed of Devaki. Kansa shall take you and hold you up to dash you against a stone; but you shall escape into the sky, where Indra shall meet and do homage to you through reverence of me."

When Devaki gives birth to her eighth son, Vasudeva takes the child, and, eluding the vigilance of the guards, hurries through the city, with the serpent Sesha following. On reaching the river Yamuna, which he has to cross, though ordinarily both wide and deep, it assists him in his flight, the water only rising to his knees. Just as he reaches Nanda's house, Yasodā had given birth to her child, which Vasudeva seizes, and, leaving Devaki's child in its place, returns to his prison home, and manages to re-enter unobserved. Soon after this the cry of the new-born child being heard by the guard, Kansa is quickly informed of its birth, and, rushing into the room, seized and dashed it against a stone. But fate was too strong for him. Immediately the child touched the ground, "it rose into the sky, and, expanding into a gigantic figure, having eight arms, each wielding some formidable weapon, laughed and said to Kansa, 'What avails it thee to have hurled me to the ground? He is born that shall kill thee, the mighty one amongst the gods, who was formerly thy destroyer.'" The reference of the last sentence as taught by other Purānas is to the fact that Kansa was no other than Kālanemi, whom Vishnu had slain when incarnate as Rāma.

Greatly alarmed by the unexpected frustration of his plans, Kansa collects his friends, and, addressing them, said: "The vile and contemptible denizens of heaven are assiduously plotting against my life; they dreading my prowess, I hold them of no account. Have I not seen the king of the gods, when he had ventured into the conflict, receiving my shafts upon his back, and not bravely upon his breast? Now, it is my determination to inflict still deeper degradation upon these evil-minded and unprincipled gods. Let therefore every man who is notorious for liberality (in gifts to gods and Brāhmans), every man who is remarkable for his celebration of sacrifices, be put to death; that thus the gods shall be deprived of the means by which they subsist. The goddess who has been born as the infant child of Devaki has announced to me that he is again alive who in a former being was my death. Let therefore active search be made for whatever young children there may be upon earth, and let every boy in whom there are signs of unusual vigour be slain without remorse." Soon after this, as he feared nothing more from them, he released Vasudeva and Devaki from their confinement, and, in dread of meeting his great enemy, withdrew into the inner apartments of his house.

On regaining his liberty, Vasudeva speedily sought out Nanda, who of course was unaware of the change of children effected by Vasudeva, and, after congratulating him on the birth of a son, suggested the advisability of his returning home; as, having paid his taxes, there was nothing to detain him in the city. He feared lest the spies of Kansa should notice the peculiar excellences of the child, and destroy him according to Kansa's order. At the same time he took his other child by Kohini (Balarāma), and placed him under the care of Nanda to be brought up as his own child. By this means, as Rāma and Lakshman were inseparable companions in the previous incarnation, Krishna and Balarāma were as intimately connected in this.

The herdsman Nanda and his family had not been long settled at Gokula before efforts were made to destroy the infant Krishna. A female fiend named Putanā, the sucking of whose breast was instant death to an infant, came by night, and, taking the child in her arms, offered him her breast. Krishna seized it with both hands, and sucked with such violence that the hideous being roared with pain, and giving way in every joint fell down dead. The villagers hearing the shrieks rushed into the house to see what was the matter. Yasodā waved a cow's tail brush over him, whilst Nanda put dried cow-dung upon his head, and, placing an amulet on his arm, besought

Vishnu to protect the child.

There are many legends connected with his boyhood, which teach his extraordinary power. On one occasion, when a mere infant, lying under Nanda's wagon, he cried for the breast, and, being impatient because his mother did not come quickly, kicked the wagon over, to the great astonishment of the bystanders. He and Balarāma played with and tormented the calves to such an extent, that Yasodā became angry; and to prevent its repetition, tied Krishna to a heavy wooden mortar in which corn is threshed, and went on with her work. Krishna, trying to free himself from this, dragged it until it became wedged fast between two Arjuna trees, and with a strong pull the trees were uprooted. The people, astonished because the trees fell when no storm was blowing, thought the place must be unlucky, and moved away to Vrindāvana. The Bhāgavata says that these trees were

Kkishna Slaying Bakāsuka

two sons of Kuvera, the god of riches, who, owing to a curse of the sage Nārada, were thus metamorphosed, and that it was for the purpose of liberating them that Krishna accomplished this feat,

Krishna and Balarāma, "the guardians of the world, were keepers of cattle in the cowpens of Vrindāvana," until they were seven years of age, during which years, according to the "Bhāgavata Purāna," the boys were full of childish tricks: stealing butter from the neighbouring cowherds appears to have been their favourite pastime.

In the "Bhāgavata Purāna" there are legends also of attempts being made by Kansa to rid himself of his dreaded foe. One day a demon was sent who hoped to surprise him when wandering with the cattle in the woods; but the boy, seeing through his disguise, seized him by the foot, swung him round his head and dashed him so violently on the ground that he immediately died. The next day, another demon, assuming the form of an immense crane, seized Krishna with its bill; but he became so hot that the crane immediately released him: Krishna then crushed its beak under his foot. Yet another came as a great serpent, and swallowed Krishna and his companions, the cowherds, with their cows; but he was no sooner in the reptile's stomach than he expanded himself, and burst open his prison. Krishna was not always defending himself; often he benefited his companions. When Brahmā stole some calves, and carried off the boys who tended them, Krishna made other calves and other boys, so that the theft was never known by the cowherds.

We now return to the narrative of the "Vishnu Purāna." The river Yamuna was the home of the serpent Kaliya, who made its waters boil with the fires of passion, so that the trees on its banks were blighted by its fumes, and birds were killed by its heat. Krishna, seeing how his friends at Vrindavana were inconvenienced by this, plunged into the stream, to the dismay of the cowherds, and, after challenging the serpent to fight, was about to slay him. Moved, however, by the intercession of the lady serpents, he allowed him to live on condition that he and his family forsook the Yamuna, and took up their abode in the sea.

On one occasion Krishna wished to annoy Indra. Seeing the Gopas (cowherds) preparing to worship the giver of rain, he dissuaded them from it, and urged them rather to worship the mountain that supplied their cattle with food, and their cattle that yielded them milk. Acting upon this advice, they presented to the mountain Govarddhana "curds, milk, and flesh." This was merely a device by which Krishna diverted the worship of Indra to himself; for "upon the summit of the mountain Krishna appeared, saying, 'I am the mountain,' and partook of much food presented by the Gopas; whilst in his own form as Krishna he ascended the hill along with the cowherds, and worshipped his other self." Having promised them many blessings, the mountain-person of Krishna vanished. Indra, greatly incensed at the disregard shown him by Nanda and others, sent floods to destroy them and their cattle; but Krishna, raising the mountain Govarddhana aloft on one hand, held it as an umbrella and thus sheltered his friends from the storm for seven days and nights. Indra then visited Krishna and praised him for what he had done; and his wife Indrāni entreated Krishna to be a friend of their son Arjuna.

Krishna did not by any means confine his attention to the wants of the cowherds amongst whom he spent his early days. On one occasion Satrajit, a worshipper of the Sun, who had received from his lord a magnificent jewel named Syamantaka, came to visit Krishna at Dwaraka, adorned with his jewel, which shone so brightly that the inhabitants thought the Sun himself was present. It was a most marvellous gem, for its possessor received through it "eight loads of gold daily, and was free from all fear of portents, wild beasts, fire, robbers, and famine;" but there was this strange condition attached to its possession: "although it was an inexhaustible source of good

Krishna holding up mount Govarddhana

to a virtuous person, when worn by a man of bad character it was the cause of his death." Thinking it possible that Krishna, on learning the excellence of the gem, might wish to keep it, Satrajit gave it to his brother Prasena. When this brother was hunting, having taken the gem with him, he was killed by a lion. Jambavat, the king of the bears, seeing the gem in the lion's mouth, killed him and took possession of the jewel. When Prasena did not return as he was expected, the Yadavas (Krishna's tribesmen) began to think that Krishna had slain him. To convince them of his innocency, taking a number of his brethren, he traced the horse upon which Prasena rode to the place where the lion slew its rider, and was acquitted of all blame in the matter. He then followed Jambavat to his cave, and finding the bear-prince Sukumāra playing with the gem, he entered and fought with his father the king for twenty-one days. As no tidings of him reached his home at Dwaraka, his friends concluded that he must be dead; but the food and water offered in the performance of his funeral ceremonies supporting him during his lengthened conflict, enabled him to overcome Jambavat, who gave him his daughter Jambavati to wife. He returned home in triumph, carrying the gem with him, which he restored to Satrajit, and received from him his daughter Satyabhāma. This gem, after causing several other disputes, was finally given to a good king, Akrura. When it was offered to Krishna he confessed that as he had 16,000 wives it was not possible for him to retain it; and also that his wife Satyabhāma would not comply with the conditions imposed upon its possessor.

The Gopis (wives of the cowherds) are represented as being madly in love with Krishna. As he and Balarāma played the flute, they came to dance with them; but as all could not hold Krishna's hand as they danced, he multiplied himself into as many forms as there were women, each woman believing she held the hand of the true Krishna.* On one occasion he watched the Gopis as they went to bathe in the Yamuna river, and, stealing their clothes, sat in a tree and refused to restore them until each came in the form of a suppliant with uplifted hands to fetch them. The Bhāgavata teaches that these women, impelled though they were by passion to seek Krishna, obtained through him final emancipation from sin. "In whatever way a man may worship him he will obtain deliverance. Some knew

---

*It is this incident in Krishna's history which is celebrated yearly at the Rāsajattra.

and sought him as a son, some as a friend, some as an enemy, some as a lover, but in the end all obtained the blessing of deliverance and emancipation."

Of all these women Krishna's favourite was Rādhā, the wife of Āyanagosha. Her sister-in-law told her brother of his wife's misconduct, and Rādhā was in fear lest he should murder her. When, however, she communicated her fears to her lover, he easily reassured her. He told her that when her husband came, he (Krishna) would transform himself into Kāli, and instead of finding her with a lover, he would see her engaged in worshipping a goddess. Her husband happening to pass that way soon after, noticed Rādhā bowing down, and joined in worshipping Krishna, whom he mistook for Kāli. It is Rādhā whose name is ever associated with Krishna in hymns, songs, prayers, and pictures, and whilst the wives of the deity are forgotten, Rādhā is worshipped along with her lover.

Rādhā worshipping Krishna as Kāli

As Krishna was dancing on one occasion with these women, a demon named Arishta, in the form of a fierce bull, savagely attacked him. Krishna quietly waited its approach, and, seizing him as an alligator would have done, held him by the horns whilst he pressed his sides with his knees; he then wrung his neck as if it had been a piece of wet cloth, and at last tearing off his horns beat him to death with them.

After some years Kansa is informed of Krishna's existence, and, as we have noticed above, sent various demons to slay him; but as these efforts failed, the king determined on a grand scheme by which he hoped to rid himself of his dreaded foe. He accordingly sent Akrura, one of the few good men in his kingdom, with a most polite invitation to Krishna and Balarāma to visit him at his capital, to witness some athletic sports; and, in the hope that they, being off their guard, would fall an easy prey, ordered a demon named Kesin, in the form of a horse, to attack them on the road. But Krishna is more than a match for the fiend; he meets the horse and fearlessly thrusts his hand in its mouth, and, causing it to swell, bursts the animal into two parts: hence one of Krishna's many names is Kesava, the slayer of Kesin.

Akrura, having told Krishna of the ill-feeling of Kansa and of the plots he had made against his life, was greatly encouraged with the assurance that in three days Kansa and his adherents would be slain. He took leave of the guests when they approached the city of Mathura. Entering the city unattended, and dressed as poor country people, they meet a washerman of Kansa at work, whom they first annoy by throwing his clothes on the ground, and, when he expostulates with them, kill him, and robe themselves in Kansa's garments. Seeing the gaily dressed, strong, and good-looking young men, a flower-seller presents them with some of his choicest flowers; for his generosity Krishna bestows rich blessings upon him in this life and promises heaven after death. After this they meet a deformed girl named Kubja, carrying ointments and perfumes to the palace, some of which, at his request, she gives to Krishna. For her kindness her deformity is cured, she is made beautiful, and invites the brothers to her home.

The day following was fixed for the sports. The lists were prepared, the trumpets sounded, and two fierce wrestlers were commanded by fair means or foul to slay Krishna and his brother; and in case they should fail to do this, an enormous elephant was in readiness to trample them to death. But wrestlers and elephant were themselves slain. Seeing his grand scheme signally fail, the king lost his temper and called out loudly to his guards to slay the youths; instead of this, however, Krishna rushed upon and slew the king in the midst of the assembly, and falling at the feet of his father and mother, Vasudeva and Devaki, placed Ugrasena, Kansa's father, upon the throne, and with his brother took up his abode at Mathura.

Krishna is of immense service to the people of Mathura, for very soon after his arrival there, Jarāsandha, Kansa's father-in-law, attacks them, and is beaten eighteen times by his prowess. When the people were almost exhausted with these protracted struggles, a new enemy appears in Kalayāvana, King of the Yāvanas, who wish to try their strength with the Yādavas under Krishna. He, thinking that by a struggle with two foes at once the people would be exhausted, provided a new city, so strong that women could protect it, to which he conducted the inhabitants of Mathura. No sooner had he made the people secure than he went forth unarmed and alone, and attracted the attention of the King of the Yavanas, whose army still surrounded the city. Krishna, seeing the king was following him, entered a cave, and concealed himself; the king seeing a man lying at its entrance, thinking it must be Krishna, kicked it, and in an instant became a heap of ashes. The secret of his destruction was this: a man named Muchukunda had received as a boon from the gods the power to sleep for a long period, with this condition, that whoever awoke him should be instantly consumed by fire emanating from his body. Unwittingly the

King of the Yāvanas kicked him and received the penalty of his ignorance; whilst Krishna escaped, and seized the army and treasures left without an owner.

Amongst many others, Krishna fell in love with Rukmini, the daughter of Bhismaka, King of Vidhabha (Berar); but her brother Rukmin hated him, and refusing to give his consent, at the advice of Jarāsandha, she was betrothed to Sisupāla. This Sisupāla was no other than Hiranyakasipu and Rāvana, whom in previous incarnations Vishnu had slain. On the eve of the wedding Krishna carries off Rukmini, leaving Balarāma and his friends to take care of themselves; and when Rukmin follows him with an immense army, Krishna easily destroys his companions, and, but for the intercession of Rukmini, would have killed his brother-in-law too. This Rukmini was none other than Lakshmi, Sitā and others, who, in her earlier incarnations, had stood in a similar relationship to him.

Soon after this occurrence, Indra pays a visit to Krishna, to enlist his sympathy and help against Naraka, King of Pragyotisha, who was inflicting all kinds of evil upon the whole creation. "Carrying off maidens belonging to gods, saints, demons and kings, he shuts them up in his own palace. He has taken away Varuna's umbrella, the celestial nectar-dropping earrings of my mother Aditi, and now demands my elephant." Krishna at once consents to help, marches off to meet the king, conquers his forces, slays Naraka and obtains the stolen property, for which on its restoration he receives the thanks of its owners. In the women's apartment he finds 16,100 damsels, and "at an auspicious moment received the hands of all, according to the ritual, in separate houses; 16,100 was the number of the maidens, and into so many forms did the foe of Madhu multiply himself; so that each of the damsels thought he had wedded her in his single person, and he abode severally in the dwelling-place of each of his wives. It was as a present from Umā, the wife of Siva, that he received these wives."

There was once a severe conflict between Krishna and

Siva. Aniruddha, a grandson of Krishna, was enamoured of Usha, a daughter of Bāna, a devout worshipper of Siva, whom he visited secretly. Being caught by Bāna's guard, the prince was imprisoned, and, as the king would not release him, Krishna attacked him; but Siva and his son Kartikeya fought for Bāna. After a severe encounter, as Siva sat weary in his car, and Kartikeya had fled from the field, Krishna, tired of using ordinary weapons, let fly his wonderful discus, which never failed of accomplishing his wish, and cut off the hundred arms of Bāna. When about to throw it a second time, Siva came and interceded for the life of his friend; to whom, in granting his request, Krishna said, "You are fit to apprehend that you are not distinct from me; that which I am, thou art."

As Krishna was marching towards Sonitapura, the city in which his grandson was confined, as narrated above, a strange enemy met him. "Fever, an emanation from Maheshwara (Siva), having three feet and three heads, fought desperately with Krishna in defence of Bāna. Baladeva (Balarāma), upon whom his ashes were scattered, was seized with burning heat, and his eyelids trembled; but he obtained relief by clinging to the body of Krishna. Contending thus with the divine holder of the bow, the Fever emanating from Siva was quickly expelled from the body of Krishna by Fever which he himself engendered. Brahmā, beholding the impersonated malady, bewildered by the beating inflicted by the arms of the deity, entreated the latter to desist, and the foe of Madhu refrained, and absorbed into himself the Fever he had created. The rival Fever then departed, saying to Krishna, "Those who call to memory the combat between us shall be exempt from febrile diseases."

Krishna was not without a rival. A man named Paundraka professed that he was the true incarnation of Vishnu, and that Vāsudeva (son of Vasudeva) was a pretender. The King of Benares was induced to believe in this false Krishna, and at his request sent an order for the real Krishna to come and do him homage, and at the same time to bring with him his discus and other insignia of office. Krishna did not hesitate. Setting off next day, he destroyed the army of his rival in a moment, and addressing Paundraka himself said, "You desired me by your envoy to resign to you my insignia: I now deliver them to you. Here is my discus, here my mace, here is Garuda; let him mount upon thy standard." The discus did its work, the rival of Krishna was cut to pieces; but, as the Rāja of Benares continued to fight, his head was cut off, and fell in the city. The people in their distress cried to Siva, who, in answer, sent a fierce female form to their help. But the discus, obedient to Krishna's command, pursued her, and its radiancy, unfortunately, was such that it consumed the whole city in which she had hid herself.

When Krishna had finished his work, and had destroyed demons and wicked men, especially Kansa, the time came for him to return to heaven; but, before his departure, owing to a curse pronounced by angry Brahmans, it was necessary that the Yadava race from which he sprang should pass away. This curse was pronounced to avenge an insult offered by some Yādu boys to Nārada and other Rishis when engaged with their devotions. These boys, as a joke, dressed up a son of Krishna, named Sāmba, in woman's clothes, and taking him to the Rishis asked, "What child will this female give birth to?" The Rishis, greatly annoyed, said, "She will bring forth a club which shall crush the whole Yādava race." Accordingly a club came from Sāmba's body, which King Ugrasena ordered to be ground to powder and thrown into the sea. The dust that fell on the shore became rushes, but a small part of the club, like a lance head, could not be broken: this was thrown into the sea, was swallowed by a fish, which was caught by a fisherman, and made into an arrow point by a huntsman named Jara.

A messenger from the gods now visited Krishna, telling him that, as his work was done, he should ascend to his home. This he was quite willing to do; but, wishing to save his race from the threatened destruction, advised the Yādavas to forsake their city and go to Prabhāsa. By his advice he unintentionally hastened their end; for on reaching the seashore they indulged in liquor and began to fight violently amongst themselves, and for arms seized the rushes which sprang from the dust of the fatal club that came from Sāmba. Krishna and Balarāma trying to make peace between the combatants only led to their swifter destruction, until at last the two brothers were left alone of their race. Whilst sitting and talking on the banks of a river, a serpent crawled out of Balarāma's mouth—the serpent Sesha, of which he was an incarnation, and so his end was come. Krishna, left alone, sat meditating, with his foot upon his knee, when the hunter Jara, armed with the fatal arrow, passed by, and taking Krishna for a deer, shot him, and thus his death was unwittingly caused by the last part of the cursed club. Jara, seeing his mistake, fell at Krishna's feet and asked forgiveness, to whom Krishna said, "Fear not thou in the least. Go, hunter, through my favour to heaven, the abode of the gods." Immediately a celestial car appeared, in which the man ascended to heaven; and Krishna abandoned his mortal body.

In this account of Krishna we have followed the "Vishnu Purāna," with which the Bhāgavata agrees; though the latter has many additional legends, similar to those given above. The writers of these Purānas have no doubt regarding his divinity; in fact a large part of these books is occupied with praises and prayers addressed to him as supreme. In the Mahābhārata, however, Krishna is little more than a hero, excepting in those passages which are believed to be of much later origin than the body of the book. By the writers of that age Krishna is described as a worshipper of Siva, from whom he received the chief blessings he enjoyed.

Amongst the references to Krishna in the Mahābhārata are the following:*—" Krishna then reverenced Siva with voice,

---

*Muir, O. S. T., iv. 184.

mind, understanding, and act;" *i.e.* when he accompanied
Arjuna to Siva's abode to beg heavenly weapons. Siva replies,
"I have been duly worshipped by Krishna, wherefore no one
is dearer to me than Krishna." In a hymn Krishna thus praises
Siva: "I know Mahādeva, and his various works of old. For he
is the beginning, middle, and end of (all) creatures." Bhisma
says, "Through his devotion to Rudra, the world is pervaded
by the mighty Krishna. This Mādhava performed austerities for
a full thousand years, propitiating Siva, the god who bestows
boons." It was through propitiating Siva that Krishna had a
son by Jambavati; from him he received the discus Sudarsana,
and from him he received eight boons, to which Umā added
eight others: among the eight granted by Siva were "a hundred
hundreds of sons," and by Umā sixteen thousand one hundred
wives. According to Krishna, Siva "is the most excellent of
beings in the three worlds." "As he is the greatest of gods, he
is called Mahādeva, since he constantly prospers all men in all
their acts: seeking their welfare (Siva), he is called Siva."

The following legend will show that the belief in Krishna's
divinity was not by any means common at the time the
Mahābhārata was written. When King Yudhishthira offered a
sacrifice, it was proposed, that Krishna, as the greatest chief
present, should receive the presents that were made. Sisupāla
strongly objected to this, and supported his objection by a
recital of Krishna's misdeeds. Krishna listened patiently for a
time, but at last declared that the time had come when he must
slay his detractor. He said, "I have promised to forgive him a
hundred offences—he has now offended more than a hundred
times;" and then the never-failing discus did its work. In other
passages of the Mahābhārata, Siva praises Krishna in almost as
extravagant language as that employed by Krishna to him; but
this is so thoroughly opposed to his general position throughout
the poem, there can be little doubt that these passages were
introduced when the worship of Krishna had to a large extent
superseded that of Siva.

Krishna, as described in the Mahābhārata, was not above employing deception, and leading others to do it too. On one occasion during the great war between the Kurus and Pāndavas, the Pāndavas were in great distress, owing to the bravery and skill of a Kuru chief named—Dronāchārjya. This chief had a son whom he deeply loved, named Ashwatthama; and it was thought that if a report could be spread to the effect that this son was slain, his father would be too distressed to fight. Dronāchārjya at last heard the rumour, but refused to believe it unless Yudishthira confirmed it. At first the good king refused to speak an untruth; but at Krishna's suggestion he repeated the words, "Ashwatthama is dead," meaning an elephant of that name, yet wishing the father to understand he referred to his son. The trick succeeded; but the king as a punishment for his prevarication had to endure the sight of the lost in hell, whilst being conducted to heaven.

Amongst Krishna's many names the following are the most common:—

Gopal, "The Cowherd."

Gopinath, "The Lord of the Milkmaids."

Mathuranāth, "The Lord of Mathura."

8A. THE BALARĀMA AVATĀRA

According to some accounts of Vishnu's incarnations, Balarāma is the *eighth*; Krishna in that case not being called an incarnation, but an appearance of the deity himself; whilst, according to others, the two brothers together form the eighth, Krishna having been produced from a black and Balarāma from a white hair of Vishnu. As they were constant companions during their stay on earth, many of the exploits in which Balarāma shared have already been narrated in speaking of Krishna. There are a few legends,* however, referring chiefly to Balarāma.

---

*"Vishnu Purāna," book v.

Balarāma is an incarnation of the serpent Sesha,* who himself was part of Vishnu, and thus is said to be "a part of a part" of that deity. When appealed to by the distressed gods to

Balarāma

appear on earth to save them from their oppressor Kansa, Vishnu, a year before his own birth, transferred by means of

---

*Sesha (the end), or Ananta (endless), the serpent deity, has a thousand heads, and forms the couch on which Vishnu reposes during the intervals of creation. The world is said to rest on the head of Sesha, who stands upon a tortoise; when, therefore, the tortoise moves his feet, or Sesha yawns, earthquakes result. It was this serpent that formed the rope at the churning of the ocean; and by fires that issue from his body the world is destroyed at the end of each age, or Kalpa. He is sometimes called a son of Kasyapa and Kadru, a daughter of Daksha.

Yoganindra, the embryo of Balarāma from Devaki to Rohini, another wife of Vasudeva, residing at Gokula, to save it from the cruel anger of Kansa, who had ordered the destruction of Devaki's children as soon as they were born. When about a year old, this child was placed under the care of a herdsman named Nanda and his wife Yasodā, the reputed parents of Krishna, that the two boys might be brought up together; Vasudeva, on the night of Krishna's birth, having carried him to the house of Nanda, and substituted him for the infant daughter of these people.

Balarāma was second only to Krishna in the possession of miraculous powers. One day, as he was with the young cow-keepers in a wood, his companions asked him to shake some fruit trees belonging to a demon called Dhenuka, that they might enjoy the fruit. As he was complying with their request, the demon, in the form of a monster ass, appeared. As he tried to kick Balarāma, the hero seized him by his hind legs, swung him round his head, and threw him to the ground with such force that he died immediately: the dead body Balarāma threw to the top of a palm tree, and the demon's relatives who came to his rescue received similar treatment at his hands. After Dhenuka's death, his orchard became a favourite spot of the cowherds. Whilst they were playing there, a demon named Pralamba came in the form of a boy, and joining them in their game, persuaded Balarāma to get upon his shoulders. No sooner had he mounted than the demon ran off with him, and, feeling the hero to be heavy, he increased his bulk until he became like a mountain in size, causing Balarāma to tremble with fear, and to call upon Krishna for help. Krishna reminding him of his divine nature says, "Calling to memory who thou art, O being of illimitable might, destroy the demon yourself. Suspending awhile your mortal character, do what is right." Balarāma acting upon this advice, squeezed the demon with his knees, and pommelled him with his fists so fiercely that he fell down dead. When boxing with Kansa's wrestler in the lists at Mathura he easily managed to slay his antagonist.

After Balarāma had dwelt for some time in Dwaraka, a city Krishna had provided for the safety of the people of Mathura, Krishna sent him to Vraja to see their old friends the herdsmen, with whom they had been brought up as boys. During his stay there, Varuna, addressing Varuni his wife, said, "Thou, Madira, art ever acceptable to the powerful Ananta (Sesha); go therefore and promote his enjoyments." Thus ordered by her husband, she took up her abode in a Kadamba tree in the forest of Vrindāvana. Balarāma, in his walks smelling the pleasant fragrance of the liquor produced from that tree, resumed his ancient passion for strong drink. Whilst in a state of intoxication caused by this juice he ordered the river Yamuna to come to him that he might bathe in her. As she refused, he threw his ploughshare into the stream, and dragging her towards him, made her follow him wherever he went, until, his anger being appeased, he set her free.

On his return to Dwaraka, after this visit to his friends, he married Revati, daughter of King Raivata. This king wishing to obtain a suitable husband for his daughter repaired to Brahmā for advice, who, expatiating on the glories of Vishnu, detained his suppliant in heaven for ages. On his return, he was surprised to find that during his long absence men had deteriorated in goodness, size, and strength; but following Brahmā's counsel, he went to Dwaraka, and offered his daughter to Balarāma, who accepted the offer. Balarāma was astonished at her immense height, but by the use of his ploughshare, however, managed to reduce her to a proper size. On one occasion, as Balarāma and Devaki were together, they were greatly annoyed by a demon named Dwivida, who had the power to assume various forms. He came as a monkey, and being a source of annoyance to gods and men, chiefly through interrupting the sacrifices, was felled by a blow of Balarāma's heavy fist.

Though the brothers Krishna and Balarāma were generally the best of friends, there was once a most violent quarrel between them. A man named Satadhanwan was suspected of stealing a most valuable jewel.* Krishna and Balarāma pursuing him, came to a part of the country where the roads were so bad that the horses could not drag their chariot. Balarāma therefore remained behind, whilst Krishna followed the supposed thief on foot. When within reach, the never-missing discus was thrown, and the man fell headless, but the gem was not to be found. On Krishna's return to his brother without the jewel, Balarāma, believing he had stolen it, "flew into a violent rage, and said to Vasudeva: 'Shame light upon you to be thus greedy of wealth! I acknowledge no brotherhood with you. Here lies my path; go whither you please, I have done with you, with Dwaraka, with all our house. It is of no use to seek to impose on me with your perjuries." Balarāma proceeded to Videha, where for three years he remained the guest of King Janaka; then, his anger being appeased, he acknowledged that he had misjudged his brother, and returned to his home at Dwaraka.

As the two brothers died about the same time an account of Balarāma's end will be found in the chapter descriptive of Krishna.

9. THE BUDDHA AVATĀRA

This incarnation of Vishnu is "originally foreign to the cycle of the Avatāras of Vishnu, and therefore is only briefly alluded to in some of Purānas. Where this is done, the intention must have been to effect a compromise between Brāhmanism and Buddhism, by trying to represent the latter religion as not irreconcilably antagonistic to the former." † Colonel Kennedy, ‡ on the other hand, argues that the Buddha of the Purānas and Buddha the founder of the Buddhist system of religion have

---

*For a fuller account of this jewel, see p. 207.
†Goldstücker, Chambers's Cyclopædia.
‡"Hindu Mythology," p. 248.

nothing in common but the name, and that the attempted identification of these two is simply the work of European

Buddha

scholars, who have not been sufficiently careful to collect information, and to weigh the evidence they have had before them. There can be little doubt that Colonel Kennedy's view is untenable. Seeing the bitter antagonism that existed between the advocates of the rival systems, it need occasion no surprise that full accounts of Buddha are not to be found in Brāhmanical books, nor that the meagre accounts that are there should try to represent him as a despicable character. The Brāhmanical writers were far too shrewd to admit that one who exerted such immense influence, and won so many disciples, could be other than an incarnation of deity; but as his teaching was opposed to their own they cleverly say that it was to mislead the enemies of the gods that he promulgated his doctrine, that they, becoming weak and wicked through error, might be led once again to seek the help and blessing of those whom they had previously neglected.

Buddhist Temple and Dagoba at Kelaniya, Ceylon

The Purānic account of Buddha will be given, supplemented by further particulars of his life and work from Buddhist writings.

In the "Bhāgavata Purāna"* are only four short passages respecting him. "At the commencement of the Kali-yuga will Vishnu become incarnate in Kikata, under the name of Buddha, the son of Jina, for the purpose of deluding the enemies of the gods." "The Undiscernible Being, having assumed a mortal form, preached heretical doctrines in the three cities founded by Māya (and in Kāsi), for the purpose of destroying, by deluding them, the enemies of the gods, steadfast in the religion prescribed by the Vedas." "Praise to the pure Buddha, the deluder of the Daityas and the Dānavas." "By his words, as Buddha, Vishnu deludes the heretics."

In the Skanda,† the legend, of which the Bhāgavata gives but the merest outline, is more fully given. There was a dire famine in the earth, owing to the failure of rains for six successive years. On this account Brahmā in great distress visited a prince named Ripanjaya, and told him that if he would become king, the gods would serve him, and his name should be changed to Divodāsa. On asking why he was chosen before all others, Brahmā tells him, "All other kings are wicked, and the gods will not shower rain upon the earth unless you accept the government. Divodāsa accedes to Brahmā's request on condition that that deity would assist him and that all the other gods would forsake the earth, so that he might reign without a rival, and be the only one who could confer happiness on men. Brahmā, in fulfilling this condition, with some difficulty persuaded Siva to forsake Kāsi (Benares), his favourite dwelling-place.

Divodāsa fixed his throne at Kāsi, where for 8000 years he ruled with the greatest benefit to men. The gods becoming jealous of his power went to Vrihaspati, their preceptor, and, whilst they spoke well of the effects of the king's government, complained that he, and not the gods, was benefited by it. Siva

---

*Kennedy, "Hindu Mythology," p. 250.
†Ibid., p. 423.

especially was annoyed at his enforced absence from Kāsi; for although he sent several times to make inquiries about its inhabitants, his messengers were too happy on earth to return to their lord in heaven. Vishnu, accompanied by Lakshmi and Garuda, at Siva's request, "then proceeded to Kāsi, a little to the north of which he formed by his divine power a pleasant abode named Dharma-kshetra, and there, attended by his lovely spouse, did he reside under the form of Buddha, while Lakshmi became a female recluse of that sect. Garuda also appeared under the name of Panyakirti, as a pupil with a book in his hand, and attentively listening to the delusive instructions of his preceptor (Buddha), who with a low, sweet, and affectionate voice taught him various branches of natural and supernatural religion."

Vishnu, as Buddha, taught that "the universe was without a creator; it is false therefore to assert that there is one universal and Supreme Spirit, for Brahmā, Vishnu, Rudra, and the rest are names of mere corporeal beings like ourselves. Death is a peaceful sleep: why fear it?" He further taught that "we should guard as our own life the life of another; that pleasure is the only heaven, and pain the only hell, and liberation from ignorance the sole beatitude. Sacrifices are acts of folly." Through the exertions of Panyakirti, these doctrines soon spread through the city; whilst Lakshmi deluded the women by teaching them to "place all happiness in sensual pleasures; as the body must decay, let us, before it becomes dust, enjoy the pleasures which it gives. The distinction of castes has been vainly imagined." As Lakshmi gave numerous boons to her disciples, her influence was great, and her teaching spread widely.

As a result of the dissemination of these doctrines in the city, Divodāsa became dispirited. Vishnu in the form of a Brāhman appeared to him, and hears an account of his troubles, and is delighted as he expresses a wish to resign his crown, The king mentions a number of cases in which virtuous men have had to suffer, owing to the power of the gods, and inquires how he can obtain final beatitude. Vishnu informs him that he has acted unwisely in compelling Siva to forsake Kasi, and advises him to consecrate an image of that god, by worshipping which he will obtain the fulfilment of his desires. Divodāsa follows this counsel, inaugurates his son as king, and as he is worshipping the Linga he had set up, Siva appears and conducts him to Kailasa (Siva's heaven). It is the common belief of the people in the west of India, that when Vishnu had effected the apostasy of Divodāsa, he was prevailed upon to terminate the propagation of his heretical opinions, and disappeared in a deep well at Gya.

The following legend from the "Siva Purāna"* gives another reason for the rise of Buddhism. A famous Rishi named Gautama, with his virtuous wife named Ahalyā, performed during a thousand years a severe *tapas* (penance) in the southern country near the mountain Brahmādri. During this time there was a severe drought, to remove which, Gautama worshipped Varuna for six months with great fervour, when the deity promised to grant any boon that should be asked. Gautama asked for rain, but Varuna said, "How can I transgress the divine command? Ask some boon, which it is in my power to grant." Gautama then desired Varuna to cause a surpassingly beautiful hermitage to appear, shaded from the sun by fragrant and fruit-bearing trees, where holy men and women by meditation shall be liberated from pain, sorrow, and anxiety; "and as thou art lord of water, let it enjoy a perennial fountain." Varuna granted this request, and the hermitage of Gautama became "the loveliest on the terrestrial orb."

One day as the disciples of Gautama went to the fountain, some Brāhman women tried to prevent them drawing water until they had filled their own pots. Ahalyā going herself was subjected daily to the same annoyance: the Brāhman women would not allow her to draw water before they had themselves obtained all they required. These women, not satisfied with

---

*Kennedy, "Hindu Mythology," p. 253.

annoying the ascetics, complained to their husbands of the unkind treatment they alleged they had received from Ahalyā.

Their husbands resorted to Ganesa for advice, who being pleased with their devotion promised a boon; they asked that Gautama might be made to leave his hermitage without their incurring the sin of driving him away. To this Ganesa reluctantly consented; and in order to effect this object he transformed himself into a poor debilitated cow, and walked into a field of rice where Gautama was standing, and began to eat the grain. The sage, knowing nothing of this disguise, took up a straw and tried to drive the cow away; no sooner did he touch it than it fell down dead. Having incurred the enormous guilt of killing a cow, the poor man had to leave the neighbourhood.

Gautama and his wife removed to a distance; but until he had expiated his sin they could not perform acceptable worship. Gautama seeks the Brāhmans, and asking how he can be free from his crime, is told to walk round the mountain of Brahmā a hundred times; bathe in the Ganges, and consecrate and worship ten million images of Siva. As he is propitiating him, Siva, delighted with the man's earnestness, appears, informs him of the trick by which Ganesa had driven him from the hermitage, and brings the Ganges so near that he can bathe in it easily. Tradition says that Gautama was so disgusted with the conduct of the Brāhmans that he separated himself from their communion, and established a new system of religion, which for a time eclipsed Brāhmanism.

The following extracts, giving an account of Buddha, are from the "Lalita-Vistara,"* a Buddhist work from which M. Barthélemy St. Hilaire has taken the materials for his work, "La Boudda et sa Religion."

"Buddha, or more correctly The Buddha—for Buddha is an

---

*Max-Müller, "Chips," vol. i. p. 210 ff.

appellative, meaning enlightened—was born at Kapilavastu, the capital of a kingdom of that name, situated at the foot of the mountains of Nepal, north of the present Oude. His father, the King of Kapilavastu, was of the family of the Sākyas, and belonged to the clan of the Gautamas. His mother was Māyādevi, daughter of King Suprabuddha, and need we say that she was beautiful, as he was powerful and just? Buddha was

Buddha

therefore by birth of the Kshattriya, or warrior caste, and he took the name of Sākya from his family, and that of Gautama from his clan, claiming a kind of spiritual relationship with the honoured race of Gautamas. The name of Buddha, or The Buddha, dates from a latter period of his life, and so probably does Siddhārtha (he whose objects have been accomplished), though we are told that it was given him in his childhood.

His mother died seven days after his birth, and the father confided the child to the care of his deceased wife's sister, who, however, had been his wife even before the mother's death. The child grew up a most beautiful and most accomplished boy, who soon knew more than his masters could teach him. He refused to take part in the games of his playmates, and never felt so happy as when he could sit alone, lost in meditation in the deep shadows of the forest. It was there that his father found him when he had thought him lost; and, in order to prevent the young prince from becoming a dreamer, the king determined to marry him at once. When the subject was mentioned by the aged ministers to the future heir to the throne, he demanded seven days for reflection, and, convinced at last that not even marriage could disturb the calm of his mind, he allowed the ministers to look out for a princess. The princess selected was the beautiful Gopā, the daughter of Dandapani. Though her father objected at first to her marrying a young prince who was represented to him as deficient in manliness and intellect, he gladly gave his consent when he saw the royal suitor distancing all his rivals in feats of arms and power of mind. Their marriage proved one of the happiest, but the prince remained, as he had been before, absorbed in meditations on the problems of life and death. 'Nothing is stable on earth,' he used to say; 'nothing is real. Like is like the spark produced by the friction of wood. It is lighted and is extinguished—we know not whence it came, or whither it goes. It is like the sound of a lyre, and the wise man asks in vain from whence it came and whither it goes. There must be some supreme intelligence where we can find rest. If I attained it I could bring light to man; if I were free myself, I could deliver the world.' The king, who perceived the melancholy mood of the young prince, tried everything to divert him from his speculations; but all was in vain. Three of the most ordinary events that could happen to any man proved of the utmost importance in the career of Buddha.

"One day, when the prince with a large retinue was driving through the Eastern gate of the city on the way to one of his parks, he met on the road an old man, broken and decrepit. One could see the veins and muscles over the whole of his body; his teeth chattered, he was covered with wrinkles, bald, and hardly able to utter hollow and unmelodious sounds. He was bent on his stick, and all his limbs and joints trembled. 'Who is this man?' said the prince to his coachman. 'He is small and weak, his flesh and his blood are dried up, his muscles stick to his skin, his teeth chatter, his body is wasted away; leaning on his stick, he is hardly able to walk, stumbling at every step. Is there something peculiar in his family, or is this the common lot of all created beings?'

"'Sir,' replied the coachman, 'that man is sinking under old age, his senses have become obscure, suffering has destroyed his strength, and he is despised by his relations. He is without support and useless, and people have abandoned him, like a dead tree in a forest. But this is not peculiar to his family. In every creature youth is defeated by old age. Your father, your mother, all your relations, all your friends, will come to the same state: this is the appointed end of all creatures.'

"'Alas!' replied the prince,' are creatures so ignorant, so weak and foolish, as to be proud of the youth by which they are intoxicated, not seeing the old age which awaits them? As for me, I go away. Coachman turn my chariot quickly. What am I, the future prey of old age—what have I to do with pleasure?' and the young prince returned to the city without going to the park.

"Another time the prince was driving through the Southern gate to his pleasure-garden, when he perceived in the road a man suffering from illness, parched with fever, his body wasted, covered with mud, without a friend, without a home, hardly able to breathe, and frightened at the sight of himself and the approach of death. Having questioned his coachman, and received from him the answer which he expected, the young prince said: 'Alas! health is but the sport of a dream, and the fear of suffering must take this frightful form. Where is the wise man, who, after having seen what he is, could any longer think of joy and pleasure?' The prince turned his chariot, and returned to the city.

"A third time he was driving to his pleasure-garden through the Western gate, when he saw a dead body on the road, lying on a bier and covered with a cloth. The friends stood about crying, sobbing, tearing their hair, covering their heads with dust, striking their breasts, and uttering wild cries. The prince, again calling his coachman to witness this painful scene, exclaimed: 'Oh, woe to youth, which must be destroyed by old age! Woe to health, which must be destroyed by so many diseases! Woe to this life, where a man must remain for so short a time!' Then, betraying for the first time his intentions, the young prince said, 'Let us turn back; I must think how to accomplish deliverance.'

"A last meeting put an end to his meditation. He was driving through the Northern gate on the way to his pleasure-gardens, when he saw a mendicant who appeared outwardly calm, subdued, looking downwards, wearing with an air of dignity his religious vestment and carrying an alms-bowl.

"'Who is this man?' asked the prince.

"'Sir,' replied the coachman, 'this man is one of those who are called *bhikshus* or mendicants. He has renounced all pleasures, all desires, and leads a life of austerity. He tries to conquer himself. He has become a devotee. Without passion, without envy, he walks about asking for alms.'

"'This is good and well said,' replied the prince. 'The life of a devotee has always been praised by the wise. It will be my refuge, and the refuge of all other creatures. It will lead us to a real life, to happiness and immortality.' With these words, the young prince turned his chariot and returned to the city.

"After having declared to his father and his wife his intention of retiring from the world, Buddha left his palace one night when all the guards that were to have watched him were asleep. After travelling the whole night, he gave his horse and his ornaments to his groom, and sent him back to Kapilavastu. 'A monument,' remarks the author of the 'Lalita-Vistara,' 'is still to be seen on the spot where the coachman turned back.' Hiouen Thsang saw the same monument at the edge of a large forest, on his road to Kusinagara, a city now in ruins, and situated about fifty miles E.S.E. from Gorakpore.

"Buddha first went to Vaisali, and became the pupil of a famous Brāhman, who had gathered round him 300 disciples. Having learnt all that the Brāhman could teach him, Buddha went away disappointed. He had not found the road to salvation. He then tried another Brāhman at Rājagriha, the capital of Magadha or Behar, who had 700 disciples, and there, too, he looked in vain for the means of deliverance. He left him, followed by five of his fellow-students, and for six years retired into solitude, near a village named Uruvilva, subjecting himself to the most severe penances, previous to his appearing in the world as a teacher. At the end of this period, however, he arrived at the conviction that asceticism, far from giving peace of mind and preparing the way to salvation, was a snare and a stumbling-block in the way of truth. He gave up his exercises, and was at once deserted as an apostate by his five disciples. Left to himself, he now began to elaborate his own system. He had learned that neither the doctrines nor the austerities of the Brāhmans were of any avail for accomplishing the deliverance of man, and for freeing him from the fear of old age, disease, and death. After long meditations and ecstatic visions, he at last imagined that he had arrived at that true knowledge which discloses the cause, and thereby destroys the fear, of all the changes inherent in life. It was from the moment when he arrived at this knowledge that he claimed the name of Buddha the enlightened. Buddha hesitated for a time whether he should keep his knowledge to himself or communicate it to the world. Compassion for the sufferings of man prevailed, and the young prince became the founder of a religion which, after more than 2000 years, is still professed by 455,000,000 of human beings.

"The further history of the new teacher is very simple. He

proceeded to Benares, which at all times has been the principal seat of learning in India, and the first converts he made were the five fellow-students who had left him when he threw off the yoke of the Brāhmanical observances. Many others followed, but as the 'Lalita-Vistara' breaks off at Buddha's arrival at Benares, we have no further consecutive account of the rapid progress of his doctrine. From what we can gather from scattered notices in the Buddhist canon, he was invited by the King of Magadha, Bimbisāra, to his capital, Rājagriha. Many of his lectures are represented as having been delivered at the monastery of Kalavataka, with which the king or some rich merchant had presented him; others on the Vulture Peak, one of the five hills which surround the ancient capital.

"Three of his most famous disciples—Sarrputra, Kātyāyana, and Maudgalyāyana—joined him during his stay in Magadha, where he enjoyed for many years the friendship of the king. The king was afterwards assassinated by his son Ajātāsatru, and then we hear of Buddha as settled for a time at Srāvasti, north of the Ganges. Most of Buddha's lectures were delivered at Srāvasti, the capital of Kosala, and the King of Kosala himself, Prāsenagit, became a convert to his doctrine. After an absence of twelve years, we are told that Buddha visited his father at Kapilavastu, on which occasion he performed several miracles, and converted all the Sākyas to his faith. His own wife became one of his followers, and, with his aunt, offer the first instance of female Buddhist devotees in India.

"We have fuller particulars again of the last days of Buddha's life. He had attained the good age of three-score years and ten, and had been on a visit to Rājagriha, where the king, Ajātāsatru, the former enemy of Buddha and the assassin of his own father, had joined the congregation, after making a public confession of his crimes. On his return he was followed by a large number of disciples, and when on the point of crossing the Ganges, he stood on a square stone, and, turning his eyes back towards Rājagriha, he said, full of emotion, 'This is the last time that I shall see that city.' He likewise visited Vaisali, and, after taking leave of it, he had nearly reached the city of Kusināgara, when his vital strength began to fail. He halted in a forest, and, while sitting under a Sāl tree, he gave up the ghost, or, as a Buddhist would say, entered into Nirvāna."

The following verses by Dr. Muir* are a translation of part of the "Lalita-Vistara," from which the quotations given above were made:—

> "On Himālaya's lonely steep
>   There lived of old an holy sage,
>   Of shrivelled form, and bent with age,
> Inured to meditation deep.

> "He—when great Buddha had been born,
>   The glory of the Sākya race,
>   Endowed with every holy grace,
> To save the suffering world forlorn—

> "Beheld strange portents, signs which taught
>   The wise that that auspicious time
>   Had witnessed some event sublime,
> With universal blessing fraught.

> "The sky with joyful gods was thronged:
>   He heard their voice with glad acclaim
>   Besounding loudly Buddha's name,
> While echoes clear their shouts prolonged.

> "The cause exploring, far and wide
>   The sage's vision ranged; with awe,
>   Within a cradle laid, he saw
> Far off the babe, the Sākyas' pride.

---

*O. S. T., ii. 496.

"With longing seized this child to view
 At hand, and clasp, and homage pay,
 Athwart the sky he took his way
By magic art, and swan-like flew;

"And came to King Suddhōdan's gates;
 And entrance craved—'Go, royal page,
 And tell thy lord an ancient sage
To see the king permission waits.'

"The page obeyed, and joined his hands
 Before the prince, and said, 'A sage
 Of shrivelled form, and bowed with age,
Before the gate, my sovereign, stands,

"'And humbly asks to see the king.'
 To whom Suddhōdan cried, 'We greet
 All such with joy; with honour meet
The holy man before us bring!'

"The saint beside the monarch stood,
 And spake his blessing—' Thine be health,
 With length of life, and might, and wealth;
And ever seek thy people's good.'

"With all due forms and meet respect
 The king received the holy man
 And bade him sit; and then began—
'Great sage, I do not recollect

"'That I thy venerable face
 Have ever seen before; allow
 That I inquire what brings thee now
From thy far distant dwelling-place.'

"'To see thy babe,' the saint replies,
 'I come from Himālaya's steeps.'
 The king rejoins, 'My infant sleeps;
A moment wait until he rise.'

"'Such great ones ne'er,' the Rishi spake,
 'In torpor long their senses steep,
 Nor softly love luxurious sleep;
The infant prince will soon awake.'

"The wondrous child, alert to rise,
 At will his slumbers light dispelled.
 His father's arms the infant held
Before the sage's longing eyes.

"The babe beholding, passing bright,
 More glorious than the race divine,
 And marked with every noble sign,
The saint was whelmed with deep delight;

"And crying, 'Lo! an infant graced
 With every charm of form I greet!'
 He fell before the Buddha's feet,
With fingers joined, and round him paced.

"Next round the babe his arms he wound,
 And 'One,' he said, 'of two careers
 Of fame awaits in coming years
The child in whom these signs are found.

"'If such an one at home abide,
 He shall become a king, whose sway
 Supreme a mighty armed array
On earth shall 'stablish far and wide.

"'If, spurning worldly pomp as vain,
  He choose to lead a tranquil life,
  And wander forth from home and wife,
He then a Buddha's rank shall gain.'

"He spoke, and on the infant gazed,
  When tears suffused his aged eyes;
  His bosom heaved with heavy sighs;
Then King Suddhōdan asked, amazed—

"'Say, holy man, what makes thee weep
  And deeply sigh? Does any fate
  Malign the child await?
May heavenly powers my infant keep!'

"'For thy fair infant's weal no fears
  Disturb me, king,' the Bishi cried;
  'No ill can such a child betide;
My own sad lot commands my tears.

"'In every grace complete, thy son
  Of truth shall perfect insight gain,
  And far sublimer fame attain
Than ever lawgiver has won.

"'He such a wheel of sacred lore
  Shall speed on earth to roll, as yet
  Hath never been in motion set
By priest, or sage, or god of yore.

"'The world of men and gods to bless,
  The way of rest and peace to teach,
  A holy law thy son shall preach—
A law of stainless righteousness.

"'By him shall suffering men be freed
    From weakness, sickness, pain, and grief;
    From all the ills shall find relief
Which hatred, love, illusion breed.

"'His hands shall loose the chains of all
    Who groan in earthly bonds confined;
    With healing touch the wounds shall bind
Of those whom pain's sharp arrows gall.

"'His words of power shall put to flight
    The dull array of leaden clouds
    Which helpless mortals' vision shrouds,
And clear their intellectual sight.

"'By him shall men, who, now untaught,
    In devious paths of error stray,
    Be led to find a perfect way—
To final calm at last be brought.

"'But once, O king, in many years,
    The fig-tree somewhere flowers, perhaps;
    So, after countless ages lapse,
A Buddha -once on earth appears.

"'And now, at length, this blessed time
    Has come: for he, who cradled lies
    An infant there before thine eyes,
Shall be a Buddha in his prime.

"'Full, perfect insight gaining, he
    Shall rescue endless myriads tost
    On life's rough ocean waves, and lost,
And grant them immortality.

"'But I am old, and frail, and worn;
   I shall not live the day to see
   When this thy wondrous child shall free
From woe the suffering world forlorn.

"'Tis thus mine own unhappy fate
   Which bids me mourn, and weep, and sigh;
   The Buddha's triumph now is nigh,
But, ah! for me it comes too late!'

"When thus this aged saint, inspired,
   Had all the infant's greatness told,
   The king his wondrous son extolled,
And sang, with pious ardour fired—

"'Thee, child, th' immortals worship all,
   The great Physician, born to cure
   All ills that hapless men endure;
I, too, before thee prostrate fall!'

"And now—his errand done—the sage,
   Dismissed with gifts and human due,
   Athwart the ether swanlike flew,
And reached again his hermitage."

Buddhism, the system of religion taught by Buddha, starts with the doctrine common to it and Hinduism of transmigration.* It then goes on to say that pain and pleasure

---

*In Hinduism it is the transmigration of souls from the lowest to the highest scale, until they become fit for absorption into the Divine from whence they came. At its close each life is carefully judged, and when next the person returns to the earth he is born in a higher stage if good preponderated; in a lower if the evil turned the scale. In Buddhism, which denies the existence of souls, the transmigration is somewhat different in form. As soon as a person dies a new being

are simply the result of Karma (works), no notice whatever being taken of the existence or non-existence of God. It assumes that existence is and must be miserable; and that the highest conceivable good is to obtain entire exemption from existence. Death does not necessarily bring this exemption; it may be but an entrance into a worse form of it than is at present endured. Buddha's four "Sublime verities," containing the germ of his system, are as follows:—The first is that pain exists; the second, that desire is the cause of pain; the third, that pain can be ended by Nirvāna, or exemption from existence, practical annihilation; the fourth shows the way that leads to Nirvāna. The great thing is to get rid of desire, and when this is accomplished, the soul is ready for complete Nirvāna, and a man dying in this state will not again be born. He taught the evil of caste distinctions, and all who embraced his tenets became members of a great brotherhood. Instead of the painful mortifications and costly sacrifices by which the Hindus were compelled to make expiation for sin, he taught that confession and promise of amendment were all that was necessary. Its moral code is one of the most perfect in the world: the spring of all virtue is Maitri, which can only be translated as charity or love. "It does not express friendship, or the feeling of particular affection which a man has for one or more of his fellow-creatures, but that universal feeling which inspires us with good-will towards all men and constant willingness to help them."*

There is one peculiarity of the followers of Buddha as

---

is produced in a more or less miserable condition, according to the "Karma," the sum total of the good or evil in all its many previous lives. Practically there is no great difference between these views. For though the Hindu believes that the same soul passes through countless changes in successive lives, there is no memory of previous experience, so that each life is separate and distinct from what went before. It is a formal rather than a real difference.

*Burnouf, quoted by Max-Müller, "Chips," i. 222.

compared with the Hindus, viz. the preservation of and veneration for relics of their founder. With the exception of a legend stating that Krishna's bones were placed in the image of Jagannāth, and another teaching that Vishnu cut the dead body of Sati into fifty-one parts, each of which is now enshrined in a temple, we have no record of relics being preserved by the Hindus. But the Buddhists profess to have carefully preserved parts of their great leader, and enshrine them in Dagobas. One of the most celebrated of these is represented on page 226. A tooth of Buddha is believed to be kept in it; in others a single hair is most religiously guarded. These Dagobas are not temples, though in some cases they form part of buildings that are, or have been, used for worship.

10. THE KALKI AVATĀRA

This incarnation, unlike those already described, has yet to be made. It is the hope of the Hindus, that he who has so frequently visited the earth to restore order and happiness will come yet again to inaugurate a reign of universal goodness, peace, and prosperity. When Vishnu in the form of Krishna reascended to heaven, the Fourth or Kali Yuga commenced, which, as its name implies, is an age of strife and dissension. In the "Vishnu Purāna" the character of this age is vividly described in words that seem prophetic. At its termination Vishnu is expected to come again, bearing the name Kalki, to put an end to wickedness, and establish a kingdom of righteousness similar to the First or Kritā Yuga —the age of Truth. These four ages, in the same order and with similar characteristics, will again and again be experienced until the final end of all things shall come. The following extract from the "Vishnu Purāna"* will give an idea of the evils of the present age, which Kalki is to remove.

---

*Page 622.

In Magadha a sovereign named Viswasphatika will extirpate the Kshattriya race, elevate fishermen, barbarians, Brāhmans, and other castes to power; whilst Sudras, outcasts and barbarians will be masters of the Indus, Darvika, Chandrabhāgā, and Kashmir. "The kings will be of churlish

Kalki

spirit, violent temper, and ever addicted to falsehood and wickedness. They will inflict death on women, children, and cows; they will seize the property of subjects, be of limited power, and will, for the most part, rapidly rise and fall; their lives will be short, their desires insatiable, and they will display but little piety. The people of various countries intermingling with them will follow their example; and the barbarians being powerful in the patronage of princes, whilst purer tribes are neglected, the people will perish. Wealth and piety will decrease day by day, until the world shall be wholly depraved. Property alone will confer rank, wealth will be the only source of devotion passion will be the sole bond of union between the sexes falsehood will be the only means of success in litigation and women will be the objects merely of sensual gratification. Earth will be venerated only for its mineral treasures (i.e. no spot will be peculiarly sacred); the Brāhmanical thread will constitute a Brāhman; external types will be the only distinctions of the several orders of life, dishonesty will be the universal means of subsistence, weakness will be the cause of dependence, menace and presumption will be the subterfuge for learning, liberality will be devotion, simple ablution will be purification (i.e. gifts will be made from the impulse of ordinary feeling, not in connection with religious rites or as an act of devotion, and ablution will be performed for pleasure or comfort, not religiously with prescribed ceremonies and prayers). Mutual assent will be marriage, fine clothes will be dignity, and water afar off will be esteemed a holy spring. The people, unable to bear the heavy burdens imposed upon them by their avaricious sovereigns, will take refuge among the valleys, and be glad to feed upon wild honey, herbs, roots, fruits, flowers, and leaves; their only covering will be the bark of trees, and they will be exposed to cold and wind, and sun and rain. No man's life will exceed three-and-twenty years. Thus in the Kali Age shall decay flourish, until the human race approaches annihilation." It is rather strange that the condition of men, in what appeared to the writer of this Purāna as the most miserable he could imagine, where their dress was bark and their food consisted of roots and fruits, was in the earliest ages regarded as the most desirable. It was thus the old Rishis lived, who are held in the greatest esteem.

"When the practices taught by the Vedas and the institutes of law shall nearly have ceased, and the close of the Kali Age shall be nigh, a portion of that divine being who exists of his own spiritual nature in the character of Brahmā, and who is the beginning and the end, and who comprehends all things, shall descend upon the earth. He will be born in the family of Vishnuyasas, an eminent Brāhman of Sambhal village, as Kalki, endowed with the eight superhuman faculties. By his irresistible might he will destroy all the Mlechchhas (outcasts), thieves, and all whose minds are devoted to iniquity. He will then re-establish righteousness upon earth; and the minds of those who live at the end of the Kali Age shall be awakened and be made pellucid as crystal. The men who are changed in virtue of that particular time shall be as the seeds of human beings, and shall give birth to a race who shall follow the laws of the Krita Age, or Age of Purity."

In the descriptions of Kalki, and in pictures, he is represented as a white man riding upon or bowing down before a white horse, and with a sword in his hand: he is the purifier of the present degenerate age, and the restorer of purity and goodness.

JAGANNĀTH

This deity is not reckoned as one of the Avataras of Vishnu in the Puranic lists. Tradition declares him to be, and common belief accepts him as, an appearance of Vishnu himself, and not the incarnation of a portion of his essence. There is, however, considerable reason for doubting whether originally Jagannāth—the Lord of the World—had any connection with Vishnu. It is possible that he was the local divinity of some now unknown tribe, whose worship was engrafted into Hinduism; and the new god, when admitted into the Pantheon, was regarded as another manifestation of Vishnu; or what is more probable, as Puri was a head centre of Buddhism, when that system was placed under a ban and its followers persecuted, the temple was utilized for Hinduism, and Jagannāth, nominally a Hindu deity, was really Buddhistic; the strange, unfinished image being nothing else than a disguised form of the symbols of the central doctrine of the Buddhist faith. Possibly, in order to be free from persecution, it was taught that this was a form of

Vishnu. There are several legends professing to account for the form in which he is worshipped, and for the peculiar sanctity of Puri, the chief place of his worship. There is a peculiarity

Jagannāth

in the phraseology employed by the people who visit his shrine: they speak of going to see Jagannāth, not to worship him as is the case with other gods; and it is the sight of the image in the temple, or as it is being bathed, or drawn in its ponderous car, that is so eagerly desired as a means by which sin in the worshipper is destroyed.

Professor Goldstücker* gives the following legend from the Ain-i-Akbari, in which some of the ordinary notions of the people respecting Jagannāth are described. A king desirous of founding a city sent a learned Brāhman to select a proper site. The Brāhman after a long search reached the seashore, and there saw a crow diving into the water, which, having washed its body, made obeisance to the sea. Understanding the language of birds, he learned from the crow that if he remained there

---

*Chambers's Cyclopædia, *s.v.*

a short time, he would comprehend the wonders of the land. The king, apprised of this occurrence, built a large city and temple on the spot near where the crow had appeared. One night the Rāja in a dream heard a voice saying to him: "On a certain day cast thine eyes on the seashore, when there will arise from the water a piece of wood 52 in. long and 18 in. broad: this is the true form of the deity; take it up and keep it hidden in thine house seven days, and in whatever shape it shall then appear, place it in the temple and worship it." The Rāja acted upon the advice given in his dream; and, when he had set up the image received from the sea, called it Jagannāth, the Lord of the World, and it became the object of worship of all ranks of people.

Ward* gives a somewhat fuller account. When Kishna was accidentally shot by the hunter Jara, his bones were left to rot under the tree where he died, until some pious person collected and placed them in a box.† There they remained, until Indradhumna, a king who was earnestly striving to propitiate Vishnu, was directed to form an image, and place in it these bone,; with the assurance that he would afterwards obtain a rich reward for his religious deeds. Indradhumna wishing to follow this advice, prayed to Visvakarma to assist him by making the image. The architect of the gods consented to do this, but was most careful in explaining to the king that if any one looked at him, or in any way disturbed him whilst he was at

---

*Vol. ii. 163.

†What appears far more likely is that some valued relics of Buddha were placed in the image, but as it was dangerous at that time to avow any connection with him and his worship, these relics were said to be the bones of Krishna. To touch a dead body', according to Hinduism, is pollution; it seems, therefore, altogether opposed to the spirit of Hinduism to enshrine a bone in an image. Only by some such fiction could the relics of Buddha be saved. There is much in the rites at Pari to countenance the idea that though professedly Hindu it is really a Buddhist shrine.

work, he would immediately desist, and leave the image in an unfinished state. The king promised to observe this condition, and Visvakarma commenced his work. In one night he raised a grand temple in the blue mountains of Orissa, and then began to make the image. For fifteen days the king managed, with difficulty, to restrain his impatience, but then foolishly tried to see the god at work. The angry deity at once ceased, as he had threatened, and the image was left with a most ugly face, and without hands or feet. The king, exceedingly grieved as he saw the result of his curiosity, went in his distress to Brahmā, who comforted him with the promise that he would render the image famous in its present form. The king invited the gods to be present at its inauguration. Several accepted the invitation, Brahmā himself officiated as priest, and gave eyes and a soul to the god. Thus the fame of Jagannāth was completely established. The original image of this deity is closely copied in other places besides Puri; and by his side there is generally an image of Krishna's favourite brother Balarāma, and his sister Subhadrā.

The following is translated from a Bengali account of Jagannāth: Nārāyana (Vishnu) and his wife having taken up their abode in the blue mountains of Orissa, where he was known by the name of Nilmādhava, was visited by great numbers of gods and men, and the neighbourhood obtained the name of Mokshyakhettra (the field of emancipation from births). A king named Indradhumna, a son of the Sun, a devout worshipper of Vishnu, being anxious to pay a visit to Nilmādhava, before starting, sent Vidyapati, the brother of his family priest, to learn the way to Orissa, that he might act as guide. On his return he gave such an account of all he had seen, that the king was more anxious to go than ever. Having made his arrangements, taking his family with him, the king went under the guidance of Vidapati, but, on his arrival there, was most grievously disappointed to learn that the god had withdrawn himself from the public gaze. As he cried with sorrow and vexation, a voice from the sky reached his ear: "As you cannot see Nilmādhava, make a wooden image and worship that; Nārāyana will inhabit it, and by the sight of the image you and others will obtain final emancipation." The king followed this advice. As he was preparing to make the image, Nārāyana himself, in the form of an old Brāhman named Visvakarma, came and offered to form the image in fifteen days. The offer was accepted, and within the specified time the image of Jagannāth, with those of his brother and sister, was made.

The peculiarity of the worship of Jagannāth is that his image is not only worshipped in its proper temple but on three days of the year is exposed to public view. On the first of these days, called the Snān Jāttra (Bathing Festival), the idol is taken from its shrine, and on a lofty platform, in sight of vast multitudes, bathed by the priests. This exposure is supposed to be productive of a cold, so that, ten days after, the Rath Jattra (Car Festival) is held; at this time the image is placed on an immense car made expressly for the purpose, and taken to the temple of another god for a change of air. The car is drawn by the excited crowd; the poorer and more ignorant people believing it to be a meritorious act to assist in dragging it. After remaining for a few days, the third festival (the Return) is held, at which, with somewhat diminished fervour, the idol is dragged back to its home. Puri is the place where it is believed the deity is seen with greater benefit to the worshippers; but it is considered that there is considerable religious merit obtained by seeing, and assisting to draw, his car in places nearer home. Every town and almost every large village has its festival of this god; and with the promise of so desirable a gift—salvation from sin—it is not to be wondered at that there should be a great wish to see him.

CHAITANYA

Chaitanya is believed by his followers to have been an incarnation of Vishnu; and as he lived in historical times, about 300 years ago, it is interesting to notice how a human being came to be regarded as divine. He is worshipped in Nadiya in Bengal, and it is a singular fact, that, at his shrine, there is a very small image of Krishna, of whom he was a disciple and apostle, whilst the image of Chaitanya is large and conspicuous. The Hindus who acknowledge this god say that, amongst the many incarnations of Vishnu, four are most important. The first, in the Satya-yuga, called the Suklavarna (the white), was Ananta; the second, in the Treta-yuga, called the Raktavarna (the red), was that of Kapiladeva; the third, in the Dwārpara-yuga, called the Krishnavarna (the black), was Krishna; and the last, in the Kali-yuga, called the Pitavarna (the yellow), was Chaitanya.

The founder of the sect, of which Chaitanya was the most illustrious member, was a Brāhman named Adaitya, who lived at Santipore in Bengal. Another leader, named Nityananda, was born at Nadiya a short time before Chaitanya. Chaitanya's father was a Brāhman, named Jagannāth Misra; his mother's name was Suchi; their first son, Visvambhara, was a religious mendicant. When their renowned son was born, his mother was rather old; and as the child seemed weak, in accordance with a custom which prevailed in those times, he was hung in a basket on a tree to die. Adaitya happening to pass by the house at the time, imagining that the child thus exposed might be the incarnation of deity he was expecting, and which he had foretold, wrote with his foot on the soft earth the incantation employed at the initiation of a disciple into the mysteries of the worship of Krishna. The mother, impressed by this act, lifted the child from the tree, who immediately took kindly to his food, which he had before neglected, and showed signs of strength and vigour.

Chaitanya made great progress in learning. At sixteen he married Vishnupriyā, with whom he lived until he was forty-four years of age, when he was persuaded by Adaitya and other mendicants to renounce his *poitā* (Brāhinanical thread) and join them in their religious life. This was to lose his high position as a Brāhman. Leaving home, parents and wife, he removed to Benares, and many thought him guilty of a great crime in forsaking a large family that was dependent upon him for support. On his arrival at that city he began to teach the doctrines of his sect and gathered many disciples. He called them Vaishnavas—worshippers of Vishnu—and although his teaching was diametrically opposed in many important matters to orthodox Hinduism he was eminently successful. Many who had formerly chiefly worshiped Siva and other deities, adopting his teaching, made Krishna the supreme. The main tenets of his teaching were these: That men should renounce a secular life, and spend their time in visiting shrines; that they abandon the distinctions of caste, and eat freely with all who joined their sect, whatever their caste might be; and that they honour the name of Vishnu, and exercise *bhakti* (or trust) in that god as the means of salvation. He allowed widows to remarry; forbade the eating of flesh and fish, and the worshipping of those deities to whom animal sacrifices were offered; and further, that his disciples should not hold fellowship with those who offered such sacrifices. It is a curious coincidence that about the same time that Luther was preaching salvation by faith, in Europe, Chaitanya in India was giving prominence to the doctrine that salvation was to be obtained through faith *(bhakti)* in Krishna.

From Benares Chaitanya went to Puri, the great shrine of Jagannāth, where he proclaimed his doctrines to the many pilgrims he met there; and whilst there it is said that he obtained four additional arms. Adaitya and Nityananda, who had induced him to assume the position of leader, remained for some years in Benares doing similar work; but though they afterwards returned to the secular state, their descendants are greatly respected by the members of this sect. It is reckoned that about one-fifth of the Hindus of Bengal are followers of this teacher. Immoral women generally profess to be his disciples. By their conduct they have excommunicated themselves from orthodox Hindu society, and being outcasts cannot secure the proper performance of their funeral rites. As members of this casteless sect these rites are not refused them.

KĀMADEVA

Kāmadeva, the Indian Cupid, is generally regarded as the son of Vishnu and Lakshmi, under the forms of Krishna and Rukmini, but he is also described in some places as a son of Brahmā. The latter account of his origin arises probably from the following. In the "Rig-Veda,"* Kāma is described as the first movement that arose in the *One,* after it had come into life through the power of fervour or abstraction. In the "Atharva-Veda," this Kāma or desire, not of sexual enjoyment, but of good in general, is celebrated as a great power superior to all the gods, and is supplicated for deliverance from enemies.

Kāmadeva

---

*Muir, O. S. T, v. 402.

According to one hymn in the "Rig-Veda," Kāma is worshipped and said to be unequalled by the gods; according to another, he is the god of sexual love, like Eros of the Greeks, and Cupid of the Latins. In the latter aspect he is thus addressed: "May Kāma, having well directed the arrow, which is winged with pain, barbed with longing, and has desire for its shaft, pierce thee in the heart." It is in this character that he appears in the Purānas.

Kāma is known in Hindu mythology as a victim of Siva's anger. A demon named Tāraka, having greatly distressed the gods, they wished to destroy him. But only a son of Siva could accomplish this. In consequence of his intense grief at the loss of his wife Sati, Siva had unfortunately become insensible to love. The gods therefore instigated Kāma to assist by wounding him with his arrows. At last he was successful, just as Pārvati (Sati in a new form) was near, who at once captivated the stricken deity. Angry with Kāma for his presumption, he caused a flame to issue from his third eye, which consumed the god who had interrupted his devotions. In the "Vamana Purāna"* is a, lengthy account of the effect of Kāma's arrows. The wounded god could find no rest. He threw himself in the Kalindi river, but "the waters were dried up and changed into blackness; and ever since, its dark stream, though holy, has flown through the forest like the string that binds a maiden's hair." As he wandered about from place to place seeking relief, the wives of the saints in the forest of Daruvanam forsook their homes and followed him.

This led their husbands to curse Siva, who, being enraged at the evil Kāma had done to him, consumed him.

The Bhāgavata† continues the story as follows:— Rati, the wife of Kāma, being almost mad with grief at the loss of her husband, entreated Parvati to intercede with Siva that he

---

*Kennedy, "Hindu Mythology."
†Kennedy, "Hindu Mythology."

might restore him to life. Pārvati encourages her by showing how her wish will be gratified. "He will be born as the son of Sri Krishna, and his name will be Pradyumna. A demon named Sambara will carry him off and cast him into the sea. Having entered the body of a fish, he will re-appear in the food of Sambara, Go, take up your abode in the house of Sambara, and when your husband arrives, take him and bring him up; eventually he will slay Sambara and will live happily with you." Acting on this advice, Rati became a servant in the house of the demon.

Siva slating Kamadeva

From the "Vishnu Purāna"* we gather the completion of this story: When Pradyumna was but six days old, he was stolen from the lying-in chamber by Sambara, terrible as death; for the demon knew (having been told by the sage Nārada) that Pradyumna, if he lived, would be his destroyer. Sambara cast him into the sea, the haunt of the huge creatures of the

---

*Page 574.

deep. A large fish swallowed him, and he was born again from his body: for the fish was caught by fishermen and by them delivered to the great asura, Sambara. His wife Māyādevi (the Bhāgavata says, servant), the mistress of his household, superintended the operations of the cooks, and, when the fish was cut open, saw a beautiful child.

Whilst wondering who this could be, and how it came there, Nārada appeared to satisfy her curiosity, and said to the graceful dame: "This is the son of him by whom the whole world is created and destroyed; the son of Vishnu, who was stolen by Sambara from the lying-in chamber, and tossed by him into the sea, where he was swallowed by the fish. He is now in thy power; do thou, beautiful woman, tenderly rear the jewel of mankind." Thus counselled by Nārada, Māyādevi took charge of the boy, and carefully reared him from childhood, being fascinated by the beauty of his person. The affection became still more impassioned when he was decorated with the bloom of adolescence. The gracefully-moving Māyādevi, then fixing her heart and eyes upon the high-minded Pradyumna, gave him, whom she regarded as herself, all her magic and illustrative arts.

"Observing these marks of passionate affection, the son of Krishna said to the lotus-eyed Māyādevi: 'Why do you indulge in feelings so unbecoming the character of a mother?" To which she replied: 'Thou art not a son of mine; thou art the son of Vishnu, whom Kāla Sambara carried away and threw into the sea; thou wast swallowed by a fish, but wast rescued by me from its belly. Thy fond mother is still weeping for thee.' When the valiant Pradyumna heard this, he was filled with wrath, and defied Sambara to battle. In the conflict the son of Mādhava slew the hosts of Sambara. Seven times he foiled the delusions of the enchanter, and, making himself master of the eighth, turned it against Sambara and killed him. By the same faculty he ascended into the air, and proceeded to his father's house, where he alighted, along with Māyāvati, in the inner apartments. When the women beheld Pradyumna, they thought it was Krishna himself. Rukmini, her eyes dimmed with tears, spoke tenderly to him, and said: 'Happy is she who has a son like this, in the bloom of youth. Such would be the age of my Pradyumna, if he were alive. Who is the fortunate mother adorned by thee? And yet from thy appearance, and from the affection I feel for thee, thou art assuredly the son of Hari.'

"At this moment Krishna and Nārada arrived; and the latter said to Rukmini: 'This is thine own son, who has come hither after killing Sambara, by whom when an infant he was stolen. This is the virtuous Māyāvati, his wife, and not the wife of Sambara. Hear the reason. When Manmatha (Kāma), the deity of love, perished, the goddess of beauty, desirous to secure his revival, assumed a delusive form, and by her charms fascinated the demon Sambara, and exhibited herself to him in various illusory enjoyments. This thy son is the descended Kāma; and this is the goddess Rati, his wife.'"

Kāma is usually represented as a beautiful youth, holding in his hands a bow and arrows of flowers. He travels about through the three worlds accompanied by his wife Rati, the cuckoo, the humming-bee, spring personified, and gentle breezes. Although in Bengal no images are made to represent him, he is worshipped at the time of marriage, and happiness in the married state, and offspring, are sought from him. Part of the hymn referred to above from the "Atharva-Veda" is recited in the Hindu marriage ritual.

Kāma has many names indicative of the influence he is supposed to exert amongst men. Amongst others may be mentioned:—

Madan, "He who intoxicates with love."
Manmatha, "He who agitates the mind."
Māra, "He who wounds."
Pradyumna, "He who conquers all."
Ananga, "He who is without a body."

Kushumesu, "He whose arrows are flowers."

Chapter VI
Siva

Siva is the third person of the Hindu Triad. As Brahmā was Creator, Vishnu Preserver, in order to complete the system,

Siva

as all things are subject to decay, a Destroyer was necessary; and destruction is regarded as the peculiar work of Siva. This seems scarcely in harmony with the form by which he is usually represented. It must be remembered, however, that, according to the teaching of Hinduism, death is not death in the sense of passing into non-existence, but simply a change into a new form of life. He who destroys, therefore, causes beings to assume new phases of existence— the Destroyer is really a re-Creator; hence the name Siva, the Bright or Happy One, is given to him, which would not have been the case had he been regarded as the destroyer in the ordinary meaning of that term.

In the later Hinduism, as taught in the Epics and Purānas, Siva plays a most important part, several books having been written for the purpose of celebrating his praise; yet his name as that of a god does not occur in the Vedas. In order, therefore, to gain greater reverence for him amongst men, he is declared to be the Rudra of the Vedras. In some passages in the Vedras, Rudra is identified with Agni; yet "the distinctive epithets applied to him in the Rig-Veda appear sufficiently to prove that he was generally discriminated from Agni by his early worshippers."*

"Between the texts from the Brāhmanas relative to Rudra, and the earliest descriptions of the same deity which we discover in the Epic poems, a wide chasm intervenes, which, as far as I am aware, no genuine ancient materials exist for bridging over. The Rudra of the Mahābhārata is not indeed very different in his general character from the god of the same name who is portrayed in the Satarudriya, but in the later literature his importance is immensely increased, his attributes are more clearly defined, and the conceptions entertained of his person are rendered more distinct by the addition of various additional features and illustrated by numerous

---

*Muir, O. S. T., iv. 404.

Siva Temple at Benares

legends. Instead of remaining a subordinate deity, as he was in the Vedic Age, Rudra has thrown Agni, Vāyu, Surya, Mitra, and Varuna completely into the shade; and although Indra still occupies a prominent place in the Epic legends, he has sunk down into a subordinate position, and is quite unable to compete in power and dignity with Rudra, who, together with Vishnu, now engrosses the almost exclusive worship of the Brāhmanical world."*

In the following texts from the Vedas,† referring to Rudra, will be seen the germs of some of the legends found in the later books concerning Siva:—"What can we utter to Rudra, the intelligent, the strong, the most bountiful, which shall be

---

*Muir, O. S. T., iv. 404.
†Ibid., iv. 299 ff.

most pleasant to his heart, that so Aditi may bring Rudra's healing to our cattle, and men, and kine, and children? We seek from Rudra, the lord of songs, the lord of sacrifices, who possesses healing remedies, his auspicious favour; from him who is brilliant as the sun, who shines like gold, who is the best and most bountiful of the gods." "We invoke with obeisance the ruddy boar of the sky, with spirally braided hair, a brilliant form." "Far be from us thy cow-slaying and man-slaying weapon." In the same hymn Rudra is called the father of the Maruts or Storm-gods; to explain which the commentator introduces a legend of a later date which is found in the account of the Maruts.* In another hymn Rudra is thus addressed : "Thou fitly holdest arrows and a bow; fitly thou [wearest] a glorious necklace of every form [of beauty]." The name Siva may have been connected with Rudra from a verse in the Vajasaneyi recension of the white "Yajur Veda," wherein Rudra is thus addressed: "Thou art gracious (Siva) by name."† Other epithets, which are afterwards extended into legends, are seen in a prayer in the same Veda: "Shine upon us, dweller in the mountain, with that blessed body of thine which is auspicious."‡ "May he who glides away, blue-necked and red-coloured, be gracious unto us." "Reverence to the blue-necked, to the thousand-eyed, to the bountiful, and to the lord of spirits, and to the lord of thieves."

In the following account of Rudra's birth, he is identified with Agni:—"The lord of beings was a householder, and Ushas (The Dawn) was his wife. A boy was born (to them) in a year. The boy wept. Prajāpati said to him, 'Boy, why dost thou weep, since thou hast been born after toil and austerity?" The boy said, 'My evil has not been taken away, and a name has not been given to me. Give me a name.' Prajāpati said,

---

*Part i. chap. vii.
†Muir, O. S. T., iv. 322.
‡Ibid., P. 326.

'Thou art Rudra.' Inasmuch as he gave him that name, Agni became his form, for Rudra is Agni. He was Rudra because he wept (from *rud*, to weep)."* This account of the birth of Rudra agrees with that of the Vishnu and Mārkandeya Purānas, and to some extent with that of others.

It is impossible to give a connected account of the life of this deity. His career was not clearly defined like an Avatāra of Vishnu, of which we have a history of his birth, life, and death. Though he often appeared on earth in human form, and frequently dwelt at his favourite city, Benares, his heavenly home was at Kailāsa on the Himālayas. All that can be done is to give a few out of the many legends found in the sacred books in which his character and works are described. From these we may learn something of the idea of the age in which they were written respecting Siva.

Rudra, according to the Rāmāyana, married Umā, the daughter of Daksha, who reappears in various stages of the life of Siva as Pārvati, Durgā, Kāli, etc. Fearing that the children of such parents would be dangerous to live with, the gods entreated Siva and Umā to live a life of chastity: to this they consented. The request, however, came too late to prevent the birth of Kartikeya. Umā declared that the wives of the other gods should also be childless. Rudra took a prominent position at the churning of the ocean; he drank the poison, as nectar, that was produced before the amrita, which caused his neck to become dark-coloured—hence one of his names is Nilkanta, "the blue-necked."

As Umā was sitting with her husband in their home on Mount Kailāsa, seeing the gods driving by in their chariots, she was told that they were proceeding, at her father's invitation, to take part in a great sacrifice he was about to make. As Siva had offended him, Daksha had not invited him. The "Bhāgavata

---

*Ibid., iv. 341.

Purāna"* gives the cause of this slight upon Siva: "On one
occasion the gods and Rishis were assembled at a sacrifice
celebrated by the Prajāpatis. On Daksha's entrance, all rose to
salute him excepting his father Brahmā and Mahādeva (Siva).
Daksha, after making his obeisance to Brahmā, sat down by his
command, but was offended at the treatment he received from
Siva. Seeing him previously seated, Daksha did not brook this
want of respect; but looking at him obliquely with his eyes, as
if consuming him, thus spake: 'Hear me, ye Brāhman Rishis,
with the gods and the Agnis, while I, neither from ignorance
nor passion, describe what is she practice of virtuous persons.
But this shameless being (Siva) detracts from the reputation of
the guardians of the world—he by whom, stubborn as he is, the
course pursued by the good is transgressed. He assumed the
position of my disciple, inasmuch as, like a virtuous person,
in the face of Brāhmans and of fire, he took the hand of my
daughter who resembled Savitri. This monkey-eyed [god],
after having taken the hand of [my] fawn-eyed [daughter],
has not even by word shown suitable respect to me, whom
he ought to have risen and saluted. Though unwilling, I yet
gave my daughter to this impure and proud abolisher of rites
and demolisher of barriers, like the word of a Veda to a Sudra.
He roams about in dreadful cemeteries, attended by hosts of
ghosts and sprites, like a madman, naked, with dishevelled
hair, wearing a garland of dead men's [skulls] and ornaments
of human bones, pretending to be Siva (auspicious), but in
reality Asiva (inauspicious), insane, beloved by the insane,
the lord of Bhutas (spirits), beings whose nature is essentially
darkness. To this wicked-hearted lord of the infuriate, whose
purity has perished, I have, alas! given my virtuous daughter,
at the instigation of Brahmā.' Having thus reviled Siva, who
did not oppose him, Daksha, having touched water, incensed,
began to curse him: 'Let this Bhava (Siva), lowest of the gods,

---

*Muir, O. S. T., iv. 378 ff.

never at the worship of the gods receive any portion along with the gods Indra, Upendra (Vishnu), and others.'

"Daksha then left the assembly. After his departure a follower of Mahādeva pronounced a curse upon him, and the Brāhmans who sympathized with him: 'Let Daksha, brutal, be excessively devoted to women, and have speedily the head of a goat. Let this stupid being continue to exist in this world in ceremonial ignorance!' Upon this, Bhrigu (a brother of Daksha, and a Rishi) launched a counter-curse upon the followers of Siva: 'Let those who practise the rites of Bhava be heretics and opponents of the true scriptures. Having lost their purity, deluded in understanding, wearing matted hair and ashes and bones, let them undergo the initiation of Siva, in which spirituous liquors are the deity.' Hearing this imprecation, Siva and his followers left the assembly, while Daksha and the other Prajāpatis* celebrated for a thousand years the sacrifice in which Vishnu was the object of veneration."

The enmity thus commenced between Siva and Daksha continued; and in consequence, at the great sacrifice made when his father-in-law was appointed chief of the Prajāpatis, Siva was not invited. Umā was greatly grieved, as her husband told her, "The former practice of the gods has been that in all sacrifices no portion should be divided to me. By custom, established by the earliest arrangement, the gods lawfully allot me no share in the sacrifice." According to the Mahābhārata, he then sets off for the assembly and with his attendants puts an end to the sacrifice, which, taking the form of a deer, is followed by Siva into the sky. A drop of perspiration falls from his forehead, from which a fire proceeds, out of which issues a dreadful being Jvara (Fever), which burns up the other things prepared for the sacrifice, and even puts to flight the gods. Brahmā now appears to Siva, promises that the gods shall

---

* The Prajāpatis, seven, ten, or twenty-one in number, according to various authorities, are the fathers of the human race.

henceforth give him a share in the sacrifices, and proposes that Jvara shall be allowed to range over the earth.

The Bhāgavata* gives a more lengthy and somewhat different account of the termination of Daksha's ceremony. Sati (Umā) was most anxious to attend it. Though her husband tries to dissuade her, she "disregards his warning and goes; but, being slighted by her father, reproaches him for his hostility to her husband, and threatens to abandon her corporeal frame by which she was connected with her parent. She then voluntarily gives up the ghost. Seeing this, Siva's attendants, who had followed, rush on Daksha to slay him." This, however, is prevented, and Siva's followers are put to flight. When Siva heard of his wife's death, he was greatly angered, and "from a lock of his hair a gigantic demon arose (named Virabhadra), whom he commanded to destroy Daksha and his sacrifice." This was accomplished. He plucked out Bhrigu's beard, tore out Bhaga's eyes, knocked out Pushan's teeth, and cut off Daksha's head. In their distress, the gods are advised to propitiate Siva. For this purpose they resort to Kailāsa, where they see Siva "carrying the linga desired by devotees, ashes, a staff, a tuft of hair, an antelope's skin, and a digit of the moon, his body shining like an evening cloud." Siva in part relents, and allows Daksha to have a goat's head: the sacrifice is completed, and Vishnu gives an address in which he shows that he is the supreme deity, and that the troubles of his worshippers arise from imagining themselves to be different from him. Daksha himself worships Siva, and Umā, who had voluntarily given up herself to the flames, and thus become a *Sati*† was re-born as Pārvati, being then the daughter of Himavat, the god of the Himālayas and Menā.

---

*Muir, O. S. T., iv. 382.

†It is in imitation of the wifely devotion of Umā, that widows were burned alive with the dead body of their husbands. Hence they were called Satis—faithful ones.

Siva adopted the garb, and lived the life of an ascetic. Though generally worshipped under the form of the linga, he "is represented in human form, living in the Himālayas along with Pārvati, sometimes in the act of trampling on or destroying demons, wearing round his black neck a serpent, and a necklace of skulls, and furnished with a whole apparatus of external emblems, such as a white bull on which he rides, a trident, tiger's skin, elephant's skin, rattle, noose, etc. He has three eyes, one being in his forehead, in allusion either to the three Vedas, or time past, present and future. He has a crescent on his forehead, the moon having been given to him as his share of the products of the churning of the ocean. Again, Mahādeva, or the great deity Siva, is sometimes connected with humanity in another personification very different from that just noted, viz. that of an austere ascetic, with matted hair, living in a forest and teaching men by his own example, first, the power to be obtained by penance (tapas), mortification of the body and suppression of the passions; and, secondly, the great virtue of abstract meditation, as leading to the loftiest spiritual knowledge, and ultimately to union, or actual identification with the great spirit of the universe."*

The following legend from the "Vāmana Purāna,"† describes the ordinary life of Siva as an ascetic. Devi (Pārvati), oppressed with violent heat, thus addressed her lord: "O Isha! the heat increases in violence; hast thou no house to which we might repair, and there abide, protected from the wind, the heat, the cold?" Sankara replied: "I am, O lovely one, without a shelter, a constant wanderer in forests." Having thus spoken, Sankara with Sati remained during the hot season under the shade of trees, and when it was passed, the rainy season with its dark clouds succeeded. On beholding which, Sati said to Siva, "Heart-agitating winds do blow, O Maheshwara, and

---

*"Indian Wisdom," p. 325.
†"Hindu Mythology," p. 293.

rushing torrents roar; let me entreat thee to build a house on Kailāsa, where I may abide with thee in comfort." Siva replied, "O my beloved, I have no riches for the erection of a house, nor am I possessor of aught else than an elephant's skin for a garment, and serpents for my ornaments." The soul of Siva, having heard these harsh words, seemingly true, but devoid of truth, was alarmed, and looking on the ground with bashfulness and anger said, "Then say, O Sambhu, how can we pass in comfort the rainy season under the shade of trees?" Siva replied, "With our bodies covered with a cloud, O lovely one, shall the rainy season pass without any rain falling on thy tender frame." Having thus spoken, Siva stopped a cloud, and with the daughter of Daksha, fixed his abode within it, and hence has he since been celebrated in heaven under the name of Jimula-Kitu (he whose banner is a cloud). When the rains were over, they took up their abode in Mount Mandara.

The home life of Siva and his spouse does not appear to have been of the happiest. As they could each bestow gifts upon their worshippers, it sometimes happened that the one wanted to bless those whom the other wished to curse. In the Rāmāyana and Mahābhārata* is an account of a dispute between them in connection with the struggle between Rāma and Rāvana. In the earlier part of the contest, Rāma being unable to overthrow his enemy because of the assistance afforded him by Siva, the gods whom Rāvana had oppressed went, with Rāma at their head, to ask him to withdraw his help. Siva consented to accompany them on the seventh day of the conflict to witness the destruction of their foe. Durgā (Pārvati) severely reproached her husband, asking how he could witness the destruction of his own worshipper, a worshipper who had stood praying to him in the most sultry weather surrounded by four fires; who had continued his devotions in the chilling cold, standing in water; and had persevered in his

---

*Ward, ii. 179.

applications, standing on his head, amid torrents of rain. She then poured forth a torrent of abuse, calling him a withered old man, who smoked intoxicating herbs, lived in cemeteries and covered himself with ashes, and asked if he thought she would accompany him on such an errand. Siva now gets angry, and reminds his wife that she was only a woman and therefore could know nothing; and further that she does not act like a woman, because she too wandered, about from place to place, engaged in war, was a drunkard, spent her time in the company of degraded beings, killed giants, drank their blood and hung their skulls around her neck. Durgā became so enraged at these reproaches, that the gods were frightened. They entreated Rāma to join them in supplication to her, or Rāvana would never be destroyed. He did so; she then became propitious and consented to the destruction of the demon. Durgā is represented in the Sivopākhyana as being exceedingly jealous because her husband, in his begging excursions, visited the quarters of the town inhabited by women of ill-fame, and in the Rāmāyana is an account of a terrible quarrel between them because Parasurāma beat her sons Kartikeya and Ganesa.

In the "Vāmana Purāna"* is a legend explaining why Siva adopted the dress and habits of a religious mendicant. Formerly, when all things had been destroyed, and naught remained but one vast ocean, that lord who is incomprehensible (Brahmā) reposed in slumber for a thousand years. When the night had passed, desirous of creating the three worlds, the skilled in the Vedas, investing himself with the quality of impurity, assumed a corporeal form with five heads (Brahmā). Then also was produced from the quality of darkness another form with three eyes, and twisted locks, and bearing a rosary and a trident. Brahmā next created Ahankara (consciousness of individual existence), which immediately pervaded the nature of both gods; and under its influence Rudra said to

---

*Kennedy, "Hindu Mythology," p. 296.

Brahmā, "Say, O lord! how camest thou hither, and by whom wert thou created?" Brahmā asks in return, "And where have you come from?" The result is a terrible quarrel, in which Siva, inflamed with anger, cut off the fifth head of Brahmā, which had uttered the boastful words. But when Siva tried to throw the head to the ground it would not fall, but remained in his hand. Brahmā then created a giant to slay Siva in his weakened state, which was caused by the sin of injuring Brahmā, the father of Brāhmans. To escape from him Siva fled to Benares. The peculiar sanctity of Benares arises from the fact that it was there Siva became absolved from his great sin, and was freed from the dissevered head of Brahmā, which, as a penance, he was doomed to carry with him wherever he went. It was his attempts to get free from the sin of Brāhmanicide that made Siva a wandering mendicant.

The ordinary name by which Siva is known is Mahādeva, the great god; the origin of this is taught in the Mahābhārata.* The asuras had a boon bestowed by Brahmā, that they should possess three castles which could be "destructible only by the deity who was able to overthrow them by a single arrow." Owing to this defence, they became hateful to the other gods, who, in their distress, went to Brahmā, and he again conducts them to Mahādeva. Siva tells them that he alone cannot destroy these castles, but that with the aid of half his strength, they themselves would be able to accomplish this. They answered that as they could not sustain half his strength, they proposed that he should undertake the work aided by half their strength. Mahādeva consented to this, and thus became stronger than all the gods, and was thenceforward called Mahādeva. Notwithstanding this, in the account of Parasurāma a legend is given in which Vishnu's superiority to Siva is shown; whilst in the Purānas devoted to Siva's praise it is distinctly affirmed that Brahmā and Vishnu are inferior to him.

---

* Muir, O. S. T., iv. 223.

The unity of the various deities is taught in the following legend.* As Lakshmi and Durgā were sitting together in the presence of Siva, Lakshmi contended that her husband (Vishnu) was greater than Siva, because Siva had worshipped him. As they were conversing, Vishnu himself appeared, and, in order to convince his wife that he and Siva were equal, entered his body, and they became one. Another form of this story is found in the "Skanda Purāna."† Siva asked Vishnu on one occasion to assume the form of a beautiful woman, such as he did at the churning of the ocean to attract the attention of the asuras whilst the gods drank the amrita. Vishnu consenting, Siva became excited and sought to embrace her. As Vishnu ran away, Siva followed him, and though Vishnu resumed his proper form, Siva clasped him so tightly that their bodies became one, and a name Har-Hari, is given to the deities thus united.

Siva is always represented as having a third eye situated in the middle of his forehead; the reason of this peculiarity is given in the Mahābhārata.‡ As he was seated on the Himālayas, where he had been engaged in austerities, Umā, attended by her companions, and dressed as an ascetic, came behind him and plalyfully put her hands over his eyes. The effect was tremendous. Suddenly the world became dark, lifeless and destitute of oblations. The gloom, however, is as suddenly dispelled. A great flame burst from Mahādeva's forehead, in which a third eye, luminous as the sun, was formed. By fire from this eye the mountain was scorched, and everything upon it consumed. Umā hereupon stands in a submissive attitude before her husband, and in a moment, the Himālaya, her father, is restored to his former condition.

---

*Ward, ii. 190.
†Ibid.
‡Muir, iv. 269.

Har-Hari.

Each god is represented as having special fondness for some bird or animal, on which he is supposed to travel, and which therefore is called his Vāhan or vehicle. The bull is Siva's; and the image of his favourite bull, Nandi, is seen in front of many of the shrines sacred to Mahādeva. Owing probably to this circumstance, a curious custom prevails, similar in many respects to the setting loose of the scapegoat by the Israelites. At the death of a worshipper of Siva, if his friends are pious and can afford it, they set a bullock loose, and allow it to wander at will. By the Hindus generally it is considered a meritorious act to feed these sacred bulls, and a sin to injure them. In country places many of them are seen, and they become a great nuisance to the cultivators into whose fields they wander; for though they do much damage, as they have no owner, no compensation can be obtained. If a man were specially devout, or his friends eminently pious, as many as seven bulls are set loose at his decease. The idea seems to be this: as Siva was delighted with Nandi, he will graciously receive into his presence those on whose behalf these bullocks are given.

As Siva himself lived the life of an ascetic, and practised severe penance, a similar life is supposed to be pleasing to him; hence many of the Saivites, or worshippers of Siva, practise great austerities, and resort to cruel rites as a means of gaining his favour. Wandering through the country are tens of thousands of Sanyāsis, or pilgrims, who subsist upon charity, and expose themselves to cold and heat and many discomforts, in the belief that their life is pleasing to this deity. Some of them inflict upon themselves great physical pain by retaining their arms or legs in one posture for years, until it has become impossible to move them; others allow the thumb nail to grow through their finger; others gaze into the sun until they become blind; others again impose upon themselves a vow of silence, until at length they cannot speak. At certain festivals held in his honour, the lower orders of the people used to swing from bamboos, having iron hooks forced into their bodies, whilst others threw themselves from a height upon sharp knives; at the present time, though these cruel practices are prohibited by the Government, in out-of-the-way places they are still carried on. To assist them to bear the pain, an intoxicating drug made from hemp is freely indulged in; the authority for this practice being the life of the god, as described in the Purānas. As Krishna is believed to be pleased with songs and dances, not always of a highly moral character, Siva is believed to delight in the cruel practices of his ignorant and intoxicated worshippers.

Siva Slaying an Asura

The following extract from the Bhāgavata, descriptive of Siva's appearance and conduct, countenances much that now forms part of his worship. Understanding that one of his worshippers was in distress, Siva "assumed half the body of Pārvati, fastened up his matted hair, rubbed his body over with ashes, ate a large quantity of hemp, swallow-wort and thorn-apple; and wearing a Brāhmanical thread composed of white snakes, clad in an elephant's hide, with a necklace of beads, and a garland of skulls, riding upon Nandi, accompanied by ghosts, goblins, spectres, witches, imps, sprites and evil spirits, Bholonāth came forth. On his forehead was the moon; he placed the Ganges on his head,* and his eyes were very red. His most destructive weapon was a trident: with this he slew the foe who was obnoxious to his follower."

Though Siva's appearance is repeatedly described with considerable minuteness in the Purānas, and in pictures he is usually represented in the human form, it is in the form of the Linga that he is almost universally worshipped. This image does not suggest anything offensive to those unacquainted with its symbolic meaning, and some writers speak of its being innocuous to the Hindus themselves. But it is impossible for any one acquainted with the legends which account for its being the symbol of Siva, to see and worship it without impure thoughts being suggested. It is intended to represent the male and female reproductive organs.

Several legends are given to explain how it came to be the representative of Siva. The probability is that it was an object of worship of some aboriginal tribe, incorporated into Hinduism. The "Padma Purāna"† teaches that it was the result of a curse pronounced by Bhrigu. When that Sage was sent to discover which of the three gods was the greatest, he came to Siva's abode, but was prevented from entering immediately he arrived by a doorkeeper, who informed him that his master was with Devi his wife. After waiting for some time, Bhrigu's patience being exhausted, he said, "Since thou, O Sankara! hast treated me with contempt, in preferring the embraces of Pārvati, your forms of worship shall be the Linga and Yoni."

The Vāmana‡ makes it the result of a curse pronounced by a number of Sages. When Sati died at Daksha's sacrifice,

---

*See "Gangā," part iii. chap. v.
†Kennedy, "Hindu Mythology," p. 301.
‡Kennedy, "Hindu Mythology," p. 299.

Siva wandered from place to place like a madman, mourning her absence. He travelled from hermitage to hermitage, but could find no rest. When the hermits' wives saw him they fell desperately in love with him and followed him from place to place. Their husbands, incensed at this, cursed the god, and deprived him of his manhood. A great commotion followed. Brahmā and Vishnu interceded on his behalf with the hermits, who consented to withdraw their curse on condition that the offender should be represented by the Linga; and thus it became an object of worship to gods and men.

As a specimen of the legends by which the worship of Siva under this form is inculcated, I give the following extract from the "Siva Purāna."* A Rākshas named Bhima, have obtained invincible might as a boon from Rāma, commenced exerting his newly acquired power by attacking the king of Kāmrupa. Having conquered the king, and seized his kingdom and riches, he placed him in chains in a solitary prison. The king, being eminently pious, notwithstanding his confinement, continued daily to make clay figures of the Linga, and to worship Siva with all the prescribed rites and ceremonies. Meanwhile the Rākshas continued his conquests, and everywhere abolished religious observances, and the worship enjoined in the Vedas. The gods being reduced by his power to great distress, appealed to Siva for help, and propitiated him by the worship of clay Lingas.

Sāmbhu assured them that he would effect the destruction of their enemy by means of the king of Kāmrupa, then a prisoner. At this very moment the prisoner was engaged in profound meditation before a Linga, when one of the guards, seeing him thus occupied, went and informed the Rākshas that his captive was performing some improper ceremonies in order to injure him. Hearing this, the monster, enraged, seized his sword and hastening to the prison, thus addressed the king:

---

*Ibid., p. 310.

"Speak the truth, and tell me who it is that thou worshippest, and I will not slay thee; otherwise I will instantly put thee to death!"

The king, placing firm reliance on the protection of Siva, undauntedly replied, "In truth, I worship Sankara; do then what thou pleasest!" The Rākshas asked, "What can Sankara do to me? I know him well, that he was once obliged to become the servant of my uncle (Rāvana); and thou trusting in his power didst endeavour to conquer me; but defeat was the result of thy attempt. However, until thou showest me thy lord, and convincest me of his might, I will not believe in his divinity!" The king replied, "Vile as I am, what power have I over the god? But mighty as he is, I know he will never forsake me!" To which the Rākshas said, "How can that delighter in ganja, and inebriation, that wandering mendicant, protect his worshippers? Let but thy lord appear, and I will immediately engage with him in battle." He then ordered the attendance of his army; and reviling the king, the mighty Rākshas smiting the Linga with his sword, said, laughing, "Now, behold the power of thy lord!" Scarcely had his sword touched the Linga than Hara issued from it, and exclaimed, "Behold I am Iswara (god), who appears for the protection of his worshipper, on whom he always bestows safety and happiness; now learn to dread my might!" Siva then attacked the Rākshas, and with the glory which issued from his third eye, consumed him and his army to ashes.

Siva is said to have a thousand names; in addition to those already mentioned thefollowing are most common:—

Maheswara, "The great god."

Ishwar, "The glorious."

Chandrashekara, "He who wears a half-moon on his forehead."

Bhuteswara, "Lord of Bhuts, or goblins."

Mritunjaya, "He who conquers death."

Sri Kanta, "He whose neck is beautiful."

Smarahāra, "The destroyer of Smara or Kāmdeva."

Gangadhara, "He who holds Gangā (the Ganges) in his hair."

Sthānu, "The everlasting."

Girisha, "The lord of the hills."

Digambara, "He who is clothed with space (naked)."

Bhagavat, "The lord."

Isāna, "The ruler."

Mahakāla, "The great time."

Tryambaka, "The three-eyed."

PANCHĀNANA

This is a form of Siva in which he is represented, as his name teaches, with five faces; the appearance of his body and the ascetic's dress being the same as in his ordinary forms. It is under this name that prayers for recovery from sickness are

Panchānana

addressed to him as the physician or healer. In places where there is no temple, and no image of this deity, worship is offered to him before a shapeless stone, painted red, placed under a tree. This is a very common form of worship in the villages of Bengal. Some shrines of Panchānana have acquired considerable celebrity, to which women resort to obtain the gift of children as well as other blessings. In times of sickness offerings are made to this deity without scruple, though the sufferer is not ordinarily a worshipper of Siva. In cases of epilepsy it is the common belief that the victim is possessed by Panchānana, and offerings are made to induce him to depart; recovery is believed to be the result of the god's departure.

Chapter VII

Umā

Umā is the name by which the consort of Siva is first known. In the sacred books she appears in many forms, and is known by many names; but as there are legends giving the circumstances connected with the names and forms more generally known, these will be given as far as possible in chronological order.

When Devi (the goddess) appears as Umā, she is said to be the daughter of Daksha, a son of Brahmā. Her father was at first very unwilling that his daughter should marry a mendicant, but his scruples were overcome by the persuasion of Brahmā. As Siva is styled Mahādeva, Umā is frequently called simply Devi. At this period of her existence she is also called Sati, in allusion to the fact that when her father slighted her husband by not inviting him to the great sacrifice he made, she voluntarily entered the sacrificial fire and was burned to death in the presence of the gods and Brāhmans; or, according to another account, was, under the same circumstances, consumed by her own glory. The name Sati means "the true, or virtuous woman, and is given to those widows who ascend the funeral pile of their husbands, and undergo a voluntary death by being burned with his corpse. Ambikā, another name of Umā, in one of the earliest books, is said to be the sister of Rudra; and yet in the later ones she is declared to be his wife.

"The earliest work, so far as I am aware, in which the name of Umā appears, is the Talavakāra, or Kena Upanishad. In the third section of that treatise it is mentioned that on one occasion Brahmā gained a victory for the gods. As, however, they were disposed to ascribe the credit of their success to themselves, Brahmā appeared for the purpose of disabusing them of their mistake. The gods did not know him, and commissioned first Agni and then Vāyu, to ascertain what this apparition was. When, in answer to Brahmā's inquiry, these two gods represented themselves, the one as having power to burn, and the other to blow away anything whatever, he desired them respectively to burn and blow away a blade of grass; but they were unable to do this, and returned without ascertaining who he was. Indra was then commissioned to ascertain who this apparition was. 'So be it,' he replied, and approached that being, who vanished from him. In the sky he came to a woman, who was very resplendent, Umā Haimavati. To her he said: 'What is this apparition?' She said, 'It is Brahmā; in this victory of Brahmā exult.' By this he knew that it was Brahmā. The commentators on this passage declare that Umā, means 'knowledge,' and speak of Umā as the impersonation of 'divine knowledge.'" *

Professor Weber† says: "As in Siva, first of all two gods, Agni and Rudra are combined, so too his wife is to be regarded as a compound of several divine forms; and this becomes quite evident as we look over the mass of her epithets. While one set of these as Umā, Ambikā, Pārvati, Haimavati, belong to the wife of Rudra, others as Kāli carry us back to the wife of Agni; while Gauri and others perhaps refer to Nirriti the goddess of all evil." And he adds: "The most remarkable instance of this

---

*Muir, O. S. T. iv. 420.
†Ibid., iv. 425.

is to be found in the Mahābhārata in the hymn of Yudhishthira
to Durgā, where he calls her Yasodā Krishna, 'born in the
cowherd family of Nanda,' 'sister of Vasudeva,' 'enemy of
Kansa,' and as 'having the same features as Sankarshana.'
Some such explanation is certainly necessary when we see
that Kāli is said to be the same with Umā, the embodiment of
'heavenly wisdom.'"

In the following passage from the Rāmāyana,* Umā is said
to be the daughter of Himavat and Mena; the two forms of
Umā, and Pārvati being confounded in the writer's mind. "To
Himavat, the chief of mountains, the great mine of metal, two
daughters were born in beauty unequalled upon earth. The
daughter of Meru, Mena by name, the pleasing and beloved
wife of Himavat, was their slender-waisted mother. Of her
was born Gangā, the eldest daughter of Himavat, and his
second daughter was Umā, who, rich in austere observances,
having undertaken an arduous rite, fulfilled a course of
severe austerity. This daughter Umā, distinguished by severe
austerity, adored by the worlds, the chief of the mountains
gave to the matchless Rudra. These were the two daughters of
the King of the Mountains: Gangā, the most eminent of rivers,
and Umā the most excellent of goddesses."

"The Harivansa† mentions three daughters of Himaval
and Menā, but Gangā is not amongst them. "Their (the Pitris)
mental daughter was Menā, the eminent wife of the great
mountain Himavat. The King of the Mountains begat three
daughters upon Menā, viz. Aparnā, Ekapamā, and Ekapātalā.
These three performing very great austerity, such as could not
be performed by gods or Dānavas, distressed [with alarm] both
the stationary and the moving worlds. Ekaparnā (one leaf) fed
upon one leaf. Ekapātalā took only one pātala (Bignonia) for
her food. One (Aparnā) took no sustenance; but her mother,

---

* Muir, O. S. T., iv. 430.
†Ibid., iv. 432.

distressed through maternal affection, forbade her, dissuading her with her words *umā* (Oh, don't). The beautiful goddess, preforming arduous austerity, having been thus addressed by her mother, became known in the three worlds as Umā. In this manner the contemplative goddess became renowned under that name. All these three had mortified bodies, were distinguished by the force of contemplation, and were all chaste, and expounders of divine knowledge. Umā was the eldest and most excellent of the three. Distinguished by the force derived from deep contemplation, she obtained Mahādeva [for her husband]."

Several of the names under which Umā is now known and worshipped are to be found in the older writings of the Hindus, though at that time they did not refer to Siva's wife. Umā, as we have already seen, was "Wisdom;" Ambikā was a sister of Rudra; Durgā "in a hymn of the Taittiriya Āranyaka is an epithet of the sacrificial flame; and Kāli, a word which occurs in the Mandaka Upanishad, is the name of one of the seven flickering tongues of Agni, the god of fire."*

Umā is called the mother of Kartikeya, and in a certain sense of Ganesa too; but it is not at all clear whether it was really as Umā or in her succeeding birth as Pārvati that she had these children.

The "Kurmā Purāna"† has an account of Umā's creation which takes us bank, a stage anterior to her birth as a daughter of Daksha. "When Brahmā was angry with his sons for adopting an ascetic life [and refusing to perpetuate the human race], a form half male and half female was produced from that anger, to whom Brahmā said, 'Divide thyself,' and then disappeared. The male half became Rudra, and the female, at the command of Brahmā, became the daughter of Daksha under the name of Sati, and was given in marriage to Rudra, and when she

---

*Goldstücker, Chambers's Cyclopædia, *s.v.* "Umā."
†Kennedy, "Hindu Mythology," p. 329.

subsequently gave up her life on being treated with disrespect by her father, she was born a second time as the daughter of Himavat and Menā, and named Pārvati."

It should be noticed that although Umā is called the *wife* of Siva, it is understood that she represents the energy or active power of that deity; she assumed a body in order that she might be united to him in due form; in like manner Vishnu's energy became incarnate in Lakshmi, Sita, etc.

PĀRVATI

The goddess in this form is the constant companion of her husband, but few independent actions are ascribed to her. In the Purānas, Siva and Pārvati are generally represented as engaged in making love to each other, or (rather a singular change) as seated on Mount Kailāsa discussing the most abstruse questions of Hindu philosophy. Occasionally, however, quarrels arose between them, and on one occasion Siva reproached her for the blackness of her skin. This taunt so grieved her that she left him for a time, and, repairing to a deep forest performed a most severe course of austerities, until Brahmā granted her as a boon that her complexion should be golden, and from this circumstance she is known as Gauri.*

The following legend from the "Vāraha Purāna" † describes her origin. Brahmā when on a visit to Siva on Mount Kailāsa is thus addressed by him: "Say quickly, O Brahmā, what has induced you to come to me?" Brahmā replies, "There is a mighty asura named Andhaka (Darkness), by whom all the gods, having been distressed, came for protection, and I have hastened to inform you of their complaints." Brahmā then looked intently at Siva, who by thought summoned Vishnu into their presence. As the three deities looked at each other,

---

*Kennedy, "Hindu Mythology," p. 334.
†Ibid., p. 209.

"from their three refulgent glances sprang into being a virgin of celestial loveliness, of hue cerulean, like the petals of a blue lotus, and adorned with gems, who bashfully bowed before

Siva and Pārvathi.

Brahmā, Vishnu, and Siva. On their asking her who she was, and why she was distinguished by the three colours black, white, and red, she said, "From your glances was I produced; do you not know your own omnipotent energies?" Brahmā then praising her, said, "Thou shalt be named the goddess of three times (past, present and future), the preserver of the universe, and under various appellations shalt thou be worshipped, as thou shalt be the cause of accomplishing the desires of thy votaries. But, O goddess, divide thyself into three forms, according to the colours by which thou art distinguished." She then, as Brahmā had requested, divided herself into three parts; one white, one red, and one black. The white was "Sarasvati, of a lovely, felicitous form, and the co-operator with Brahmā in creation; the red was Lakshmi, the beloved of Vishnu, who with him preserves the universe; the black was Pārvati, endowed with many qualities and the energy of Siva." In the preceding legend it was narrated how Pārvati, originally black, became golden-coloured.

The "Vaivarta Purāna"* relates the circumstance which led to the re-appearance on earth of Umā, who had sacrificed herself and became a Sati, under the form of Pārvati. Siva, hearing of the death of his wife, fainted from grief; on his recovery he hastened to the banks of the river of heaven, where he beheld "the body of his beloved Sati arrayed in white garments, holding a rosary in her hand, and glowing with splendour bright as burnished gold. No sooner did he see the lifeless form of his spouse, than, through grief for her loss, his senses forsook him." When he revived, gazing on her beautiful countenance, with tears in his eyes and sorrow in his voice, he thus addressed her: "Arise, arise, O my beloved Sati! I am Sankara, thy lord; look therefore on me, who have approached thee. With thee I am almighty, the framer of all things, and the giver of every bliss; but without thee, my energy! I am like a corpse, powerless and incapable of action: how then, my beloved, canst thou forsake me? With smiles and glances of thine eyes, say something sweet as amrita, and with the rain of thy gentle words sprinkle my heart, which is scorched with grief. Formerly, when thou didst see me from a distance, thou wouldst greet me with the fondest accents; why then to-day art

---

*Kennedy, "Hindu Mythology," p. 331.

thou angry, and wilt not speak to me, thus sadly lamenting?'
O lord of my soul, arise! O mother of the universe, arise! Dost
thou not see me here weeping? O beauteous one! thou canst
not have expired. Then, O my faithful spouse! why dost thou
not honour me as usual? And why dost thou thus, disobedient
to my voice, infringe thy marriage vow?"

'Siva, having thus spoken, raised the lifeless body, and in
the anguish of separation pressed it to his bosom, and kissed
it again and again. Lip to lip, and breast to breast, Sankara
clasped the corpse of his beloved; and, after frequent faintings,
arose, and, pressing Sati closely to his bosom, rushed forward
maddened with grief. Like a man deprived of his senses, the
preceptor of the universe wandered over the seven *dwipas,*
until, exhausted by fatigue and anguish, he fell down in a
swoon at the foot of a banyan tree. The gods, seeing Siva in this
state, were greatly astonished, and, accompanied by Brahmā
and Vishnu, hastened to the spot where he lay. Vishnu placed
the head of the fainting Siva on his bosom and wept aloud;
after a little time he encouraged his friend by saying,' O Siva!
recover thy senses, and listen to what I say. Thou wilt certainly
regain Sati, since Siva and Sati are as inseparable as cold from
water, heat from fire, smell from earth, or radiance from the
sun!"

"Hearing these words, Siva faintly opened his eyes,
bedewed with tears, and said: 'O form of splendour! who art
thou? Who are these that accompany thee? Who am I, and where
are my attendants? Where art thou and these going? Where am
I, and where proceeding?' As Vishnu heard these words he
wept, and his tears, uniting with those of Siva, formed a lake,
which hence became a famous place of pilgrimage. Vishnu at
length calmed Siva, who, delighted with his words, beheld
Sati, seated before him in a gem-adorned car, accompanied by
numerous attendants, arrayed in costly garments, resplendent
with ornaments, her placid face being irradiated with a gentle
smile. The anguish of separation ceased, and joy filled his

soul as Sati thus addressed him: 'Be firm, O Mahādeva! lord of my soul! In whatever state of my being I may exist, I shall never be separated from my lord; and now have I been born the daughter of Himavat in order to become again thy wife; therefore no longer grieve on account of our separation.' Having thus consoled Siva, Sati disappeared."

In another chapter of the same Purāna we have an account of their reunion.* "Sati soon obtained another birth in the womb of Himavat's wife; and Siva, collecting the bones and ashes from her funeral pile, made a necklace of the bones and covered his body with the ashes, and thus preserved them as memorials of his beloved. Not long after this, Sati was born

Pārvati worshipping the Linga

as the daughter of Menā, excelling in beauty and virtue all created beings, and she grew up in her mountain home like the young moon increasing to its full splendour. Whilst still a girl, she heard a voice from heaven saying, 'Perform a severe

---

*Kennedy, "Hindu Mythology," p. 334.

course of austerity, in order to obtain Siva for a husband, as
he cannot otherwise be obtained.' Pārvati, proud of her youth,
smiling disdainfully at this instruction, thought within herself,
'Will he who, on account of the grief he felt for my having
formerly consumed myself, not accept me as his spouse when
redolent of life? And how can disjunction exist between those
who have been predestined from their first being to be husband
and wife?' Confident in her youth, loveliness, and numerous
attractions, and persuaded that on the first mention of her
name Siva would be anxious to espouse her, Pārvati did not
seek to gain him by the performance of austerity, but night
and day gave herself to joyous sports with her companions."
Her hopes, however, were disappointed. She had to perform
most severe penance before she was reunited to her husband;
and it was only by the assistance of Kāmadeva, who, at the
instigation of the gods, wounded him with his arrows as he
was engaged in meditation, whilst Pārvati was seated in front
of him, that her wish was gratified. Siva at first was anything
but grateful for this interference; and as before narrated he
rewarded Kāma by destroying him with a flame of glory that
issued from his third eye.

In a Bengali account of Durgā, a legend is given from a
later work than the Purāna from which the above extract was
taken. It is to the following effect:—When Siva raised the
dead body of Sati in his arms he began to dance in a frantic
manner. The earth trembled beneath the weight of such a load;
and Vishnu, fearing there would be an utter destruction of the
universe if this were allowed to continue, let fly his wonder-
working discus, and cut the body into fifty-one pieces. These
fell in different places, a leg here, a hand there; but wherever
a part touched the earth, the spot became sacred, an image of
the goddess was set up, and a temple rose—in some places
it is said they *grew* to her honour—which pilgrims still visit
as shrines. The renowned temple at Kāli Ghat, near Calcutta,
is said to possess the big toe of her left foot; and the other

principal shrines of Pārvati profess to contain a relic of her body. Pārvati is represented in pictures as a fair and beautiful woman, with no superfluity of limbs. Few miraculous deeds are claimed for her. It is when she appears as Durgā, Kāli, etc., that she manifests divine powers, and exhibits a very different spirit from that which appears in her as Pārvati. Hence the supposition that these were originally distinct deities, though now believed to be one and the same.

DURGĀ.

The consort of Siva now assumes a very different character from that in which she has so far been represented. In those incarnations, though the wife of Siva, she acted as an ordinary woman, and manifested womanly virtues; as Durgā she was a most powerful warrior, and appeared on earth, under many names, for the destruction of demons who were obnoxious to gods and men.

She obtained the name Durgā because she slew an asura named Durga, the name of the goddess being the feminine form of the demon's name. The "Skanda Purāna" gives the following account of this occurrence. Kartikeya, being asked by Agastya, the sage, why his mother was called Durgā, says: "A giant named Durga, the son of Ruru, having performed penance in favour of Brahmā, obtained his blessing, and grew so mighty that he conquered the three worlds, and dethroned Indra and the other gods. He compelled the wives of the Rishis to sing his praise, and sent the gods from heaven to dwell in the forests, and by a mere nod summoned them to reverence him. He abolished religious ceremonies, Brāhmans through fear of him gave up the reading of the Vedas; rivers changed their course; fire lost its energy, and the terrified stars retired from sight. He assumed the shape of the clouds, and gave rain whenever he pleased; the earth, through fear, yielded an abundant harvest, and the trees flowered and gave fruit out of the proper season."

The gods in their distress appealed to Siva. Indra, their king, said, "He has dethroned me!" Surya said, "He has taken my kingdom!" Siva, pitying them, desired Pārvati to go and destroy this giant. She, accepting the commission willingly, calmed the fears of the gods, and first sent Kālarātri (Dark Night), a female whose beauty bewitched the inhabitants of the three worlds, to order the demon to restore things to their ancient order. He, however, full of fury, sent his soldiers to lay hold of Kālarātri; but by the breath of her mouth she reduced them to ashes. Durga then sent 30,000 other giants, who were such monsters in size that they covered the surface of the earth. At the sight of these giants, Kālarātri fled to Pārvati, followed by the giants. Durga, with 100,000,000 chariots, 120,000,000,000 elephants, 10,000,000 swift-footed horses, and innumerable soldiers, went to fight Pārvati, on the Vindhya mountain. As soon as he drew near, Pārvati assumed 1000 arms, called to her assistance different beings, and produced a number of weapons from her body (a long list of these is given in the Purāna). The troops of the giant poured their arrows on Pārvati as she sat on the mountain Vindhya, thick as the drops of rain in a storm; they even tore up trees, mountains, etc., and hurled them at her; in return she threw a weapon which carried away the arms of many of the giants. Durga himself then hurled a flaming dart at the goddess, which she turned aside; another being sent, she stopped it by a hundred arrows. He next aimed an arrow at Pārvati's breast; this too she repelled, and two other weapons, a club and a pike. At last coming to close quarters, Pārvati seized Durga and set her left foot on his breast, but he, managing to disengage himself, renewed the fight.

Pārvati then caused a number of helpers to issue from her body, which destroyed the soldiers of the giants. In return, Durga sent a dreadful shower of hail, the effect of which Pārvati counteracted by an instrument called Sosuna. The demon now assumed the shape of an elephant as large as a mountain, and approached the goddess; but she tied his legs, and, with her nails, which were like scimitars, tore him to pieces. He rose again in the form of a buffalo, and with his horns cast stones, trees, and mountains, tearing up the trees by the breath of his nostrils. Pārvati then pierced him with her trident; he reeled to and fro, and, renouncing the form of a buffalo, assumed his original body as a giant, with a thousand arms, having a weapon in each. Approaching Pārvati, she seized him by his arms, and carried him into the air, whence she threw him to the ground with fearful force. Seeing that the fall had not destroyed him, she pierced him in the breast with an arrow, whereupon blood issued from his mouth in streams, and he died. The gods were delighted at the result, and soon regained their former splendour.

Still another account of the origin of Durgā is found in the Chandi, a part of the "Mārkandeya Purāna."* Mahisha, king of the giants, at one time overcame the gods in war, and reduced them to such a state of want that they wandered through the earth as beggars. Indra first conducted them to Brahmā, and then to Siva; but as these gods could render no assistance, they turned to Vishnu, who was so grieved at the sight of their wretchedness, that streams of glory issued from his face, whence came a female figure named Mahāmāya (another name of Durgā). Streams of glory issued from the faces of the other gods also, which in like manner entered Mahamāyā; in consequence of which she became a body of glory, like a mountain of fire. The gods then handed their weapons to this dreadful being, who with a frightful scream ascended into the air, slew the giant, and gave redress to the gods.

The account, as found in the "Vāraiana Purāna,"† differs in some details. When the gods had sought Vishnu in their distress, he, and at his command Sankara (Siva), Brahmā,

_____

*Ward, ii. 88.
†Kennedy, "Hindu Mythology," p.336.

and the other gods, emitted such flames from their eyes and countenances that a mountain of effulgence was formed, from which became manifest Katyayini, refulgent as a thousand suns, having three eyes, black hair, and eighteen arms. Siva gave her his trident, Vishnu a discus, Varuna a conch-shell, Agni a dart, Vāyu a bow, Surya a quiver full of arrows, Indra a thunderbolt, Kuvera a mace, Brahmā a rosary and water-pot, Kala a shield and sword, Visvakarma a battle-axe and other weapons. Thus armed, and adored by the gods, Katyayini proceeded to the Vindhya hills. Whilst there, the asuras Chanda and Manda saw her, and being captivated by her beauty they so described her to Mahisha, their king, that he was anxious to obtain her. On asking for her hand, she told him she must be won in fight. He came, and fought; at length Durgā dismounted from her lion, and sprang upon the back of Mahisha, who was in the form of a buffalo, and with her tender feet so smote him on the head that he fell to the ground senseless, when she cut off his head with her sword.

In pictures and images Durgā is represented as a golden-coloured woman, with a gentle and beautiful countenance. She has ten arms; in one hand she holds a spear, with which she is piercing the giant Mahisha; with one of her left hands she holds the tail of a serpent, with another the hair of the giant whose breast the snake is biting; her other hands are filled with various weapons. Her lion leans against her right leg, and the giant against her left. The images of Lakshmi, Sarasvati, Kartikeya, and Ganesa are frequently made and worshipped with that of Durgā. The frontispiece is a representation of Durgā and the other goddesses and gods, as they are made in Bengal at the time of the great autumnal festival.

In Bengal the worship of this goddess forms the most popular of all the Hindu festivals; it continues for three days, and is the great holiday of the year. At this season, as at Christmas in England, the members of the family whom business detains from home during the year return; and with the worship of

Durgā, is associated all that is bright and cheerful. Sacrifices of buffaloes and goats are made to her; feasting, singing, and dancing are continued through the greater part of the night. Though her chief festival is in the autumn, she is also worshipped, though not so generally, in the spring. The reason of this as taught in a Bengali account is as follows:—Rāvana was a devout worshipper of Durgā, and had the Chandi (an extract from one of the Purānas) read daily. When, therefore, Rāma attacked him, the goddess assisted her servant. It was in the spring that Rāvana observed her festival. Rāma, seeing the help his enemy received from this goddess, began himself to worship her. This was in the autumn. Durgā was delighted with the devotion of Rāma, and at once transferred her aid to him.

Dasabhujā

Durgā is said to have assumed ten forms for the destruction

of two giants, Sumbha and Nisunibha; the "Mārkandeya Purāna" describes these incarnations in the following order:—
(1) As Durgā, she received the message of the giants; (2) As Dasabhujā (the ten-armed) she slew part of their army; (3) As Singhavāhini (seated on a lion) she fought with Raktavija; (4) As Mahishā-mardini (destroyer of a buffalo) she slew Sumbha in the form of a buffalo; (5) As Jagaddhatri (the mother of the world) she overcame the army of the giants; (6) As Kali (the black woman) she slew Raktavija; (7) As Muktakesi (with flowing hair) she overcame another of the armies of the giants; (8) As Tāra (the saviour) she slew Sumbha in his own proper shape; (9) As Chinnamustaka (the headless) she killed Nisumbha; (10) As Jagadgauri (the golden-coloured lady renowned through the world) she received the praises and thanks of the gods.*

The great conflict for success in which Durgā, assumed so many forms is described as follows in the "Mārkandeya Purana."† At the close of the Treta Age, two giants, named Sumbha and Nisumbha, performed religious austerities for 10,000 years, the merit of which brought Siva from heaven, who discovered that by this extraordinary devotion, they sought to obtain the blessing of immortality. He reasoned long with them, and vainly endeavoured to persuade them to ask for any other gift. Being denied what they specially wanted, they entered upon still more severe austerities, for another thousand years, when Siva again appeared, but still refused to grant what they asked. They now suspended themselves with their heads downwards over a slow fire, till the blood streamed from their necks: they continued thus for 800 years. The gods began to tremble, lest, by performing such rigid acts of holiness, these demons should supplant them on their thrones. The king of the gods thereupon called a council, and imparted to them his fears. They admitted that there was ground for anxiety, but

---

*Ward, ii. 101.
†Ibid., p. 98.

asked what was the remedy.

"Acting upon the advice of Indra, Kandarpa (the god of love), with Rambhā and Tilatamā, the most beautiful of the celestial nymphs, were sent to fill the minds of the giants with sensual desires. Kandarpa with his arrow wounded both; upon which, awaking from their absorption, and seeing two beautiful women, they were taken in the snare, and abandoned their devotions. With these women they lived for 5000 years; after which they saw the folly of renouncing their hopes of immortality for the sake of sensual gratifications. They suspected this snare must have been a contrivance of Indra; so, driving back the nymphs to heaven, they renewed their devotions, cutting the flesh off their bones, and making burnt offerings of it to Siva. They continued in this way for 1000 years, till at last they became mere skeletons; Siva again appeared and bestowed upon them his blessing—that in riches and strength they should excel the gods.

"Being exalted above the gods, they began to make war upon them. After various successes on both sides, the giants became everywhere victorious; when Indra and the gods, reduced to a most deplorable state of wretchedness, solicited the interference of Brahmā and Vishnu. They referred them to Siva, who declared that he could do nothing for them. When, however, they reminded him that it was through his blessing they had been ruined, he advised them to perform religious austerities to Durgā. They did so; and after some time the goddess appeared, and gave them her blessing; then disguising herself as a common female carrying a pitcher of water, she passed through the assembly of the gods. She then assumed her proper form, and said, 'They are celebrating my praise.'

"This new goddess now ascended Mount Himālaya, where Chanda and Manda, two of Sumbha and Nisumbha's messengers, resided. As these demons wandered over the mountain, they saw the goddess; and being exceedingly struck with her charms, which they described to their masters, advised them to engage her affections, even if they gave her all the glorious things which they had obtained in plundering the heavens of the gods.

"Sumbha sent Sugriva as messenger to the goddess, to inform her that the riches of the three worlds were in his palace; that all the offerings which used to be presented to the gods were now offered to him, and that all these offerings, riches, etc., would be hers, if she would come to him. The goddess replied that the offer was very liberal, but that she had resolved that the person she married must first conquer her in war, and destroy her pride. Sugriva, unwilling to return unsuccessful, pressed for a favourable answer, promising that he would conquer her in war, and subdue her pride; and asked in an authoritative strain: 'Did she know his master, before whom none of the inhabitants of the worlds had been able to stand, whether gods, demons, or men? How then could she, a female, think of resisting his offers? If his master had ordered him, he would have compelled her to go into his presence immediately.' She agreed that this was very correct, but that she had taken her resolution, and exhorted him, therefore, to persuade his master to come and try his strength with her.

"The messenger went and related what he had heard. On hearing his account, Sumbha was filled with rage, and, without making any reply, called for Dhumlochana his commander-in-chief, and gave him orders to go to Himālaya and seize the goddess and bring her to him, and, if any attempted a rescue, utterly to destroy them.

"The commander went to Himālaya, and acquainted the goddess with his master's orders. She, smiling, invited him to execute them. On the approach of this hero, she set up a dreadful roar, by which he was reduced to ashes. After which she destroyed the army of the giant, leaving only a few fugitives to communicate the tidings. Sumbha and Nisumbha, infuriated, sent Chanda and Manda, who, on ascending the mountain, perceived a female sitting on an ass, laughing. On seeing them she became enraged, and drew to her ten, twenty, or thirty of their army at a time, devouring them like fruit. She next seized Manda by the hair, cut off his head, and holding it over her mouth, drank the blood. Chanda, on seeing the other commander slain in this manner, himself came to close quarters with the goddess. But she, mounted on a lion, sprang on him, and, despatching him as she had done Manda, devoured part of his army, and drank the blood of the slain.

"The giants no sooner heard this alarming news than they resolved to go themselves, and collecting their forces, an infinite number of giants, marched to Himālaya. The gods looked down with astonishment on this vast army, and the goddesses descended to help Mahāmāya (Durgā), who, however, soon destroyed her foes. Raktavija, the principal commander under Sumbha, and Nisumbha, seeing all his men destroyed, encountered the goddess in person. But though she covered him with wounds, from every drop of blood which fell to the ground a thousand giants arose equal in strength to Raktavija himself. Hence innumerable enemies surrounded Durga, and the gods were filled with alarm at the amazing sight. At length Chandi, a goddess who had assisted Kāli (Durgā) in the engagement, promised that if she would drink the giant's blood before it fell to the ground, she (Chandi) would engage him and destroy the whole of his strangely-formed offspring. Kāli consented, and the commander and his army were soon despatched.

"Sumbha and Nisumbha, in a state of desperation, next engaged the goddess in single combat, Sumbha making the first onset. The battle was inconceivably dreadful on both sides, till at last both the giants were slain, and Kāli sat down to feed on the carnage she had made. The gods and goddesses chanted the praises of the celestial heroine, who in return bestowed a blessing on each."

It seems scarcely correct to speak of these forms of Durgā as incarnations; they are rather epithets descriptive of her appearance or method of fighting at different times during the great conflict. There is, however, so great a difference in appearance and character between Pārvati and Kāli that it is not easy to regard them as the same being; yet Durgā, whilst represented as a warrior fully armed, has the calm features and golden colour of the goddess in her earlier manifestation. It appears a reasonable hypothesis that Kāli was originally altogether distinct from Umā or Pārvati.

In the following hymn of Arjuna to Durgā in the Mahābhārata,* her many names are mentioned:— "Reverence be to thee, Siddha-Senāni (generaless of the Siddhas), the noble, the dweller on Mandara, Kumāri (Princess), Kāli, Kapāli, Kapilā, Krishnapingalā. Reverence to thee, Bhadrakāli; reverence to thee, Mahā Kāli, Chandi, Chandā, Tārini (deliveress), Varavarini (beautiful-coloured). O fortunate Kālyāyani, O Karāli, O Vijayā, O Jayā (victory), younger sister of the chief of cowherds (Krishna), delighting always in Mahisha's blood! O Umā, Sakambhari, thou white one, thou black one!

O destroyer of Kaitabha! Of sciences, thou art the science of Brahma (or of the Vedas), the great sleep of embodied beings. O mother of Skanda (Kartikeya), divine Durgā, dweller in wildernesses! Thou, great goddess, art praised with a pure heart. By thy favour let me ever be victorious in battle." In another verse of this same book she is said to dwell perpetually in the Vindhya hills, and "to delight in spirituous liquors, flesh, and sacrificial victims."

The statement that Durgā was the younger sister of Krishna refers to the fact that it was she who took Krishna's place in Devaki's womb after Vasudeva had carried the infant Krishna to Nanda, and whom Kansa attempted to destroy by dashing her against a stone immediately after her birth. Krishna promised, if she would take his place as Devaki's child, "becoming assimilated to him in glory, she would obtain

---

*Muir, O. S. T., iv. 432.

an eternal place in the sky, be installed by Indra amongst the gods, obtain a perpetual abode on the Vindhya mountains, where meditating upon him (Vishnu) she would kill two demons, Sumbha and Nisumbha, and would be worshipped with animal sacrifices."*

THE CHIEF FORMS OF DURGĀ

1. Durgā received Chanda and Manda, the messengers of the giants; they, struck with her beauty, spoke so rapturously of her to their lords that Sumbha sent her an offer of marriage by Sugriva.

2. Dasabhujā,† the ten-handed, destroyed Sumbha's army under the commander-in-chief Dhumlochana. Of these troops only a few fugitives escaped to carry the news of their defeat to their master.

Jagaddhāri

---

*Muir, 0. S. T., iv. 34.
†See illustration, p. 301.

3. Singhavāhini (riding on a lion) fought with Chanda and Manda, and has four arms only. She drank the blood of the leaders, and devoured a large part of their troops.

4. Mahishamārdini (the slayer of Mahisha) slew Sumbha as he attacked her in the form of a buffalo. She had eight or, according to other accounts, ten arms. There is little to distinguish the account of this form from that of Durgā.

5. Jagaddhāthi (the mother of the world) destroyed another army of the giants; is dressed in red garments, and is seated on a lion. She, too, has four arms only, and is very similar to Singhavāhini; the difference being in the weapons she wields. As Singhavāhini, she carries a sword and spear, and with two hands is encouraging her worshippers; as Jagaddhātri, she carries a conch-shell, discus, bow and arrow. In all the above forms she is represented as a fair, beautiful, gentle-looking lady.

6. Kāli (the black woman), or, as she is more commonly called, Kāli Mā, the black mother, with the aid of Chandi, slew Raktavija, the principal leader of the giant's army. Seeing his men fall, he attacked the goddess in person; when from every drop of blood that fell from his body a thousand giants equal in power to himself arose. At this crisis another form of the goddess, named Chandi, came to the rescue. As Kāli drank the giant's blood and prevented the formation of new giants, Chandi slew the monster herself.

Kāli is represented as a black woman with four arms; in one hand she has a sword, in another the head of the giant she has slain, with the other two she is encouraging her worshippers. For earrings she has two dead bodies; wears a necklace of skulls; her only clothing is a girdle made of dead men's hands, and her tongue protrudes from her mouth. Her eyes are red as those of a drunkard, and her face and breasts are besmeared with blood. She stands with one foot on the thigh, and another on the breast of her husband. This position of Kāli is accounted for by the fact that, when her victory over the giants was won, she danced for joy so furiously that the earth trembled beneath her weight. At the request of the gods Siva asked her to desist, but as, owing to her excitement, she did not notice him, he lay down amongst the slain. She continued dancing until she caught sight of her husband under her feet; immediately she thrust out her tongue with shame at the disrespect she had shown him.

Kāli

In the "Adhyatma* Rāmāyana," † is a legend giving quite a different origin of Kāli; the object of the writer evidently being to enhance the glory of Sita, by showing that Kāli was but a form that she had assumed. On Rāma's return from the destruction of Rāvana, he was boasting of his prowess, when Sita smiled and said, "You rejoice because you have slain Rāvana with ten

---

*There are four recensions of the Rāmāyana: Valmiki's, Vyasa-deva'a, the Adhuta, and the Adhyatma.
†Ward, ii. 116.

heads, but what would you say to a Rāvana with a thousand?" "Destroy him too," said Rama. Sita advised him to remain at home; but he collected his army of monkeys, and with his wife and brothers set off for Satadwipa to meet this new Rāvana. Hanumān was despatched to discover the residence of the monster, and to gather all the information he could about him, and on his return Rama went to the attack. The giant regarded the army of his assailant as so many children. He shot three arrows.

Kāli dancing ox Siva

One of these sent all the monkeys to their home at Kiskindha; a second drove the giants and demons to Lanka; whilst the third despatched the soldiers to Ayodha, Rāma's capital. Rāma was thunderstruck as he found himself alone, and, imagining that all his forces were destroyed, began to weep. Sita, laughing at her husband, assumed the terrific form of Kāli, and furiously attacked the thousand-headed Rāvana. The conflict lasted ten years, but at length she slew the giant, drank his blood, and began to dance and toss about the limbs of his lifeless body. Her dancing shook the earth to its centre; but not until Siva lay on the ground, and her attention was called to the disrespect she was showing him, could she be prevailed upon to desist. Thus Siva saved the universe; and Sita, assuming her proper form, went home with Rāma and his brothers.

The "Skanda Purāna"* explains that Chandi, who came to the rescue and assisted Kāli in the destruction of Raktavija, was a form of Devi, assumed on another occasion for the destruction of Chanda. It is interesting to see that these leaders of Sumbha's army reappear, although they were slain, and their blood was drunk by Singhavāhini. Two asuras, named Chanda and Manda, through a boon received from the divine mothers, became so powerful as to subdue the three worlds. The gods besought Devi, who appeared to them under the form of Chandi, to deliver them; she replied, "that she could do nothing for them until she had propitiated Siva." To accomplish this she retired to a forest, and, whilst engaged in worship, Siva first appeared, under the form of a vast Linga, and then, in answer to Chandi's prayer, revealed himself, and in answer to her praises thus addressed her: "O goddess! Thou art celebrated in the three worlds as Parasakti (the energy of the supreme being). Wherever thou art, there am I; and wherever I am, there is Chandikā. There is no difference between us. What shall I do for you?" Chandi replies: "Formerly I slew Chanda and Manda in battle; but they have been born again as mighty asuras, and have oppressed the three worlds. It is therefore to be enabled to destroy them that I seek thy protection." Siva promises his help, and sends her in the guise of a messenger to challenge them to fight. They accept the challenge, and are

---

*Kennedy, "Hindu Mythology," p. 338.

slain by Siva.

The "Linga Purāna"* seems to teach that Kāli, though produced by Durgā, was yet distinct from her. Formerly a female asura named Dārukā had through devotion obtained such power that she consumed like fire the gods and Brāhmans. But as she was attended by a host of female asuras, Vishnu and the gods feared to attack her, lest they should be guilty of the great sin of slaying a woman. Siva is then appealed to, who, addressing Devi, said, "Let me request, O lovely one! that thou wouldst effect the destruction of this Dārukā." Pārvati, having heard these words, created from her own substance a maiden of black colour, with matted locks, having an eye in her forehead, bearing in her hand a trident and a skull; she was of aspect terrible to behold, was arrayed in celestial garments, and adorned with all kinds of ornaments. On beholding this terrific form of darkness, the gods retreated in alarm. Pārvati then created innumerable ghosts, goblins, and demons; attended by these, Kāli, in obedience to her order, attacked and destroyed Dārukā.

Maurice† gives another account of Kāli: "The origin of this singular deity is perfectly in union with her life and history. Arrayed in complete armour, she sprang from the eye of the dreadful war-bred goddess Durga, the vanquisher of demons and giants, at the very instant that she was sinking under their united assaults. Kāli joining her extraordinary powers to those of her parent, they renew the combat and rout their foes with great slaughter."

The "Mārkandeya Purāna"‡ makes Kāli a production of Lakshmi. The origin of all things is Mahā Lakshmi, who visibly or invisibly pervades and dwells in all that is. Separating from herself the quality of darkness, she gave origin to a

---

*Kennedy, "Hindu Mythology," p. 337.
†"Indian Antiquities," ii. 184.
‡Kennedy, "Hindu Mythology," p. 210.

form black as night, with dreadful tusks and large eyes, and holding a sword, a goblet, a head and a shield, and adorned with a necklace of skulls. She is distinguished by the names of Mahākāli, Ekāvirā, Kālarātri, and other similar appellations. Then from the quality of purity she produced Sarasvati. As soon as they were formed, Mahā Lakshmi thus addressed Mahākāli and Sarasvati: "Let us from our own forms produce twin deities." She then generated a male and female, named Brahmā and Lakshmi; in the same manner Mahākāli produced Siva and Sarasvati, and Sarasvati produced Gauri and Vishnu. Mahā Lakshmi then gave in marriage Sarasvati to Brahmā, Gauri to Siva, and Lakshmi to Vishnu.

In the accounts of the forms of Durgā, and also in those of the other deities, if the writer of the book is commending Lakshmi, as in the last quotation, she is declared to be the source of all: if the book is in praise of Durgā, she is equally declared to be the source. Unless this is borne in mind the varying origins of the deities become somewhat confusing. But when it is ascertained on whose special behalf a book was written, it may be expected that he or she will be described as the source, the greatest of all.

There can be no doubt that human sacrifices were formerly offered to Kāli, though now they are forbidden both by British law and the Hindu scriptures; the prohibition in Hindu books, however, is in a more recent class of books than those in which they were ordained. In the "Kālika Purāna,"* from which the following extracts are made, nothing could be clearer than the instruction regarding this cruel practice. Siva is addressing his sons the Bhairavas, initiating them in these terrible mysteries.

"The flesh of the antelope and the rhinoceros give my beloved (Kāli) delight for five hundred years. By a human sacrifice, attended by the forms laid down, Devi is pleased for a thousand years; and by the sacrifice of three men, a hundred

---

*Moor's "Hindu Pantheon," 144 ff.

thousand years. By human flesh Kāmākhyā, Chandikā, and Bhairavā, who assume my shape, are pleased a thousand years. An oblation of blood which has been rendered pure by holy texts, is equal to ambrosia; the head and flesh also afford much delight to Chandikā. Blood drawn from the offerer's own body is looked upon as a proper oblation to the goddess Chandikā.

"Let the sacrificer repeat the word Kāli twice, and say, 'Hail, Devi! goddess of thunder; hail, iron-sceptred goddess!' Let him then take the axe in his hand, and again invoke the same by the Kālarātri text, as follows: 'Let the sacrificer say, Hrang, Hrang! Kāli, Kāli! O horrid-toothed goddess! Eat, cut, destroy all the malignant; cut with this axe; bind, bind; seize, seize; drink blood! Spheng, spheng! secure, secure. Salutation to Kāli.' The axe being invoked by this text, called the Kālarātri Mantra, Kālarātri herself presides over the axe, uplifted for the destruction of the sacrificer's enemies.

"Different mantras (or forms) are used in reference to the description of the victim to be immolated. If a lion, this—

"' O Hari! who in the shape of a lion bearest Chandikä, bear my evils and avert my misfortunes. Thy shape, O lion! was assumed by Hari [in the Nrisingha incarnation of Vishnu] to punish the wicked part of the human race; and under that form, by truth, the tyrant Hiranyakasipu was slain!'

"Females are not to be immolated, except on very particular occasions; the human female never.

"Let princes, ministers of State, councillors, and vendors of spirituous liquors make human sacrifices, for the purpose of attaining prosperity and wealth. Let the victim offered to Devi, if a buffalo, be four years old; and if human, twenty-five. On these occasions this is the mantra to be used: 'Hail! three-eyed goddess, of most terrifying appearance, around whose neck a string of human skulls is pendent; who art the destroyer of evil spirits; who art armed with an axe and a spear, salutation to thee with this blood.'

"An enemy may be immolated by proxy, substituting a

buffalo or a goat, and calling the victim by the name of the enemy through the whole ceremony, thereby infusing, by holy texts, the soul of the enemy into the body of the victim; which will when immolated deprive the foe of life also. On this occasion, let the sacrificer say: 'O goddess of horrid forms! O Chaadikā! Eat, devour such an one my enemy. Consort of fire! salutation to fire. This is the enemy who has done me mischief, now personated by an animal—destroy him, O Mahāmāri!'"

A great variety of regulations and invocations, rites, etc., are laid down for the performance of sanguinary offerings, whether the immolation of a victim, or an offering of the sacrificer's own blood, or burning his flesh. Until very recent times commonly, and in some quiet places even now, at certain festivals, the worshippers cut their flesh and burn their bodies in order to please this cruel deity. Before the Thugs set out on their murderous projects they first sacrificed to Kāli to obtain her blessing; and, on their return, paid a portion of the spoils as an offering for her help.

7.   Muktakesi* (having flowing hair) destroyed another part of the giant's forces. In appearance there is little to distinguish her from Kāli: she has four arms; holds a sword and a helmet in her left hands, and with her right she is bestowing a blessing and dispelling fear. She, too, is standing upon the body of her husband.

8.   Tāeā (the saviour) slew Sumbha, and holds his head in one hand and a sword in another. Her appearance, too, is similar to that of Kāli. She must not be confounded with Tārā, the wife of Vrihaspati; or Tārā, the wife of Bāli, the asura king.

9.   Chinnamustaka (the beheaded) slew Nisumbha, the other giant. It is evident from her appearance that she found her task rather difficult, for her head is half- severed from her body. She is painted as a fair woman, naked, and wearing a

---

*Ward, ii. 101-117.

garland of skulls, standing upon the body of her husband.

10. Jagadgauri (the yellow woman [renowned] through the world) received the thanks and praises of the gods and men for the deliverance she wrought; in her four hands she holds a conch-shell, a discus, a club, and a lotus.

Images are made of Durgā at different seasons of the year in nearly all of these forms, and various blessings are sought from her by her worshippers. In addition to these she is worshipped under other names; some of the more generally known will now be given. It should be noticed that the Hindus who worship Durgā in any of her forms, and the other female deities, when they represent the Sakti, or energy of their husbands, are called Saktas, and form a class distinct from the Hindus generally. An exception, however, must be made in respect to Sarasvati, Lakshmi, and the autumnal worship of Durgā; this particular form of worship being common to almost all Hindus.

11. Pratyangirā (the well-proportioned one). Of this form of Durgā no images are made, but at night the officiating priest, wearing red clothes, offers red flowers, liquors, and bloody sacrifices. The flesh of animals dipped in some intoxicating drink is burned; the worshipper believing that the flesh of the enemy for whose injury the ceremony is performed will swell, as the flesh of the sacrifice swells in the fire.

12. Annapurnā (she who fills with food) is represented as a fair woman, standing on a lotus, or as sitting on a throne. In one hand she holds a rice bowl, and in the other a spoon used for stirring rice when it is being boiled. Siva, as a mendicant, is receiving alms from her. She is the guardian deity of many Hindus, who have a proverb to the effect that a sincere disciple of this deity will never want rice. It is in connection with this form of Durgā that the "Linga Purāna"* gives a legend explaining an image called Ardhanāri-shwara, which represents Siva and Durgā as together forming one body. Siva as a mendicant

---

*Ward, ii. 187.

supported his wife and children by begging; but on one occasion, owing to his use of intoxicating herbs, he was unable to go his rounds. Durgā told him there was nothing in the house to eat; half the previous day's contributions they had eaten; Ganesa's rat and Kartikeya's peacock having finished the rest.

Annapirxā

Siva then went out to beg, and Durgā started for her father's house with the children, but was met by Nārada, who advised her, as Annapurnā, to lay an embargo on the food of the houses where Siva asked for alms. The result was no one would give him anything. Nārada meeting him advised him to go home;

Annapurnā met him at the door, and so pleased him by giving him food, that he pressed her to his breast with such force that they became one body.

13. GANESAJANANI (the mother of Ganesa) is worshipped with her infant in her arms.

14. KKISHNAKRORA (she who holds Krishna on her breast). When Krishna fought with the serpent Kaliya in the river Yamuna, he was bitten, and in pain called upon Durgā for help. She heard his cry, and, by sucking him from her breast, restored him to health.

This list might be almost indefinitely enlarged. From the number of her names, it is evident she is largely worshipped in North India; and from the number of Hindus bearing one or other of her names, it is certain she is most popular. It is a common custom for the Hindus to give their children names indicating the god or goddess through whose favour they are believed to have been given, and Durgā seems to have had a part in the bestowal of a very large proportion of the children in Bengal. "By the favour of Kāli, or Durgā, or Tāra," is expressed in the names of multitudes, and every day witnesses the payment of vows made to this goddess when some desired good is granted, or threatened evil averted.

THE SAKTIS

Although a full account of the three chief goddesses, Sarasvati, Lakshmi, and Pārvati, has already been given, there still remains something to be said in order to indicate the position they occupy in the Pantheon. By far the greater part of the Hindus in Bengal, and a considerable number in other provinces, devote their chief, almost their exclusive worship to the wives of the gods rather than to their husbands; and by these people they are declared to be the source and support of all things. Of the three, Pārvati, chiefly in her more dreadful forms, is by far the most popular. Comparatively few assign to the other two a similarly exalted position.

All the Hindus acknowledge the consorts of the gods in a general way, and on the days commonly devoted to their worship are careful to present the customary offerings. But the sects now under consideration are not content with this. As the goddesses fill their field of vision, their husbands are almost entirely neglected. Originally the term Sakti signified the energy, or power of a deity. In process of time this energy was supposed to dwell in the wife, and as a result the devotion of the worshippers was transferred to her. And for many centuries a special name has been given to those who pay their supreme worship to the energy of the gods that are, so to speak, incarnated in their wives. These are known as Saktas, just as those who make Siva their chief object of adoration are Saivites; or those who regard Vishnu as the supreme are Vaishnavas.

There is a respectable and recognized cult of Sakti worship, known as the right-handed; and there is one that is quite the opposite, known as the left-handed. The rites and ceremonies in the one case are openly performed, and do not greatly differ from those in common with other Hindu sects. But amongst the left-handed sects the greatest care is taken to keep secret, from the uninitiated, the doctrines and practices that regulate and form their worship. But enough is known to make the members generally ashamed of their connection with the system. Meat, strictly prohibited by ordinary Hinduism, intoxicating drinks, also strictly forbidden by the same authority, and grossly obscene acts are performed as part of the worship that is offered to the deity. Of old, without doubt, human sacrifices were offered at such festivals. But as this forms part of Hindu worship, rather than of mythology, it does not call for further notice here. The goddesses, and especially Devi, or Durgā, the wife of Siva, are the supreme objects of worship amongst the Saktas; and they are worshipped as the incarnation of the energy or force of their divine husbands. The authority for this form of Hinduism are the Tantras, not the Purānas. As in the case of the more modern deities an attempt is made to identify them with the older, so expressions in the more ancient books are caught up and explained in such a way as to make it appear that the Tantric teaching is in harmony with, or a legitimate development of them.

Chapter VIII
Sons of Siva and Pārvati

1. GANESA

G ANESA is usually regarded as the elder son of Siva and Pārvati, but the Purānas differ very considerably in their

Ganesa

accounts of his origin. Sir W. Jones says* that "Ganesa, the Indian god of Wisdom, has the same characteristics as Janus of the Latins. All sacrifices and religious ceremonies, all serious compositions in writing, and all worldly affairs of importance are begun by pious Hindus with an invocation to Ganesa; a word composed of Isa, the governor or leader, and gana, a company (of deities). Instances of opening business auspiciously by an ejaculation to him might be multiplied with ease. Few books are begun without the words, 'Salutation to Ganesa;' and he is first invoked by Brāhmans who conduct the trial by ordeal, or perform the ceremony of the homa or sacrifice to fire." M. Sonnerat represents him as highly revered on the coast of Coromandel, where, according to him, "the Indians would not on any account build a house without having placed on the ground an image of this deity, which they sprinkle with oil and adorn every day with flowers. They set up his image in all their temples, in the streets, in the high roads, and in the open plains at the foot of some tree, so that persons of all ranks may invoke him before they undertake any business, and travellers worship him before they proceed on a journey." What is true of the Coromandel coast, is true of most parts of India so far as the worship of this deity is concerned.

"Ganesa is the Hindu god of Prudence and Policy. He is the reputed eldest son of Siva and Pārvati (the 'Padma Purāna' alone declares that he was the actual child of these deities), and is represented with an elephant's head—an emblem of sagacity—and is frequently attended by, or is riding upon, a rat. He has generally four hands, but sometimes six, or eight, or only two." † He is always described as being very corpulent; and pictures or images of him are seen over the doors of most shopkeepers. It is not easy to see why Ganesa has become so universally worshipped, as there are few legends in the

---

*"Asiatic Researches," i. 227.
†Moor's "Hindu Pantheon," p. 169.

Purānas attesting his divine power.

The "Brahmāvaivarta Purāna"* gives the following-account of his birth :—" Pārvati, after her marriage with Siva, being without a child, and very desirous to obtain one, was advised by her husband to perform the Panyā-kavrāta. This is the worship of Vishnu, to be begun on the thirteenth day of the bright fortnight of Māgha, and continued for a year, on every day of which flowers, fruits, cakes, vessels, gems, gold, etc., are to be presented, and a thousand Brāhmans fed; and the performer of the rite is to observe most carefully a life of inward purity, and to fix the mind on Hari (Vishnu). Pārvati having, with the aid of Sanat Kumāra, as directing priest, accomplished the ceremony on the banks of the Ganges, returns after some interval, in which she sees Krishna, first as a body of light, and afterwards as an old Brāhman, come to her dwelling. The reward of her religious zeal being delayed, she is plunged in grief, when a viewless voice tells her to go to her apartment, where she will find a son who is the lord of Goloka, or Krishna, that deity having assumed the semblance of her son as a recompense for her devotions.

"In compliment to this occasion, all the gods came to congratulate Siva and Pārvati, and were severally admitted to see the infant. Amidst the splendid cohort was Sani, the planet Saturn, who, although anxious to pay his homage to the child, kept his eyes stedfastly fixed on the ground. Pārvati asking him the reason of this, he told her that, being immersed in meditation upon Vishnu, he had disregarded the caresses of his wife, and in resentment of his neglect, she had denounced upon him the curse that whomsoever he gazed upon he should destroy. To obviate the evil consequences of this imprecation, he avoided looking any one in the face. Pārvati, having heard his story, paid no regard to it, but, considering that what must be, must be, gave him permission to look on her son. Sani,

---

*Wilson's Works, iii.

calling Dharma to witness his having leave, took a peep at
Ganesa, on which the child's head was severed from his body,
and flew away to the heaven of Krishna, where it re-united
with the substance of him of whom it formed a part.

"Durgā, taking the headless trunk in her arms, cast herself
weeping on the ground, and the gods thought it decent to
follow her example, all except Vishnu, who mounted Garuda,
and flew off to the river Pushpabhadra, where, finding an
elephant asleep, he took off his head, and, flying back with
it, clapped it on to the body of Ganesa; hence the body of
that deity is crowned with its present uncouth capital. On the
restoration of Ganesa to life, valuable gifts were made to the
gods and Brāhmans by the parents, and by Pārvati's father,
the personified Himālaya. The unfontunate Sani was again
anathematized, and, in consequence of Pārvati's curse, has
limped ever since.

"In another part of the same Purāna, further particulars
are given somewhat at variance with the above. Siva, offended
with Aditya (the sun), slew him, and although he restored him
to life incurred the wrath of the sage Kasyapa, who doomed
his (Siva's) son to lose his head. The elephant whose head was
placed upon Ganesa's body was Indra's elephant, which was
decapitated because Indra threw over his neck the garland of
flowers which the sage Durvasas gave him, and the disrespect
of which, with the consequent degradation of Indra, is noticed
in various Purānas, although with different results. Indra was
no loser of an elephant by this transaction, as Vishnu, moved
by the prayers of his wife, gave him another in place of that
which he took away.

"Ganesa has only one tusk, and hence is called Ekadanta.
The reason of this is as follows:—Parasurāma, who was a
favourite disciple of Siva, went to Kailasa to visit his master.
On arriving at the inner apartment, his entrance was opposed
by Ganesa, as his father was asleep. Parasurāma nevertheless
urged his way, and, after a long dialogue, the two came to

blows. Ganesa had at first the advantage, seizing Parasurāma in his trunk, and giving him a twirl that left him sick and senseless. On recovering, Rāma threw his axe at Ganesa, who, recognizing it as his father's weapon—Siva having given it to Parasurāma—received it with all humility upon one of his tusks, which it immediately severed, and hence Ganesa has but one tusk. Pārvati was highly incensed at this, and was about to curse Rāma, when Krishna, of whom he was a worshipper, appeared as a boy and appeased her indignation. Brahmā is said to have promised that her son should be worshipped before the other gods. This result of his contest with Rāma was in consequence of a curse pronounced upon him by the sage Tulasi, with whom he had quarrelled."

We have quite a different account of the origin of Ganesa in the "Matsya Purāna."* When Pārvati was bathing, she took the oil and ointments used at the bath, together with the impurities that came from her body, and formed them into the figure of a man, to which she gave life by sprinkling it with the water of the Ganges. This figure had the head of the elephant. The "Siva Purāna" relates that, after giving Ganesa life, Pārvati placed him at her door to prevent intrusion whilst she was bathing. On his refusal to allow Siva to enter, a struggle ensued, in which that deity cut off Ganesa's head; but when Pārvati showed her husband that it was by her orders that the door was closed, and wept because of the loss of her son, Siva ordered the first head that could be found to be brought to him; this happened to be an elephant's, which he fitted to the headless trunk and resuscitated his son.

In the "Vārāha Purāna"† Ganesa is said to have been produced by Siva alone. "The immortals and holy sages observing that no difficulty occurred in accomplishing good or evil deeds which they and others commenced, consulted

*Kennedy, "Hindu Mythology," p.353.
†Kennedy, "Hindu Mythology," p. 353.

together respecting the means by which obstacles might be opposed to the commission of bad actions, and repaired to Siva for counsel, to whom they said: "O Mahādeva! God of gods, three eyed, bearer of the trident, it is thou alone who canst create a being capable of opposing obstacles to the commission of improper acts.' Hearing these words, Siva looked at Pārvati, and whilst thinking how he could effect the wishes of the gods, from the splendour of his countenance there sprang into existence a youth shedding radiance around, endowed with the qualities of Siva, and evidently another Rudra, and captivating by his beauty the female inhabitants of heaven.

"Umā seeing his beauty was excited with jealousy, and in her anger pronounced this curse: 'Thou shalt not offend my sight with the form of a beautiful youth; therefore assume an elephant's head and a large belly, and thus shall all thy beauties vanish.' Siva then addressed his son, saying, 'Thy name shall be Ganesa, and the son of Siva; thou shalt be chief of the Vinayakas and Ganas; success and disappointment shall spring from thee; and great shall be thine influence amongst the gods, and in sacrifices and all affairs. Therefore shalt thou be worshipped and invoked the first on all occasions, otherwise the object and prayers of him who omits to do so shall fail.

"The origin and purpose of Ganesa's existence are more fully taught in the Skanda.* Siva addressing Parvati says, "During the twilight that intervened between the Dwarpara and Kali Yugas, women, barbarians, Sudras, and other workers of sin obtained entrance to heaven by visiting the celebrated shrine of Someswara (Somnāth). Sacrifices, ascetic practices, charitable gifts, and all the other prescribed ordinances ceased, and men thronged only to the temple of Siva. Hence old and young, those skilled in the Vedas and those ignorant of them, and even women and Sudras, ascended to heaven, until at length it became crowded to excess. Then Indra and the gods,

---

*Kennedy, "Hindu Mythology," p. 354.

afflicted because thus overcome by men, sought the protection of Siva, and thus addressed him: 'O Sankara! by thy favour heaven is crowded with men, and we are nearly expelled from it. These mortals wander wherever they please, exclaiming, "I am the greatest, I am the greatest;" and Dharmarāja (Yama), beholding the register of their good and evil deeds, is lost in astonishment. The seven hells were intended for their reception; but, having visited thy shrine, their sins have been remitted, and they have attained to a most excellent future!' Siva replied, 'Such was my promise to Soma, nor can it be infringed; all men, therefore, who visit the temple of Someswara must ascend to heaven; but supplicate Pārvati, and she will contrive some means for extricating you from this distress.'

"The gods then invoked Pārvati in laudatory strains: 'Praise be to thee, O supreme of goddesses! Supporter of the universe, praise be to thee, who createst and destroyest! Grant us thy aid, and save us from this distress!' Having heard the prayer of Indra and the gods, thou, O goddess! wert moved with compassion; and gently rubbing thy body, there was produced a wondrous being with four arms and an elephant's head, and then thou didst thus address the gods: 'Desirous of your advantage, have I created this being, who will occasion obstacles to men, and, deluding them, will deprive them of the wish to visit Somnāth, and thus shall they fall into hell.' Hearing this, the gods returned to their homes delighted.

"The Elephant-faced then, addressing Devi, said, 'Command, O lovely goddess! what shall I now do?' Thou didst reply, 'Oppose obstacles to men's visiting Somnāth, and entice them to give up such a purpose by the allurements of wives, children, possessions, and wealth. But from those who propitiate thee with the following hymn, do thou remove all obstacles, and enable them to obtain the favour of Siva, by worshipping his shrine at Somnāth: — "Om, I praise thee, O lord of difficulties! The beloved spouse of Siddhi (knowledge) and Buddhi (understanding); Ganapati, invincible, and the giver of victory; the opposer of obstacles to the success of men who do not worship thee! I praise thee, O Ganesa! The dreadful son of Umā, but firm and easily propitiated! O Vinayaka! I praise thee! O elephant-faced, who didst formerly protect the gods, and accomplish their wishes, I praise thee!" Thus,' continued Pārvati, 'shalt thou be praised and worshipped.' And whoever previously invokes the god Vinayaka, no difficulties shall impede the attainment of his purposed object, and a most beneficial result shall he derive from sacrifices, pilgrimages, and all other devotional acts."

The following extract from the "Ganapati Upanishad"* is a specimen of the addresses to Ganesa used by the Ganapatyas:† "Praise to thee, O Ganesa! Thou art manifestly the truth; thou art undoubtedly the Creator, Preserver, and Destroyer, the Supreme Brahma, the eternal Spirit. I speak what is right and true; preserve me therefore, when speaking, listening, giving, possessing, teaching, learning; continually protect me everywhere. By thee was this universe manifested; for thou art earth, water, fire, air and ether. Thou art Brahmā, Vishnu, and Rudra. We acknowledge thy divinity, O Ekadanta! and meditate on thy countenance; enlighten, therefore, our understanding. He who continually meditates upon thy divine form, conceiving it to be with one tooth, four hands, bearing a rat on thy banner, of a red hue, with a large belly, anointed with red perfumes, arrayed in red garments, worshipped with offerings of red flowers, abounding in compassion, the cause of this universe, imperishable, unproduced and unaffected by creation, becomes the most excellent of Yogis. Praise, therefore, be to thee, O Ganapati. Whoever meditates upon this figure of the 'Atharva Siras' (the name of the Upanishad of which the Ganapati forms a part) never will be impeded by difficulties, will be liberated from the five great sins, and all lesser ones;

---

*Kennedy, "Hindu Mythology," p. 493.
†Hindus of whom Ganesa is the supreme object of worship.

and will acquire riches, the objects of his desires, virtue and final beatitude."

Ganesa is said to have written the Mahābhārata at Vyāsa's dictation. In the Ādiparva of that book it is declared that when the sage was about to compose it Brahmā advised him to ask Ganesa to become his amanuensis. Vyāsa at first gave a few difficult sentences to puzzle him, which to this day the composer only and his disciple Suka have been able to understand. As Ganesa paused to think out the meaning of what he was writing, Vyāsa composed other difficult passages.

In recent times there has been a supposed incarnation of Ganesa, whose descendant and representative was visited by Captain E. Moor during the present century. The following is the account of his visit:*—"Muraba Goseyn was a Brāhman of Poona who by abstinence, mortification, and prayer, merited above others the favourable regards of the Almighty. Ganapati accordingly vouchsafed to appear to him at Chinchoor in a vision by night; desired him to arise and bathe; and, whilst in the act of ablution, to seize and hold sacred to the Godhead the first tangible substance that his hand encountered. The god covenanted that a portion of his Holy Spirit should pervade the person thus favoured, and be continued as far as the seventh generation to his seed, who were to become successively hereditary guardians of this sacred substance, which proved to be a stone, in which the god was understood as mystically typified. This type is duly reverenced, carefully preserved, and has ever been the constant companion of the sanctified person inheriting with it the divine patrimony. This annunciation happened about A.D. 1640; and at the time Captain Moor visited the place, the sixth descendant was the representative of the Deity.

"It does not now appear what was the precise extent of the divine energy originally conceded, but it is inferred to have

---

*"Asiatic Researches," vii. 381.

been a limited power of working miracles, such as healing sickness, answering the prayers of pious suppliants, and the faculty of foretelling future events. These gifts were enjoyed in a more extensive degree by the earlier representatives of the god; but the person whom Moor saw professed to have performed several miracles. The third in descent is reported to have performed a wonderful work. It was in his time that the Moghul army of Hyderabad so successfully invaded the Mahratta country. After plundering and burning Poona, a party proceeded to Chinchoor, the residence of this Deity, to lay it under contribution. To this the Deo refused to submit, confiding in the divine influence wherewith he was invested. The Mussulmans derided such superstition, and with a view of rendering it ridiculous offered to send a Nuzur (present) to the Deo. The offer was accepted, the Deo betook himself to prayers, and the insulting bigots deputed certain persons to see the result, as apparently a decorous and appropriate present was given. It consisted, however, of cow's flesh, an abomination in the eyes of a Hindu. When the trays were uncovered, they were greatly astonished to find that, instead of the cow's flesh, the trays were filled with the finest and most sacred flowers of the Hindus. The Mussulmans, seeing this, recognized the finger of God in the transaction, and so struck were they with the reality of the miracle that a valuable grant of land was made to the Deo, which his temple enjoys to this day."

The Deo eats, sleeps, marries, and lives the life of an ordinary mortal; and though he is regarded as a fool in worldly matters, he is worshipped as a god. On special occasions his actions and movements are most carefully watched, as they are transient manifestations of the divine will, and are regarded as prophetic. Thus, on a particular night of the year, should he remain in peaceful sleep, national repose is predicted; should his slumbers or his waking moments be disturbed, national calamities are expected. If he start wildly from his seat, seize a sword, or make any warlike movement, war may be looked for."

2. KARTIKEYA

Kartikeya, the god of war, and generalissimo of the armies of the gods, though called the younger son of Siva and Pārvati, according to most of the Purānic legends, is their son only in the sense that they formed him. Brahmā arranged for his birth

Kartikeya

in answer to the prayers of the gods for a competent leader of their forces, The Rāmāyana* says: "While Siva, the lord of the gods, was performing austerities, the other deities went

---

*Muir, O. S. T., iv. 364.

to Brahmā and asked for a general in the room of Mahadeva, who, it seems, had formerly acted in that capacity. 'He,' said they, 'whom thou didst formerly give as a leader of our armies (Mahādeva), is now performing great austerities, along with Umā.' Brahmā says that in consequence of the curse of Umā no son could be born of any wives of the gods, but that Agni should have a son by the river Gangā, who should be their general."

In the following extract from the Mahābhārata* is an explanation of the statement in the preceding paragraph that Agni was to be the father of this god. Kartikeya has just been installed as general, when, "the god whose banner is a bull (Siva), arriving with his goddess, paid him honour, well pleased. Brāhmans called Agni Rudra, consequently he (Kartikeya) is the son of Rudra. Having seen him thus honoured by Rudra, all the deities consequently call him, who is the most excellent of the gifted, the son of Rudra For this child was produced by Rudra when he entered into fire. Skanda (Kartikeya), that most eminent deity, being born of Agni, [who was] Rudra, and from Svāhā (Umā) [and] the six wives [of the Rishis], was the son of Rudra."

This quotation will be more intelligible after reading what precedes it: "Indra being distressed at the defeat of the armies of the gods by the Dānavas, is meditating on this subject, when he hears the cry of a female calling for help, and asking for a husband to protect her. Indra sees that she has been seized by the demon Kesin, with whom he remonstrates; but the demon hurls his club at Indra, who, however, splits it with his thunderbolt. Kesin is disabled in the next stage of the combat, and goes off. Indra then finds out from the female that her name is Devasenā (army of the gods), that she has a sister named Daityasenā (army of the daityas), and that they are both daughters of Prajāpati. She wishes Indra to find her

---

*Ibid., iv. 350.

a proper husband, who shall be able to overcome the enemies of the gods. Indra takes Devasenā with him to Brahmā, and desires him to provide her with a martial husband; and Brahmā promises that a helpmate of that description shall be born. It happened that Vasishtha and other Rishis had been offering a sacrifice, whither the gods, headed by Indra, proceeded to drink the Soma-juice. Agni, too, being invoked, descended from the region of the sun, entered into the fire, received the oblations of the Rishis, and presented them to the gods.

"Issuing forth [from the fire], he beheld the wives of these great [Rishis] reclining in their own hermitages, and sweetly sleeping, resembling golden altars, pure as beams of the moon, like to flames of fire, all wonderful as stars. Perceiving that his senses became agitated, beholding the wives of the Rishis, Agni was overcome with desire. Again and again he said, 'It is not proper that I should be thus agitated; they are not in love with me. Entering into the domestic fire, I shall gaze upon them close at hand.' Entering the domestic fire, touching, as it were, with his flames, all of them, and beholding them, he was delighted. Dwelling thus there for a long time, fixing his attention on these beautiful women, and enamoured of them, Agni was overcome.

"Agni failing to obtain the Brāhmans' wives, resolved to abandon his corporeal form, and went into the forest. Then Svālā, the daughter of Daksha, first fell in love with him. This amorous and blameless goddess for a long time sought for his weak point, but could not find any. But being aware that he had gone into the wood, and that he was really disturbed by desire, the amorous goddess thus reflected: 'I, who am distressed with love, will take the forms of the seven Rishis' wives, and will court the affection of Agni. By doing so he will be pleased, and I shall obtain my desire.' Assuming first the form of Siva, the wife of Angiras, the handsome goddess went to Agni, and thus addressed him: 'Agni, thou oughtest to love me, who am disturbed with love for thee; if thou wilt not do so, look upon

me as dead Agni, I, Siva, the wife of Angiras, have come, sent
by virtuous women.' Agni replied : 'How dost thou, and how
do the other beloved wives of the seven Rishis, know that I am
distressed with love?''

Agni was not able to resist the temptation. After the
interview, lest the wives of the Rishis should be blamed for
their misconduct if she happened to be seen in their form,
she assumed the figure of Garuda, the bird of Vishnu, and
unnoticed, as she thought, flew from the forest. She visited
Agni a second time, as the wife of another Rishi, and so on
until she had paid six visits. The germs obtained from Agni
she deposited in a golden reservoir, which, "being worshipped
by the Rishis, generated a son. Kuaāra (Kartikeya) was born
with six heads, a double number of ears, twelve eyes, arms,
and feet, one neck and one belly.

"Kartikeya marries Devasenā. The six Rishis' wives, his
mothers, afterwards come to him, complaining that they had
been abandoned by their husbands, and degraded from their
former positions, and asking him to secure their admission into
paradise (Swarga). When Skanda had done what was gratifying
to his mothers, Svāhā said to him, 'Thou art my genuine son.
I desire the love difficult to obtain which thou givest.' Skanda
then asked her, 'What love dost thou desire?' Svāhā replied, 'I
am the beloved daughter of Daksha, by name Svāhā. From my
childhood I have been enamoured of Agni; but, my son, Agni
does not thoroughly know me, who am enamoured of him.'
Skanda replied, 'Whatever oblation of Brāhmans is introduced
by hymns, they shall always, goddess, lift and throw it into
the fire, saying Svāhā (happiness). Thus, O beautiful goddess,
Agni shall dwell with thee continually." Then Brahmā Prajāpati
said to Skanda, 'Go to thy *father Makādeva*, the vexer of Tripura.
Thou, unconquered, hast been produced for the good of all
worlds by Rudra, who had entered into Agni, and Umā, who
had entered into Svāhā.'"

The allusion to Rudra's entering into Agni is explained

in the Rāmāyana. The gods, fearing that the descendants of such a pair as Siva and Pārvati would be too dreadful to live with, entreated those deities not to have offspring. Siva consented, but Umā, being angry, declared that as she could not have children the other goddesses should suffer similar deprivation. Unfortunately, the gods came too late to prevent the production of Kartikeya; the germ from which he was born having been received by the earth. Agni and Vayu entered it, and deposited it with Gangā, the sister of Umā, and thus this deity was produced.

The "Siva Purāna"* gives a different account of his origin, and teaches that he was produced to effect the destruction of Tārika. This demon, who was King of Tripura, was "exceedingly ambitious and oppressive. He forced Brahmā, by his penance and austerities, to promise him any boon that he should demand. Among his austerities he went through the following series, each of the eleven specific mortifications continuing 100 years:—1. He stood on one foot, holding the other and both hands up towards heaven, with his eyes fixed on the sun. 2. He stood on one great toe. 3. He took only water as sustenance. 4. He lived similarly on air. 5. He remained in water. 6. He was buried in the earth, but continued as under the last infliction, in incessant adoration. 7. The same in fire. 8. He stood on his head. 9. He hung on a tree by his hands. 10. He bore the weight of his body on one hand. 11. He hung on a tree with his head downwards.†

"Such merit was irresistible, and Indra and a host of demi-gods, alarmed lest their sovereignty should be usurped through the potency of this penance, resorted to Brahmā for consolation. Brahmā, however, said that, although he could

---

*Moor's "Hindu Pantheon," p. 51.
†Many of these forms of penance are resorted to, with some modifications, at the present time; these devotees may be seen at Benares, and other shrines.

not resist such austerities, he would, after rewarding them by granting the boon demanded, devise a method of rendering it ultimately inoffensive to them.

"The demand by Tārika was that he should be unrivalled in strength, and that no hand should slay him but that of a son of Mahādeva. He now became so arrogant that Indra was forced to yield to him the white eight-headed horse Ukhisrava; Kuvera gave up his thousand sea-horses; the Rishis were compelled to resign the cow Kāmdhenu, that yielded everything that could be wished. The Sun in dread gave no heat, and the Moon in terror remained always at full. The Winds blew as he dictated, and, in short, he usurped the entire management of the universe.

"Nārada prophesied the marriage whence should arise the deliverer of the world; but at first Mahādeva could not be influenced with the passion of love. Indra persuaded Kāma to lie in ambush, and contrived that Pārvati should be seen by Siva while engaged in the amiable and graceful act of gathering flowers, wherewith to decorate his image. Kāma, accompanied by his wife Rati (Desire), and his bosom friend Vasantu (the Spring), took his aim, and launched an arrow at Mahādeva, who, enraged at the attempt (to interrupt his devotion), reduced Kāma, to ashes by a beam of fire that issued from his third eye. At length, however, by ardent devotion and austerities, Pārvati propitiated Siva, and the deity consented to espouse his persevering devotee."

For some time after their marriage, as there was no child born to them, the distressed and disappointed deities who had been anxiously expecting a deliverer, renewed their lamentations and complaints.

"Agni arrived in the presence of Mahādeva, having been deputed to express the desires of the other gods, that he would provide them with a son, who should destroy Tārika. Siva had just left his wife, and Agni, assuming the form of a dove, received from Mahādeva the germ from which Kartikeya arose. Unable to carry it further, he let it fall into the Ganges, on the banks of which river arose a boy, beautiful as the moon, and bright as the sun, who was called Agnibhuva (produced from Agni), Skanda, Kartikeya, etc.

"It happened that six daughters (the Pleiades) of as many Rājas, coming to bathe, saw the boy, and each called him her son; and, offering the breast, the child assumed to himself six mouths, and received nurture from each; whence he is called Sasthimātriya (having six mothers). But in fact the child had no mother, for he came from his father alone. In course of time a conflict ensued between Kartikeya and Tārika, in which the demon was slain."

A story is told showing how Kartikeya was outwitted by his brother Ganesa. As the two brothers fell in love with two ladies named Siddhi and Buddhi, it was agreed that whoever first travelled round the world should have them. Ganesa proved by his logical talents and aptness at quotation that he had done this, and obtained the prize long before his brother returned from his weary pilgrimage, to the disquiet of both families when Ganesa's sophistry was discovered.

We have still another account* of the origin of Kartikeya: "Siva emitted sparks of fire from his eyes, which, being thrown into the lake Saravana, became six infants, who were nursed by the wives of the Rishis, who are seen in the sky as the Pleiades. When Pārvati saw these children, she was transported with their beauty, and embraced all of them together so forcibly that their six bodies became one; while their six heads and twelve arms remained."

Kartikeya is better known in South India under the name of Subramanya. The "Skanda Purāna" gives a full account of his war with Sura, and relates how he was sent by his father to interrupt Daksha's sacrifice; and how, at the instigation of the latter, he was delayed on his journey by beautiful damsels,

---

*Garrett's "Classical Dictionary of India."

who entertained him with dance and song. Hence it is the practice for dancing girls, who are attached to the pagodas, to be betrothed and married to him; and, though allowed to prostitute themselves, cannot marry any one.

Chapter IX

The Purānic Account of The Creation

Before passing on to the inferior deities, an account of the creation will be given. It is not at all easy to make out a consistent one from the Hindu scriptures, because the imagination of the writers seems to have run wild on this subject; not having any authority, each writer has written what seemed good to himself. As in the accounts of the deities, the germs are found in the older books of what is told at considerable length in the more recent. The following hymn from the Rig-Veda* describes the primal condition of things before the creative power of the Deity was exercised :—

> "There was neither aught nor naught, nor air, nor sky
>   beyond.
> What covered all? Where rested all? In watery gulf
>   profound?
> Nor death was then, nor deathlessness, nor change of
>   night and day.
> The One breathed calmly, self-sustained; nought else

---

*Muir, O. S. T., v. 350.

beyond it lay.

"Gloom, hid in gloom, existed first—one sea, eluding
  view.
That One, a void in chaos wrapt, by inward fervour
  grew.
Within it first arose desire, the primal germ of mind,
Which nothing with existence links, as sages searching
  find.

"The kindling ray that shot across the dark and drear
  abyss—
Was it beneath? or high aloft? What bard can answer
  this?
There fecundating powers were found, and mighty
  forces strove—
A self-supporting mass beneath, and energy above.

"Who knows, who ever told, from whence this vast
  creation rose?
No gods had then been born—who then can e'er the
  truth disclose?
Whence sprang this world, and whether framed by hand
  divine or no—
Its lord in heaven alone can tell, if even he can show."

This hymn contains perhaps the earliest speculations of the
Hindus respecting the creation that have come down to us; and
the wise conclusion was arrived at that God alone knew how
the world came into being. But as time went on this confession
of ignorance did not satisfy the cravings of the human mind:
hence succeeding ages sought by its conjectures, which are
given with the assurance of exact knowledge, to throw light
upon the unknowable.

The next quotation is from the "Purusha Sakta" of the

Rig-Veda, which from its thought and language is generally believed to be of much later origin than the preceding hymn.

"Purusha has a thousand heads, a thousand eyes, a thousand feet. On every side enveloping the earth, he overpassed (it) by a space of ten fingers. Purusha himself is this whole (universe), whatever has been and whatever shall be. He is also lord of immortality, since (or when) by food he expands. All existences are a quarter of him, and three-fourths of him are that which is immortal in the sky. With three-quarters Purusha mounted upward. A quarter of him was again produced here. From him was born Virāj; and from Virāj, Purusha. When the gods performed a sacrifice, with Purusha as the oblation, the spring was its butter, the summer its fuel, and the autumn its (accompanying) offering. From that universal sacrifice were provided curds and butter. From that universal sacrifice sprang the Rich and Sāman verses, the metres and the Yajush; from it sprang horses and all animals with two rows of teeth, kine, goats and sheep. When (the gods) divided Purusha, into how many parts did they cut him up? The Brāhman was his mouth, the Rajanya was made his arms, the being (called) Vaisya was his thighs, and the Sudra sprang from his feet. The morn sprang from his soul (manas), the sun from his eye, Indra and Agni from his mouth, and Vāya from his breath. From his navel arose the air, from his head the sky, from his feet the earth, from his ear the (four) quarters; in this manner (the gods) formed the worlds."*

Now follows an extract from the "Sātapatha Brāhmana," which gives the words used at the creation. "(Uttering) 'bhūh,' Prajāpati generated this earth. (Uttering) 'bhuvah,' he generated the air; and (Uttering) 'svah,' he generated the sky. This universe is coextensive with these worlds. Saying 'bhūh,' Prajāpati generated the Brāhman; (saying) 'bhuvah,' he generated the Kshattra; (and saying) 'svah,' he generated the

---

*Muir, O. S. T., i. 9.

Vis. All this world is as much as the Brāhman, Kshattra and Vis. (Saying) 'bhūh,' Prajāpati generated himself; (saying) 'bhuvah,' he generated offspring; (saying) 'svah,' he generated animals. This world is so much as self, offspring, and animals."*

The "Taittiriya Brāhmana" says, "This entire (universe) has been created by Brahmā," and gives an account of the creation of the asuras, pitris (or fathers), and gods. "Prajāpati desired, 'May I propagate.' He practised austerity. His breath became alive. With that breath (asu) he created asuras. Having created the asuras, he regarded himself as a father. After that he created the fathers (pitris). That constitutes the fatherhood of the fathers. Having created the fathers, he reflected. After that he created men. That constitutes the manhood of men. He who knows the manhood of men becomes intelligent. To him, when he was creating men, day appeared in the heavens. After that he created the gods."†

The "Sātapatha Brāhmana" relates the creation of men and animals. "Prajāpati was formerly this (universe) only. He desired, 'Let me create food, and be propagated.' He formed animals from his breaths, a man from his soul, a horse from his eye, a bull from his breath, a sheep from his ear, a goat from his voice. Since he formed animals from his breaths, therefore men say, 'The breaths are animals.' The soul is the first of breaths. Since he formed a man from his soul, therefore they say. 'Man is the first of the animals and the strongest.' The soul is all the breaths; for all the breaths depend upon the soul. Since he formed man from his soul, therefore they say, 'Man is all the animals;' for all these are man's."‡

In another passage this Brāhmana gives quite a different account. Purusha, as the soul of the universe, was alone. Hence "he did not enjoy happiness. He desired a second. He caused

---

*Ibil.,i. 17.
†Muir, O. S. T., i. 23.
‡Ibid„ i. 24.

this same self to fall asunder into two parts. Thence arose a husband and wife. From them men were born. She reflected, 'How does he, after having produced me from himself, cohabit with me? Ah! let me disappear!' She became a cow, and the other a bull; from them kine were produced. The one became a mare, the other a stallion; the one a she-ass, the other a male-ass. From them the class of animals with undivided hoofs were produced. The one became a she-goat, the other a he-goat; the one an ewe, the other a ram. From them goats and sheep were produced. In this manner pairs of all creatures whatsoever, down to ants, were created."*

Again, this Brāhmana says, "Prajāpati created living beings. From his upper vital airs he created the gods; from his lower vital airs, mortal creatures."†

Manu's account of the creation most probably follows the preceding one in order of time; and it will be noticed that he has developed some germs of thought expressed there. "He (the self-existent) having felt desire, and willing to create various living beings from his own body, first created the waters, and threw into them a seed. That seed became a golden egg, of lustre equal to the Sun; in it he himself was born as Brahmā, the parent of all the world. The waters are called narah, for they are sprung from Nara; and as they were his first sphere of motion (ayana, *i.e.* path), he is therefore cal'ed Nārāyana. Produced from the imperceptible, eternal, existent and non-existent cause, that male (purusha) is celebrated in the world as Brahmā. After dwelling for a year in the egg, the glorious being, by his own contemplation, split in twain...Having divided bis own body into two parts, the lord (Brahmā) became, with the half a male, and with the half a female; and in her he created Viraj. Know, O most excellent twice-born men, that I, whom that male Viraj himself created, am the creator of all this world."

---

*Muir, O. S. T., i. 20.
†"Vishnu Purāna," p.31.

The Purānas enter very minutely into the details of the creation. It is one of the specified topics of which a Purāna ought to treat. The first book of the "Vishnu Purāna" is largely filled with the accounts of this work, In his preface* to the translation of the "Vishnu Purāna,' Wilson says: "The first book of the six into which the work is divided is occupied chiefly with the details of creation, primary and secondary; the first explaining how the universe proceeds from Prakriti, or eternal crude matter; the second, in what manner the forms of things are developed from the elementary substance previously evolved, or how they reappear after their temporary destruction. Both these creations are periodical, but the termination of the first occurs only at the end of the life of Brahmā; when not only all the gods and other forms are annihilated, but the elements are again merged into primary substance; besides which one only spiritual being exists: the latter takes place at the end of every Kalpa, a day of Brahmā, and affects only the forms of inferior creatures and lower worlds, leaving the substance of the universe entire, and sages and gods unharmed."

The account in the "Vishnu Purāna" was, according to that authority, "originally imparted by the great father of all (Brahmā) in answer to the questions of Daksha and other venerable sages, and repeated by them to Purukutsa, a king who reigned on the banks of the Narmadā."† "Who can describe him who is not to be apprehended by the senses? He is Brahma, supreme, lord, eternal, unborn, imperishable. He then existed in the form of Purusha and of Kāla. Purusha (Spirit) is the first form of the supreme; next proceeded two other forms, the discreet and indiscreet; and Kāla (time) was the last. These four—Pradhāna (primary or crude matter), Purusha (Spirit), Vyakta (visible substance), and Kāla (time)— in their due proportions, are the causes of the production of

---

*Ibid., p. 39.
†"Vishnu Purāna," p. 9.

the phenomena of creation, preservation, and destruction. The supreme Brahma, the supreme soul, the substance of the world, the lord of all creatures, the universal soul, the supreme ruler Hari (Vishnu), of his own will having entered into matter and spirit, agitated the mutable and immutable principles, the season of creation having arrived, in the same manner as fragrance affects the mind from its proximity merely, and not from any immediate operation upon mind itself; so the supreme influenced the elements of creation."*

After giving an account of the creation, or rather the evolution of the elements, the "Vishnu Purāna"† goes on to say: "Then (the elements) ether, air, light, water and earth, severally united with the properties of sound, and the rest existed as distinguishable according to their qualities as soothing, terrific, or stupefying; but possessing various energies, and being unconnected, they could not without combination create living beings, not having blended with each other. Having combined, therefore, with one another, they assumed, through their mutual association, the character of one mass of entire unity; and from the direction of spirit, with the acquiescence of the indiscreet principle, intellect, and the rest, to the gross elements inclusive, formed an egg, which gradually expanded like a bubble of water. This vast egg, compounded of the elements, and rasting on the waters, was the excellent natural abode of Vishnu in the form of Brahmā; and there Vishnu, the lord of the universe, whose essence is inscrutable, assumed a perceptible form, and even he himself abided in it in the character of Brahmā. Its womb, vast as the mountain Meru, was composed of the mountains; and the mighty oceans were the waters that filled its cavity. In that egg were the continents and seas and mountains, the planets and divisions of the universe, the gods, demons, and mankind.

---

*"Vistula Purāna," p. 13.
†Page I8.

"Affecting then the quality of activity, Hari the lord of all, himself becoming Brahmā, engaged in the creation of the universe. Vishnu, with the quality of goodness and of immeasurable power, preserves created things through successive ages, until the close of the period termed a Kalpa; when the same mighty deity, invested with the quality of darkness, assumes the awful form of Rudra, and swallows up the universe. Having thus devoured all things, and converted the world into one vast ocean, the supreme reposes upon his mighty serpent couch amidst the deep: he awakes after a season, and again, as Brahmā, becomes the author of creation."

The Purāna next gives an account of the creation in the present Kalpa or age. This is a secondary creation, for water and the earth also are already in existence; it is not creation properly speaking, but the change of pre-existing matter into their present forms. Vishnu knew that the earth lay hidden in the waters; he, therefore, assuming the form of a boar,* raised it upon his tusks.

In answer to a request for a full account of the creation of gods and other beings, the following passages† occur:—
"Created beings, although they are destroyed (in their original forms) at the periods of dissolution, yet, being affected by the good or evil acts of former existence, are never exempted from their consequences; and when Brahmā creates the world anew, they are the progeny of his will, in the fourfold condition of gods, men, animals, and inanimate things. Brahmā then, being desirous of creating the four orders of beings—termed gods, demons, progenitors, and men—collected his mind into itself.

"Whilst thus concentrated, the quality of darkness pervaded his body, and thence the demons (the asuras) were first born, issuing from his thigh. Brahmā then abandoned that form which was composed of the rudiment of darkness, and which,

---

*See *ante,* p. 144.
†"Vishnu Puriimi," p. 39.

being deserted by him, became night. Continuing to create, but assuming a different shape, he experienced pleasure, and thence from his mouth proceeded the gods. The form abandoned by him became day, in which the good quality predominates; and hence by day the gods are most powerful, and by night the demons. He next adopted another person (form) in which the rudiment of good men also prevailed; and thinking of himself as the father of the world, the progenitors (or Pitris) were born from his side. The body, when he abandoned it, became the Sandhya, or evening twilight. Brahmā then assumed another person, pervaded by the quality of foulness; and from this, men in whom foulness (or passion) predominates, were produced. Quickly abandoning that body, it became the dawn. At the appearance of this light of day men feel most vigour; whilst the progenitors are most powerful in the evening.

"Next from Brahmā, in a form composed of the quality of foulness, was produced hunger, of whom anger was born; and the god put forth in darkness beings emaciated with hunger, of hideous aspect and with long beards. These beings hastened to the deity. Such of them as exclaimed, 'Oh, preserve us,' were thence called Rākshasas (from Raksha, to preserve); others who cried out,' Let us eat,' were denominated from that expression Yākshas (from Yaksha, to eat). Beholding them so disgusting, the hairs of Brahmā were shrivelled up, and first falling from his head were again renewed upon it; from their falling they became serpents, called Sarpa (Srip, to creep), from their creeping, and Ahi (from Hā, to abandon), because they had deserted the head. The creator of the world, being incensed, then created fierce beings, who were denominated goblins, bhutas, malignant fiends, and eaters of flesh. The Gand-harvas (choristers) were next born: imbibing melody, drinking of the goddess of speech, they were born, and hence their appellation.

"The divine Brahmā, influenced by their material energies, having created these beings, made others of his own will. Birds he formed from his vital vigour; sheep from his heart; goats from his mouth; kine from his belly and sides; and horses, elephants, sarabhas, gayals, deer, camels, mules, antelopes, and other animals from his feet: whilst from the hairs of his body sprang herbs, roots, and fruits." In this manner all things are said to have sprung from Brahmā; they were with him in the egg: hence this is an account of evolution, rather than of creation. The creation of man, as divided into four castes, is described in this Purāna, in similar terms to those in Manu.

Following this is the account of the mind-born sons of Brahmā—Bhrigu, Daksha, and others—nine in number, who became the progenitors of men.* Next "Brahmā created himself as Manu Swāyambhu, born of, and identical with, his original self, for the protection of created beings: and the female portion of himself he constituted Satarūpā, whom austerity purified from the sin (forbidden nuptials), and whom the divine Manu Swayambhu took to wife." After this follows a long account of the descendants of these mind-born sons; and it is then shown how by the production of the amrita at the churning of the ocean the gods obtained immortality, and the work of creation for this age was complete.

With some variations this is the story of the creation as told in the Purānas. In some, greater prominence is given to parts that are only lightly touched upon in this account; whilst other incidents are more fully described here than in the other Puranas.

---

*See part iii. chap. i.

Chapter X

The Purānic Divisions of Time

The three main divisions of time employed in the Hindu Scriptures are YUGAS, MANVANTARAS, and KALPAS.* These will now be described.

There are four Yugas, which together extend to 12,000 *divine* years. Their respective duration is as follows : —

The Krita Yuga	= 4,800	divine years.	
The Tretā Yuga	= 3,600	"	"
The Dvāpara Yuga	= 2,400	"	"
The Kali Yuga	= 1,200	"	"

"One year of mortals is equal to one day of the gods." As 360 is taken as the number of days in the year—

The Krita Yuga	= 4,800 x 360 = 1,728,000 years of mortals.
The Tretā Yuga	= 3,600 x 360 = 1,296,000 " "
The Dvāpara Yuga	= 2,400 x 360 = 864,000 " "
The Kali Yuga	= 1,200 x 360 = 432,000 " "

---

*See "Vishnu Purāna." book i. ehap. iii., and book vi. chap. i.

One Mahāyuga, or Great Age, including the four lesser Yugas, therefore, being 12,000 divine years = 4,320,000 years of mortals. "A thousand such Mahāyugas are a day of Brahmā," and his nights are of equal duration; a *Kalpa,* therefore, or Day of Brahmā extends over 4,320,000,000 ordinary years. "Within each Kalpa 14 Manus reign; a Manvantara, or period of a Manu, therefore, is consequently one-fourteenth part of a Kalpa, or day of Brahmā.

"In the present Kalpa, six Manus, of whom Swyambhuva was the first, have already passed away; the present being Vaivasata. In each Manvantara (period of a Manu), seven Rishis, certain deities, an Indra and a Manu, and the kings, his sons, are created and perish. A thousand systems of the four Yugas occur coincidentally with these fourteen Manvantaras, and consequently about 71 systems of four Yugas elapse during each Manvantara, and measure the lives of the Manus and the deities of the period. At the close of this day of Brahmā, a collapse of the universe takes place, which lasts through a night of Brahmā, equal in duration to his day, during which period the worlds are converted into one great ocean, when the lotus-born god (Brahmā), expanded by his deglutition of the universe, and contemplated by the Yogis and gods in Janaloka, sleeps on the serpent Sesha. At the end of that night he awakes and creates anew.

"A year of Brahmā is composed of the proper number of such days and nights, and a hundred of such years constitute his whole life. The period of his life is called *Para,* and the half of it *Parārddha,* or the half of a *Para.* One Parārddha, or half of Brahmā's existence, has now expired, terminating with the great Kalpa called the Padma Kalpa. The now existing Kalpa, or day of Brahmā, called Varāha (or that of the boar), is the first of the second Parārddha of Brahmā's existence. The dissolution which occurs at the end of each Kalpa, or day of Brahmā, is called *naimittika,* incidental, occasional, or contingent."*

The dissolution of existing beings is of three kinds : "incidental, elemental, and absolute."† The first is *naimittika,* occasional, incidental, or Brāhmya, as occasioned by the intervals of Brahmā's days; the destruction of creatures, though not of the substance of the world, occurring during the night. The second is the general resolution of the elements into their primitive source, or Prakriti, the Prākritika destruction, and occurs at the end of Brahmā's life. The third, the absolute, or final, Ālyantika, is individual annihilation, Moksha, exemption for ever from future existence.

The process of destruction is described as follows :—

"At the end of a thousand periods of four ages the earth is for the most part exhausted. A total death then ensues, which lasts a hundred years, and in consequence of the failure of food all beings become languid and exanimate, and at last entirely perish. The eternal Vishnu then assumes the character of Rudra, the destroyer, and descends to reunite all his creatures with himself. He enters into the seven rays of the sun, drinks up all the waters of the globe, and causes all moisture whatever, in living bodies or in the soil, to evaporate, thus drying up the whole earth. The seas, the rivers, the mountain-torrents, and springs are all exhaled, and so are all the waters of Pātāla, the regions below the earth.

"Thus fed, through his intervention, with abundant moisture, the seven solar rays dilate to seven suns, whose radiance glows above, below, and on every side, and sets the three worlds and Pātāla on fire. The three worlds, consumed by these suns, become rugged and deformed throughout the whole extent of their mountains, rivers, and seas; and the earth, bare of verdure and destitute of moisture, alone remains, resembling in appearance the back of a tortoise. The destroyer

---

* Muir, O. S. T., i. 45.
†"Vishnu Purāna," p. 630, note.

of all things, Hari, in the form of Rudra, who is the flame of time, becomes the scorching breath of the serpent Sesha, and thereby reduces Pātāla to ashes. The great fire, when it has burnt all the divisions of Pātāla, proceeds to the earth and consumes it also. A vast whirlpool of eddying flame then spreads to the region of the atmosphere and the sphere of the gods, and wraps them in ruin. The three spheres show like a frying-pan amidst the surrounding flames, that prey upon all movable or stationary things. The inhabitants of the two upper spheres, having discharged their functions, and being annoyed by the heat, remove to the sphere above, or Maharloka. When that becomes heated, its tenants, who after the full period of their stay, are desirous of ascending to higher regions, depart for the Janaloka."*

The "Vāyu Purāna"† gives more explicit teaching on this subject.

"Those sainted mortals who have diligently worshipped Vishnu and are distinguished for piety, abide at the time of dissolution in Maharloka, with the Pitris, the Manus, the seven Rishis, the various orders of celestial spirits and the gods. These, when the heat of the flames that destroy the world reaches to Maharloka, repair to Janaloka in their subtle forms, destined to become re-embodied in similar capacities as their former, when the world is renewed, at the beginning of the succeeding Kalpa. This continues throughout the life of Brahmā; at the expiration of his life all are destroyed; but those who have then attained a residence in the Brahmaloka, by having identified themselves in spirit with the Supreme, are finally resolved into the sole existing Brahma."

The "Vishnu Purāna"‡ continues as follows: "Janārddana, in the person of Rudra, having consumed the whole world,

---

*"Vishnu Purāna,"Ip. 631.
†Ibid., P. 632, note.
‡Page 633.

breathes forth heavy clouds. Mighty in size, and loud in thunder, they fill all space. Showering down torrents of water, these clouds quench the dreadful fires which involve the three worlds, and then they rain uninterruptedly for a hundred years and deluge the whole world. Pouring down in drops as large as dice, these rains overspread the earth, and fill the middle region and inundate heaven. The world is now enveloped in darkness, and all things, animate and inanimate, having perished, the clouds continue to pour down their waters for more than a hundred years."

The four Yugas mentioned above—viz. the Krita, Tretā, Dvāpara, and Kali—have characteristic qualities. The Krita is the golden, and Kali the iron age. The Mahābhārata* gives these characteristics very distinctly. Hanumān, the monkey-god, is the speaker, describing the four ages to Bhīmasena, one of the Pandus.

"The Krita is that age in which righteousness is eternal. In the time of that most excellent of Yugas (everything) had been done *(Krita)*, and nothing (remained) to be done. Duties did not then languish, nor did the people decline. Afterwards through (the influence of) time, this Yuga fell into a state of inferiority. In that age there were neither gods, Dānavas, Gandharvas, Yākshasas, Rākshasas, nor Pannagas; no buying and selling went on, no efforts were made by men; the fruit (of the earth was obtained) by their mere wish righteousness and abandonment of the world (prevailed). No disease or decline of the organs of sense arose through the influence of age; there was no malice, weeping, pride, or deceit; no contention, no hatred, cruelty, fear, affliction, jealousy, or envy. Hence the Supreme Brahma was the transcendent resort of these Yogins. Then Nārāyana, the soul of all beings, was white. In that age were born creatures devoted to their duties. They were alike in the object of their trust, in observance, and in their knowledge.

---

*Muir, 0. S. T., i. 144.

At that period the castes, alike in their functions, fulfilled their duties, were unceasingly devoted to one deity, and used one formula (mantra), one rule, and one rite. They had but one Veda.

"Understand now the Tretā, in which sacrifice commenced, righteousness decreased by a fourth, Vishnu became red; and men adhered to truth, and were devoted to a righteousness dependent on ceremonies. Then sacrifices prevailed, with holy arts and a variety of rites. In the Tretā men acted with an object in view, seeking after reward for their rites and their gifts, and no longer disposed to austerities, and to liberality from (a simple feeling of) duty. In this age, however, they were devoted to their own duties and to religious ceremonies.

"In the Dvāpara age righteousness was diminished by two quarters, Vishnu became yellow, and the Veda fourfold. Some studied four Vedas, some three, others two, and some none at all. The scriptures being thus divided, ceremonies were celebrated in a great variety of ways; and the people, being occupied with austerity and the bestowal of gifts, became full of passion *(rājasī)*. Owing to ignorance of the one Veda, Vedas were multiplied. And now from the decline of goodness *(Sattva)*, few only adhered to truth. When men had fallen away from goodness, many diseases, desires, and calamities, caused by destiny, assailed them, by which they were severely afflicted, and driven to practise austerities. Others, desiring enjoyments and heavenly bliss, offered sacrifices. Thus,, when they had reached the Dvāpara, men declined through unrighteousness.

"In the Kali, righteousness remained to the extent of one-fourth only. Arrived in that age of darkness, Vishnu became black; practices enjoined by the Vedas, works of righteousness, and rites of sacrifices ceased. Calamities, diseases, fatigue, faults, such as anger, etc., distresses, anxiety, hunger, fear, prevailed. As the ages revolve, righteousness again declines; when this takes place, the people also decline. When they decay, the impulses which actuate them also decay. The practices generated by this declension of the Yugas frustrate men's aims. Such is the Kali Yuga, which has existed for a short time. Those who are long-lived act in conformity with the character of the age." In the "Bhishmaparvan" there is a paragraph in which it is said that "Four thousand years are specified as the duration of life in the Krita Yuga, three thousand in the Tretā, and two thousand form the period at present established on earth in the Dvāpara. There is no fixed measure in the Tishya (Kali)."*

It should be noticed that the immense duration of the ages as quoted above from the "Vishnu Purāna" is peculiar to the Purānas. In the text of the Mahābhārata "no mention is made of the years comprising the different Yugas being *divine years*,"† though the earlier books certainly favour far more extravagant notions of chronology than those which Western nations accept.

It is interesting to notice that in the account of the Krita Yuga, or Age of Righteousness, it is said that the castes were alike in their functions. This must evidently mean that the modern caste distinctions did not then exist, and that all were devoted to the worship of one deity with one rule and one rite, evidently pointing to the time when their forefathers were monotheists. And in the judgment of the writer this happy condition was in the age of which the prevailing characteristic was righteousness.

---

*Muir, 0. S. T., i. 148.
†Ibid., i. 148.

PART III

THE INFERIOR DEITIES

The Tulsi

Chapter I
The Divine Rishis

1. BHRIGU

"WHEN Brahmā wished to populate the world, he created mind-born sons, like himself; viz. Bhrigu, Pulastya, Pulaha, Kratu, Angiras, Marichi, Daksha, Atri, and Vasishtha: these are the nine Brahmās or Brahmā-rishis celebrated in the Purānas."* Originally seven only were mentioned in the Mahābhārata; but the lists found in different parts of that Epic do not agree with each other. These seven are supposed to be visible in the Great Bear, as their wives shine in the Pleiades. These Brahmārishis are also called Prajāpatis (lords of offspring), Brahmāputras (sons of Brahmā), and Brāhmanas. The "Vishnu Purāna" teaches that Bhrigu married his niece Khyāti, a daughter of Daksha, who bore to him Sri or Lakshmi; but as it was the common belief that she was one of the products of the churning of the ocean, the reciter of the Purāna is asked to explain this discrepancy. The substance of his answer was, that "of gods, animals, and man, Hari is all that is called male, Lakshmi is all that is termed female."

---

*"Vishnu Purāna," p. 40.

In his account of the creation, Manu mentions ten Maharishis as having been created by himself, one of whom is Bhrigu, who in his turn created seven other Manus, from whom all that is has sprung.* The Mahābhārata says: "Six great Rishis are known as the mind-born sons of Brahmā;" but Bhrigu is not named amongst them. In another passage it describes him as a son of Varuna, but Brahmā is there identified with Varuna. At a sacrifice at which Brahmā officiated, a portion of Varuna was thrown into the sacrificial fire, whence there arose three men endowed with bodies. Bhrigu sprang first from *bhrik* (the blazing of the fire), Angiras from the cinders, and Kavi from a heap of ashes. The god called Mahādeva, Varuna, and Pavana, claimed these three as his own. Agni and Brahmā also claimed them.† It was agreed that Bhrigu was Varuna's son. Agni received Angiras, and Brahmā took Kavi. In another part of that poem it is said, "We have heard that the great and venerable Rishi Bhrigu was produced by Brahmā from fire at the sacrifice of Varuna."‡ The "Bhāgavata Purāna" says that "he sprang from the skin of the Creator;" and the Mahābhārata, in another verse, declares that "the venerable Bhrigu, having split Brahmā's heart, issued forth."

At the great sacrifice of Daksha, to which Siva was not invited, Bhrigu officiated as priest; and because he reviled that god and his followers, and justified Daksha in slighting him, he suffered the loss of his beard.

The Mahābhārata gives a legend of Bhrigu cursing Indra. The Indra of that age, named Nahusha, being filled with pride, lost the benefit of his previous good works, and in his presumption caused the Rishis to carry him about. When it came to Agastya's turn to carry him, Bhrigu said to him, "Why do we submit to the insults of this wicked king of the gods?"

---

*Muir, 0. S. T., i. 30.
†Ibid., i. 445.
‡Ibid.

Agastya replied that none of the Rishis had cursed Nahusha, because he had received as a boon the power to subject to his service anyone on whom he fixed his eye; but that at the same time he was quite ready to act upon any suggestion Bhrigu might make. Bhrigu then told him that he had been sent by Brahmā to take vengeance on Nahusha, who would that very day attach Agastya to his car and kick him; but incensed at this insult, he (Bhrigu) would by a curse condemn the oppressor to become a serpent.

The mighty Nahusha summoned Agastya from the banks of the Sarasvati to carry him. The glorious Bhrigu then said to Maitiāvarum (Agastya), "Close thy eyes, whilst I enter into the knot of thy hair!" With the view of overthrowing the king, Bhrigu hid himself in the hair of Agastya, who then stood motionless as a stock. Nahusha came to Agastya, when the sage desired to be attached to the vehicle, and agreed to carry the king of the gods wherever he pleased. Nahusha attached him, but Bhrigu did not venture to look at him, knowing his power of subduing by a glance. Agastya kept his temper; even when urged by a goad, he remained unmoved. The king at last kicked him; then Bhrigu, invisible in the hair of Agastya, became enraged, and violently cursed him: "Since, fool, thou hast in thine anger smitten the great Muni on the head with thy foot, therefore become a serpent, and fall swiftly to the earth."*
Thus cursed, Nahusha fell to the earth; had the sage been seen by Indra, he would have been unable to punish the oppressor.

Bhrigu on another occasion cursed Agni. The Mahābhārata says:—A woman named Pulomā was betrothed to a demon; Bhrigu, seeing her beauty, married her according to Vedic rites, and carried her off secretly. The demon, by the aid of Agni, discovered the bride's hiding-place, and took her away to his home. For rendering the demon this assistance, Bhrigu, cursing Agni, said, "From this day, you shall eat everything."

---

*Muir, O. S. T., i. 314.

Agni asked Bhrigu why he had cursed him, seeing that by speaking the truth he had simply done his duty; and reminded him that "when a person is asked a question, and intentionally speaks what is false, he, with seven preceding and seven succeeding generations, is cast into hell; and that he who withholds information is equally guilty." He goes on to say, "I, too, can curse, but respecting Brahmāns restrain my anger. I am really the mouth of the gods and ancestors. When *ghī* is offered to them, they partake of it through me as their mouth; how then can I be said to eat everything?" Bhrigu hearing this consented to modify his curse, by saying that, "as the Sun by his light and heat purifies all nature, so Agni should purify all that passed through him."

Bhrigu is said to have performed a most wonderful deed; the transforming of a Kshattriya king into a Brāhman. The Mahābhārata* gives the following account of this unique work :—"Divodāsa, King of Kāsi (Benares), was attacked by the sons of Vitāhavya, and all his family slain in battle. The afflicted monarch therefore resorted to the sage Bharadvāja, who performed for him a sacrifice, in consequence of which a son named Pratardana was born to him. Pratardana, becoming an accomplished warrior, was sent by his father to take vengeance on the Vitāhavyas. Vitāhavya had now to fly to another sage, Bhrigu, who promised his protection. The avenger Pratardana, however, followed, and demanded that the refugee should be given up. Bhrigu, the most eminent of religious men, filled with compassion, said, 'There is no Kshattriya here; all these are Brāhmans.' Hearing this true assertion of Bhrigu, Pratardana was glad, and, gently touching the sage's feet, rejoined, 'Even thus, O glorious saint, I have gained my object, for I have compelled this king to relinquish his caste.' This Vitāhavya, by the mere word of Bhrigu, became a Brāhman Rishi, and an utterer of the Vedas."

---

*Muir, O. S. T., i. 229.

The names of nineteen Bhrigus are given in the "Matsya Purāna," who are said to be composers of hymns; Bhrigu himself being one of the narrators of the Mahābhārata. Professor Roth* speaks of the Bhrigus as a class of mythological beings, who belonged to the aërial or middle class of gods. They were the discoverers of fire, and then brought it to men. He adds that the race has a connection with history, as one of the chief Brāhmanical families bears the name, and allusions are made to the fact in the hymns of the Rig-Veda.

In the Rāmāyana there are not many references to Bhrigu; he is there called a Maharishi; and Rama is induced to slay a female demon by the remembrance that Vishnu slew Brigu's wife when she aspired to Indra's throne. He is the saint whom the childless wives of Sāgar worshipped in order to obtain a son; and he gave to one lady one, to the other sixty thousand. Parasurāma was one of his most illustrious descendants.

2. PULASTYA

Pulastya, another of Brahmā's mind-born sons, is reverenced because it was through him that the Purānas were made known to men. The reason of his being regarded as the Revealer of Scripture is taught in the "Vishnu Purāna," † where the narrator Paiāsara, in answer to a question of his disciple Maitreya, says: "You recall to my mind what was of old narrated by my father's father, Vasishtha. I had heard that my father had been devoured by a Rākshas, employed by Visvamitra: violent anger seized me, and I commenced a sacrifice for the destruction of the Rākshasas; hundreds of them were reduced to ashes by the rite, when, as they were about to be entirely extirpated, my grandfather Vasishtha thus spake to me: 'Enough, my child; let thy wrath be appeased; the Rākshasas are not culpable: thy

---

*Muir, 0. S- T., i. 442.
†Page 4.

father's death was the work of destiny.'"

Paiāsara ceased from his sacrifice, and his grandfather was pleased; then Pulastya coming said to him: "Since, in the violence of animosity, you have listened to the words of your progenitor, and exercised clemency, you shall become learned in every science. Since you have forborne, even though incensed, to destroy my posterity, I will bestow on you another boon; you shall become the author of a summary of the Purānas, shall know the true nature of the deities, and your understanding through my favour shall be perfect and free from doubts." Paiāsara relates the Purāna as told him formerly "by Vasishtha and the wise Pulastya."

Pulastya married Prithi, a daughter of Daksha, by whom he had a son, the sage Agastya; the Bhāgavata calls his wife Havisbhu, whose sons were Agastya and Visravas, the father of Kuvera, Rāvana, and other Rakshasas.

The reason of Parāsara's attack upon the Rākshasas is given in a legend in the Mahābhārata. King Kalmā-shapada, meeting with Sakti (Parāsara's father) in a narrow path in a forest, wished him to get out of his way. This the sage refused to do; whereupon the king thrashed him with his whip; in return Sakti cursed him, and he became a cannibal Rākshas. When in this form, the king killed and ate Sakti and all the other sons of Vasishtha. Sakti's wife being pregnant at the time of his death, Parāsara was born soon after and brought up with his grandfather. When he grew up, he commenced the slaughter of the Rākshasas, but was restrained by Vasishtha, Pulastya, and others.

3. PULAHA

This Rishi does not figure largely in Hindu mythology. He married a daughter of Daksha named Kshamā (Patience), by whom he had three sons.

4. KRATU

Kratu is no more widely known than Pulaha. He married Sannati (Humility), another daughter of Daksha, by whom he had "sixty thousand Bālakhilyas, pigmy sages no bigger than the joint of the thumb; chaste, pious, and resplendent as the rays of the sun."*

5. ANGIKAS

Angiras is famed as the author of several hymns of Rig-Veda. He first married Smriti (Memory), by whom he had four daughters, and afterwards he married Swaddha (Oblation) and Sati, also Daksha's daughters. His so-called daughters, the Pratyangirasa Richas, are thirty-five verses addressed to presiding divinities. There is some ambiguity in the use of his name; it comes from the same root as Agni, of which deity it is used as an epithet; it is also used of Agni's father, and is the name of a son of Agneya, Agni's daughter. Angiras is supposed to have been associated with Bhrigu in introducing fire-worship into India.

6. MARICHI

Marichi is better known through his descendants than from any work of his own, his most illustrious child being Kasyapa, as a son of whom Vishnu came, in his incarnation as a dwarf. Amongst Kasyapa's thirteen wives were Diti and Aditi, who by him became the mothers of gods. "There were twelve celebrated deities in a former age called Tushitas, who, on the approach of the present period, or during the reign of the last Manu Chakshusa, said amongst themselves, 'Come, let us quickly enter into the womb of Aditi, that we may be born

---

*"Vishnu Purāna," p. 83.

in the next Manvantara, for thereby we shall again enjoy the rank of gods. Accordingly they were born the sons of Kasyapa, the son of Marichi by Aditi; thence named the twelve Ādityas, whose names were Vishnu, Sakra, Aryaman, Dhuti, Tvastri, Pushan, Vivas vat, Savitri, Mitra, Varuna, Ansa, and Bhaga."*

An explanation of the fact that gods undergo successive births is found in the "Vāyu Purāna." In the beginning of the Kalpa, twelve gods, named Jayas, were created by Brahmā as his deputies and assistants in creation. They, lost in meditation, neglected his commands, on which he declared that they should be reborn in each Manvantara until the seventh.† The writer of the "Vishnu Purāna" tries to explain this fact: "These classes of divinities are born again at the end of a thousand ages according to their own pleasure, and their appearance and disappearance are spoken of as a birth and death; but they exist age after age in the same manner as the sun sets and rises again."

By his wife Diti, Kasyapa had two sons, Hiranyākasipu and Hiranyāksha, whom Vishnu, here said to be the son of her sister Aditi, became incarnate to destroy; these mortal enemies were therefore cousins.

7. ATRI

Atri was the author of many Vedic hymns, especially those "praising Agni, Indra, the Asvins, and the Viswadevas." He married Anasūyā, who bore him Durvāsas, the sage who was slighted by Indra. Soma, the moon, is said to proceed from the eyes of his father Atri.

When this sage and his wife were old, they received a visit at their hermitage from Rāma, Sita, and Lakshman, who were then wandering from place to place—

---

*"Vishnu Purāna," p. 122.
†Page 123.

"He came to Atri's pure retreat,
Paid reverence to his holy feet,
And from the saint such welcome won
As a fond father gives his son."*

Atri, in introducing his wife to his illustrious guests, thus describes her—

"Ten thousand years this votaress, bent
On sternest rites of penance, spent;
She, when the clouds withheld their rain,
And drought ten years consumed the plain.
Caused grateful roots and fruits to grow
And ordered Gangā here to flow;
So from their cares the saints she freed,
Nor let these checks their rites impede.
She wrought in heaven's behalf, and made
Ten nights of one, the gods to aid."†

Anasūyā then joins with her husband in welcoming the exiles to their hermitage, and, delighted with the princess, tells her to ask a boon. As, however, Sitā appeared to want nothing particular, the aged saint said—

"My gift to-day
Thy sweet contentment shall repay:
Accept this precious robe to wear,
Of heavenly fabric, rich and rare;
These gems thy limbs to ornament,
This precious balsam sweet of scent.
O Maithil dame ! this gift of mine
Shall make thy limbs with beauty shine,

---

*Griffiths's "Rāmāyana," ii. 468.
†Griffiths's "Rāmāyaua," ii. 473.

And, breathing o'er thy frame, dispense
Its pure and lasting influence.
This balsam, on thy fair limbs spread,
New radiance on thy lord shall shed,
As Lakshmi's beauty lends a grace
To Vishnu's own celestial face."*

8. DAKSHA

Daksha, the father of Umā, the consort of Siva, has attained pre-
eminence amongst his brethren largely through the greatness
of his son-in-law. He, too, is a mind-born son of Brahmā;
or, according to other accounts, sprang from the thumb of
his father. He is one of the chief Prajāpatis. Before speaking
of Daksha, as the term Prajāpati is of frequent occurrence, it
will not be out of place here to describe the position of these
beings.

Daksha

---

*Ibid., ii. 474.

The term Prajāpati means a lord of creatures; the Prajāpatis, therefore, are regarded as the progenitors of mankind. The word is used in much the same manner as Patriarch in the Christian Scriptures. Sometimes Brahmā alone is intended by the term Prajāpati; he is *the* "lord of creatures;" sometimes it is employed for the first-formed men from whom the human race sprang. The word was originally employed as an epithet of Savitri and Soma, as well as of Hiranyāgarbha, or Brahmā. It afterwards, however, came to denote a separate deity, who appears in three places in the Rig-Veda. Prajāpati is sometimes identified with the universe, and described (in the same way as Brahma, or entity, or non-entity in other places) as having alone existed in the beginning, as the source out of which creation was evolved: "*e.g.* Prajāpati was this universe; Vach was a second to him. She became pregnant, she departed from him, she produced these creatures. She again entered into Prajāpati."* At the same time he is "sometimes described as a secondary or subordinate deity, and treated as one of thirty-three deities."

By the time Manu wrote, creation had come to be regarded as the special work of Brahmā, hence the term Prajāpati is applied to him in the Dharmasastra, and in the later writings it is given to those who sprang from him, and carried on his work of populating the world.

The Mahābhārata† gives two distinct accounts of the origin of Daksha:—"Daksha, the glorious Rishi, tranquil in spirit, and great in austere fervour, sprang from the right thumb of Brahmā. From the left thumb sprang the great Muni's wife, by whom he begot fifty daughters." "Born with all splendour, like that of the great Rishis, the ten sons of Prachetas (another Prajāpati) are reputed to have been virtuous and holy, and by them the glorious beings (trees, plants, etc.), were formerly burnt up by

---

*Muir, O. S. T., v. 390.
†Ibid. i. 224.

fire springing from their mouth. From them was born Daksha Prāchetasa; and from Daksha, the parent of the world, (were produced) these creatures. Cohabiting with Virini, the Muni Daksha begat a thousand sons like himself, famous for their religious observances." In the Harivansa, Vishnu is identified with Daksha. At the end of a thousand Yugas the Brāhmans of a previous age, "perfect in knowledge and contemplation, became involved in the dissolution of the world. Then Vishnu, sprung from Brahma, removed beyond the sphere of sense, absorbed in contemplation, became the Prajāpati Daksha, and formed numerous creatures."*

Fuller particulars of Daksha's origin we find in the "Vishnu Purāna."† "From Brahmā, continuing to meditate, were born mind-engendered progeny, with forms and faculties derived from his corporeal nature, embodied spirits produced from the person of that all-wise deity. But as they did not multiply themselves, Brahmā created other mind-born sons like himself, viz. Bhrigu, etc. Considerable variety prevails in this list of Prajāpatis, but the variations are of the nature of additions made to an apparently original enumeration of but seven, whose names generally occur. The names mentioned in all the Purānas make up altogether seventeen. The simple statement that the first Prajāpatis sprang from the mind or will of Brahmā has not contented the depraved taste of the mystics, and in some of the Purānas, as the Bhāgavata, Vāyu and Linga, they are said to be derived from the body of their progenitor; Bhrigu from his skin, Marichi from his mind, Atri from his eyes, Angiras from his mouth, Pulastya from his ear, Pulaha from his navel, Kratu from his hand, Vasishtha from his breath, Daksha from his thumb, and Nārada from his lips. They do not exactly agree, however, in the [description of the

---

*Muir, O. S. T., i. 153.
†Page 49.

places] whence these beings proceed."*

The "Vishnu Purāna" † also speaks of Daksha as a son of the Prāchetasas, and gets over the difficulty by the statement that he was born first as a son of Brahmā, and afterwards as the son of the Prāchetasas. These progenitors of Daksha were the sons of a mighty patriarch named Prachinaverhis, so called "from his placing upon the earth the sacred grass pointing to the East." At the termination of a season of rigid penance, he married Savarnā, the daughter of the ocean, who had by him ten sons, styled Prāchetasas, who were skilled in military science; "they all observed the same duties, practised religious austerities, and remained immersed in the bed of the sea for ten thousand years." The reason for this prolonged penance was the fact that their father had been enjoined by Brahmā to increase the human family. In harmony with his promise of obedience, he told his sons that the performance of severe penance was the best way of fulfilling Brahmā's order; "for whoever worships Vishnu, the bestower of good, attains undoubtedly the object of his desires: there is no other mode."

As the sons were immersed in the ocean, intent on the worship of Vishnu, that deity appeared to them, and, hearing their request, said, "Receive the boon you have desired; for I, the giver of good, am content with you." Whilst the Prāchetasas were absorbed in their devotions, "the trees grew and overshadowed the unprotected earth, the people perished, the winds could not blow, the sky was shut out from view by the boughs, and mankind unable to labour for ten thousand years. When the sages saw this, wind (which tore up the trees) and flames (which then consumed them) issued from their mouths, and the forests were soon cleared away. Soma, the sovereign of the vegetable world, seeing nearly all the trees destroyed, went to the patriarchs and said, 'Restrain your

---

*Wilson in note, p. 49, "Vishnu Purāna."

†Page 116.

indignation, and listen to me. I will make an alliance between you and the trees. Prescient of futurity, I have nourished this maiden, the daughter of the woods. She is called Mārishā, and, as your bride, she shall be the multiplier of the race of Druva. From a portion of your and my lustre the patriarch Daksha shall be born, who, endowed with a part of me and composed of your vigour, shall be resplendent as fire, and shall multiply the human race.'"

Soma then informs the brothers respecting Mārishā's origin. "There was formerly a sage named Kandu, eminent in wisdom and austerity, on the banks of the Gomati. Indra sent the nymph Pramlochā to divert the sage from his devotions: they lived together for 150 years, during which time the Muni was given up to pleasure. The nymph at the close of this period asked leave to depart, but the Muni entreated her to continue with him. And though at the end of several centuries she preferred the same request, again and again she was asked to remain.

"On one occasion, as the sage was going forth from their cottage in a great hurry, the nymph asked where he was going. 'The day,' he replied, 'is drawing fast to a close. I must perform the Sandhya worship, or a duty will be neglected.' The nymph smiled mirthfully as she rejoined, 'Why do you talk, grave sir, of this day drawing to a close; your day is a day of many years, a day that must be a marvel to all: explain what this means.' The Muni said, 'Fair maiden, you came to the river-side at dawn. I beheld you then, and you entered the hermitage. It is now the revolution of evening, and the day is gone. What is the meaning of this laughter? Tell me the truth.' Pramlochā answered, 'You say rightly, venerable Brāhman, that I came hither at morning dawn, but several hundred years have passed since the time of my arrival. This is the truth.'" She informed him that they had lived together nine hundred and seven years, six months, and three days. The Muni sees now that the nymph must have been sent by Indra purposely to interrupt his devotions, and deprive him of the divine knowledge he had desired. And though very angry with her at first, he bids her depart in peace, as he says, "The sin is wholly mine."

"Thus addressed by the Muni, Pramlochā stood trembling, whilst big drops of perspiration started from every pore, till he angrily cried to her, 'Begone, begone!' She then, reproached by him, went forth from his dwelling, and, passing through the air, wiped the perspiration from her person with the leaves of the trees. The nymph went from tree to tree, and as with dusky shoots that crowned their summits she dried her limbs, which were covered with moisture, the child she had conceived by the Rishi came forth from the pores of her skin in drops of perspiration. The trees received the living dews, and the winds collected them into one mass. 'This,' said Soma, 'I matured by my rays, and gradually it increased in size, till the exhalation that had rested on the tree-tops became the lovely girl named Mārishā. The trees will give her to you, Prāchetasas; let your indignation be appeased. She is the progeny of Kandu, the child of Pramlochā, the nursling of the trees, the daughter of the wind and moon.'"

Soma then informs the Prāchetasas that Mārishā, in her previous birth, was the widow of a prince, but left childless. She therefore earnestly worshipped Vishnu, who told her to desire some boon. She replied, "I pray thee that in succeeding births I may have honourable husbands, and a son equal to a patriarch among men,…and may I be born out of the ordinary course." Vishnu promised her: "In another life you shall have ten husbands of mighty prowess, and renowned for glorious acts; and you shall have a son magnanimous and valiant, distinguished by the rank of a patriarch, from whom the various races of men shall multiply, and by whose posterity the universe shall be filled. You, virtuous lady, shall be of marvellous birth, and delighting the hearts of men." Thus having spoken, the deity disappeared, and Soma informs his hearers that it was this princess who was born as Mārishā.

"Soma having concluded, the Prāchetasas took Mārishā, as he had enjoined them, righteously to wife, relinguishing their indignation against the trees, and upon her they begot the eminent patriarch Daksha, who had (in a former life) been born as the son of Brahmā. This great sage, for the furtherance of creation and the increase of mankind, created progeny. Obeying the command of Brahmā, he made movable and immovable things, the bipeds and quadrupeds,, and subsequently by his will gave birth to females, ten of whom he bestowed on Dharma, thirteen on Kasyapa, and twenty-seven, who regulate the course of time, on Soma (the moon). Of these the gods, the Titans, the snake gods, cattle and birds, the singers and dancers of the courts of heaven, the spirits of evil and other beings, were born. From that period forward living creatures were engendered in an ordinary manner; before the time of Daksha, they were variously propagated by the will, by sight, by touch, and by the influence of religious austerities by devout sages and holy saints."

Daksha's first attempts at populating the world were unsuccessful. A thousand sons were born to him by Asikni, but these were induced byNārada not to propagate offspring. A thousand other sons by the same wife were born, who also were advised by Nārada not to be troubled with children. The Prajāpati, incensed, cursed Nārada, and proceeded to create sixty daughters by Asikni, whom he gave to various husbands, by whom they had children. At length, when a time of peace and prosperity prevailed on. the earth, and the gods had their proper places assigned to them, to Daksha was given the position as chief of the Prajāpatis—progenitors of mankind.

In the account of Siva it was noticed that as a punishment for the insults Daksha had offered to his illustrious son-in-law, the great god changed his head for that of a goat; a perpetual sign of his ignorance and stupidity.

9. VASISHTHA

Vasishtha, together with Pulastya, is said to have narrated the "Vishnu Purāna," and he, too, is believed to have been the writer of many of the Vedic hymns. It was he who allayed the anger of Panāsara when that sage was about to extirpate the Rākshas race, because one of their kings had slain his father. He is said to have been the Vyāsa, or arranger of the Vedas, in the Dvāpara Age; this work of arranging having a different agent in each age.

Vasishtha served as the family priest of several kings. One of these, named Saudāsa, when out hunting, seeing a couple of tigers, shot one of them with an arrow. It happened that these tigers were really Rākshasas, for, as the one shot by Saudāsa was dying, it assumed a fiendish shape; the other, threatening vengeance, disappeared. Not long after this, as the king was engaged in a sacrifice, Vasishtha being out of the room, the Rākshas who escaped, assuming the form of Vasishtha, came to the king and said, "Now that the sacrifice is ended, give me something to eat; let it be cooked, and I will presently return." The Rākshas next transformed himself into the cook, and, having prepared a dish of human flesh, brought it to the king. When the real Muni entered, the king offered him the dish; but he discovered, by the force of meditation, that it was human flesh that was presented to him. Indignant at the insult, cursing the king, he said, "Your appetite shall be excited by similar food to that now offered me." The king was astonished at this outburst of anger, and Vasishtha, seeing this, by further meditation, discovered the whole trick; but as he could not entirely recall the effects of his curse, he modified it so that it was to work for twelve years only.* It was this same king who was cursed by Vasishtha's son Sakti to become a Rākshas, and who, in that state, devoured the sage that cursed him.

Vasishtha also cursed a king named Nimi. As the king was about to commence a sacrifice that was to continue for a

---

*"Vishnu Purāna," p. 381.

thousand years, he asked Vasishtha to officiate as priest; but the Muni being engaged in a similar work for Indra, he could not do so for the next five hundred years. The king proceeded with his sacrifice, engaging Gautama as priest. As soon as his engagement was over with Indra, the sage, coming to conduct Nimi's sacrifice, found another priest had been appointed. He was so angry that, cursing the king, he declared that he should cease to exist in a bodily form. On learning what was done, the king in return pronounced a similar curse upon the sage. Both took effect; but as Vasishtha's spirit became united to the spirits of Mitra and Varuna, when these deities were smitten with the beauty of the nymph Urvasi, the spirit of the sage fell from them, and he became again incorporated through her.* A verse in the Rig-Veda ascribes Vasishtha's birth to Mitra and Varuna, in harmony with the legend just quoted: "Thou, O Vasishtha, art a Son of Mitra and Varuna, born a Brāhman from the soul of Urvasi. All the gods placed in the vessel thee—the drop which had fallen through divine contemplation."

There are several stories of quarrels between this sage and Visvamitra, who was anxious to obtain the position of priest to Saudāsa, which was held by Vasishtha. At another time, when he was priest to Harischandra, he was so greatly incensed at the treatment the king had received at Visvamitra's hands that he cursed him, and he became a crane. His rival returned the compliment, and he too became a bird. In this form the sages fought so violently that it was necessary for Brahmā to pacify them. The real cause of all this unpleasantness was the fact that Visvamitra was a Kshattriya by birth, who, by penance and various rites, had obtained admission into the Brāhmanical caste. Previous to his exaltation he was a king. Being desirous of obtaining a wonderful cow that belonged to Vasishtha, which had the power to grant whatever her owner desired, as he could not overcome the Brāhmans, owing to their superhuman

---

*"Vishnu Purāna," p. 388.

power, he first sought to raise himself to equality with them, and at length his efforts were crowned with success.

10. NĀRADA

Nārada's name is not found in the list of Brahmā's sons in the "Vishnu Purāna," yet he is generally regarded as one, though, according to some authorities, he had a different origin. He is the messenger of the gods, and is often described as imparting information that was only known to them. It was he who persuaded the sons of Daksha not to beget offspring, and who was cursed for his interference; it was he who informed Kansa of the approaching birth of Krishna, which led that king to slay the children of Vasudeva: hence his common name is Kalikāraka, the strife-maker, and in modern plays he is introduced as a spy and marplot. The name Nārada is frequently employed as a term of abuse. It is used to describe a quarrelsome, meddling person.

"A distinguished son of Brahmā, named Nārada, whose actions are the subject of a Purāna, bears a strong resemblance to Hermes or Mercury. He was a wise legislator, great in arts and arms, an eloquent messenger of the gods, either to one another or to favoured mortals, and a musician of exquisite skill. His inventing the *vina,* or Indian lute, is thus described in the poem entitled 'Māgna:' 'Nārada sat watching from time to time his large *vina,* which, by the impulse of the breeze, yielded notes that pierced successively the regions of his ear, and proceeded by musical intervals.' The Law Tract, supposed to have been revealed by Nārada, is at this hour cited by Pundits, and we cannot therefore believe him to have been the patron of thieves, though an innocent theft of Krishna's cattle, by way of putting his divinity to the test, he strangely imputed, in the 'Bhāgavata Purāna,' to his father Brahmā."*

---

*Sir W. Jones, "Asiatic Researches," i. 264.

The accounts of Nārada's origin vary considerably. According to the Bhāgavata, he was the third incarnation of Vishnu. Manu declares that he was one of the Maharishis whom he created at the beginning of the age. Moor* quotes as follows: "Brahmā said, 'Rise up, Rudra, and form man to govern the world.' Rudra obeyed; but the men he made were fiercer than tigers, having nothing but the destructive quality in their composition. Anger was their only passion. Brahmā, Vishnu, and Rudra then joined their different powers, and created ten men whose names were Nārada," etc. The "Siva Purāna" teaches that Nārada sprang from the thigh of his father: "Brahmā, in view of peopling the world, produced four beings, who, being refractory, caused their parent to weep. To comfort him, Siva, in the character of Rudra, issued from a fold in his forehead, with five heads and ten arms, and, endowing Brahmā with additional might, he (Brahmā) produced Bhrigu and the seven Rishis, and after that Nārada from his thigh." †

In another birth Nārada was the son of Kasyapa‡ and a daughter of Daksha. Daksha was greatly incensed when he dissuaded the Prajāpati's sons from peopling the world, and declared that he should not have a resting-place; hence his wandering nature.

On one occasion Nārada was cursed by his own father, and he in return cursed Brahmā. "Brahmā exhorted his son Nārada to take a wife, and assist in peopling the world. Nārada, who was a votary of Krishna, becomes angry, affirms that devotion to that god is the sole way to attain felicity, and denounces his father as an erring instructor. Brahmā, in reply, curses Nārada, and dooms him to a life of sensuality, and subjection to women. Nārada pays back the imprecation as follows: 'Wretch! become no object of adoration: how shall any one be devoted to the

---

*"Hindu Pantheon," p. 91.
†Ibid., p. 78.
‡"Vishnu Purāna," p. 118.

forms of thy worship? Thou shalt without doubt lust after her who is no fit object of thy desires!' Through this curse of Nārada, the creator of the world ceased to be an object of worship. Beholding the beauty of his daughter, he ran after her. Nārada, having made obeisance to his lotus-born father, forsook his Brāhmanical body, and became a Gandharva,* a chorister of Indra's heaven."

In the Mahābhārata, Nārada figures as a religious teacher; and in the "Uttara Kānda" of the Rāmāyana is a specimen of his teaching.† A Brāhman, carrying the dead body of his son, came to the door of Rāma's palace at Ayodha; and bewailing his loss, as he himself was unconscious of any fault, he believed it to be owing to some misconduct on the part of the king. Rāma summoned his councillors, when the divine sage Nārada spoke as follows : "Hear, O king, how the boy's untimely death occurred; and, having heard the truth regarding what ought to be done, do it." The story, briefly told, is as follows: "A presumptuous Sudra, paying no regard to the fact that during the age in which he lived the prerogative of practising self-mortification had not descended to the humble class to which he belonged, had been guilty of seeking to secure a store of religious merit by its exercise. Rāma, after considerable search, comes upon a person who was engaged in the manner described by Nārada. The Sudra avows his caste, and his desire to conquer for himself the rank of a god, by the self-mortification he was undergoing. Rāma instantly cuts off the offender's head; the gods applaud the deed, and, having been encouraged by them to ask a boon, Rāma requests that the Brāhman's boy may be resuscitated. He is informed that he was restored to life the very moment that the Sudra was slain."

Nārada was the friend and companion of Krishna, and was

---

*"Nārada Pancharatna," Muir, O. S. T., preface, iv. p. 6.
†Ibid. i. 117.

famed for his musical talents, but, becoming presumptuous on account of them, he emulated the divine strains of Krishna, who severely punished him for his presumption by placing his *vina* in the paws of a bear, when it emitted sounds far sweeter than those of the minstrelsy of the mortified musician. Krishna played many practical jokes on his friend; on one occasion he went so far as to metamorphose him into a woman.*

Great honour is given to Nārada because he is said to have revealed to Valmiki the "Rāmāyana," which opens as follows:—

> "To sainted Nārad, prince of those
> Whoso lore in words of wisdom flows,
> Whose constant care and chief delights
> Were scripture and ascetic rites,
> The good Valmiki, first and best
> Of hermit saints, these words addressed:
> 'In all the world, I pray thee, who
> Is virtuous, heroic, true?
> Firm in his vows, of grateful mind,
> To every creature good and kind?
> Bounteous and holy, just and wise,
> Alone most fair to all men's eyes?
> *   *   *   *
> Grant, saint divine, the boon I ask,
> For thee, I ween, an easy task,
> To whom the power is given to know
> If such a man breathes here below.'
> Then Nārad, clear before whose eye
> The present, past, and future lie,
> Made ready answer!"†

---

*Moor, "Hindu Pantheon," p.205.
†Griffiths's "Rāmāyana," i.3.

Nārada proceeds to narrate the life of Rāma to Valmiki, who feels that the task of writing down what was told him is too great a work for his powers, until Brahmā himself appears, and encourages him to proceed—

> "Then come, O best of seers, relate
> The life of Rāma, good and great;
> The tale that saintly Nārad told
> In all its glorious length unfold."*

Chapter II
Kuvera

Kuvera, the god of riches, does not occupy a very conspicuous position in the mythology of the Hindus. No images or pictures of him are to be had, though he is frequently referred to in the Rāmāyana as the lord of gold and wealth. "Brahmā had a mental son named Pulastya, who again had a mental son named Gaviputra Vaisravana (Kuvera). The latter deserted his father, and went to Brahmā, who as a reward made him immortal, and appointed him to be the god of riches, with Lanka for his capital, and the car Pushpaka for his vehicle.* This car was of immense size, and moved at its owner's will at a marvellous speed; Rāvana took it by force from Kuvera, at whose death it was restored by Rāma to its original possessor.

"Pulastya being incensed at this desertion (of his son Kuvera) reproduced the half of himself in the form of Vaisravas, who looked upon Vaisravana with indignation. The latter strove to pacify his father, and with this view gave him three elegant Rākshasīs to attend on him: Pushpotkatā, who had two sons, Rāvana and Kumbhakarna; Mālinī, who bore Vibhīshana; and Rākā, who bore Khara and Sūparnakha.

---

*"Mahābhārata:" Muir, O. S. T., iv. 481.

These sons were all valiant, skilled in the Vedas and observers of religious rites, but, perceiving the prosperity of Vaisravana, were filled with jealousy. Excepting Khara and Sūparnakha, they began to practise austerities to propitiate Brahmā, and at the end of a thousand years Rāvana cut off his own head and threw it as an oblation into the fire. Brahmā appeared to put a stop to their austerities, and to offer them boons (except that of immortality). He ordained that Rāvana should have heads and shapes at will and be invincible, except by men; that Kumbha-karna should enjoy a long sleep. Having obtained these powers, Rāvana expelled Vaisravana from Lanka. Kuvera retired to Gandamārdana. Rāvana having been installed as king, and begun to exercise his power tyrannically, the Rishis resort to Brahmā, who promises that, as Rāvana could not be killed by gods or asuras, the four-armed Vishnu, the chief of warriors, should by his (Brahmā's) appointment descend to earth for his destruction."*

The Rāmāyana (Uttara Kānda)† makes Kuvera the grandson, not the son, of Pulastya. In the Krita Yuga the pious Pulastya, being teased with the singing and dancing of different damsels, proclaimed that any one of them whom he saw near his hermitage should become a mother. This threat had not been heard by the daughter of Trinavindu, who came near the hermitage, and incurred Pulastya's threatened punishment. Her father, on learning her condition, gave her as wife to Pulastya, and she bore him a son named Visravas; who, becoming a sage, married a daughter of the Muni Bharadvāja, whose son Brahmā named Vaisravana (Kuvera). He performed austerities for thousands of years, and received as a boon from Brahmā that he should be the god of riches, and one of the guardians of the world. At the suggestion of his father Visravas, he took possession of Lanka for his abode, which was formerly

---

* Muir, 0. S. T., v. 483.
†Ibid., iv. 488.

built by Visvakarma for the Rakshasas, who through fear of Vishnu had recently forsaken it.

A Rākshas prince named Sumali, who had been driven to Pātāla, happening to visit the earth, saw Kuvera travelling in his chariot to visit his father. This leads him to devise a plan by which he might regain his former position. He sends his daughter Kaikasi to woo Visravas; she is kindly received and becomes the mother of Rāvana, Kumbhakarna, Sūparnakha and Vibhishana. When Kaikasi saw the splendour of Kuvera, she urges Rāvana to resemble him in glory; who, in order to effect this, undergoes most severe austerities for a thousand years, when Brahmā grants him as a boon invincibility against all beings more powerful than men, and other gifts. Kuvera on Rāvana's demand yields the city of Lanka.

It was noticed above that Kuvera was one of the guardians of the world; these are commonly said to be four in number. Rāma mentions their names:

> "May he whose hands the thunder wield [Indra],
> Be in the East thy guard and shield:
> May Yama's care the South befriend,
> And Varuna's arm the West defend;
> And let Kuvera, Lord of Gold,
> The North with firm protection hold."*

When eight guardians are spoken of, the additional four are these: Agni has charge of the South-East, Surya of the South-West, Soma of the North-East, and Vayu of the North-West.

Kuvera is called the King of the Yākshasas—savage beings who, because the moment they were born said, "Let us eat," were called Yākshasas. These beings were ever on the watch for prey, and ate those they slew in battle.

Throughout the Rāmāyana there are brief references to

---

*Griffiths's "Rāmāyana," ii. 20.

Kuvera as the giver of riches, and also to the beauty of his palace and gardens. Thus Bharadvāja the sage, desirous of giving Rāma and Lakshman a fitting reception, said—

"Here let Kuvera's garden rise, Which far in Northern Kuru lies; For leaves let cloth and gems entwine, And let its fruit be nymphs divine."*

His garden is a place "where the inhabitants enjoy a natural perfection, attended with complete happiness, obtained without exertion. There is there no vicissitude, nor decrepitude, nor death, nor fear; no distinction of virtue and vice, none of the inequalities denoted by the words 'best,' 'worst,' and 'intermediate,' nor any change resulting from the succession of the four Yugas. There is neither grief, weariness, anxiety, hunger, nor fear. The people live in perfect health, free from every suffering, for ten or twelve thousand years."† As Sugriva was sending forth his armies to search for Sita, he thus speaks of this garden to Satabal, the leader of the army of the North—

> "Pursue your onward way, and haste
> Through the dire horrors of the waste,
> Until triumphant with delight
> You reach Kailāsa's glittering height.
> There stands a palace decked with gold,
> For King Kuvera wrought of old,
> A home the heavenly artist planned,
> And fashioned with his cunning hand.
> There lotuses adorn the flood
> With full-blown flower and opening bud,
> Where swans and mallards float, and gay
> Apsarasas‡ come down to play.

---

*Griffiths's "Rāmāyana," ii. 358.
†"Bhāgavata Purāna:" Muir, O. S. T., i. 492.
‡Nymphs of Paradise.

There King Vaisravan's self, the lord
By all the universe adored,
Who golden gifts to mortals sends,
Lives with the Guhyakas,* his friends."†

As Rāma and Lakshman were wandering in the forest, they were attacked by a giant named Virādha; but as they could not slay him with their weapons, they buried him alive, and as a result he regained his proper form. Formerly Kuvera had cursed him, for "loving Rambhā's charms too well," to assume the hideous form in which Rāma met with him, and the only relief Kuvera would give him was—

"When Rāma, Dasaratha's son, Destroys thee, and the fight is won, Thy proper shape once more assume, And heaven again shall give thee room."‡

When Rāvana had risen to the summit of his power, he made the gods perform various offices in his house : thus Indra prepared garlands, Agni was his cook, Surya gave light by day and Chandra by night, and Kuvera became his cash-keeper.

Kuvera married Yakshi or Charvi; and two of his sons, through a curse of the sage Nārada, became trees, in which condition they remained until Krishna, when an infant, uprooted them. Nārada met with them in a forest, bathing with their wives, in a state of intoxication. The wives, ashamed of themselves, fell at Nārada's feet and sought for pardon; but as their husbands disregarded the presence of the sage, they suffered the full effects of his curse.

---

*Guardians of treasures.
†Griffiths's "Rāmāyana," iv. 24.
‡Ibid., iii. 14.

Chapter III

The Demigods of The Rāmāyana

1. SUGRIVA

Over the mighty leaders of the Monkey army associated with Rāma in the destruction of Rāvana was King Sugriva.

Sugriva

When Vishnu, before leaving heaven to become incarnate as Rama, asked the gods to—

> "Make helps, in war to lend him aid,
> In forms that change at will arrayed,
> Of wizard skill and hero might,
> Outstrippers of the wind in flight,"*

they consented, and "begot in countless swarms brave sons disguised in sylvan forms." Of Sugriva it is said—

> "That noblest fire,
> The Sun, was great Sugriva's sire."†

When Rāma finds this King of the Monkeys, he was an exile, having been driven from his throne by his brother Bāli. Kabandha, a giant slain by Rāma, gives the following description of the king to the wandering hero:—

> "O Rāma, hear my words and seek
> Sugriva, for of him I speak.
> His brother Bāli, Indra's son,
> Expelled him, when the fight he won.
> With four great chieftains, faithful still,
> He dwells on Rishyanuka's hill.
>   * * * *
> Lord of the Vānars, just and true,
> Strong, very glorious, bright to view,
> Unmatched in counsel, firm and meek,
> Bound by each word his lips may speak,
> Good, splendid, mighty, bold and brave.
> Wise in each plan to guide and save.

---

*Griffiths's "Rāmāyana," i. 92.
†Ibid., i. 93.

His brother, fired by lust of sway,
Drove forth the king in woods to stray;
  In all thy search for Sitā, he
Thy ready friend and help will be."*

Rāma discovers his retreat, hears the story of his wrongs, promises to slay Bali, the usurper, and assist Sugriva to regain his throne; Sugriva on his part solemnly promises to aid Rāma in his search and to enable him to release Sitā from Rāvana's bonds. Rāma very soon fulfils his part of the compact. He marches with Sugriva and the others to Bāli's city; Sugriva challenges Bali to fight, and just as he is getting the worst of it, Rāma lets fly his arrow, which gives Bāli his mortal wound. Ere this chief dies, he strongly reproves Rāma for slaying one who had never harmed him and for slaying him too in a secret and cowardly manner. He asks—

"What fame, from one thou hast not slain
In front of battle, canst thou gain,
Whose secret hand has laid me low,
When madly fighting with my foe?
　　*　　　*　　　*　　　*
I held that thou wouldst surely scorn
To strike me as I fought my foe,
And thought not of a stranger's blow.
But now thine evil heart is shown,
A yawning well, with grass o'ergrown.
Thou wearest virtue's badge,† but guile
And meanest sin thy soul defile."‡

Rāma reminds Bāli that Fate had ordained his death,

---

*Ibid., iii. 337.
†The dress of a hermit.
‡Griffiths's "Rāmāyana," iv. 91.

against which it was useless to contend, with which statement Bāli agrees, and, withdrawing his unkind words, asks for Rāma's forgiveness.

Monkeys constructing the bridge at Lanka

On the death of Bāli, Sugriva is again installed as King of the Vānars, and Rāma gives him four months for the enjoyment of his long-lost wife and kingdom. At its expiration, as Sugriva appeared to be so absorbed with pleasure as to forget his engagement to assist Rāma, Lakshman reminds him of his duty in no measured terms. At length the order is given to collect the forces. An army of monkeys, bears, etc., goes forth in search of Sitā, who, it is discovered, is somewhere in the southern district over which Hanumān is supposed to rule, who after diligent inquiry learns her whereabouts. The army marches to the seashore; a bridge connecting the island of Lanka (Ceylon) with the mainland is erected by Nala, and the attacking army surrounds the city. No sooner were they in sight of the city of the foe than

> "Up sprang Sugriva from the ground,
> And reached the turret at a bound.
> Unterrified the Vānar stood,
> And wroth, with wondrous hardihood,
> The king in bitter words addressed,
> And thus his scorn and hate expressed:
> 'King of the giant race, in me
> The friend and slave of Rāma see.
> Lord of the world, he gives me power
> To smite thee in thy fenced tower.'
> While through the air his challenge rang,
> At Rāvan's face the Vānar sprang,
> Snatched from his head the kingly crown,
> And dashed it in his fury down.
> Straight at his foe the giant flew,
> His mighty arms around him threw,
> With strength resistless swung him round,
> And dashed him panting to the ground.
> Unharmed amid the storm of blows,
> Swift to his feet Sugriva rose.
> Again in furious fight they met;
> With streams of blood their limbs were wet,
> Each grasping his opponent's waist."*

They continue to fight with uncertain result until Rāvana calls to his aid his magical arts—

> "But brave Sugriva, swift to know
> The guileful purpose of his fee,
> Gained with light leap the upper air,
> And breath, and strength, and spirit there;

---

*Griffiths's "Rāmāyana," v. 121.

> Then, joyous as for victory won,
> Returned to Raghu's royal son."*

In the course of the great fight, a giant named Kurnbhakarna, a brother of Rāvana, came forth from the city and did great execution amongst the Vānar host, devouring his victims as fast as they were slain, though they were numbered by thousands. Some idea of the size of this monster may be gained from the fact that

> "There was no respite then, no pause:
> Fast gaped and closed his hell-like jaws:
> Yet prisoned in that gloomy cave,
> Some Vānars still their lives could save;
> Some through his nostrils found a way,
> Some through his ears resought the day." †

Bāli's son Angad tried to rally the Vānar host, but he was soon "dashed senseless on the ground." Hanumān had already been severely wounded by the monster. And now he attacks Sugriva, who hurled a hill at him, but

> "The giant's chest the stroke repelled." ‡

This compliment the monster returns by throwing his spear, which Hanumān caught as it flew, and broke it across his knee. Then

> "At Sugriva's head he sent
> A peak from Lanka's mountain rent.
> The rushing mass no might could stay:

---

* Griffiths's "Rāmāyana," v. 122.
†Ibid., v. 197.
‡Ibid., V. 198.

Sugriva fell, and senseless lay.
The giant stooped his foe to seize,
And bore him thence, as bears the breeze
A cloud in autumn through the sky."*

The giant enters Lanka with his captive, and is greatly lauded by the people; but his triumph was of short duration, for

"By slow degrees the Vānars' lord
Felt life, and sense, and strength restored.
He heard the giant's joyful boast:
He thought upon his Vānar host.
His teeth and feet he fiercely plied,
And bit and rent the giant's side,
Who, mad with pain and smeared with gore,
Hurled to the ground the load he bore.
Regardless of a storm of blows,
Swift to the sky the Vānar rose,
Then lightly, like a flying ball,
High overleapt the city wall."†

Lakshman tried to slay this monster; but it was left for Rāma to finish the work, whose arrows cut off limb after limb, and at last severed head from body. After his death, two brothers, Nikumbha and Kumbha, came forth to do battle for their chief. Sugriva seized Kumbha and hurled him into the sea; on his reaching the shore he struck Sugriva such a blow on his chest that he broke his own wrist with the shock. Sugriva returned the blow by another beneath the neck, which proved fatal. His brother now attacked Sugriva;

---

*Ibid., v. 199.
†Ibid., v. 229.

"And red with fury flashed his eye.
He dashed with mighty sway and swing
His axe against the Vānar king;
But shattered on that living rock,
It split in fragments at the shock.
Sugriva, rising to the blow,
Raised his huge hand and smote his foe,
And in the dust the giant lay,
Gasping in blood his soul away."*

Sugriva and his heroic army continued faithful to their king's promise until Rāma's victory was won, though death had considerably thinned their ranks; but this loss was made good as, in answer to Rāma's prayer, Yama gave up the whole of the Vānars who had died in the struggle. When Rāma was about to return home in the magic car, Sugriva asked that he and the Vānar chiefs might accompany him to his capital. Their request being granted, they took part in the installation of Rāma as king, and received from that grateful monarch rich presents as a reward for their faithful service.

2. HANUMĀN.

Hanumān, on the whole the most useful of the Monkey leaders of the expedition to Ceylon, was the son of Vāyu, by a Vānar or monkey mother. His birth is thus described—

"An Apsaras, the fairest found
Of nymphs, for heavenly charms renowned,
Sweet Punjikasthalā, became
A noble Vānar's wedded dame.
Her heavenly title heard no more,
Anjanā was the name she bore,

---

*Griffiths's "Rāmāyana," v. 199.

When, cursed by gods, from heaven she fell,
In Vānar form on earth to dwell.

  * * * * *

In youthful beauty wondrous fair,
A crown of flowers about her hair.
In silken robes of richest dye,
She roamed the hills that kiss the sky.
Once in her tinted garments dressed,
She stood upon the mountain crest.
The god of wind beside her came,
And breathed upon the lovely dame;
And as he fanned her robe aside,
The wondrous beauty that he eyed,

Hanumān

In rounded lines of breast and limb,

And neck and shoulders, ravished him,
And captured by her peerless charms,
He strained her in his amorous arms.
Then to the eager god she cried,
In trembling accents, terrified,
'Whose impious love has wronged a spouse
So constant to her nuptial vows?'
He hoard, and thus his answer made:
'Oh, be not troubled, nor afraid,
But trust, and thou shalt know ere long
My love has done thee, sweet, no wrong.
So strong, and brave, and wise shall be
The glorious son I give to thee;
Might shall be his, that nought can tire,
And limbs to spring as springs his sire.'
Thus spoke the god: the conquered dame
Rejoiced in heart, nor feared the shame."*

At length the son was born. When a child, seeing the sun rising, and thinking it to be the fruit of a tree, he sprang up three hundred leagues to clutch it. On another occasion Indra let a bolt fly at him which caused him to fall violently on a rock. The fall shattered his check, and hence the name Hanumān, the long-jawed one, was given to him. His father seeing this became angry, and the breezes ceased to blow, until the gods in terror came to appease Vāyu: Brahmā promised that this boy should not be slain in battle, and Indra declared that his bolts should never injure him in the future.

The Monkey leader rendered most valuable service to Rama. It was he who discovered Sita's abode, and carried a message to her from Rāma. It was he who set fire to Lanka and caused fear to enter the hearts of the Rākshasas dwelling there. It was he who bore Rāma on his shoulders as he crossed over

---

*Griffiths's "Rāmāyana," iv. 272.

from India to Lanka. Hanumān thus speaks of his wondrous
power:

> "Sprung from that glorious Father, I
> In power and speed with him may vie.
> A thousand times, with airy leap,
> Can circle loftiest Meru's steep:
> With my fierce arms can stir the sea
> Till from their beds the waters flee,
> And rush at my command to drown
> This land with grove and tower and town.
> I through the fields of air can spring
> Far swifter than the feathered king,
> And leap before him as he flies
> On sounding pinions through the skies.
> I can pursue the Lord of Light
> Uprising from the eastern height,
> And reach him ere his course be sped,
> With burning beams engarlanded."*

All these powers he devoted to the service of Rāma; for,
when that hero and his brother were wounded in the fight,
and nothing else could restore them, Hanumān fled to the
Himālayas from Ceylon, and returned almost immediately
with the medicinal herbs that grew there, though, on reaching
the hills, he had some difficulty† in finding them:

---

*Griffiths's "Rāmāyana," iv. 275.
†In seeking for these leaves, Hanumān was exposed to considerable
danger. Kālanemi, an uncle of Rāvana, was promised the half of the
kingdom if he would slay Hanumān. To effect this, he went to the
Himālayas and, disguised as a devotee, invited Hanumān to eat with
him. Hanumān refused; but on entering a tank near, a crocodile seized
his foot. This reptile Hanumān dragged out of the tank and killed it,
from whose body a lovely Apsaras arose, whom Daksha had cursed
to live in that form until her release was accomplished by Hanumān.

"But when he thought to seize the prize,
They hid them from his eager eyes.
Then to the hill in wrath he spake:
'Mine arm this day shall vengeance take
If thou wilt feel no pity, none,
In this great need of Raghu's son.'
He ceased: his mighty arms he bent,
And from the trembling mountain rent
His huge head, with the life it bore,
Snakes, elephants, and golden ore.
O'er hill and plain and watery waste
His rapid way again he traced,
And mid the wondering Vānars laid
His burden, through the air conveyed.
The wondrous herbs' delightful scent
To all the host new vigour lent.
Free from all darts, and wounds, and pain,
The sons of Raghu lived again;
And dead and dying Vānars, healed,
Rose vigorous from the battle-field."*

Hanumān is described in the "Uttara Kānda" of the Rāmāyana,† as a being possessed of great learning. "The chief of the monkeys, measureless, seeking to acquire grammar, looking up to the sun, bent on inquiry, went from the mountain where the sun rises to that where he sets, apprehending the mighty collection. The chief of the monkeys is perfect: no one equals him in the Sāstras, in learning, and in ascertaining the

---

This nymph, in gratitude for his kindness, warned Hanumān of his danger. The monkey god went to Kālanemi, and telling him that he saw through his disguise, took him by the feet, and whirled him through the air to Lanka, where he fell before the throne in Rāvana's palace.
*Griffiths's "Rāmāyana," iv. 225.
†Muir, O. S. T., iv. 490.

sense of the Scriptures. In all sciences, in the rules of austerity, he rivals the preceptor of the gods."

Rāma himself thus speaks of Hanumān's knowledge of the Scriptures, when he came to the exile as Sugriva's envoy:

> "One whose words so sweetly flow,
> The whole Rig-Veda needs must know,
> And in his well-trained memory store
> The Yajush and the Sāman's lore.
> He must have bent his faithful ear
> All grammar's varied rules to hear.
> For his long speech how well he spoke!
> In all its length no rule he broke."*

To this day Hanumān is regarded as divine, and in some parts of India is largely worshipped. Living monkeys are regarded as his representatives: hence many temples swarm with them, and it is regarded a meritorious act to feed them, and a sacrilegious act to injure them.

3. NALA.†

Nala, another of the monkey chiefs, was a son of Visvakarma; and as the son of the architect of the gods, the builder of their beautiful cities, and the forger of their wonder-working weapons, as might have been expected, his work was of a similar nature to that for which his illustrious parent was celebrated. When the army reached the sea, and the difficulty of crossing to Lanka presented itself, as Rāma was preparing

---

*Griffiths's "Rāmāyana," iv. 25.

† This Nala must not be confounded with another person of the same name, whose history is given in the Mahābhārata. Nala of the Mahābbārata was King of Nishadha, the husband of Damayanti, whom he obtained in marriage, although Indra, Agni, Varuna, and Yama were amongst the suitors for her hand.

to shoot one of his mighty arrows to dry up the ocean, the Sea Deity presented himself, amidst a great commotion of the elements, and thus addressed him;

> "Air, ether, fire, earth, water, true
> To Nature's will, their course pursue;
> And I, as ancient laws ordain,
> Unfordable must still remain.
> Yet, Raghu's son, my counsel hear:
> I ne'er for love, or hope, or fear,
> Will pile my waters of a heap,
> And leave a pathway through the deep.
> Still shall my care for thee provide
> An easy passage o'er the tide,
> And like a city's paven street
> Shall be the road beneath thy feet."*

His first word of advice was this, that Rāma, instead of shooting at the sea, should direct his arrow towards the North, to destroy a race of demons who were hateful to him, and then he went on to say—

> "Now let a wondrous task be done
> By Nala, Visvakarma's son,
> Who, born of one of Vānar race,
> Inherits by his father's grace
> A share of his celestial art.
> Call Nala to perform his part,
> And he, divinely taught and skilled,
> A bridge athwart the sea shall build."†

Nala declares that he has the will and power to accomplish

Griffiths' "Rāmāyanā," v. 66.
†Griffiths's "Rāmāyana," v. 67.

this great and necessary work; and as an encouragement to
Rāma to believe that he will complete it, said—

> "My mother, ere she bore her son,
> This boon from Visvakarma won:
> 'O Mandarī, this child shall be
> In skill and glory next to me.'
> But why unbidden should I fill
> Thine ear with praises of my skill?
> Command the Vānar hosts to lay
> Foundations for the bridge to-day."*

Rāma trusts Nala's skill, and orders the Vānars to bring
materials for the bridge:

> "Up sprang the Vānars from their rest,
> The mandate of the king obeyed,
> And sought the forest's mighty shade.
> Uprooted trees to earth they threw,
> And to the sea the timber drew.
>
>   *   *   *   *
>
> With mighty engines piles of stone
> And seated hills were overthrown:
> Imprisoned waters sprang on high,
> In rain descending from the sky:
> And ocean with a roar and swell
> Heaved wildly when the mountains fell.
> Then the great bridge of wondrous strength
> Was built, a hundred leagues in length.
> Rocks, huge as autumn clouds, bound fast
> With cordage from the shore, were cast,
> And fragments of each riven hill,
> And trees whose flowers adorned them still.

---

*Ibid., v. 68.

Wild was the tumult, loud the din,
As ponderous rocks went thundering in.
Each set of sun, so toiled each crew,
Ten leagues and four the structure grew;
The labours of the second day
Gave twenty more of ready way,
And on the fifth, when sank the sun,
The whole stupendous work was done.
O'er the broad way the Vānars sped,
Nor swayed it with their countless tread."*

4. NĪLA

This chief is said to have sprung from Agni, and is described
as

"Bright as flame,
Who in his splendour, might, and worth,
Surpassed the sire who gave him birth."†

Though thus eulogized, no very special feats of his are
recorded in the Rāmāyana. He held a post of honour as the
leader of a division of the array, and his special work appears
to have been to provide sentries, and generally to guard the
forces of Sugriva from the sudden attacks of the enemy. As the
son of Agni he was able to see clearly, and by his watchfulness
rendered good service.

5. SUSHENA

Varuna aided Rāma by the gift of this leader, who was the father

---

of Tārā, the wife of Bāli, Sugriva's brother and the usurper of his throne. To him was given the command of the army of the West. Sugriva, addressing him, said—

> "Two hundred thousand of our best
> With thee, my lord, shall seek the West."*

After searching in vain for traces of the missing princess, he and the other unsuccessful leaders returned to Rāma and Sugriva, and said—

> "On every hill our steps have been,
> By wood, and cave, and deep ravine;
> And all the wandering brooks we know,
> Throughout the land that seaward flow;
> Our feet by thy command have traced
> The tangled thicket and the waste,
> And dens and dingles hard to pass
> For creeping plants and matted grass." †

Though they could not learn the exact spot where Sitā was hidden, they discovered that she had been carried towards the South, the quarter under Hanumān's special charge, and thus considerably narrowed the sphere of the quest. In the great encounter with the foe, Sushena did good service; for when Rāma and Lakshman were overcome by Indrajit's magical noose, Sugriva and his comrades were greatly distressed. The Vānar king, however, being aware that Garuda could release them from the spell by which they were bound, told Sushena, when they regained their strength and senses, to fly with them to Kishkindha hermitage, where they could dwell in safety, whilst he himself fought against Rāvana, and rescued the royal

---

*Griffiths's "Rāmāyana," iv. 208.
†Ibid., iv. 224.

lady. Then Sushena, as the physician, said—

> "Hear me yet:
> When gods and fiends in battle met,
> So fiercely fought the demon crew,
> So wild a storm of arrows flew,
> That heavenly warriors, faint with pain,
> Sank smitten by the ceaseless rain.
> Vrihaspati, with herb and spell,
> Cured the sore wounds of those who fell,
> And, skilled in arts that heal and save,
> New life and sense and vigour gave.
> Far, on the milky ocean's shore,
> Still grow those herbs in boundless store;
> Let swiftest Vānars thither speed
> And bring them for our utmost need.
> Let Panas and Sampati bring,
> For well the wondrous leaves they know
> That heal each wound and life bestow.
> Beside that sea, which, churned of yore,
> The Amrit on its surface bore,
> Where the white billows lash the land,
> Chandra's fair height and Drona stand.
> Planted by gods, each glittering steep
> Looks down upon the milky deep.
> Let fleet Hanumān bring us thence,
> Those herbs of wondrous influence."*

These plants were brought by Hanumān; the wounded recovered, and fought with renewed vigour.

**Griffiths's "Rāmāyana," v. 152.

Chapter IV

The Demigods of The Mahābhārata

As these heroes are so intimately connected with each other, a separate account of each would necessitate frequent repetition; they will therefore be noticed together, in a brief outline of the main story of the Mahābhārata.*

In the fifth generation from Soma (the Moon), the progenitor of the Lunar race, who reigned at Hastināpur, came two sons, Puru† and Yadu; from whom proceeded two branches of the

---

*This account of the Mahābhārata is taken in an abbreviated form almost entirely from Lecture XIII. of Monier Williams's "Indian Wisdom."

†An interesting story is told of Puru. His father, Yayāti, married Devayāni, daughter of Sukra, the preceptor of the Daityas. Her husband loving her servant Sarmisthā also, Puru was born as their youngest son. The wife being highly indignant at the unfaithfulness of her husband, returning to her father's home, so excited the old priest that he cursed Yayāti with old age; but afterwards consented to withdraw the curse provided one of his sons would bear it for him. They all refused to do this excepting Puru. As a reward for his piety, his father disinherited his other sons, and made Puru sole heir to his dominions.

Lunar line. In the account of Krishna and Balarāma, who were born in the Yadu tribe, we have seen the end of that branch of the family. Sixteenth from Puru, the founder of the other branch, came Bharata, from whom India takes its name, Bharatvarsha (the country of Bharata), in the present day. Twenty-third from Bharata came Sāntanu. This Sāntanu had two sons, Bhishma, by the goddess Gangā (the Ganges), and Vichitravīrya, by Satyavati.* Satyavati had a son named Vyāsa before her marriage with Sāntanu; so that Bhishma, Vichitravīrya, and Vyāsa were half-brothers. Bhishma became a Brahmāchari (i.e. took a vow of celibacy). Vyāsa retired to the wilderness to live a life of contemplation, but promised his mother that he would obey her in everything.

Now it so happened that Vichitravīrya died childless, and Satyavati was therefore obliged to ask her son Vyāsa to marry the childless widows. The result was that the one wife, Ambikā, had a son who was born blind, named Dhritarāshtra. This blindness is said to have been caused by the fact that Vyāsa, coming in from his ascetic life, was so repulsive in appearance that Ambika kept her eyes closed all the time he remained with her. The other wife, named Ambālika, had a son who was born of a pale complexion, and named Pāndu; this paleness was the result of the fear that Vyāsa caused to the mother. Satyavati, not satisfied with either of these children, wished for another and perfect child. But Ambikā, dressing up one of her slaves, sent her to Vyāsa in her stead; the result was that this girl had a son who was called Vidura. After fulfilling his mother's

---

*Satyavati was the daughter of an Apsaras named Adrikā, who was condemned to live on earth in the form of a fish. Parasāra, a sage, met her daughter as he was crossing the river Yamunā, and Vyāsa was the result. He was born on an island of the river, and hence he had the name Dwaipāyana (who moves on an island). Vyāsa is said to have been the arranger of the Vedas, the compiler of the Mahābhārata and the Purātanas, and the founder of the Vedānta system of philosophy.

commands, Vyāsa returned to his ascetic life in the forest.

Bhishma, the uncle of these children, conducted the government of Hastināpur in their name during their minority, and their education was also entrusted to him. Dhritarāshtra, though blind, is described as excelling the others in strength; Pāndu, as being skilled in the use of the bow; and Vidura, as pre-eminent in virtue and wisdom.

When the boys came of age, Dhritarāshtra was disqualified for the throne by reason of his blindness; Vidura could not be king because his mother was a Sudra; Pāndu was therefore installed as king. Dhritarāshtra married Gāndhāri (also called Saubaleyi, or Saubali), daughter of Subala, King of Gāndhāra. Pāndu married Prithā (or Kunti), the adopted daughter of Kuntibhoja. This Prithā, "one day, before her marriage, paid such respect and attention to a powerful sage named Durvāsas, a guest in her father's house, that he gave her a charm, and taught her an incantation, by virtue of which she might have a child by any god she liked to call into her presence. Out of curiosity, she invoked the Sun, by whom she had a son who was born clothed in armour. But Prithā, fearing the censure of her relatives, deserted her offspring, after exposing it in the river. It was found by Adhirata, a charioteer, and nurtured by his wife Rādhā; whence the child was afterwards called Rādheya, though named by his fosterparents Vasushena. When he was grown up, the god Indra conferred upon him enormous strength, and changed his name to Kama." He is also called Vaikartana, being the son of Vikartana (the Sun).

Pāndu, at his uncle Bhishma's request, next marries Mādrī, sister of Salya, King of Madra. Soon after this marriage, Pāndu undertook a great campaign, and extended his kingdom to the dimensions it had reached in the time of his great ancestor Bharata. He then, with his two wives, retired to the woods, that he might indulge in his passion for hunting. The blind Dhritarāshtra, with Bhishma as regent, ruled in his stead.

Dhritarāshtra had a hundred sons. The story of their

birth is as follows: "One day, the sage Vyāsa was hospitably entertained by Queen Gāndhāri, and in return granted her a boon. She chose to be the mother of a hundred sons. After two years she produced a mass of flesh, which was divided by Vyāsa into a hundred and one pieces, as big as the joint of a thumb. From these, in due time, the eldest, Duryodhana, was born. The miraculous birth of the remaining ninety-nine occurred in due course. There was also one daughter, named Duhsala." These sons of Dhritarāshtra are generally called "The Kurus," or Kauravas.

Pāndu's children were of divine origin. This circumstance happened in the following manner: Pāndu, as noticed above, was addicted to hunting. One day, he "transfixed with five arrows a male and female deer. These turned out to be a certain sage and his wife, who had assumed the form of these animals. The sage cursed Pāndu, and predicted that he would die in the embraces of one of his wives. In consequence of this curse, Pāndu took the vow of a Brahmāchari, gave all his property to the Brāhmans, and became a hermit."

Upon this, Prithā, his wife, with his approval, employed the charm and incantation given to her by Durvāsas, and had three children: by the god Dharma, Yudhishthira; by Vāyu, Bhīma; and by Indra, Arjuna. Mādrī, the other wife of Pāndu, was now anxious to have children, and, acting on the advice of Prithā, she thought of the Asvins, who appeared to her according to her wish, through whom she became the mother of twin sons, Nakula and Sahadeva. Soon after this, Pāndu, forgetting the curse of the sage, died in the embraces of his wife Mādrī, who was burned with the dead body of her husband.

Prithā and the five children, generally known as the Pāndus, or Pāndavas, now returned to Hastināpur, and informed Dhritarāshtra of the death of his brother; he seemed to be deeply moved by the event, and the Pāndus were allowed to live with his own sons, the Kurus.

But even when the cousins were children, enmity arose,

and on one occasion the jealousy of Duryodhana was excited to such a pitch that he tried to poison Bhīma, and, when under its effect, threw him into the water. "Bhīma, however, was not drowned, but descended to the abode of the Nāgas (or serpent demons), who freed him from the poison, and gave him a liquid to drink which endued him with strength of ten thousand Nāgas. From that moment he became a second Hercules." Several schemes were formed for the destruction of the Pāndus, but without success.

"The characters of the five Pāndavas are drawn with much artistic delicacy of touch, and maintained with general consistency throughout the poem. The eldest, Yudhishthira (the son of Dharma, virtue), is the Hindu ideal of excellence — a pattern of justice; calm, passionless composure; chivalrous honour and cold heroism." As the name implies (firm in battle), "he was probably of commanding stature and imposing presence. He is described as having a majestic, lion-like gait, with a Wellington-like profile and long lotus-eyes.

"Bhīma (the son of Vāyu) is a type of brute courage and strength; he is of gigantic stature, impetuous, irascible, somewhat vindictive, and cruel even to the verge of ferocity, making him, as his name implies, 'terrible.' It would appear that his great strength had to be maintained by plentiful supplies of food, as his name Vrikodara, 'wolf-stomached,' indicates a voracious appetite; and we are told that at the daily meals of the five brothers, half of the whole dish had to be given to Bhīma. But he has the capacity for warm, unselfish love, and is ardent in his affection for his mother and brothers.

"Arjuna (the son of Indra) rises more to the European standard of perfection. He may be regarded as the real hero of the Mahābhārata, of undaunted bravery, generous, with refined and delicate sensibilities, tender-hearted, forgiving, and affectionate as a woman, yet of superhuman strength, and matchless in arms and athletic exercises. Nakula and Sahadeva (sons of the Asvins) are both amiable, noble-hearted, and spirited. All five are as unlike as possible to the hundred sons of Dhritarāshtra, who are represented as mean, spiteful, dishonourable, and vicious." Karna (the son of the Sun), though half-brother of these five Pāndus, in the great conflict is a valuable ally of the Kurus; though in character he is entirely their opposite. "He exhibited in a high degree fortitude, chivalrous honour, self-sacrifice, and devotion. Especially remarkable for a liberal and generous disposition, he never stooped to ignoble practices, like his friends, the Kurus, who were emphatically bad men."

The cousins were educated together at Hastināpur by a Brāhman named Drona; all were instructed in arms, but Arjuna, "by the help of Drona, who gave him magical weapons, excelled all." Both Bhīma and the Kuru Duryodhana learnt the use of the club from their cousin Balarāma; Prithā, Bhīma's mother, was a sister of Vasudeva, and therefore aunt of Krishna. When their education was completed, a tournament was held, in which the youths displayed their skill in archery; in the management of chariots, horses, and elephants; in sword, spear, and club exercises, and in wrestling. "Arjuna, after exhibiting prodigies of strength, shot five arrows simultaneously into the jaws of a revolving iron boar, and twenty-one arrows into the hollow of a cow's horn, suspended by a string." When he had accomplished this feat, Karna came and did precisely the same deeds of skill, and challenged Arjuna to single combat; but as he could not tell his parentage, he was not considered worthy to enter the lists with the royal youth.

After the tournament was over, Yudhishthira was installed as heir apparent, and soon made his name even more famous than his father's had been. The people wished Yudhishthira to be crowned king at once, but the Kurus tried hard to prevent it. First of all, the Pāndus and their mother were sent to a house at Vāranāvata, in which a quantity of combustible materials was placed, with the intention of burning the whole family. The Pāndus were informed of this by Vidura, and escaped;

but the man who conducted them, and a woman with her five sons, whom Bhīma led there in a state of intoxication, were consumed instead. By this device, the Kurus were under the impression that their plan had been successful. The brothers, with their mother, now hastened to the woods, where Bhīma slew a giant named Hidimba, and then married his sister.

By the advice of Vyāsa they now went to live in the city of Ekaehakrā, disguised as mendicant Brāhmans. Near this city was a Rākshas named Vaka, who compelled the citizens to send him a dish of food daily, and the messenger who took it was devoured as the daintiest morsel of the whole. One day it happened that the turn came to a Brāhman to supply the Rākshas with a meal. The man determined to go himself, but his wife and daughter each asked to be allowed to go with him. Lastly, the little son, too young to speak distinctly, in prattling accents said, "Weep not, father; sigh not, mother." Then, breaking off and brandishing a pointed spike of grass, he exclaimed, "With this spike will I slay the fierce, man-eating giant." Bhīma, overhearing this, offered to go; he went, and killed the giant.

After this occurrence, Vyāsa appeared to his grandsons, and informed them that Draupadi, the daughter of Drupada, King of Panchāla, was destined to be their common wife. This girl, in a former birth, was the daughter of a sage, and had performed a most severe penance in order that she might have a husband. Siva, pleased with her devotion, said, "You shall have five husbands; for five times you said, 'Give me a husband.'" When the brothers returned from Draupadi's Svayambara (a tournament in which the princess chose for herself a husband), Arjuna having been selected from amongst many suitors on account of his skill in archery, their mother, hearing their footsteps, and, fancying they were bringing alms, said, "Divide it amongst yourselves." The word of a mother could not be set aside, so Vyāsa showed them that it was appointed that Draupadi should be the wife of each. At this tournament Arjuna displayed great skill in the use of the bow, by piercing a fish that was suspended in the air, without looking directly at the object; he saw its image only, reflected in a pan of water on the ground.

Arjuna shooting at the fish

Vyāsa, seeing the discrepancy between the conduct of the five brothers having a wife in common and that which prevailed in his day, explains it by the fact that Arjuna was really a portion of the essence of Indra, and his brothers portions of the same god, whilst Draupadi herself was a form of Lakshmi; as, therefore, the five brethren were parts of Indra, there was no impropriety in their having but one wife. It is a fact to be noticed, that to this day polyandry prevails amongst some of the hill-tribes of India. Draupadi is said to have had a son by each of the brothers, and the brothers had other wives besides Draupadi. It was noticed above that Bhīma married Hidimbā. Arjuna married Krishna's sister, Subhadrā, and also a serpent nymph named Uludi, and Chitrāngadā, daughter of the King of Manipura.

When the Pāndus, by their marriage with Draupadi, had allied themselves with the King of Panchāla, they threw off their disguise, and their uncle Dhritarāshtra divided the kingdom: to his sons he gave Hastināpur; to the Pāndus a district near the Yamuna (Jumna), called Khāndavaprastha. Here they built Indraprastha (Delhi), and, under Yudhishthira, their kingdom grew.

Arjuna wandered in the. forest alone for twelve years, in fulfilment of a vow, and there met Krishna, who invited him to Dwāraka, where he married Subhadrā. Krishna was invited to a great festival in honour of the inauguration of Yudhishthira as sovereign. Acting on Nārada's advice, Bhishma proposed that an oblation should be made to the best and strongest person present, and selected Krishna. Sisupāla objected, and, as he openly reviled Krishna, the deity struck off his head with his discus.

After this, a festival was held at Hastināpur, to which the Pāndus were invited. Yudhishthira was induced to play; and having staked his kingdom, his possessions, and, last of all, Draupadi, he lost everything. A compromise was effected. Duryodhana was made ruler over the whole kingdom for twelve years; whilst the Pāndus with Draupadi were to live in the forest for the same period, and to pass the thirteenth year under assumed names, in various disguises. "Whilst enjoying this forest life, Arjuna went to the Himālayas to perform severe penance in order to obtain celestial arms. "After some time, Siva, to reward him and prove his bravery, approached as a Kirātā,* or wild mountaineer, at the moment that a demon named Mūka, in the form of a boar, attacked him. Siva and Arjuna shot together at the boar, which fell dead, and both

---

*The Kirātās were mountaineers, or foresters. In the Rāmāyana they are described as "islanders, who eat raw flesh, live in the waters, and are men-tigers."

claimed to have hit him first. This served as a pretext for Siva to have a battle with him. Arjuna fought long with the Kirātā but could not conquer him. At last he recognized the god, and threw himself at his feet, when Siva, pleased with his bravery, gave him the celebrated weapon Pāsupata, to enable him to conquer Kama and the Kuru princes in war."

In the thirteenth year of exile the Pāndus journeyed to the court of King Virāta, and entered his service in disguise. Yudhishthira called himself a Brāhman, and took the name of Kanka. Arjuna called himself Vrihanalā, and, pretending to be a eunuch, adopted a sort of woman's dress, and taught music and dancing. One day when Virāta and four of the Pāndus were absent, Duryodhana and his brother attacked Virāta's capital, and carried off some cattle. Uttara, the king's son, followed them, having Arjuna as his charioteer. When they came in sight of the enemy, Uttara's heart failed him. Arjuna changed places with him, having told him who he was. This gave him courage, the Kuru army was defeated, and the stolen cattle reclaimed. Arjuna asked Uttara to keep the secret of his real character for the present. A short time afterwards, at a great assembly called by Virāta, the Pāndus took their places amongst the princes, and were welcomed heartily by the king.

A council of princes was soon held, at which Krishna and Balarāma were present, to consider how the Pāndus could regain their possessions. Some were for immediate war; Krishna and Balarāma urged that attempts at negotiation should first be made. This advice was acted upon, but without result. In the mean time, Krishna and his brother returned to Dwāraka. Not long after his arrival at his capital, Duryodhana, the Kuru prince, visited Krishna to ask his aid in the coming struggle; and on the same day, Arjuna, the Pānda prince, arrived there for the same purpose. And "it happened that they both reached the door of Krishna's apartment, where he was asleep, at the same moment. Duryodhana succeeded in entering first, and took up his station at Krishna's head; Arjuna followed, and

stood reverently at his feet." Krishna, on awaking, first saw
Arjuna; and when the cousins mentioned the object of their
visit, he gave the right of choice to Arjuna. He offered himself
to one side, but said he should not himself fight; and to the
other side his army of a hundred million warriors. Arjuna
at once chose Krishna, and Duryodhana was delighted with
the prospect of having Krishna's immense army on his side.
Duryodhana then asked Balarāma's aid, but was informed
that both the brothers had decided to take no active part in
the conflict. Krishna, however, consented to act as Arjuna's
charioteer, and joined the Pāndus at Virāta's capital.

Battle of the Kuru and the Pāndavas

Fresh negotiations were commenced, and Krishna himself
went as mediator to the Kurus; but although in the assembly
he assumed his divine form, and "Brahmā appeared in his
forehead, Rudra on his breast, the guardians of the world
issued from his arms, and Agni from his mouth"—although

the other gods were visible in and about his person—his attempt at reconciliation failed. War was determined on between the cousins. Bhishma was made the commander-in-chief of the Kuru army; and Dhrishtadyumna, son of Drupada, was the leader of the Pāndus. Vyāsa offered to give sight to Dhritarāshtra, to enable him to witness the conflict, but, as the blind man declined the offer, he gave to his charioteer, Sanjaya, the faculty of knowing everything that took place, made him invulnerable, and bestowed on him the power to transport himself by a thought to any part of the field of battle.

The armies met on Kurukshetra, a plain to the north-west of the modern Delhi, and we are told that "monstrous elephants career over the field, trampling on men and horses, and dealing destruction with their huge tusks; enormous clubs and iron maces clash together with the noise of thunder; rattling chariots dash against each other; thousands of arrows hurtle in the air, darkening the sky; trumpets, kettledrums, and horns add to the uproar; confusion, carnage, and death are everywhere."

The Pāndus are described as performing prodigies of might. Arjuna killed five hundred warriors simultaneously, covered the plain with dead, and filled rivers with blood: Yudhishthira "slaughtered a hundred men" in a mere twinkle: Bhīma annihilated a monstrous elephant, including all mounted upon it, and fourteen foot soldiers besides, with one blow of his club: Nakula and Sahadeva, when fighting from their chariots, cut off heads by the thousand, and sowed them like seed upon the ground. Of the weapons employed, about a hundred are named; and the conch shell which served as the trumpet of each leader had its distinct name, as had also the weapons of each of the chiefs.

The first great single combat was between Bhishma and Arjuna, which resulted in Bhishma being so transfixed with arrows that "there was not a space of two fingers' breadth on his whole body unpierced. Falling from his chariot, his body could not touch the ground, as it was surrounded by countless arrows, and thus it reclined on its arrowy couch. He had received from his father the power of fixing the time of his own death, and now declared that he intended retaining life till the sun entered the summer solstice. The warriors on both sides ceased fighting that they might view the wonderful sight and do homage to their dying relative. As he lay on his uncomfortable bed, with his head hanging down, he begged for a pillow, whereupon the chiefs brought him soft supports; these the hardy old soldier sternly rejected. Arjuna then made a rest for him with three arrows, which Bhishma quite approved; and soon afterwards asked him to bring a little water. Arjuna struck the ground with an arrow, and forthwith a pure spring burst forth, which so refreshed Bhishma that he called for Duryodhana, and begged him, before it was too late, to restore half the kingdom to the Pāndavas."

Drona, the tutor of the princes, is appointed to take the command of the Kuru army after the fall of Bhishma; and a number of single combats are described. Bhīma's son by the Rākshasi Hidimbā is slain by Kama; Drupada's son, Dhrishtadyumna, the leader of the Pāndus, overcomes Drona; Drona being a Brāhman, When overpowered by his foe, voluntarily laid down his life, and is conducted to heaven "in a glittering shape like the sun" to save Dhrishtadyumna from the enormous crime of killing a Brāhman. Kama was then made leader of the Kurus in place of Drona. Bhīma next slew Duhsāsana, and remembering how this prince had insulted Draupadi, he drank the blood of his fallen foe. Arjuna then slew Kama, and Salya, King of Madra, was appointed to fill the vacant post. Bhima challenges Salya, and the following is the account of their encounter:—

> "Soon as he saw his charioteer struck down,
> Straightway the Madra monarch grasped his
>   mace,

And like a mountain, firm and motionless,
Awaited the attack. The warrior's form
Was awful as the world-consuming fire,
Or as the noose-armed god of death, or as
The peaked Kailāsa, or the Thunderer
Himself, or as the trident-bearing god,
Or as a maddened forest elephant.
Him to defy did Bhima hastily
Advance, wielding aloft his massive club.
A thousand conchs and trumpets, and a shout,
Firing each champion's ardour, rent the air.
From either host, spectators of the fight,
Burst forth applauding cheers: 'The Madra king
Alone,' they cried, 'can bear the rush of Bhīma;'
'None but heroic Bhīma can sustain
The force of Salya.' Now like two fierce bulls
Sprang they towards each other, mace in hand.
And first, as cautiously they circled round,
Whirling their weapons as in sport, the pair
Seemed matched in equal combat. Salya's club.
Set with red fillets, glittered as with flame,
While that of Bhīma gleamed like flashing
     lightning.
Anon the clashing irons met, and scattered round
A fiery shower; then, fierce as elephants
Or butting bulls, they battered each the other.
Thick fell the blows, and soon each stalwart
     frame,
Spattered with gore, glowed like the Kinsuka,
Bedecked with scarlet blossoms; yet beneath
The rain of strokes, unshaken as a rock,
Bhīma sustained the mace of Salya, he
With equal firmness bore the other's blows.
Now, like the roar of crashing thunder-clouds,
Sounded the clashing iron; then, their clubs

Brandished aloft, eight paces they retired,
And swift again advancing to the fight,
Met in the midst like two huge mountain crags
Hurled into contact. Nor could either bear
The other's shock; together down they rolled,
Mangled and crashed, like two tall standards
    fallen."

Yudhishthira then fought with and eventually slew Salya. After suffering continual reverses, the Kurus rallied for a final charge, which led to so great a slaughter, that only four of their leaders, Duryodhana, Asvatthāman (son of Drona), Kritavarman, and Kripa remained, whilst "nothing remained of eleven whole armies." Whereupon Duryodhana resolved upon flight, and taking refuge in a lake, by his magical power supported it so as to form a chamber round his body. The Pāndus discovered his retreat; but when taunted by them, he told them to take the kingdom, as, his brothers having all been slain, he had no pleasure in life. At last, enraged by the sarcasms of his cousins, he came forth and fought with Bhīma, from whom he received his death-wound. The remaining three Kuru chiefs left their wounded companion and took refuge in a forest.

Whilst resting under a tree at night, Asvatthāman, seeing an owl approach stealthily and kill numbers of sleeping crows, the thought occurred to him that in this manner he might destroy the Pāndu forces. Accordingy he quietly entered their camp, leaving Kripa and Kritavarman to watch the gates. Under cover of darkness they slew the whole army: the Pāndu princes and Krishna, happening to be stationed outside the camp, alone escaped. These three then return to Duryodhana, and tell him what they had done. Hearing their narrative, his spirit revived for a moment; he thanked them, bade them farewell, and expired.

The funeral obsequies of the chief are performed, and

Yudhishthira is installed as King of Hastināpur. But he is most unhappy as he thinks of the great slaughter that has taken place. Acting on Krishna's advice, he and his brothers visit Bhishma, who is still lingering on his "spiky bed." For fifty-eight nights he had lain there, and ere his departure gave utterance to a series of most lengthy didactic discourses, after which his spirit ascended to the skies.

As Yudhishthira was entering the capital in triumph, an incident occurred to lessen his joy in victory. A Rākshas named Chārvāka, disguised as a Brāhman, met him and reproached him for the slaughter he had caused; but the Brāhmans, discovering the imposture, consumed the Rākshas to ashes with fire from their eyes. Yet even now the spirit of the king is not at rest. After a little time, he resigns his kingdom, and, together with his brothers and Draupadi, starts on his journey towards Indra's heaven on Mount Meru.

> "When the four brothers knew the high resolve of King
> 　　Yudhishthira
> Forthwith with Draupadi they issued forth, and after
> 　　them a dog
> Followed; the king himself went out the seventh from
> 　　the royal city,
> And all the citizens and women of the palace walked
> 　　behind;
> But none could find it in their heart to say unto the king,
> 　　'Return.'
> And so at length the train of citizens went back, bidding
> 　　adieu."

These went, "bent on abandonment of worldly things; their hearts yearning for union with the Infinite." In their journey they reach the sea, and there Arjuna cast away his bow and quiver. At last they came in sight of Mount Meru, and Draupadi "lost hold of her high hope, and faltering fell upon the earth." One by one the others fall, until only Yudhishthira, Bhīma, and the dog are left. Bhīma cannot understand why such pure beings should die: his brother informs him that Draupadi's fall was the result of her excessive affection for Arjuna; that Sahadeva's death was the result of pride in his own knowledge; that Nakula's personal vanity was his ruin, and that Arjuna's fault was a boastful confidence in his power to destroy his foes. Bhīma now falls, and is told that the reason of his death is his selfishness, pride, and too great love of enjoyment. Yudhishthira, left alone with the dog, is walking on:

> "When, with a sudden sound that rang through earth
>   and heaven, the mighty god
> Came towards him in a chariot, and he cried, 'Ascend, O
>   resolute prince.'
> Then did the king look back upon his fallen brothers,
>   and addressed
> These words unto the Thousand-eyed in anguish: 'Let
>   my brothers here
> Come with me. Without them, O god of gods, I could
>   not wish to enter
> E'en heaven! and yonder tender princess Draupadi, the
>   faithful wife,
> Worthy of endless bliss, let her come too. In mercy hear
>   my prayer.'"

Indra informs him that the spirits of Draupadi and his brothers are already in heaven, but that he alone is permitted to enter in bodily form. The king asks that the dog may accompany him. But as this is refused, he declines to go alone. Indra says, "You have abandoned your brothers; why not forsake the dog?" Yudhishthira replies, "I had no power to bring them back to life: how can there be abandonment of those who no longer live?" It now appears that the dog was no other than his father Dharma in disguise; who, assuming his proper form, enters with him.

On reaching heaven, though Duryodhana and his cousins are already in bliss, as he does not see Arjuna and the rest, Yudhishthira declines to remain there without them. An angel accompanies him to hell, where he hears their voices calling upon him for help. He therefore bids the angel depart, as he prefers to suffer in hell with his brethren rather than to remain in heaven without them. As soon as his resolution is taken, the scene suddenly changes, and it appears that this was simply a trial of his faith. He bathes in the heavenly Ganges, and in heaven, with "Draupadi and his brothers, finds the rest and happiness that were unattainable on earth."

Chapter V
The Planets

"A T the great festivals of the Hindus a small offering is made to all the planets at once; but, excepting on these occasions, they are never worshipped together. They are, however, frequently worshipped separately by the sick and unfortunate who suppose themselves to be under the baneful influence of one or other of them. At these times they are worshipped one after the other in regular succession."* Seven of the planets give names to the days of the week; the other two represent the ascending and descending nodes. Surya and Chandra (Soma) have already been noticed at length among the Vedic Deities; they are again described briefly along with the planets, under the names they bear in this connection.

"To Surya or Ravi are offered the burnt sacrifice of small pieces of the shrub *arka* (*Asclepias gigantica*); to Chandra those of the *palasa* (*Butea frondosa*); to Mangala (Mars) those of the *khudiru* (*Mimosa catechu*); to Budha (Mercury) those of the *apārmārga* (*Achry-ranthes aspera*); to Vrihaspati (Jupiter) those of the *asvattha* (*Ficus religiosa*); to Sukra (Venus) those of the *ūrumbara*; to Sani (Saturn) those of the *Sami* (*Mimosa albida*); to

---

*Ward, ii. 70.

Rāhu (the ascending node) blades of *Lurva* grass; and to Keta (the descending node) blades of *Kusa* grass."*

"The image of Surya is a round piece of mixed metal twelve fingers in diameter; of Chandra, a piece like a half-moon, a cubic from end to end; of Mangala, a triangular piece six fingers in width; of Budha, a golden bow two fingers in breadth; of Vrihaspati, a piece like a lotus; of Sukra, a square piece of silver; of Sani, an iron scimitar; of Rāhu, an iron makara (a fabulous animal, half stag and half fish); and of Ketu, an iron snake."†

1. Ravi (the Sun), hence Ravibāra (Sunday), is the son of Kasyapa and Aditi. Though as Surya he is daily worshipped, as Ravi he is only worshipped at the greater festivals. "The 'Jyotish-tatwa,' a great work on astrology, says that if a person is born under the planet Ravi, he will possess an anxious mind, be subject to disease and other sufferings, be an exile, a prisoner, and suffer the loss of wife, children, and property."‡

2. Chandea or Soma, hence Somavāra (Monday). "If a person be born under the planet Soma he will have many friends; will possess elephants, horses, and palanquins; be honourable and powerful; will live on excellent food, and rest on superb couches." A race of kings are said to be the descendants of Soma, by his wife Rohini (the Hyades), who are called the children of the moon.

3. Mangala, hence Mangalavāra (Tuesday), is represented as a red man with four arms, riding on a sheep; he wears a red necklace and clothes of the same colour. "If a person be born under the planet Mangala, he will be full of anxious thoughts, wounded with offensive weapons, imprisoned, oppressed with fear of robbers, fire, etc., and will lose his lands, trees, and good name." This deity is identical with Kartikeya.

---

*Ward, ii. 70.

†Ibid., 71.

‡Page 72

4. Budha,* hence Budhavāra (Wednesday), was the son of Soma by Tāra, the wife of Vrihaspati, the preceptor of the gods. At his birth, on the confession of his mother that he was Soma's son, her husband reduced her to ashes. Brahmā afterwards raised her to life, and, being purified by the fire, her husband received her back. Samudra (the Sea), incensed at his son for the great crime of dishonouring his preceptor's wife, disinherited him; but owing to his sister† Lakshmi's influence, part of his sin was removed, and he became bright as the moon when three days old; and, through her intercession with Pārvati, he was restored to heaven, by being placed on Siva's forehead, who, thus ornamented, went to a feast of the gods. Vrihaspati on seeing Chandra again in heaven was greatly incensed, but was appeased on Brahmā's declaring that the lascivious god should be excluded from heaven and placed among the stars; and that the sin which had obscured his glory should remain for ever. "If a person be born under the planet Budha, he/will be fortunate, obtain an excellent wife," etc.

5. Vrihaspati, hence Vrihaspativāra (Thursday), was the preceptor of the gods, and is regarded as identical with Agni, almost the same epithets being applied to both in the Vedic hymns. In later times he is said to be a Rishi, a son of Angiras. "If a person be born under this planet, he will be endowed with an amiable disposition, possess palaces, gardens, lands, and be rich in money and corn. He will possess much religious merit, and have all his wishes gratified. Brāhmans, however, will not be so fortunate as those of other castes, for Vrihaspati being a Brāhman does not wish to exalt those of his own caste."

6. Sukra, hence Sukravāra (Friday), was the son of Bhrigu. He was the preceptor and the priest of the demons, and blind

---

* This Budha must not be confounded with Buddha, the Incarnation of Vishnu.

†Soma (the Moon) and Lakshmi were produced together at the churning of the ocean.

in one eye. The reason of this affliction is told in the following legend: When Vishnu, in the Dwarf Incarnation, went to Bali, king of the daityas, to solicit a blessing, Sukra, as Bali's preceptor, forbade the king to give him anything. The king being determined to give what was asked, it was the duty of the priest to read the customary formula and to pour out water from a vessel as a ratification of the gift. Sukra, anxious to prevent his master from giving what was asked, as he foresaw that it would prove his ruin, entered the water in an invisible form, and by his magical powers prevented it from falling. Vishnu, aware of the device, put a straw into the vessel, which, entering Sukra's eye, gave him so much pain that he could remain there no longer; so the water fell, the gift was ratified, and Sukra lost an eye. "If a person be born under the planet Sukra, he will have the faculty of knowing things past, present, and future. He will have many wives, a kingly umbrella (an emblem of royalty), and other kings will worship him."

Sukra is said to have possessed the power of raising the dead, as the following legend* shows:—Devajāni, the daughter of Sukra, was deeply in love with Kacha, a son of Vrihaspati and a pupil of her father, who had been sent to Sukra for the express purpose of learning from him the incantation for raising the dead. One day Devajāni sent Kacha to gather flowers from a wood belonging to some giants, who, on previous occasions had eaten him; but Sukra, by the above incantation, had restored him to life. The giants now resolved to make Sukra himself eat the boy; for which purpose, they cut him into small pieces, boiled him in spirits, and invited Sukra to an entertainment. As Kacha did not return with the flowers, Devajāni' with many tears told her father that, if he did not restore her lover, she would certainly destroy herself. Sukra learned by the power of meditation that he had eaten the boy, but did not know how to restore him to life, without

*Ward, ii. 71.

the attempt being fatal to himself. At length, whilst the boy was in his stomach, he restored him to life, and then taught him the incantation he was so wishful to learn. Kacha, tearing open Sukra's stomach, came forth, and immediately using the wonderful incantation restored his teacher to life.

7. Sani, hence Sanivāra (Saturday), is said to be the son of Surya, and Chhāya, the servant whom his wife Savarnā substituted for herself; or, according to other accounts, he sprang from Balarāma and Revati. He is represented as a black man, clothed in black garments, riding on a vulture, with four arms. "If a person be born under the planet Sani, he will be slandered, his riches dissipated, his son, wife, and friends destroyed; he will live at variance with others and endure many sufferings." Many stories are told of his evil influence, consequently the Hindus are under fear of evil from this planet. It was Sani who was said to have burnt off Ganesa's head.

8. Rāhu (the ascending node) was the son of Vrihaspati and Sinhikā. He is described as a black man, riding on a lion. "If a person be born under the planet Rāhu, his wisdom, riches, and children will be destroyed; he will be exposed to many afflictions and be subject to his enemies." According to the popular notions of the Hindus, at the time of an eclipse Rāhu devours the sun and moon; hence, as soon as an eclipse is noticed, the people make a dreadful noise, shouting, blowing horns, and beating drums, to cause Rāhu to restore these luminaries. The reason of this custom is probably found in the following story: Rāhu was originally an asura or giant, who took his present form at the churning of the sea. As the gods and demons churned, Surya and Chandra, who were sitting together, hinted to Vishnu, when the amrita appeared, that one of the demons had tasted it. Vishnu immediately cut off the head of the offender; but as he had drunk of the water of life, neither head nor trunk could perish. The head, taking the name of Rāhu, and the trunk, that of Ketu, were placed in heaven as the ascending and descending nodes, and leave was

granted, as a means of revenge on Surya and Chandra, that on certain occasions Rāhu should approach these gods and render them unclean, so that their bodies at these times become thin and black.*

*Ward, ii. 81.

Chapter VI
The Asuras

In the Purānas and other of the later writings of the Hindus, and also in the popular mind, the asuras are powerful evil beings; in translations the word is represented by such terms as demons, giants, etc. As the suras* were the gods, the a-suras were not-gods, and therefore the enemies or opponents of the gods. In the Vedas the name asura is applied more frequently to the gods themselves than to their enemies, whilst it is also used very much in the same manner as in the later writings. In the Rig-Veda, Varuna is accosted as follows: "King Varuna has made a highway for the sun to go over. O thou wise asura and king, loosen our sins!" Again: "The all-knowing asura established the heavens, and fixed the limits of the earth. He sat as the supreme ruler of all worlds. These are the works of Varuna." "Asura stands for the Supreme Spirit," in another verse, and "also as an appellative for Prajāpati or creation's lord."† Again and again Varuna alone, and also in conjunction with Mitra, is called an asura. "All the Vedic gods have shared

---

*Originally the suras were a class of inferior deities, connected with Surya; afterwards the term was employed to signify the gods generally.

†Dr. Bauerjea, *Bengal Magazine*, April, 1880,

the same title, not excepting even goddesses." "Varuna was the all-knowing asura, Prajāpati the Supreme Being; Indra, the Maruts, Tvastri, Mitra, Rudra, Agni, Vāyu, Pushan, Savitri, Parjanya, the sacrificial priests, were all asuras. In fine, Deva (god) and asura were synonymous expressions in a multitude of texts."*

On the other hand, in the Rig-Veda, Indra is the destroyer of asuras. "The same Veda which speaks of the asuras as celestial beings supplies its readers also with the Mantras, by means of which devas overcame asuras. The texts which are condemnatory of the suras as impure and ungodly are far less in number than those which recognize the term as applicable to gods and priests." Dr. Banerjea, in the most interesting and ingenious article from which the above extracts are made, suggests a means of reconciling these contradictory uses of the word "asura." Before the Indo-Aryans arrived in India, they had lived in close proximity to the Persians, the original worshippers of fire. "What could be more natural," he asks, "than that the Asura-Pracheta, or Asura-Viswaveda of the one branch, was but the translation of the Ahura-Mazda (the Wise Lord, according to the 'Zend-Avesta') of the other branch; and that the word 'Ahura,' which the one used in a divine sense, would become a household word in the other branch, in the same sense?" the word "Ahura" being changed into "Asura," in a way common to many other words. He then goes on to say, that as "Assur" was the term used in Assyria for the Supreme Lord, and the Assyrians were for some time the rulers of the Persians, it was natural that this word should find its way into Persia; the only change being this, that the Persians added Mazda (wise or good) to the term "Assur," and the Indo-Aryans received it from them. So much for the good use of the term "Asura."

But the word "Assur" was not only used for the Supreme

---

*Dr. Banerjea, *Bengal Magazine*, April, 1880.

Lord, it also represented the Assyrian nation, his worshippers, who were most cruel in their treatment of their foes; and as, later on, the bitterest hatred is known to have existed between the Indo-Aryans and the Persians, the followers of Ahura-Mazda, Dr. Banerjea concludes that owing to the cruelties perpetrated by the Assyrians on the one hand, and the hatred cherished towards them by the Persians on the other, the branch of the Aryan family that migrated into India brought with them very bitter feelings towards Assur (the Assyrian people) and Ahuri (the belongings of Ahura); and thus the term "Asura," which at one time was considered a becoming epithet for the Supreme Being, became descriptive only of those who were the enemies of the gods. In order to afford sanction for this altered sense of a word, a new derivation has been given to it. The word was originally derived from the root *as*, through *asu*, "breath," and means a spirit, or "the Great Spirit." Now, however, it is explained to be simply a compound of *a* privative, and *sura*, "god," meaning a non-god: therefore a demon.

Whatever be the cause of it, there is no doubt that at the present day, and throughout the later writings of the Hindus, the term "asura" is used only for the enemies of the gods. In the "Taittirya Sanhita"* we read "that the gods and asuras contended together, and that the former, being less numerous than the latter, took some bricks, and placing them in a proper position to receive the sacrificial fire, with the formula, 'Thou art a multiplier,' they became numerous." In the "Satapatha Brāhmana"† it is said that "the gods and asuras, both descendants of Prajāpati,‡ obtained their father's inheritance, truth and falsehood. The gods, abandoning falsehood, adopted truth; the asuras, abandoning truth, adopted falsehood.

---

*Muir, O. S. T., v. 15.

† Muir, 0. S. T., iv. 60.

‡The Mahābhārata says the asuras were the elder, the gods the younger, sons.

Speaking truth exclusively, the gods became weaker, but in the end became prosperous; the asuras, speaking falsehood exclusively, became rich, but in the end succumbed." The gods tried to sacrifice, but though interrupted at first by the asuras, at length succeeded, and so became superior to their foes. Another legend in the same book teaches that the asuras, when offering sacrifices, placed the oblations in their own mouths, whilst the gods gave their oblations to each other; at length Prajāpati giving himself to them, the sacrifices, which supply the gods with food, were henceforth enjoyed by them.

Although there were frequent wars between the gods and asuras, the suras were not averse to receive the aid of their foes at the churning of the ocean; and some of them were not inferior in power and skill to the gods. Bali, one of their number, is worshipped by the Hindus on their birthday; and Jalandhara conquered in battle even Vishnu himself; Indra and the other gods fled before him, and Siva, unaided, could not destroy him. Rāhu is an asura, and it was to destroy some of these mighty beings who distressed the gods, that Durgā, and Kāli had to put forth their strength. In the constant wars between these rivals, Sukra, the preceptor of the asuras, was frequently called to resuscitate the fallen. The following story of Jalandhara from the Uttara Khānda of the "Padma Purāna"* will illustrate the teaching of the later Hindu Scriptures respecting the asuras.

JALANDHARA

The story of Jalandhara's birth and life was narrated by Nārada to the Pāndavas to encourage them when they were in distress on account of their misfortunes. He reminds them that adversity and prosperity come to all: Rāhu, who swallows the sun, is the same Rāhu whose head was severed from his body by Vishnu; and the valiant Jalandhara, the son of the Ocean

---

*Kennedy, "Hindu Mythology," p.-457.

and the river Ganges, who on one occasion conquered Vishnu, was himself slain by Siva. The mention of this fact excites the curiosity of his hearers; and in answer to their inquiry about him, Nārada gives the following history.

Indra and the other gods, arriving at Siva's home on Mount Kailāsa to pay him a visit, informed the bull Nandi, the chief of Siva's attendants, that they had come to amuse his master with song and dance. Siva invites them to enter, and, being delighted with their music, tells Indra to ask a boon, who, in a defiant tone, asks that he might be a warrior like Siva himself. The boon is granted, and the gods depart. No sooner have they left than Siva asks his attendants if they had not noticed Indra's haughty tone, when immediately there stood before him a form of anger, black as darkness, who said to Siva, "Give me thy similitude, and then what can I do for you?" Siva tells him to incorporate himself with the river of heaven (Gangā), form a union between her and the Ocean, and conquer Indra.

In obedience to Siva's command, Gangā left the skies, and becoming united to the Ocean, from them a son proceeded, at whose birth the earth trembled and wept, and the three worlds resounded with noise. Brahmā coming to inquire the cause of this commotion, and asking to see the child, Gangā lays it in his lap, when it seized his head, and would not loose it until its father opened its hand. Brahmā, admiring the child's strength, said, "From his holding so firmly, let him be named Jalandhara," and bestowed upon him this boon, that he "should be unconquered by the gods, and enjoy the three worlds."

Jalandhara's boyhood was full of wonders. Borne up by the wind, he flew over the ocean; his pets were lions which he had caught; and the largest birds and fishes were subject to him. When he grew up to manhood, at Sukra's request, his father withdrew the sea from Jambadwipa, the residence of holy men, which became his home, and bearing his name has become celebrated.* Māya, the architect of the asuras, there built him a beautiful city, his father installed him as king, and Sukra gave him the charm by which he could raise the dead to life. He married Vrindā, the daughter of an Apsaras named Swarnā, and soon after his wedding made war upon the gods.

In order to lead to a conflict, he sent a messenger to Indra, whom he found "surrounded by three hundred and thirty-three millions of deities," to demand the restoration of the moon, the amrita, elephant, horse, gem, tree, and other things of which he said Indra had robbed him, at the churning of his uncle, the Sea of Milk; and also to resign Swarga. As Indra refuses to accede to this request, Jalandhara raises an army of warriors having the heads of horses, elephants, camels, cats, tigers and lions, with which Indra's abode is soon surrounded. The gods in their extremity resort to Vishnu for aid.

On Vishnu's arrival the battle commences. Multitudes are slain on both sides, but the gods, when wounded, resort to the mountains, where they find herbs which quickly restore them. At length the greater gods and the leaders of the daityas personally engage in conflict; Indra falls insensible, Rudra is taken prisoner, and Kuvera is laid low by a blow of a mace. After this, the tide turns in favour of the gods. When Indra struck Bali, the most costly gems dropped from his mouth; he therefore asked for his body, and with his thunderbolt cut it into many parts. "From the purity of his actions, the parts of his body became the germs of the various gems. From his bones came diamonds, from his eyes sapphires, from his blood rubies, from his marrow emeralds, from his flesh crystals, from his tongue coral, and from his teeth pearls."

Indra being in his turn attacked by Jalandhara, Vishnu comes to the rescue; and though the asuras attack him in immense numbers, and the sky is dark with their arrows,

---

*The present Jallander.

Vishnu overthrows them as if they were leaves. One of their number, named Shailaroma, losing his head, seized hold of Garuda, Vishnu's marvellous bird, when the severed head immediately rejoined his body; Garuda, seeing this wonderful event, flew off with his master. Jalandhara was prevented from following him, as he had to call in the aid of Sukra to restore his warriors to life.

Hearing that the soldiers of the gods were also restored to life through using herbs obtained from an island called Drona, situated in the Sea of Milk, he asked his uncle to submerge it. Being deprived of this means of restoration, they appealed to Vishnu, who, attacking Jalandhara, was laid low by the daitya, and would have been slain but for Lakshmi's intercession with her cousin. In return for his life Vishnu promised to remain near the Sea of Milk. Jalandhara, having now conquered the gods, enjoyed peace and happiness.

The gods, however, being expelled from heaven, and deprived of sacrifices and the amrita, did not long remain contented with their lot. They went together to Brahmā, who conducted them to Siva, whom they found "seated on a throne and attended by myriads of devoted servants, naked, deformed, curly-haired, with matted locks and covered with dust." On Brahmā stating the case for the gods, Siva declared that, if Vishnu had been unsuccessful in fighting the demon, it was impossible that he alone could overcome him; he therefore advised that the gods should unite to form a weapon by which their common enemy might be destroyed. Acting on this advice, the gods, glowing with anger, darted forth volumes of flames, to which Siva added the consuming beams of his third eye. Vishnu, too, when summoned, added his flame of anger, and asked Siva to destroy the daitya, excusing himself from the task on the ground that Jalandhara was a relative of Lakshmi. Visvakarma and the deities were alarmed as they saw the glowing mass; but Siva, placing his heel on it, whirled round with it, and formed it into the discus called Sudarsana, which sent forth such fiery beams that the gods cried out, "Preserve us!" Brahmā's beard was scorched as he took it into his hand — "such is the result of offering a gift to a blockhead" —but Siva hid it under his arm.

Nārada informed Jalandhara of the intended attack of Siva, and, enlarging on Pārvati's beauty, excited him to attack her husband that he might win her. With this object he sent Rāhu as an ambassador, to summon the god to submission. On his arrival at the court the envoy delivered his master's message to Siva, in the form of Panchānana, who did not deign to speak; but the snake Vasuki, falling to the ground from his hair, began to eat Ganesa's rat. Seeing this, Kartikeya's peacock made such an awful noise that the snake disgorged the rat and returned to his proper place.

Lakshmi then entered the assembly with a vessel *of* amrita, with which she resuscitated Brahmā's fifth head that was in Siva's hand; the head rolling on the ground uttered most boastful language, until myriads of hideous forms from Siva's locks quieted it. Rāhu, seeing all this, asked Siva to forsake his wife and children, and live a mendicant's life. At a sign from Siva, Nandi, the bull, showed him the door; this was the answer vouchsafed to the illustrious master's demand.

War being determined on, Jalandhara marched first to Kailāsa; hut finding that Siva had forsaken it and taken up a position on a mountain near Lake Manasa, he surrounded the mountain with his troops. Nandi marched against them, and spread destruction "like the waters of the deluge;" reserves, however, being brought up, the army of the gods suffers loss. Pārvati, hearing that her sons, Ganesa and Kartikeya, are hardly pressed, urged her husband to go in person and put forth his energy, though not to expose himself unnecessarily. Before leaving home, Siva carefully warned Pārvati to be on her guard during his absence, as it was possible the daitya in some disguise might visit her; after this, accompanied by Virabbadra and Manibhadra, two forms of his anger, he went to the field of battle. When the conflict between the daityas and the attendants of Siva had continued for some time, Jalandhara devised a plan by which he hoped to succeed more easily than by fighting. Giving his own form and the command of his troops to a chief, the daitya king assumed the form of Siva, changed Durwarana into Nandi, and, taking the heads of Ganesa and Kartikeya under his arms, hastened to Siva's abode. Seeing this, Pārvati was overwhelmed with grief; but having some doubt of his being the real Siva, she hid herself and would not listen to his overtures of love. To make certain of his identity, she caused one of her attendants to assume her form and visit the daitya, who, returning with the information that he was not the true Siva, Pārvati hid herself in a lotus, and her companions were changed into bees which hovered around her.

In the mean time Vishnu had been more successful with Vrindā, the wife of Jalandhara. In the guise of a Brāhman, he made a hermitage near her palace, and caused her to dream that she saw her husband's head severed from his body, his flesh eaten by wild animals, and his eyes plucked out by vultures. Distracted with her dream, in a high fever she rushed into the forest, where an ogress met her, ate her mules, and was about to attack her, when the Brāhman came to her rescue. On reaching the hermitage, Vishnu induced her to enter, changed himself into the form of her husband, and there they lived together for some time. At length Vrindā, seeing through the disguise, cursed Vishnu, telling him that, as he had wronged Jalandhara, he would himself be wronged, and, having purified herself from her sin, died. Her body was burned, her mother collected the ashes, and threw them into the Ganges. The forest in which she was burned has ever since borne the name of Vrindāvana,* near Mount Govardhana.

Jalandhara, hearing of his wife's deception and death, was

---

*Brindāban.

mad with rage; and, leaving the neighbourhood of Pārvati's home, returned to the field of battle. By Sukra's power his dead heroes were restored to life, and a grand final charge was made. At length Siva and Jalandhara personally fight; after a desperate encounter, in which the daitya employs various magical powers, Siva cuts off his head; but it is no sooner severed than it resumes its place. Siva in his extremity summonses to his aid the female forms or energies of the gods, Brāhmi, Vaishnavi and the rest, who drink up the blood of the giant, and with their aid Siva succeeds in destroying him, and the gods regain their kingdom and possessions.

Chapter VII

Sacked Animals and Birds

Some of the animals regarded as sacred have already been mentioned in connection with the deities to whom they are specially dear, and in whose worship they participate. They are regarded as the Vāhans, or vehicles, upon which these gods and goddesses travel. Thus Indra rides upon the elephant Airavata: Siva on the bull Nandi; Yama on a buffalo; Durgā, as Singhavāhini, on a lion, as Durgā on a tiger; Agni on a ram; Vāyu on an antelope; Ganesa on a rat, and Sasti on a cat. Virabhadra, the emanation of Siva which destroyed Daksha's sacrifice, rode on a dog, and Kāmadeva travelled either on the monster Makara or a parrot. The jackal is regarded as a representative of Durgā, who in this form assisted in preserving Krishna, on the night of his birth, from Kansa's anger. Monkeys, as representatives of Hanumān, are very commonly worshipped; the dog, though worshipped by some, by others is regarded as unclean.

Amongst birds, the goose is the Vāhan of Brahmā, the peacock that of Kartikeya, Sani rides upon a vulture; the Brāhmani kite is said to be a form of Durgā, and the Khanjana, or wagtail, represents Vishnu, because the mark on its throat is thought to resemble the Shālgrāma; the owl, too, is worshipped at the festivals of Kartikeya, Brahmā, and Lakshmi. Garuda, the Vāhan of Vishnu, and Jatāyus and Sampāti, the vultures who assisted Rāma, will be described separately.

The cow, though not regarded as the Vāhan of any deity, is worshipped too. Brahmā is said to have created cows and Brāhmans at the same time; the Brāhman to officiate at worship, and the cow to provide milk, ghī, etc., as offerings, whilst cow-dung is necessary for various purifying ceremonies. Regular worship of the cow takes place yearly, at which similar ceremonies are performed to those which are employed at the worship of images; the horns and bodies of the cows are painted, and they are then bathed in the rivers. Some people are said to worship the cow daily.

GARUDA

Garuda or Superna is a mythical being, half-man and half-eagle, the Vāhan of Vishnu. Though not strictly divine, he appears frequently in Vishnu's exploits, and, being worshipped together with his lord, it is necessary to give some description of his birth and deeds.

When Daksha's sons refused to people the world, he produced sixty daughters, thirteen of whom he gave to Kasyapa the sage; of these, two come into prominence in connection with Garuda. Vinatā bore him two celebrated sons, Garuda and Aruna: the former, also called Superna, was the king of the feathered tribes, and the remorseless enemy of the serpent race. Aruna became famous as the charioteer of the Sun. "The progeny of Kadru (the other sister) were a thousand powerful many-headed snakes, of immeasurable might, subject to Garuda."* The mother of Garuda is said to have laid an egg; hence her son assumed a bird-like form.

Another legend makes "Garuda the son of Kasyapa and

---

*"Vishnu Purāna," P.119.

Diti. This all-prolific dame laid an egg, which, it was predicted, would yield her a deliverer from some great evil. After the lapse of five hundred years, Garuda sprang from the egg, flew to Indra's abode, extinguished the fire that surrounded

Garuda

it, conquered its guards, and bore off the amrita, which enabled him to liberate his captive mother. A few drops of the immortal beverage falling on some *Kusa* grass, it became eternally consecrated; and the serpents greedily licking it, so lacerated their tongues with the sharp grass, that they have ever since remained forked. But the boon of immortality was ensured to them by their partaking of the amrita."* "As soon as Garuda was born, his body expanded till it touched the sky; the other animals were terrified. His eyes were like the lightning. The mountains were driven away with the wind

*Moor's "Hindu Pantheon," 341.

caused by the flapping of his wings. The rays which issued from his body set the four quarters of the world on fire; the affrighted gods imagining that Garuda must be an incarnation of Agni, resorted to that deity for protection."*

Garuda is the mortal enemy of snakes. His mother Vinatā quarrelled with her sister, Kadru, the mother of the snakes, respecting the colour of the horse that was produced at the churning of the ocean; since that time there has been constant enmity between their descendants. On the occasion of his marriage, the serpents, alarmed at the thought of his having children who might destroy them, made a fierce attack on him; but the result was that he slew them all, save one, which he has ever since worn as an ornament round his neck. To this day superstitious Hindus repeat the name of Garuda three times before going to sleep at night, as a safeguard against snakes.

The following legend from the Mahābhārata† gives the account of his liberating his mother from servitude, and of his appointment as the Vāhan of Vishnu. His mother, having lost her wager with her sister respecting the colour of the sea-produced horse, was reduced to servitude to the serpents, who, being anxious to become immortal, promised to liberate her on condition that her son Garuda should bring them Chandra (the Moon), whose bright spots are filled with amrita. Before starting on this expedition he went to his mother for food, who advised him to go to the seashore and gather whatever he could find, but entreated him to be most careful not to eat a Brāhman; adding, "Should you at any time feel a burning sensation in your stomach, be sure you have eaten a Brāhman."

After receiving this warning, he set off on his journey, Passing through a country inhabited by fishermen, he at one inspiration drew in houses, trees, cattle, men, and other animals. But among the inhabitants swallowed, one was a Brāhman,

---

*Ward, ii. 200.
†Ibid., ii. 201.

who caused such an intolerable burning in his stomach that Garuda, unable to bear it, called in the greatest haste for him to come out. The Brāhman refused unless his wife, a fisherman's daughter, might accompany him. To this Garuda consented.

Pursuing his journey, Garuda met his father Kasyapa (he shines as the Pole Star), who directed him to appease his hunger at a certain lake where an elephant and tortoise were fighting. The tortoise was eighty miles long, and the elephant one hundred and sixty. Garuda with one claw seized the elephant, with the other the tortoise, and perched with them on a tree eight hundred miles high. But the tree was unable to bear the ponderous weight, and, unhappily, thousands of pigmy Brāhmans were then worshipping on one of its branches. Trembling lest he should destroy any of them, he took the bough in his beak, continuing to hold the elephant and tortoise in his claws, and flew to a mountain in an uninhabited country, where he finished his repast on the tortoise and elephant.

Garuda having surmounted astonishing dangers, at last seized the Moon and concealed it under his wing. On his return, however, being attacked by Indra and the gods, he overcame all, excepting Vishnu. Even Vishnu was so severely put to it in the contest, that he came to terms with Garuda, made him immortal, and promised him a higher seat than his own; while on his part Garuda became the Vāhan or carrier of Vishnu. Since then, Vishnu rides upon Garuda, while the latter, in the shape of a flag, sits at the top of Vishnu's car.

In the Rāmāyana Garuda is represented as doing great service to Rāma and his followers, and his powers and peculiarities are repeatedly referred to. Thus, in the description of Hanumān it is said, that

> "Like a thunderbolt in frame was he,
> And swift as Garud's self could flee."[*]

---

[*]Griiffiths's "Rāmāyana," i. 94.

In like manner it is said of two heroes:

> "Sugriva, offspring of the Sun,
> And Bali, Indra's mighty one,
> They, both endowed with Garud's might,
> And skilled in all the arts of fight,
> Wandered in arms the forest through,
> And lions and snakes and tigers slew.'"*

When Ansumān found the ashes of the sixty thousand sons of Sāgar,† who, owing to Kapila's curse, had been destroyed, and was in distress because he could obtain no water with which to offer oblations for the dead, he sees their uncle—

> "King Garud, best beyond compare,
> Of birds who wing the fields of air.
> Then thus unto the weeping man
> The son of Vinatā began:
> 'Grieve not, O hero, for their fall,
> Who died a death approved of all.'"‡

Garuda then tells Ansumān that if he can succeed in inducing Gangā to descend from heaven, and with her streams to touch these ashes, the dead shall return to life, and finally ascend to Indra's heaven.

In the description of the city of Ayodha, when Rāma had gone into the forest, is a reference to Garuda's antipathy to snakes:—

> "The city wore
> No look of beauty as before—

---

*Ibid., i- 96.
†See Gangā, §Griffiths's
‡"Rāmāyana," i. 186.

Like a dull river or a lake
By Garud robbed of every snake."*

In the following lines is an account of Garuda's resting on
a tree when he was carrying off the elephant and the tortoise
as narrated above. Rāvana impelled by the accounts of Sitā's
beauty, goes to see her, and on his journey

> "He saw a fig-tree like a cloud,
> With mighty branches earthward bowed.
> It stretched a hundred leagues, and made
> For hermit bands a welcome shade.
> Thither the feathered king of yore
> An elephant and tortoise bore,
> And lighted on a bough to eat
> The captives of his taloned feet.
> The bough, unable to sustain
> The crushing weight and sudden strain,
> Loaded with sprays and leaves of spring,
> Gave way beneath the feathered king.
>
>   *   *   *   *
>
> The feathered monarch raised the weight
> Of the huge bough, and bore away
> The loosened load and captured prey.
>
>   *   *   *   *
>
> His soul conceived the high emprise
> To snatch the amrit from the skies.
> He rent the nets of iron first,
> Then through the jewel chamber burst,
> And bore the drink of heaven away
> That watched in Indra's palace lay." †

---

*Griffiths's "Rāmāyana," ii. 167.
†Ibid., iii. 162.

In the great conflict with Ravana, as Rama and his brother were wounded and well-nigh dead, owing to a flight of serpents sent by Indrajit, Garuda appeared to restore them, and thus enabled them to carry on the war. His approach and work are thus described:—

> "The rushing wind grew loud,
> Red lightnings flashed from banks of cloud,
> The mountains shook, the wild waves rose,
> And, smitten by resistless blows,
> Uprooted fell each stately tree
> That fringed the margin of the sea.
> All life within the waters feared:
> Then, as the Vanars gazed, appeared
> King Garud's self, a wondrous sight,
> Disclosed in flames of fiery light.
> From his fierce eye in sudden dread
> All serpents in a moment fled;
> And those transformed to shafts, that bound
> The princes, vanished in the ground.
> On Raghu's sons his eyes he bent,
> And hailed the lords omnipotent.
> Then o'er them stooped the feathered king,
> And touched their faces with his wing.
> His healing touch their pangs allayed,
> And closed each rent the shafts had made.
> Again their eyes were bright and bold;
> Again the smooth skin shone like gold."*

For this great work of restoration Rama expressed his gratitude, whereupon Garuda replied—

> "In me, O Raghu's son, behold

---

*Griffiths's "Ramiiyana," v. 153.

One who has loved thee from of old.
Garud, the lord of all that fly,
Thy guardian and thy friend am I.
Not all the gods in heaven could loose
These numbing bonds, this serpent noose,
Wherewith fierce Ravan's son, renowned
For magic arts, your limbs had bound.
Those arrows fixed in every limb
Were mighty snakes, transformed by him.
Bloodthirsty race, they live beneath
The earth, and slay with venomed teeth."

Garuda is represented in pictures and sculpture in various ways. Sometimes he has the head and wings of a bird, with a human body; sometimes he has a bird's claws; and at others he has a human face, and the body of a bird.

JATĀYUS AND SAMPĀTI.

Garuda had two sons, named Jatāyus and Sampāti, who also assisted Rāma. As he, Lakshman and Sati reached the hermitage in the forest where they intended to remain, they saw "a mighty vulture, of size and strength unparalleled." Struck with his appearance, Rāma inquired who he was, when Jatāyus informed them of his parentage, and offered to be their friend:

"Thy ready helper will I be
And guard thy house, if thou agree:
When thou and Lakshman urge the chase,
By Sita's side shall be my place."*

This offer was accepted; and when Rāma saw the stag

---

*Griffiths's "Rāmāyana," iii. 68.

which Rāvana sent to attract him from his home, he went after it with the greater sense of security because Jatāyus was there to guard his wife. When Rāvana seized Sitā, she cried out to Jatāyus—

> "Oh see, the king who rules the race
> Of giants, cruel, fierce, and base !
> Rāvan, the spoiler, bears me hence,
> The helpless prey of violence."*

Jatāyus first tries by reasoning to lead Rāvana to restore Sitā to her home, and warned him that death would result from his act of violence. When, however, neither advice nor threats availed, he prepared to fight.

Jatāyus.

"With clash and din and furious blows
Of murderous battle met the foes :

* * * *

Then fierce the dreadful combat raged,
As fiend and bird in war engaged,
As if two winged mountains sped
To dire encounter overhead."*

Jatayus succeeded in breaking Rāvana's bow, but—

"A second bow soon armed his hand,
Whence pointed arrows swift and true
In hundreds, yea, in thousands flew." †

The giant's arrows wounded the vulture; the vulture in return threw darts which injured Rāvana, struck the steeds of the chariot, and broke the chariot itself; whilst with his beak and claws he tore the coachman to pieces. Rāvana descended from his chariot and fought on foot; but gradually the strength of Jatāyus, who was weak with age, gave way. Rāvana, therefore, re-ascends the chariot, and is about to fly through the air, when the vulture a second time intercepts his flight, and—

"Swooped down upon the giant's back:
Down to the bone the talons went;
With many a wound the flesh was rent." ‡

Jatāyus was able to tear off the ten left arms of Rāvana, but unfortunately others grew to replace them. At length Rāvana seizes his sword, and, after giving the vulture a mortal blow, hurries off with Sitā to Lanka.

---

*"Griffiths's Rāmāyana," iii. 236.
†Ibid., 237.
‡Ibid., 240.

When Rāma and Lakshman commence their search for Sitā, they come upon the dying bird, and, seeing the marks of blood upon him, at first think that he has been guilty of carrying off the lady; but, after hearing from him the story of Rāvana's visit and flight, they watch the bird expire, and perform his funeral rites.

In their search, reaching the seashore, but still ignorant of Sitā's whereabouts, some of their monkey followers see an immense vulture, weak with age, who, hearing them mention Jatāyus' name, inquires of his welfare. When told that he had been slain by Rāvana, the vulture informs them that this victim of the giant was no other than his own brother; and in revenge assists them, by informing them where Rāvana and Sitā were at that moment. He told them that he had Garuda's power to see immense distances, and, mounting into the sky, saw Lanka, and told the Vānar chiefs that the object of their search was there. Hearing this, Hanumān was despatched to communicate with Sitā, and to assure her of Rāma's coming to rescue her.

The Lotus

Chapter VIII
Gangā

Gangā (the Ganges), the chief of the sacred streams of India, whose waters are said to have the power of cleansing

Gangā

from all past, present, and future sins, is believed to be divine, and the account of her birth and appearance on earth forms an interesting episode in the Ramāyana. The story is told to Rāma by the hermit Visvamitra, as he was travelling with Rāma and his brother Lakshman. As soon as they reach the banks of the sacred stream,

> "They bathed, as Scripture bids, and paid
> Oblations due to god and shade."

As soon as they were seated, Rāma said—

> "'O saint, I yearn
> The three-pathed Gangā's tale to learn.
> Thus urged, the saint recounted both
> The birth of Gangā and her growth:
> 'The mighty hill with metals stored,
> Himālaya, is, the mountains' lord,
> The father of a lovely pair
> Of daughters, fairest of the fair.
> Their mother, offspring of the will
> Of Meru, everlasting hill,
> Menā, Himālaya's darling, graced
> With beauty of her dainty waist.
> Gangā was elder-born; then came
> The fair one known by Umā's name.
> Then all the gods of heaven, in need
> Of Gangā's help their vows to speed,
> To great Himālaya came and prayed
> The mountain king to yield the maid.
> He, not regardless of the weal
> Of the three worlds, with holy zeal
> His daughter to the Immortals gave—
> Gangā, whose waters cleanse and save,
> Who roams at pleasure, fair and free,

Purging all sinners, to the sea.
The three-pathed Gangā thus obtained,
The gods their heavenly homes regained.'"*

The sage next tells Rāma that there was a mighty King of
Ayodha named Sāgara, † who, being childless and most anxious
to have a son, propitiated the saint Bhrigu (or, according to
other accounts, his grandson) by penances extending over a
hundred years. At length the saint, pleased with Sāgara's
worship, said —

"From thee, O Sāgar, blameless king,
A mighty host of sons shall spring,
And thou shalt win a glorious name,
Which none, O chief, but thou shalt claim;
One of thy queens a son shall bear,

---

*Griffiths's "Rāmāyana," i. 171.

†Sāgara's birth was supernatural. His father Bāhu, King of Ayodha,
was expelled from his kingdom. The mother of Sāgara accompanied
her husband to the forest, but, owing to a poisonous drag having been
given to her by a rival wife, she could not bring forth her son, with
whom she had been pregnant for seven years. When her husband
died, she wished to be burned with his body; but this was prevented
by a sage named Aurva, who assured her that her sou would yet
be born, and grow up to be a mighty king. When he was born,
Aurva gave him the name Sāgara (*sa*, with, and *gara*, poison). Aurva
himself was also born in an extraordinary manner. A king named
Kritavirya was very liberal to the Bhrigus, and through his liberality
they became rich. His descendants being poor, they asked help of the
Bhrigus. On this being refused them, they made an onslaught on the
Brāhmans of this family, slaying all they could find, even to children
in the womb. One woman concealed her unborn child in her thigh.
The Kshattriyas, hearing of this, tried to slay him, but he issued from
his mother's thigh with such lustre that he blinded his persecutors.
And because he was born from the thigh (*uru*) of his mother, he was
called Aurva.

> Maintainer of thy race and heir;
> And of the other there shall be
> Some sixty thousand born to thee."*

Hearing this, the wives are anxious to know which of them is to have the one son, and which the multitude; but this the Brāhman leaves them to decide. Kesini wishes for the one; and Sumati is pleased with the prospect of having sixty thousand.

> "Time passed. The elder consort bare
> A son called Ansumrān, the heir.
> Then Sumati, the younger, gave
> Birth to a gourd, O hero brave,
> Whose rind, when burst and cleft in two,
> Gave sixty thousand babes to view.
> All these with care the nurses laid
> In jars of oil; and there they stayed,
> Till, youthful age and strength complete,
> Forth speeding from each dark retreat,
> All peers in valour, years, and might,
> The sixty thousand came to light."†

After a time King Sāgara determined to make an Asvamedha, or horse sacrifice, with the object of becoming the reigning Indra, or king of the gods. Preparations for this are accordingly made, and Prince Ansumān, the son of the elder wife, is appointed by the king to follow the horse set apart for the sacrifice; for, according to the ritual, it was to be set free, and allowed to wander for a whole year wherever it would. Indra, knowing the great merit that Sāgar would obtain by this sacrifice, and fearing that he might even lose his crown,

---

*Griffiths's "Rāmāyana," i. 174.
†Griffiths's Rāmāyana," i. 175.

"Veiling his form in demon guise,
Came down upon the appointed day,
And drove the victim horse away."*

The officiating priest, being aware of this, cries out—

"Haste, king! now let the thief be slain;
Bring thou the charger back again;
The sacred rite prevented thus
Brings scathe and woe to all of us."

King Sāgara, incited by the Brāhman, urges his sons to search until they find the stolen horse:

"Brave sons of mine, I know not how
These demons are so mighty now;
The priests began the rites so well,
All sanctified with prayer and spell.
If in the depths of earth he hide,
Or lurk beneath the ocean's tide,
Pursue, dear sons, the robber's track;
Slay him and bring the charger back.
The whole of this broad earth explore,
Sea-garlanded from shore to shore;
Yea, dig her up with might and main,
Until you see the horse again."†

The sons commence their search. Each digs a league in depth, and by this means they reach the centre of the earth; but cannot see the horse. Alarmed at their destructive work, the gods repair to Brahmā, and tell him what is happening. He cheers them with the information that Vishnu, in the form

---

*Ibid., 177.
†Griffiths's "Rāmāyana," i. 177.

of Kapila, will protect the Earth, his bride, and that these sons of Sāgara will be consumed to ashes. The gods, encouraged by these words, repair to their home and patiently wait for deliverance.

After digging sixty thousand leagues into the earth without obtaining any tidings of the horse, the princes return to their father, asking what can be done. Sāgara commands them to dig on, and continue their search until the horse is found. At length they

> "Saw Vāsudeva (Vishnu) standing there.
> In Kapil's form he loved to wear;
> And near the everlasting God
> The victim charger cropped the sod.
> They saw with joy and eager eyes
> The fancied robber and the prize,
> And on him rushed the furious band,
> Crying aloud,' Stand, villain ! Stand!'
> 'Avaunt! avaunt!' groat Kapil cried,
> His bosom flusht with passion's tide;
> Then, by his might, that proud array
> All scorched to heaps of ashes lay."*

Hearing no news of his sons, the king became anxious, and sent his grandson Ansumān to look after them. He inquires of all he meets on the earth, and is encouraged by the information that he shall certainly bring back the stolen horse. At length he reaches the spot where his brothers were consumed, and is overwhelmed with grief at their fate. At this moment his uncle Garuda appears and consoles him, saying—

> "Grieve not, O hero, for their fall,
> Who died a death approved of all.

---

*Griffiths's "Rāmāyana," i. 183.

Of mighty strength they met their fate
By Kapil's hand, whom none can mate.
Pour forth for them no earthly wave,
A holier flood their spirits crave.
If, daughter of the Lord of Snow,
Gaṅgā would turn her stream below,
Her waves, that cleanse all mortal stain,
Would wash their ashes pure again.
Yea, when her flood, whom all revere,
Rolls o'er the dust that moulders here,
The sixty thousand, freed from sin,
A home in Indra's heaven shall win.
Go, and with ceaseless labours try
To draw the goddess from the sky.
Return, and with thee take the steed;
So shall thy grandsire's rite succeed."*

The prince takes the steed; the sacrifice is completed, and for 30,000 years King Sāgara was thinking how he could induce Gaṅgā to come down from heaven. At length, not having succeeded in forming a successful plan, the monarch himself went to heaven. Ansuman reigned in his stead, who, in his turn, tried to find some means of liberating his brothers. His son Dilipa also made a similar, but equally unsuccessful, effort. It was given to Dilipa's son Bhagirath to accomplish this work. Bhagirath had no son. He, in order to obtain this boon, and also to free his kinsmen from their sad fate, practised most severe austerities, until at length Brahmā said—

"Blest monarch, of a glorious race,
Thy fervent rites have won my grace.
Well hast thou wrought thine awful task:

---

*Ibid., 186.

Some boon in turn, O hermit, ask."*

To which Bhagirath replies as follows—

"Let Sāgar's sons receive from me
Libations that they long to see.
Let Gangā with her holy wave
The ashes of the heroes lave,
That so my kinsmen may ascend
To heavenly bliss that ne'er shall end.
And give, I pray, O god, a son,
Nor let my house be all undone."

To this the god replies—

"As thou prayest, it shall be.
Gangā, whose waves in Swarga (Heaven) flow,
Is daughter of the Lord of Snow.
Win Siva, that his aid be lent
To hold her in her mid descent,
For earth alone will never bear
These torrents hurled from upper air."†

Brahmā then re-ascended to the skies; but Bhagirath remained for a whole year—

"With arms upraised, refusing rest,
While with one toe the earth he prest."

Siva, pleased with this devotion, promised to sustain the shock of the descent of the waters on his head; but Gangā was not at all pleased when commanded to descend to earth:

------

*Griffiths's "Rāmāyana," i. 190.
†Ibid.

> "'He calls me,' in her wrath she cried,
> 'And all my flood shall sweep
> And whirl him in its whelming tide
> To hell's profoundest deep.'"*

Siva, however, was a match for the wrathful deity. He held her in the coils of his hair until her anger abated, and then she fell into the Vindu lake, from whence proceed the seven sacred streams of India. This lake is not known; and of the seven streams mentioned, two only are familiar to geographers, the Ganges and the Indus. One branch of this stream followed Bhagirath wherever he went On the way the waters flooded the sacrificial flame of Jahnu, a saint. In his anger he drank up its waters, and Bhagirath's work seemed to be fruitless. But at the intercession of the king and Brahmā, the saint allowed the waters to flow from his ears. From this fact one of the many names of Gangā is Jāhnavi, or daughter of Jahnu. At length Bhagirath reached the ocean, and descending to the depths where Sāgara's sons were lying, Gangā followed until her waters touched the ashes, when—

> "Soon as the flood their dust bedewed,
> Their spirits gained beatitude,
> And all in heavenly bodies dressed
> Rose to the skies' eternal rest." †

As a reward for his meritorious work, Brahmā said to him—

> "Long as the ocean's flood shall stand
> Upon the border of the land,
> So long shall Sāgar's sons remain,

---

*Grififiths's "Rāmāyana," i. 193.
†Ibid., 196.

And, god-like, rank in heaven retain.
Gaṅgā thine eldest child shall be,
Called from thy name Bhāgīrathī."*

As a consequence of faith in this legend, one of the most frequented places of pilgrimage in India is Sāgar Island, the place where the river Ganges and ocean meet.

In addition to the Ganges, there are many other rivers regarded as sacred by the Hindus; the worship of these, and bathing in them, being productive of almost as great blessings as are to be obtained from Gaṅgā herself. Some of these are considered as males and some as females. The following is not a complete list, but it contains the names of the rivers most generally worshipped.

Male rivers :—The Sona and the Brahmaputra.

Female rivers:—The Godāvarī, the Kāveri, the Atreyī, the Karaloyā, the Bahudā, the Gomatī, the Sarayu, the Gandakī, the Varahī, the Charmanwatī, the Shatadru, the Vipāshā, the Goutamī, the Karmanāshā, the Airāvatī, the Chandrabhāgā, the Vitastā, the Sindhu, the Krishnā, the Vetravatī, the Bhairava.†

---

*Griffiths's "Rāmāyana," i. 197.
†Ward, ii. 217.

Chapter IX
Sacred Trees

SEVERAL trees are regarded as sacred; they being representative of, or peculiarly dear to, some of the deities. It is a meritorious act to plant and water them, and such is the respect cherished for them, that even their withered branches

The Banyan Tree

are not allowed to be burnt. The same ceremonies are observed at the planting of these trees, or, when they have been taken care of for some time, at their consecration, as are observed at the setting up of an image. The following are the names of the sacred trees:—

The Asvatta, or Pipul Tree *(Ficus religiosa),* sacred to Vishnu.

The Vata, Banyan or Indian Fig Tree* *(Ficus Indica),* also, sacred to Vishnu.

The Vilva, or Wood-apple, or Bēl Tree *(Ægle Marmelos),* sacred to Siva.

The Vakula *(Mimusops Elengi).*

The Harltāki *{Terminalia chebula).*

The Bēl

The Amalaki, or *Emblic Myrobalans (Phyllanthus emblica).*

The Nimba, or Nim Tree *(Melia azadirachta).*

The Tulsi *(Ocimum gratissimum* or *sanctum).*

The, Tulsi is very commonly worshipped by the followers of Vishnu; and the plant is most carefully tended as his

---

*See p. 472.

representative. Every morning the ground near it is cleaned with cow-dung and water; at night a lamp is hung before it. During the two hottest months of the year, a vessel of water is hung over it so that it constantly receives moisture. When a plant dies, it is cast into a river, the same honour being given to it as to an image as soon as the worship of it is concluded. It is a common custom to place a sprig of Tulsi near the head of a dying person. The origin of the worship of this plant is said to be the following: A woman named Tulsi engaged in religious austerities for a long period, and asked, as a boon, that she might become the wife of Vishnu. Lakshmi, hearing of this, cursed her, and changed her into the plant which bears her name. Vishnu, however, comforted his follower with the assurance that he would assume the form of the Shālgrāma, and continue near her.* The Vāyu and the Padma Purānas teach that the Tulsi was one of the products of the churning of the ocean.

In addition to these trees should be mentioned the *Durva* grass *(Agrostis linearis)* and *Kusa* grass *(Poa cynosuroïdes)*, which form part of the offerings made to the gods; as do the leaves or flowers of most of the trees previously mentioned. The Mahābhārata has a legend accounting for the sacredness of the Kusa grass. When Garuda brought some of the amrita from the moon for the Nagas, or serpent deities, as the price to be paid for his mother's release from servitude, Indra tried to induce him not to give it to them lest they, becoming immortal, should oust him from his throne. Garuda would not consent to this arrangement, but told Indra that after it was given to them he could steal it.

Garuda therefore placed the amrita in a vessel on the grass, and whilst the Nāgas were bathing, Indra stole it. They, thinking that the ambrosia must be on the Kusa grass, licked it; the sharp spikes slit their tongues, and hence the serpents'

---

*Ward, ii. 204.

tongues are forked; and the grass, having been touched by the amrita, is holy.

The Fig Tree

Chapter X

Miscellaneous Minor Deities

1. SHITALA

Shitala is the Bengali name for the small-pox, and for the deity who is supposed to have charge of that disease. The meaning of the word is "She who makes cold." This goddess is

Shitala

represented as a golden-complexioned woman sitting on a lotus, or riding on an ass, dressed in red clothes. Before an image of this kind, or more commonly a pan of water merely, Shitala is worshipped in the hope that she will preserve her worshippers from this dire disease.

In the spring of the year, the Hindus formerly inoculated their children for this disease when they were about two years of age. The Brāhman who performed the operation made presents to render Shitala propitious, and promised, in case the work was successful, to give still greater gifts. At the close of the operation the flowers that were presented to the goddess were placed in the hair of the child as a charm. On behalf of those afflicted with small-pox, offerings are made daily; and when the patient is thought to be dangerously ill, he is placed in front of an image of Shitala, bathed in, and given to drink, water that has been offered to her. Beggars go about with a stone, partly gilded, which they teach is sacred to Shitala, and, in seasons when the disease is prevalent, receive presents from the superstitious.*

2. MANASĀ

Manasā is the sister of Vasuki, king of the snakes; the wife of Jaratkāru, a sage; and being the queen of the snakes is regarded as the protectress of men from those reptiles. Another name by which she is known is Vishahara, "the destroyer of poison." Generally, offerings are made to her without any image being made, a branch of a tree, a pan of water, an earthen snake being her representative; when her image is made, it is that of a woman clothed with snakes, sitting on a lotus, or standing upon a snake. A song founded upon the following story concludes the worship of this deity.

A merchant named Chānda not only refused to worship

---

*Ward, ii. 139.

Manasā, but professed the profoundest contempt for her. In process of time six of his sons died from snake-bites. To avoid a similar fate, his eldest son Lakindara dwelt in an iron house; but Manasā caused a snake to enter through a crevice, which bit him on his wedding-day and caused his death too. His widow, however, escaped, and went weeping to her mother-in-law,

Manasā

who, with the neighbours, vainly tried to induce Chānda to propitiate the goddess through whose influence so much evil had come to the family; Manasā herself urged his friends to prevail upon him not to remain so hostile to her. At last he so far yielded to their wishes as to throw a single flower with his left hand towards her image, which so delighted her that she restored his sons to life, and from that time, as men came to know of her power, her worship has become celebrated.*

The Mahābhārata gives the following particulars regarding her marriage. Jagatakāru, her husband, was an eminent sage, who had practised great austerities, bathed in all the holy tanks, abstained from matrimony, and, as a result of his penance and fasting, had a dry and shrivelled body. In the course of his wanderings, he came to a place where he saw a number of men hanging from a tree with their heads downwards over a deep abyss, with a rat gnawing the rope by which they were suspended, and learned that they were his own ancestors, doomed to endure this misery because, their children being dead, they had no one to release them (*i.e.* by performing religious ceremonies); and he, who, by having a son might have set them free, was given up to a life of austerity, and refused to marry. When they are told that Jagatakāru is the man through whose abstinence they are suffering, they entreat him to seek a wife and secure their deliverance. He consents to do so on condition that the parents of the girl he marries give her to him willingly. Vāsuki hearing of this, offers his sister to the sage, who marries her and has a son named Asika. This son effected the deliverance of his ancestors and also rendered good service to the serpent race in saving them from destruction when Janamejaya was wishful to exterminate them.

3. SASTĪ

Sastī is peculiarly the goddess of married women; she is the giver of children, assists at childbirth, and is the guardian of young children. She is represented as a golden-complexioned woman with a child in her arms, riding upon a cat; hence no Hindu woman would under any circumstances injure that animal, lest she should offend the goddess and be made to suffer for it. Six times a year festivals in honour of Sastī are

---

*Ward, ii. 142.

held; in addition to which, women who have lost their children by death worship her monthly. When a child is six days old,

Sastī

the father worships her; and when three weeks old, the mother presents offerings to her. The ordinary representative of Sastī is a stone about the size of a man's head, placed under a Banyan tree, which is decorated with flowers, and offerings of rice, fruit, etc., are made to it.*

4. THE SHĀLGRĀMA

By the worshippers of Vishnu, the Shālgrāma is regarded as a most sacred object. It does not derive its sacredness from consecrating rites, as images and other representatives of deities, but is believed to be inherently holy. It is a black

---

*Ward, ii. 143.

ammonite, found in Mount Gandakī in Nepal. The popular belief is that in this mountain there are insects which perforate the stones; and when perforated, falling into the river Gandaka, they are taken out by means of nets. The more common ones are about the size of a watch, and their price varies according to their size, hollowness, and inside colouring, according to which peculiarities special names are given. For the rarer kinds as much as ₹2000 are given; and as it is the common belief of the people that the possessor of one of these, and a shell called Dakshināvarta (*i.e.* a shell whose convolutions are towards the right), can never be poor, it is not to be wondered at that large prices should be paid for them. As it is also believed that in parting with them they invite misfortune, it is natural that few should wish to part with them; to sell them for gain is regarded as a most dishonourable deed.

A reason for the sacredness of the Shālgrāma is found in the "Bhāgavata Purāna." Sani commenced his reign with a request to Brahmā to become subject to him; Brahmā referred him to Vishnu, who asked him to call upon him the next day. When he called, finding that Vishnu had transformed himself into a mountain, he became a worm named Vajrakīta, and afflicted him for twelve years. At the expiration of that time Vishnu resumed his proper shape, and ordered that henceforth the stones of this mountain (Gandakī) should be worshipped as representatives of himself.*

The Brāhmans usually worship Vishnu in this form in their daily *puja* at home. In the hot season a vessel is suspended over it, and the water continually dropping on it keeps it cool; another vessel is placed under it to catch the water, which is drunk in the evening by the worshipper. The marks of it are shown to men when dying, in the belief that the concentration of the mind on them at this time will ensure the soul a safe

---

*For another account of the origin of the worship of the Shālgrāma, see the account of Tulsi, chap. ix.

passage to Vishnu's heaven.*

5. THE DHENKĪ.

The Dhenkī is a log of wood fixed to a pivot, used for husking rice, pounding bricks for mortar, etc. It is generally worked by women, who, by standing on the one end, raise it to a certain height and then let it fall by its own weight. It is said to be the Vāhan or vehicle of Nārada, and it is believed that, owing to his blessing, it became an object of worship. A religious teacher, when initiating a disciple into the mysteries of Hinduism, told him to say, "Dhenkī, Dhenkī." Nārada, hearing this, was delighted, and coming upon his Vāhan gave him another incantation by which he became perfect and was admitted into heaven. It is worshipped at the time of marriage, at the investiture of a son with the Poita or Brāhmanical thread, at the ceremony of giving rice to a child, and on other festive occasions. At the close of the last century a Rāja of Naladanga is said to have spent Rs. 300,000 in celebrating the worship of the Dhenki.

6. KA? WHO?

The Athenians were not alone in worshipping the "Unknown God." "The authors of the Brāhmanas had so completely broken with the past, that, forgetful of the poetical character of the hymns (of the Vedas), and the yearning of the poets after the unknown god, they exalted the interrogative pronoun itself into a deity, and acknowledged a god, Ka? or 'Who?' In the 'Taittiriya Brāhmana,' in the 'Kanshītaki Brāhmana,' in the 'Tāndya Brāhmana,' and in the 'Satapatha Brāhmana,' wherever interrogative verses occur, the author states that Ka is Prajāpati, or the lord of creatures. Nor did they stop

---

*Ward, ii. 221.

here. Some of the hymns in which the interrogative pronoun occurred were called Kadvat, *i.e.* having kad or quid. But soon a new adjective was formed, and not only the hymns, but the sacrifices also, offered to the god, were called Kāya, or 'Who-ish.' At the time of Pānini (the great grammarian), this word had acquired such legitimacy as to call for a separate rule explaining its formation. The commentator here explains Ka by Brāhman. After this, we can hardly wonder that in the later Sanskrit literature of the Purānas, Ka appears as a recognized god, with a genealogy of his own, perhaps even a wife; and that in the laws of Manu one of the recognized forms of marriage, geneially known by the name of the Prajāpati marriage, occurs under the monstrous title of Kāya."* In the Mahābhārata Ka is identified with Daksha, and in the "Bhāgavata Purāna" it is applied to Kasyapa, probably on account of their similarity to Prajāpati.

The Nim

---

*Max-Müller, quoted in Dowson's Classical Dictionary, *s.v.* "Ka?"

Chapter XI
Superhuman, Though Not Divine Beings

APSARAS AND GANDHARVAS

The Apsaras are nymphs, and the Gandharvas choristers in Indra's heaven. The Apsaras are not as a class prominently noticed in the Vedas, but Urvasi and a few others are mentioned by name. In the Institutes of Manu they are said to be the creations of the Seven Manus, the progenitors of mankind. In the Epic poems more is said about them—the Rāmāyana attributing their origin to the churning of the ocean, and with this the Purānic account of their origin agrees. It is said that when they rose from the waters neither gods nor asuras would wed them, so they became the common property of both classes. They are sometimes called "the wives of the gods," and "daughters of pleasure."

> "Then from the agitated deep up sprung
> The legion of Apsarasas, so named
> That to the watery element they owed

Their being. Myriads were they born, and all
In vestures heavenly clad, and heavenly gems;
Yet more divine their native semblance, rich
With all the gifts of grace, of youth and beauty.
A train innumerous followed; yet thus fair, Nor
god nor demon sought their wedded love;
Thus Rāghava! they still remain—their charms
The common treasure of the host of heaven."

"In the Purānas various ganas or classes of them are
mentioned; the Vāyu Parāna enumerates fourteen, the Hari
Vansa seven. They are again divided, as being *daivika*, 'divine,'
or *laukika*, 'worldly.' The former are said to be ten in number,
and the latter thirty-four, and these are the heavenly charmers
who fascinated heroes as Urvasi, allured austere sages from
their devotions and penances as Menekā and Rembhā. The
Kāsi Khand says there are forty-five millions of them, but only
one thousand and sixty are the principal. The Apsaras, then,
are fairy like beings, beautiful and voluptuous. They are the
wives or mistresses of the Gandharvas, and are not prudish
in the dispensation of their favours. Their amours upon earth
have been numerous, and they are the rewards in Indra's
heaven held out to heroes who fall in battle. They have the
power of changing their forms, and give good luck to whom
they favour."*

In the Satapatha Brāhmana is a story, which has been
copied into the Purānas, concerning Purūravas and the Apsaras
Urvasi which will give some idea of the character of these
beings. Owing to the imprecation of Indra and Varuna, Urvasi
was compelled to leave heaven. Purūravas, son of Budha and a
daughter of Manu, fell deeply in love with her; and she agreed,
on certain conditions, to live with him. She said, "I have two
rams which must always remain with me, both by day and

*Dowson, *s.v.*

night; you must never be seen by me undressed; and I must eat only *ghī,* or clarified butter." The inhabitants of heaven being anxious for her return, the Gandharvas came at night and carried off her rams. Purūravas, in order to rescue them, rushed into her room hurriedly, without being dressed, trusting to the darkness to hide him. Unfortunately a flash of lightning revealed him to her gaze, and, the condition of her remaining with him being broken, she returned to her celestial home. Purūravas was distracted at his loss, and wandered from place to place searching for her. At length he was successful in his quest, and obtained a promise that she would meet him yearly and present him with a son. After five visits, she assured him that if he offered a sacrifice with the express object of gaining her, he would succeed. He followed her advice, became a Gandharva, and so obtained eternal possession of his strange bride.

The Gandharvas, according to the Vishnu Purāna, were sons of Brahmā. "The Gandharvas were next born, imbibing melody; drinking of the goddess of speech, they were born, and thence their appellation (gām dhayantah, 'drinking speech).'"* In another place the same Purāna† makes them the offspring of Kasyapa and Arishtā, and therefore grandchildren of Brahmā. The Padma Purāna speaks of them as the children of Vach. They are said to be sixty millions in number. They defeated the Nāgas, or snake-gods, seized their jewels, and usurped their kingdom. In their distress the snakes resorted to Vishnu, who promised to enter into Purukutsa and destroy them. The Nāgas sent their sister Narmadā (the river Nerbudda) to ask the help of Purukutsa, who consented to do her bidding. As a reward the Nāgas gave this power to their sister, that whoever worshipped her and repeated her name should be safe not only from the poison of snakes, but other poison too.

---

*Page 41.
†Page 150.

It would appear from the earlier books that the Gandharvas were assistants of Indra, the Storm King, and were rewarded by the later writers with a place in his heaven. And as the deities were all provided with a wife or wives, the Gandharvas were not neglected in this respect. The beautiful though frail Apsaras were allotted to them, and when Indra was in danger of losing his throne, or the other gods were in a similar plight through the austerity of the devout, some of the more attractive were commissioned to visit them and distract their minds.

The name of these heavenly musicians and their loose matrimonial alliances with the Apsaras has come into common use to designate one of the five forms of marriage—that where the mutual consent of man and woman to live together is all that is necessary, without any civil or religious ceremony.

THE RĀKSHASAS.

These formidable beings are frequently referred to, and their actions described at some length in Hindu legend. Though Brāhmans by birth, strange to say they are described as cannibals. The goddess Pārvati gave to the whole tribe the power to arrive at maturity the moment they were born. They are said to be able to assume any form at will; and we read of them appearing as horses, buffaloes, and tigers. Some of them had a hundred heads. Amongst the most noted of them was Rāvana, the hereditary foe of Vishnu, who in several incarnations left his heavenly home to slay him. The demon reappeared on the earth after remaining some years in hell; it was therefore necessary for the god in like manner to revisit the earth to get rid of him. Some of Rāvana's relatives, such as Kumbhakarna, Vibhishena, Indrajit, and others, were almost equally notorious.

Kumbhakarna, a brother of Rāvana, as soon as he was born, stretched forth his arms, and gathered everything he could reach to stay his hunger. Later on in life, on one occasion he seized five hundred Apsaras, and at another time he laid violent hands on the wives of a hundred sages, besides cows and Brāhmans innumerable. Brahmā threatened to destroy him unless he moderated his demands. Fearing he might come to an untimely end, he commenced a life of austerity, which was to continue ten thousand years. But as this proceeded, the gods feared lest, as a result of such a penance, he should be stronger than ever, and, especially that he might obtain immortality and be able to swallow up everything, gods and men included. In their distress they appealed to Brahmā, who caused his wife Sarasvati to enter the demon's mind, and delude him so far as to lead him to ask as a boon that he might sleep for ever. The plan succeeded. But the Rākshasas were not pleased with the result, and asked Brahmā to allow him to awake once in six months for one day only, and then eat as much as he wished. This request was granted. At one meal he is said to have eaten six thousand cows, ten thousand sheep, ten thousand goats, four hundred buffaloes, five thousand deer, and drank four thousand hogsheads of spirits, with other things in proportion, and then was angry with his brother Rāvana for not providing him with more! His home in Ceylon is said to have been 20,000 miles long, and his bed occupied the full length; but according to the Rāmāyana the island itself was only 800 miles in circumference! What can be represented by these monsters? In Manu,* amongst instructions concerning sacrifice, we read: "As a preservative of the oblation to the patriarchs, let the housekeeper begin with an offering to the gods; for the Rākshasas rend in pieces an oblation which has no such preservative." According to Professor Wilson, these beings may be divided into three classes: "One is of a semi-celestial kind, and is ranked with the attendants of Kuvera, the god of wealth; another is a sort of goblin, imp, or ogre, haunting cemeteries, animating dead bodies, disturbing

---

*Manu, bk. iii.

sacrifices, and ensnaring and devouring human beings; the third kind approaches more to the Titan, or relentless and powerful enemy of the gods." Can it be that men, finding it difficult to abstain from evil and do good, have invented these mighty beings to represent the forces of evil that are arrayed against them? They are described as eating cows and also men, when, according to the ordinary belief of the people, these are the greatest imaginable crimes. May this not be a vigorous method of teaching that the enemies of God and man will not stop at anything in order to secure success in their work of destruction? It may be that the Rākshasas of the Epics were the rude barbarians of India, who were conquered by the Aryans, and their manners of life and religious ceremonies caricatured in this strange fashion. Some of the more intelligent were styled monkeys, possibly the more savage were styled Rākshasas.

The name Bhuta is given to a similar class of beings who are the common attendants of Siva; hence his name of Bhutanātha, the lord of spirits. The term Pisarch is given to beings similar to, though if possible more offensive than, the Rākshasas.

THE JAIN DEITIES

As there are considerable numbers of Jains, chiefly in the north and north-west of India, some account should be given of their objects of worship.

The origin of this sect is obscure, especially as their chronology is so wild and extravagant. Hindu notions of time are reasonable compared with those of the Jains.

In some respects, there is much in the tenets of this religion that closely resembles those of Buddhism. Both reject the divine origin and authority of the Vedas; though when a Vedic text agrees with his own belief, a learned Jain will not scruple to employ it to buttress his own teaching. Both may be regarded as heretical sects of Hinduism. Both reject the divine institution of caste, and profess to believe in the social and religious equality of man: though the Jains are not regarded as outside the pale of Hinduism. For when, as it sometimes happens, a Jain wishes to worship as an orthodox Hindu, a place is found for him in the caste system; he is not treated as an outcast. Both acknowledge in a general way the more common and modern of the Hindu deities; and very much of the worship of both is very similar to that which prevails amongst the Hindus. In both systems a number of saints have been raised to the dignity of deities, and have largely taken the place of the inferior gods of the Hindu Pantheon. In fact, at one time it was a commonly received opinion that the Jains were the present-day representatives of the Buddhists. But fuller and more correct knowledge has shown that the two religions, though strikingly similar, have distinct and separate origins. Possibly they originated about the same time, when there was considerable religious excitement in India; or it may be, that very soon after Gautama Buddha commenced his work as a teacher, some of his followers broke away from his leadership, and from that time have formed a separate and independent stream. At the present time Jains and Buddhists worship a succession of deified saints in place of the many gods adored by the Hindus: but in the two systems the names of these saints are quite different. The main lines of the religions are very similar, but the differences are sufficiently great to show that they have run a separate, though to a large extent parallel, course.

The Jain saints belonging to the present age are twenty-four in number; in a previous age there were twenty-four, and in a succeeding age there will be a similar number. These twenty-four as represented in the temples are seated in an attitude of contemplation. In features they greatly resemble each other, and in order to distinguish them, they are painted in different colours, and have either their names engraved on their pedestals, or some distinguishing sign, commonly an animal by their side. In the stories of their lives there is little of a distinctive character. But there is this noticeable fact, that in height of stature and in length of life there has been a steady decline. A brief account of the first and last two of these saints, now regarded as divine beings, may be taken as fairly representative of the whole.

1. Vrishabha, of the kingly race of Ikohwaku, was son of Nābhi and Marudeva. He is usually painted yellow, and has a bull as his characteristic mark. His stature was 500 poles in height, and he lived 8,400,000 great years. He was born at Oude. When crowned king he was 2,000,000; he reigned 6,300,000 years, and spent 100,000 in the practice of austerity, by which he became qualified for sainthood.

23. Parswanatha was also of the same race as the first. He is represented as blue in colour, and has a snake to distinguish him. Possibly this was the real founder of the Jain sect. He was born at Benares, and commenced his saintly life when he was thirty years of age, and, continuing his asceticism for seventy years, died when he was just a hundred years old.

24. Mahavir is the last and much the best known of all. His common title is "The Saint." His image is golden in colour, and his symbol a lion. He resigned his position as a god in order to obtain immortality as a saint, when there was a little over seventy-five years to run before the end of the age. His parents were Brāhmans; but as Indra considered it improper that one whom he recognized as a saint before he was born, who was to occupy such a position, should be born in a humble family, he removed the foetus to the womb of a princess of the royal race, Trisalā, wife of Siddhārta. At twenty-eight he lost his father, became king and reigned for two years. Then resigning his royal state, he entered upon a life of austerity, and after forty-two years of preparation, at the age of seventy-two he became exempt from pain for ever. In other words he died, and obtained moksha, deliverance from birth and death, absorption. According to tradition, the death of the last Jain occurred two thousand four hundred years ago.